THE LITTLE
DREAM

All my love
Lucy x♡x

ALSO BY LUCY KNOTT

One Snowy Week in Springhollow

THE LITTLE BARN OF DREAMS

LUCY KNOTT

An Aria Book

First published in the United Kingdom in 2021 by Aria,
an imprint of Head of Zeus Ltd

9 7 5 3 1 2 4 6 8

E ISBN 9781800243323
PB ISBN 9781800246232

Cover design © The Brewster Project

Aria
c/o Head of Zeus
First Floor East
5–8 Hardwick Street
London EC1R 4RG
www.ariafiction.com

Printed and bound in Great Britain by
CPI Group (UK) Ltd, Croydon CR0 4YY

MIX
Paper from
responsible sources
FSC® C020471
FSC
www.fsc.org

For JMK; and to creating the worlds we see in our heads.
I love you beyond measure.

ONE

The room looked to be derelict. It was murky and drab with strewn papers carpeting the floor. The air smelt musty, the place dark, with curtains that looked as though they hadn't been washed in decades. The young woman squinted for signs of life when she suddenly saw them: yellow diamond eyes glowing at her in the distance. She recognised the creature and knew any minute now the werewolf was sure to pounce and attack its prey. The girl would stand no chance. The werewolf would howl, she would scream, and no one would hear them. No one would save her.

Suddenly, the girl's breathing began to get heavier. She struggled to get the air to fill her lungs as a racket and whirring reverberated around the room. Yet there were still no signs of life besides the beast with whom she had just made eye contact. Heaven knows the room reeked of abandonment, like no one had stepped foot in it for centuries. Yet, the noise grew louder. The girl squinted her eyes harder in search of another intruder. She held her breath. This time a voice came loud and clear, above the beeping, frustration and a slight anger in

1

its tone. If she just ignored it, she could grab the chest and run. As the thought floated through her mind, the animal growled, a mean growl from somewhere deep in its disturbed belly.

Could this be the last noise she would ever hear? Was this to be her final excursion? Her nanna had warned her about gallivanting off into the woods on her own, but being on her own didn't scare her. She was independent, she didn't need a friend to help her find adventure, she was plenty capable of finding it herself. She was a fearless warrior, she told herself, taking a tentative step towards the small chest. Yet now an odd sensation swam around in her gut, which felt strangely like fear, as her forehead trickled with sweat and a human voice grew louder.

The girl tried to squint harder in the pitch black, only resulting in her eyes closing, for they could not draw further into a straight line, as narrow as they already were. She could feel a warm breath tickle the tip of her nose. Oh, but she couldn't leave yet, not after spotting the overturned chest in the corner, not when she was so close to retrieving it and learning what was inside. Trying to brave the formidable lurking creature and block out the distracting noises, she strained an arm to reach out, to lift the chest and make it hers.

'Flo? Flo?' Wait a second. It knew her name; whoever had come to steal the treasure too knew her name.

'Oh, for the love of God, Florence.' The voice came again in a terrifying hushed whisper that packed some force and had the desired effect on its recipient, because at the use of her full name, Florence lifted her head off her hand, snapped her elbows off her desk and jolted upright in her seat.

'What? Sorry, I mean, yes, that's me,' she replied, blinking away the shadows of the dark room and fighting the strong urge to drift back into it to see what was hiding in the dusty and damp chest. Glancing over her shoulders, to check for any signs of werewolves or beasts, Florence gave in and let her friend Olivia's face come into view, in addition to the neon lights and matching cubicles that made up her office.

Olivia's face was a pretty one. It was round in shape featuring green eyes, a button nose and thin lips – which were currently pressed into a severe line. The green eyes were wide with concern, her chin pointing down, giving Florence a stern glare.

Florence stared back, widening her blue eyes innocently. She was used to receiving this look from Olivia at least three times a day.

'Your phone has been ringing for five minutes straight,' Olivia informed her friend from across their shared cubicle in which their computer screens were back to back, their desks mirror images, except for the trinkets and frames displayed on Olivia's that were not present on Florence's side. Though Florence had been at Paperchains for five years she wasn't one for displaying family photos, allowing people to see her precious memories.

'Ooh,' Florence said as she picked up her phone. She put on her best Irish accent along with her phone voice and began her telephone narrative. This successfully caused her friend to crack a smile, for the phone had since stopped ringing. Florence placed it back on the receiver and when she looked up she was treated to an eye roll from Olivia with a sigh for good measure. But before Olivia could give Florence a lecture on professional conduct or the rules of the office – for the thousandth time – her own phone rang, which she picked up in a timely and efficient manner, meaning Florence was spared any speech for the immediate future.

With her mind now very much in the present, Florence

took a sip of tea and looked down at the few order forms she had to put through and log. She tuned in to the noise of the photocopier and the chatter from the lively office and pulled her focus to the tasks at hand. She wished Olivia knew how hard she tried to dispel her daydreams in public. Florence was aware of the looks she received, not just from her closest friend, whenever her eyes became clear again and she popped back into reality. It was odd and certainly something an adult should not do, but ever since she was a young girl, she had had trouble controlling her daydreams, not least because she didn't exactly want to. You see, Florence preferred them to reality. They were a much safer place to live, even if they did include the occasional werewolf.

* * *

'One of these days you're going to get caught twiddling your thumbs and not manning the phones. You've already had two warnings, Florence; you get your third strike and you're out of here,' Olivia said in her patronising tone as they left the office just after five p.m. It was a warm and sunny July evening, which meant that Piccadilly was packed with office workers clocking out for the day, including the kinds of people who fascinated Florence: those who, after a long hard day, ventured out into town on a work night and chose to sit in a noisy pub rather than curl up in their pyjamas with a good book. They weaved in and out of the crowd with Olivia walking a little faster than Florence, who floated behind with her hands in her pockets, not quite as fierce as Olivia in navigating the real world. Florence tended to drift, her eyes often gazed towards the sky or surveyed passers-by as she came up with stories for them in her head. She liked to smile at people, but it was scarcely returned, for people were glued to the phones in their hands. Just looking at the rectangular objects gave Florence a cold shiver that she quickly and expertly by now shook off. Returning her attention to Olivia, she skipped to catch up with her friend.

'Olivia, it has been five years and I do man the phones. I dutifully sit at my desk like a good little cable girl and I do nothing but answer phones from dusk till dawn,' Florence said quietly, her shoulders slumping as she looked down at the cobbles, dodging suitcases, and handbags, beginning to feel claustrophobic. Olivia slowed her pace allowing Florence to fall in line with her. Florence knew her friend often worried she'd get trampled on as they neared the busier tram stop. Olivia was only a year older than Florence but sometimes it felt like ten. Olivia knew Florence didn't care for crowded spaces, especially when no one paid anyone much attention and bumped and shoved, trying to get to their next destination in a rush. Olivia was always keeping an eye on her. She didn't want to lose her in the bustle or down a rabbit hole or wishing well for that matter. It was in crowded spaces where Florence could become overwhelmed and unable to stop her imagination from taking over and transporting her to a safe place.

'If Charlie were to fire me, I do so hope it would be in dramatic fashion. Maybe he would summon me to his office via messenger with a noble steed and I'd have to jump from stepping stone to stepping stone to avoid the snapping crocodiles that are ready to eat me for my sins. Or maybe, he'd storm out of his office with wizard cape and staff and diminish me to a faraway land, for I am to no use to anyone here.' Florence had gone from her quiet and regular British accent to a posh and regal one within a matter of seconds as they found a small spot of concrete with a little space around it to wait for their trams. When trying to defend herself, a little sarcasm and humour crept in. Internally she cringed as a man wearing a sharp suit, carrying a briefcase, gave her a disapproving look. If Olivia wasn't used to Florence's accents by now, she would most likely deem her crazy or fear for her sanity too, but as it was, they had become fast friends ever since Florence came to work at Paperchains five years ago. Being a confident, take-charge kind of woman, Olivia had been excited to have another woman on the team and Florence's lack of computer skills, shy demeanour and faraway eyes had intrigued her.

Olivia immediately offered a friendship, telling her that if she wanted to know all there was to know about Paperchains, then she should do as she did. So, Florence had worked with her, allowing this assertive and no-nonsense woman to teach her the ropes and introduce her to the team and, slowly, Florence had come out of her shell. But it was only Olivia who was privy to the accents. Florence had occasionally let them slip in the early days, but the sniggers and confused looks had put a stop to that. As for when Florence's eyes glazed over and she disappeared to another universe, Florence had made Olivia aware that her head was simply full of books and some-times she just liked to dip in and read them.

At first, Olivia had found it endearing and Florence would notice her smile as she studied her and got to know her, but five years later and Olivia's frustration was clearly etched in the screwed-up forehead and lowered eyelids. It appeared her friend thought it was her duty to coerce Florence into the real world and help her connect with those around her and fit in.

'You're coming out with us tomorrow night and I'm not taking no for an answer,' Olivia stated, grabbing Florence's forearms and ignoring her whole speech about crocodiles and wizards. Florence shifted uncomfortably on the spot. Her eyes darted around the tram stop in a nervous manner, searching for a friendly face. She had her hands firmly in the pockets of her vintage ankle-length dress, her sandy blonde waves were a little fuzzy in the heat of the breeze, while her mind raced with an excuse as Olivia's words landed heavy on her chest.

'Arrgh, but I cannot, for I am very busy,' Florence noted, taking a finger to the air, her posh lilt back again. After being stuck in the office all day, it was difficult to control her accents. They also had a habit of coming out when she was in a sticky situation. Though Florence was increasingly aware of how much Olivia disliked when she was "being silly", she couldn't help herself, her defences were up.

'You're not busy, Flo. Come on,' Olivia pleaded, tugging at Florence's elbow.

'Oh, but I am you see. There is this boy and he has been left on a doorstep. He has this terrible scar on his head, and I cannot possibly go a single night without knowing what is to become of him and...' Florence told Olivia, her voice dipping in and out of gasps and pauses for effect.

Olivia shifted, turning her head. 'You've got to be kidding me, Florence,' she demanded cutting her off and tipping her head back.

'I'm not kidding,' Florence said with a shrug. A wave of insecurity washed over her, but she had started her excuse now; she had to go with it. She raised her eyebrows innocently and joined her hands together in a mix of faux excitement for the little boy of whom she spoke, but also in a silent prayer for Olivia to leave her alone and not challenge her weak excuse.

'There's not a person on the face of this earth who doesn't know what happens to that little boy, least of all you. You've read *Harry Potter*, one through seven, three times over in the space of me knowing you,' Olivia said. Florence didn't miss her maddened tone. It was Florence's third excuse this week and Olivia didn't beat around the bush when it came to telling Florence that she was always scuppering plans to go out and have what Olivia deemed fun.

Florence's shoulders sunk and her voice returned to normal. 'I really don't want to go out, Olivia. Please,' she protested, less confident in the real world than she was bringing her books to life with her accents and mini theatre-like performances.

'It will do you good to get out there again and...' Olivia started.

'Do not say it Liv, I mean it, don't,' Florence implored, her voice wobbling. She shoved her hands deep into her pockets once more, looking away from her friend. These conversations were getting tiresome and Florence felt deflated that once again she was trying to defend herself to her friend.

'...and meet real people. You can't hide away because of a few bad ones,' Olivia finished, taking no notice of Florence's plea. Florence knew Olivia believed herself to be right and it wasn't that she thought her friend entirely wrong; she simply did not have what it took to be bold and confident like Olivia. Though Olivia's heart was in the right place, her bluntness occasionally only made matters worse and put the fear of God into Florence, like that time she had raised her voice and noted: *'Florence, everyone has romance troubles, but they get up and dust themselves off and try again. I don't want you dying alone under an avalanche of books.'*

'I can't, Liv. I've got to be home. My nanna needs me, OK? You have fun,' Florence said, trying a different tack. The look on Olivia's face told Florence that she knew even her nanna would guffaw at that one. The old lady was a force to be reckoned with, even after her fall. 'And people are much kinder in

8

books,' Florence muttered, more to herself, as her tram pulled up and its doors hissed open. She jumped inside, wanting to get away from the conversation as quickly as possible.

'Just please come. We'll change at work and we'll go out and have some fun. It's been ages. I want to spend time with my friend when there's not a computer screen blocking her gorgeous face,' Olivia said, walking to the window after Florence. 'Please, for me.' She added as the tram started up and moved away. Florence waved unenthusiastically with a small smile on her face.

Guilt crept over Florence as she kept her balance, holding on to the nearest handrail as the tram stopped and started at each station. It was cruel to deem all people unkind. Her nanna would admonish her for such thoughts but whenever Olivia suggested they go out, it always ended up being a surprise double date. Drew, Olivia's boyfriend, always had a friend or a friend of a friend who just happened to swing by and somehow Florence was then left on her own with said friend and it never went well, ever.

As nice as Drew was, he worked in accounting. He couldn't understand Florence's love of books and fantasy, and as for accounting, numbers gave her a headache. She simply didn't get them and after spending eight hours logging in orders, pricing up stationery and doing calculations at Paperchains, all Florence wanted to do was sniff the heavenly pages of her books and soak up all the words. Needless to say, Olivia and Drew's idea of fun was not the same as Florence's. The problem was that many of Drew's friends or friends of friends were accountants too and for some reason Olivia and Drew thought they would be a good match for Florence, like yin and yang or opposites attract. Time and time again Olivia told Florence that she needed someone who would bring logistics and realism to her otherwise imaginary world. However, just the words *logistics* and *realism* made Florence's skull throb.

The last spontaneous date had been a disaster. Florence had thought it was rather wonderful when her date had suggested visiting the garden centre and the delightful flower maze that had been built there, but her optimism was short-lived. She had been enamoured with the flowers, but her date didn't seem all that interested, giving her odd looks every time she asked his opinion, like he hadn't bargained for someone who actually cared about the flowers and wasn't sure if it was a positive or a negative. The conversation kept reaching those awkward silent moments until someone changed the topic. Florence had tried to keep up when he talked about his job. It was lovely that he was so passionate about it, but it had been hard for her to ask the right questions when she had no clue what misstatements and double entries were. She had willed her brain to focus and concentrate so she could understand the fast words spitting from his mouth, but it had been no use. Her cheeks flushed furiously, and her date had looked fed up. It simply wasn't working. The final nail in the coffin was when he asked how many followers she had on Instagram and she had to tell him that she didn't have an Instagram. He'd tried to cover his shock with a tight grin but there was no mistaking the underlying glare that said he thought she had two heads. Florence had wanted the ground to swallow her up.

That night she had spent the evening trying to work out what it was she had done wrong. Maybe she should have tried harder to look impressed by the amount of money there was to be made in accounting, or she should have patted him on the back when he told her that he had over five thousand followers on the gram, as he had called it, but she had failed miserably. She was simply not cut out for dating.

Florence let out a sigh before she unlocked the front door of her and her nanna's modest house that was nestled in a cul-de-sac in the outer edges of Manchester. Her shoulders instantly loosened, her limbs felt lighter and her spirit more joyful. She dropped her heavy bag off in the hall and breathed in the aroma of fresh basil and olive oil emanating from the kitchen. As she walked the hallway, she traced her fingers over the books that littered every available surface before she entered the kitchen where she made herself known.

'Hi, Nanna, that smells delicious,' Florence said as she picked up the book she had left on the dining table over break-fast that morning.

'How was work, dear?' her nanna asked, chopping up tomatoes and olives for the colourful salad she was preparing for dinner. Picking up from where she left off that morning, Florence curled her legs underneath her on the chair, let her dress float around her and began reading aloud, her nanna's question getting lost in the atmosphere.

The sweet old lady listened to her granddaughter, whom she treated and thought of as her own child, and her lips curved into a warm smile. How she loved to hear the girl read. But as she glanced across the table, her heart ached, for she noticed Florence's tired eyes, devoid of their usual sparkle, and her shoulders hunched after a dreary day at the office. Inwardly she sighed. She wanted the world for her only granddaughter and though she believed with all her heart that in due course it would present itself, Margot felt it was time for a little extra push. Her nose so far in books is what she had always championed and encouraged, but it was time for Florence to see the magic of her own story.

TWO

It had been another uneventful day at Paperchains if you didn't count Florence's brief escape to Hawaii sometime during mid-afternoon. The sand had been luscious and golden, the waves soothing, and delicious-looking cocktails were being served from cabanas in every direction. She had had to replace the toner in the photocopier but had got lost amidst the stacks of paper, card, and inventory of stationery, and when staring at the dull grey office wall her mind had decided to take a vacation. She hadn't been on a holiday in a terribly long time.

Of course, time had ticked on at an alarming rate meaning she received a pointed glare and a watch tap from Olivia upon returning to her seat. Florence was pleased she had made it through the workday. It wasn't a difficult job by any means: phone calls, supply forms, data input. She was good at it now, but it was far from a dream. When she had first started the job it hadn't been easy. The data was confusing, she stumbled over phone calls and trying to learn the names and numbers of everything in the catalogue had been a nightmare. Her saving grace had been Olivia, who had taken her under her wing. While Olivia might not always understand Florence's need to have a book at close proximity – and couldn't help finding it a little odd whenever she looked over and simply saw Florence's hand resting on said book while she was talking on the phone – she had been the only person to make an effort to get to know Florence in a long time and Florence had been grateful for her guidance then, and thought fondly of their friendship now.

Where Olivia might not identify with the mind of a bibliophile, Florence was occasionally baffled with the enthusiasm Olivia had for office supplies. However, where Olivia put up with Florence's acting skills and quirky style, Florence respected her friend's passion and the care she put into her work. Olivia's desk was decorated with family pictures and colourful knick-knacks and she had the friendliest manner when answering phones, embodying the phrase: "How can I help you?" Olivia's reasoning being that she loved supplying people with what they needed and making their work life easier. She had so many ideas for adding more lines to the catalogue and offering more exciting stationery that Florence hoped Olivia would soon get a promotion. Even if Olivia did try to mother Florence too much and even if she didn't always do a great job at hiding her frustration when Florence glazed over, she still deserved a promotion because when it came to having a fierce, authoritative and business-like manner, Florence felt Olivia was the perfect woman for the job.

Watching Olivia flutter around her desk or in action on phone calls kept Florence entertained, that and her own mind's escapades. It didn't always used to be like this though. Once upon a time Florence had had a job that had her up before her alarm and smiling as she laid her head down at night. She had felt like the luckiest women in the world to be one of the rare ones who could claim they loved their job so much that it never felt like work. Her job at Old Maude's Theatre had lasted eight glorious years. When she was growing up, she and her nanna would spend weekends attending theatre shows. Whenever her nanna got a little extra money, which was very rare, they would even see two shows in one day. Florence never tired of seeing the inside of Old Maude's Theatre and had been asking since she was a child if there were any jobs available. To her it was a win-win: she could help her nanna with bills and spend her days watching rehearsals and learning the magic behind the performances she adored.

Between story times and theatre shows, her nanna had created the most enchanting childhood for her. Florence never had time to dwell on her sorrows or worry about the kids at school. She kept her head down and though she still heard when the other children called her names, like Oliver Twist or speccy four eyes, she was often too wrapped up in a book or lost in a scene to ever let it get to her too much.

Being a loner and "different" only came to light when her dreams were realised at seventeen years old and Old Maude's Theatre finally offered her the job of stagehand and cleaner at her beloved playhouse. Florence would help prep the theatre for productions, which mostly involved polishing everything and anything brass until she could see her face in it, before curtain call. Then she would get to stick around and be a spare body if any of the actors needed a coffee. In the beginning the digs and comments had hurt her, for she didn't know how to be anyone but her shy self.

'Look at me when you're talking to me, dear,' one actor had scolded when Florence had offered a coffee.

'Why are you looking at the floor?' another had barked when Florence had handed over their drink.

'Earth to Florence, now's not the time,' the director had snapped, when she had missed a cue with the lighting, being so transfixed with the costumes hanging on a nearby rail.

Then one day when Florence was eighteen, after having worked at the theatre for a year, there came a voice, 'Honey, those remarkable blue eyes of yours need some focus.' Her name was Antoinette Tucci, she was the lead in the current production, and she was fabulous. Her lips were always siren red, her heels never shorter than five inches and though Florence wished to talk to her, she realised she didn't know how, as the previous ugly comments crowded her brain, making her feel insecure and far from worthy. So, captivated with the woman and inept at social interactions, she simply ogled, spacing out with the conversations she dreamt of having but couldn't quite bring to her lips, but Antoinette had come to her.

'For every chapter you go home and read tonight you will have a conversation with someone here. Heavens knows they are all dying to talk to you. A girl as precious as you should not simply get through life gazing. You are part of this whole shebang, darling. Stop blending into the backdrop and show me your sparkle, please. I'm practically bursting to see what's dancing behind those crystals of yours.' Antoinette had performed this little speech with all the razzmatazz and oomph that Florence would have expected. Yet despite the dramatic hand gestures and tone of Antoinette's voice, Antoinette's eyes never veered from Florence's. They had oozed such warmth and care, as well as a hint of fierceness, that Florence did what she had been told.

Opening up to those around her gave her a new life within

the theatre, one she had only ever experienced in her books. She held conversations, learnt about the actors from their very own mouths and not just from reading the playbill. Best of all she danced, she twirled and shared her elation at the end of each production with her new friends. Her voice mattered and she had felt accepted.

She had fallen more in love with storytelling with every month that passed and then after two years of working there she fell in love with something else, or should she say, someone else. But this wasn't something Florence liked to think or talk about and right now she was in a pickle and didn't have the time to go down memory lane. She was stuck at Paperchains, more specifically trapped in the women's toilets having to strongly resist the urge to stick her foot in the loo in the hopes that this evening it might just whisk her off to the Ministry of Magic before...

'Flo, are you there?' came Olivia's voice. No such luck today, Florence thought flushing the toilet and longingly watching the water swirl around the basin.

'Yes, I'm here.' She called out, trudging out of the cubicle and washing her hands. Olivia stood touching up her make-up in the mirror, clear excitement on her face as she tried to fix her lipstick over her lips that were grinning broadly.

Florence's stomach flipped with horrid nerves. She couldn't match Olivia's smile, no matter how hard she tried. She dived into her make-up bag pulling out her compact to powder her nose and take away its shine and to distract herself from the anxiety swimming in her belly. 'You promise me that we're just going to have a nice dinner – me, you and Drew – and that this isn't one of your surprise double dates?' Florence asked, nervously, dusting the clear powder over the tip of her nose. She had added a touch of highlight to her cheekbones, making her blue eyes shine brighter under the clear frames of her glasses and complimenting the high ruffle neck of her pastel blue floaty dress, which had replaced the button-up collared pinafore she had worn during the day for work.

'Of course,' Olivia replied, sweetly. Florence didn't miss Olivia busying herself, turning away and fishing for her mascara deep in her make-up bag to avoid her gaze when she answered. But Olivia couldn't hide the nervous blush as it crept up the back of her neck. Olivia had admitted in the past that she hated lying to Florence, but that she felt desperate and out of options. In her opinion, the longer Florence was out of the dating game, the harder it would be to get back in. Olivia had also noted that if Florence didn't dig her heels in so hard, then she wouldn't have to lie when trying to get her out on dates.

Florence's shoulders sagged. She wished it was as easy as her friend made out, but she clearly didn't have what it took to be a playing piece on the dating board game.

'Liv, you promised me you wouldn't do this, not after the last one,' Florence muttered, her voice cracking with the apprehension that was creeping into her chest.

'Florence, stop worrying. I just told you, it's just us tonight. But you do realise that you're never going to find your Prince Charming if you don't kiss a few frogs first,' Olivia said, resting her hands on Florence's shoulders to calm her. The raise of her eyebrows and the twinkle in her eye suggested that she was rather pleased with her fairy-tale reference – that and her playful wink. But Florence did not smile. Though she did appreciate her friend's attempt at using book lingo.

'I have plenty of Prince Charmings in my life, thank...' Florence began to state, her eyes wandering around the bathroom.

'In books, Flo. You need a real man,' Olivia interrupted, sternly.

'I don't need a real man. Real men are tricky and wicked creatures and I have no use for them,' Florence said reverting to her posh character to hide her emotions and try to dispel the pain in her chest. Olivia didn't notice Florence's fearful state; she simply snorted at Florence's comment.

'I can think of plenty of uses for them,' Olivia said, wiggling her eyebrows. She still had hold of Florence's shoulders and gave them a playful shake. 'Lighten up,' she added, but Florence couldn't lighten up; why couldn't she just lighten up, like everyone else? The weight of Olivia's hands on her shoulders suddenly felt too heavy. 'Come on, Drew's saving us a table. You can relax.'

* * *

It was wonderfully pleasant outside, the July air warm on Florence's skin. It appeared everyone was out celebrating the joyous occasion that was a Friday night. The laughter was loud under the quiet stars. The horses and carts click-clacked along the road giving the evening a beautiful soundtrack when suddenly the sugary-sweet scent of the bakery nearby caused Florence to turn her head, in search of the tantalising aroma. In doing so she did not see the tall and fetching gentleman walking towards her until it was too late, causing them to bump right into each other. Staggering backwards Florence gasped, but the kind man reached out, grabbing her hands ever so gently to stop her falling. As he did so their eyes met. His smile was handsome and shy, and she could not look away. Once he was satisfied that she was steady on her feet, he stepped back and lifted his hat. 'Are you all right, miss?' His voice came out like a song. Florence cleared her throat to reply...

'Ouch, ow,' Florence said under her breath as a bunch of lads barged past her, hollering and cheering with pints in their hands, knocking her out of her fantasy.

'It's busy in here tonight,' Olivia noted, keeping hold of Florence's hand as she navigated the sticky floor and crowded bar in search of Drew. Florence blinked a couple of times, trying to hide any hint that she had just disappeared into a daydream from her friend. But the way in which Olivia held her hand tighter indicated Olivia had seen the tell-tale signs. Olivia's furrowed brow and slight headshake signalled that she was getting a little fed up with her dizzy daydreams.

Words from Olivia's previous pep talks rang out through Florence's brain. 'You are going to be swallowed up and spat out repeatedly if you don't pull yourself together and accept that life isn't some fantasy land.' Her words had stung, but as Florence looked around the crowded pub, she couldn't deny the truth in them. The world around her looked nothing like her fantasy land. When would she give in and accept that? A sharp tug of her hand meant that Olivia had spotted Drew in a corner booth. He stood waving them over. Olivia picked up speed and Florence followed suit. 'Hi,' Olivia said. When they reached the table, she let go of Florence's hand as Drew leant down to kiss her.

Florence took a seat at the booth, unable to stop herself from smiling. She loved love, she loved seeing people in love, she loved romance novels – it was just that love itself did not work for her. She also couldn't help the wave of relief that hit her to find Drew on his own. Sitting back and settling in she picked up the menu; while Olivia and Drew asked each other about their days and kissed a couple more times. Florence thought their exchange sweet but couldn't help thinking about getting home to her nanna and to her book. If she picked something that was quick to eat and engaged in a little small talk, she might not have to stay too long. She was sure Olivia and Drew could occupy themselves in their loved-up state.

'I take it this is my seat?' came a gruff voice from beside her. Florence looked up to her right and peered over her menu. Her eyes found a broad man with his arm already comfortably leaning over the back of the booth, his hand awfully close to her shoulder. Her eyes then diverted from the man and scanned across the table to see Olivia and Drew innocently going over their food choices, taking no mind of the man and leaving the conversation all up to Florence. Florence inwardly groaned, she had fallen for Olivia's antics again and felt stupid, not to mention hurt.

Before Florence could offer her name, the man spoke again. 'I'm Andy. So, you're the bookworm, huh?' he commented, looking her up and down, which at least got Drew and Olivia's attention. Andy wasn't exactly gentle in his approach.

'This is Florence,' Olivia said, when Florence didn't speak. The hope in Olivia's smile was not lost on Florence but she spoke in a tone that suggested she too was now harbouring a few nervous butterflies. Florence was certain the fluttering in Olivia's stomach was nothing compared to the flapping in her own. But unlike Florence, Olivia's stubborn streak was persistent, and she kept a confident smile on her face.

'Hi,' Florence eventually managed, trying to look past Andy's initial abruptness and give him a chance. After all, her nanna had taught her not to judge; maybe Andy was nervous too and where Florence was quiet, his nerves expressed themselves in a more outgoing manner. 'Nice to meet you, Andy,' she said. Not caring to be rude, she forced a small smile and twisted her body to face him.

'Do you read all those erotic books that chicks like to read? What's that guy, that Mr Grey?' Andy said sliding into the booth next to Florence. Florence looked at him, then returned to viewing the menu. She had genuinely wanted to make an effort, but she would need food in her stomach if she was going to have to endure Andy's questions all evening.

'Not all chicks read those kinds of books, mate,' Drew said surprising Florence. He never stepped in or engaged in book talk. Did Drew even know that there were different types of books? Florence could sense Drew simply trying to defuse the tension building at the table. Olivia gave a small chuckle and waved Andy's comment away like it was nothing. Florence's stomach knotted tightly.

'There's nothing wrong with those books but Florence likes all kinds of books and theatre too,' Olivia said trying to catch Florence's eye and no doubt give her an encouraging nod, but Florence was not about to take the bait. Her mouth had gone dry and emotions were stirring in her stomach. Why did Olivia never listen? Andy sipped his beer unaware of his blunt and uneducated approach, but Olivia continued smiling, no doubt hoping she could save the evening and steer it from the gutter with a question about football that Andy ignored. Instead, he took another large gulp from his glass. Florence guessed the beer he was holding was not his first this evening. He did not take notice or apparent interest in what Olivia had asked; instead his eyes now lingered on Florence's dress.

Thinking of all the strong women she had read about in her books, Florence prayed for her brain to come up with at least a few short sentences to inform Andy that he should leave because she was not interested, but her head felt empty. She tried to swallow but her mouth had gone dry.

'Is this part of the foreplay, all the fabric and glasses? Are you like the naughty secretary and then you take it all off...' Andy didn't get to finish that thought, for Drew stood up and reached across the table, grabbing at his shirt collar at the same time Olivia threw her wine all over a shocked-looking Andy.

'Get lost, mate,' Drew said, letting go and shoving him out of the booth.

'I'm so sorry. He's a jerk, please don't listen to him,' Olivia pleaded, dabbing at her wet hands with a napkin, for the wine had splashed over her in her haste to throw it. Florence sat quietly for a moment trying to calm both the anger and pain bubbling in the pit of her stomach. Both Andy's crude remarks and Olivia and Drew standing up for her in such a way had been rather unexpected and could have been avoided had she gone home like she had wanted to after work this evening.

'We're not all like that, Florence,' Drew said, his brown eyes kind and his forehead furrowed with concern. For a minute Florence appreciated his big-brother-like manner and felt grateful for both his and Olivia's protectiveness over her in the heat of the moment, but there was no way she wanted to stick around and talk about it and have Olivia pass it off as just another frog. She placed the menu down.

'Thank you. Look, I'm going to go home, make a cup of tea for myself and my nanna and curl up with my book.' She told them, her voice soft and sweet but stern as she shuffled out of the booth. Where had that sternness been a moment ago, brain? she scolded. Florence could see a hint of worry on Olivia's face, but it was overshadowed by a smile tugging at her lips. Florence was smart enough to know that Olivia wanted to laugh it off and spend the evening dancing and encouraging her to cast it off as a silly anecdote of "boys will be boys" and Florence was in no mood for that. She didn't want to be made to feel stupid once more for feeling things more deeply and reading into everything; she just wanted to go home.

'Drew, Olivia, no more blind dates please. I know your hearts are in the right place, but I'm fine. I like being on my own. OK?' Florence nodded at her friends and offered them a forced cheerful smile before exiting the too noisy establishment, her books calling her name.

THREE

The curtains were wide open, the windows pushed open a crack, allowing the birds' morning chorus to fill the room, which lay in a soft dim glow, for the sun had not yet come out to say hello. Florence was sitting in her spot on the cushy settee that after years of wear now had the comfiest of indents that fit her bottom perfectly. She was reading under the light of a lamp that loomed over her loyally while her nanna flicked through a book over in her armchair. The antique armchair was another well-loved feature in the small living room that one could not possibly be blamed for mistaking for a library. Books filled the shelves, covered the floor by Margot's chair and Florence's settee and stacks were piled high on the coffee table. It was Florence's sanctuary.

Slowly the room became brighter, the dust on the books more prominent as the sun rose high in the sky. Florence stretched out her legs and released a yawn. 'Should we have our usual Saturday morning breakfast?' Florence asked, looking over at her nanna to find that Margot was already looking at her. 'Tea and pancakes?' Florence asked, raising her eyebrows, and smiling, knowing too well the look on her nanna's face and not wanting to address it.

'I think you should go on holiday,' Margot said. Her face was engraved with wrinkles telling of a happy, fulfilled life, but one that had not been without tragedy and deep pain. It was a face that had worn both smiles and frowns throughout Florence's life. The face that gave Florence her most favourite smile in the world while also capable of displaying a stern glare so strict Florence had never failed to do her homework or respect her elders. Her nanna was an extraordinary lady and she and Florence shared a bond more special than most. It was this bond that meant Florence had to muffle a laugh at the ridiculous suggestion Margot had just made, for her nanna's features were serious and Florence knew better than to laugh.

'Where would I go?' Florence enquired, just to play along but knowing full well that she would never take a real holiday and leave her nanna on her own. Margot had an imagination that rivalled her own and so Florence sat up in the belief that Margot might just be playing the game she used to play when Florence had been a little girl. They would lie on the carpet amongst the piles of books on the rug, look up to the ceiling and talk of all the worlds that they wished to explore and if they had a magic carpet where they would have it take them.

'Anywhere, my dear, you can go anywhere.' Her nanna smiled, placing her book on her side table and turning off her lamp, the sun now lighting up the room more boldly.

'Shall I go somewhere hot or cold? Anywhere is quite overwhelming. You'll have to help me narrow it down,' Florence teased. When her nanna's face softened, it put her own mind at ease. Maybe her nanna wasn't being serious after all and she had just wanted to play. Florence knelt up; tucking her feet underneath herself. She leant over and turned off her own lamp before resting her bookmark neatly in the pages of her book.

'Why don't you pack a small suitcase and your heart will answer that one for you?' Margot said. This had been Florence's favourite part of the game as a child. They would each take out a small suitcase and her nanna would say: "Do not overthink, follow your heart and let it pick out what it likes," and if Florence's suitcase held jumpers and knits, they would dream up the snowy mountains they would hike and name the polar bears they would meet. If Florence's suitcase was filled with dresses and sandals, they would be riding camels across the desert or splashing in the grandest swimming pool with giant floats.

'Arrgh but before I can do that, I require sustenance. One's heart cannot work if one's belly is empty and one's mind is crabby,' Florence replied. As her nanna pushed herself up from her armchair, Florence heard her stomach growl and immediately jumped up out of her chair to go and help her.

'I can do it myself, you know. You go and pack,' Margot said, unnerving Florence. Was she being serious about this holiday? Florence knew her nanna thought of herself as a spring chicken and rightly so. At eighty years old she was holding on to her independence – cooking, cleaning and constantly fussing over Florence to stop fussing over her. Florence didn't want to see her as old and less so as vulnerable but after a fall last month, her invincible nanna had been shaken and forced to slow down a little and Florence was now fussier than ever. She took her beautiful nanna by the arm and they walked slowly into the kitchen.

'So, pancakes it is. You know, change it up a bit,' Florence joked, getting back to the topic of their Saturday treat. Saturday was their day to have a leisurely morning where they stayed in their pyjamas, read their books, and indulged in pancakes and copious amounts of tea.

'Why not,' Margot said with a chuckle. She glanced up at Florence with a look of pure love, her crystal eyes large and all knowing. Distracted in her haste for pancakes and to get her nanna safely to the kitchen, Florence missed those special eyes studying her face and her nanna trying to read her. It was not often that Florence kept things from her, but Margot knew something was amiss.

Florence allowed Margot the dignity of taking the last few steps to the dining table on her own. It was true that she was capable of seating herself, so Florence saw to flicking on the kettle and retrieving all the ingredients and pans she needed for their Saturday tradition.

'Are you going to tell me what happened last night?' her nanna asked, as she poured the tea from the delicate teapot Florence had just placed on the table. Florence went back to stirring the pancake batter.

'Nothing happened last night. I just caught up with Olivia and Drew for a minute after work,' Florence said, not thinking of it as a lie. In her defence she had only agreed to go out on the premise that it was just her, Olivia and Drew having dinner. She hadn't known until the last second that that had not been on the agenda from the start.

'I always said you would make a fine actor, but Flo, my dear, I am your nanna and you buried your head so quickly in *Little Women* both last night and this morning that I would say something is very much amiss and I care to know what it is, please.' Florence could not help the smile that tugged at her lips, one for the way in which her nanna spoke – she always sounded so elegant and sophisticated – two because her nanna never missed when Florence reached for her comfort blanket that was *Little Women*, and three because her nanna was the only person who truly saw her and loved every inch of her, so much so that Florence could never not tell her the truth, eventually.

'I'm way out of my depth in the real world, Nanna. Men seem to think I'm either a dainty dame who will succumb to their every whim, for they are to be my very own Romeo, rather forgetting the charm and romance they should possess if that were the case, might I add. Or...' Florence paused to flip a pancake as her nanna watched on, sipping her tea '...or they think I'm this kinky erotic type who spends my days fantasising about millionaires in suits who have a contract for me to sign and that they just have to say the word and I will rip my glasses off and devour them, with whips, tassels and all.' Florence blushed a little but laughed a lot and out loud over her last qualm. Margot had never been one to sugar-coat anything and her nanna's rendition of the birds and the bees had been delivered with a mix of beauty and poetic prose that was not shy in its explanation of love in all its forms. Florence had known of the many bells and whistles long before she read *Fifty Shades of Grey*.

'Not to worry, my angel, not to worry,' her nanna said, chuckling into her teacup. 'Not all men mean to be so foul or cause you harm. When we do not understand something, we tend to misjudge it. The world these days is so full of variety and fancy packaging, it is hard to pause and we often forget what we are really looking for. Take our beloved books; nowadays, so much goes into the pictures on the covers that it cannot be helped that some will forget to look deeper or take the time to step in between the pages. Some men, and women mind you, see a pretty cover and they dare not ask what is inside it. All they are programmed to know is that they want it and some will go to any means necessary to get it without careful thought. They think they know what the cover is presenting them, or they misjudge it based on society's stereotypes. They do not take the time to study within.'

Florence flipped two pancakes on to her nanna's plate and made an "mmm" sound, both for the deliciousness of the golden-brown pancakes and Margot's words.

'How did you get to be so wise?' Florence asked knowing all too well the lessons her nanna had learnt over the years. Not wanting to bring up her painful past, she tried to keep the mood light.

'Age is both a beautiful and harsh teacher,' Margot replied, picking up her knife and fork to tuck in. But before she took a bite she paused, letting her fork hover at her lips as she watched Florence take her seat, adding fluffy pancakes to her own plate. 'Promise me that you will keep that mind of yours open to all possibilities and not pass judgement on others. I taught you better than that.' The old lady's blue eyes locked with her granddaughter's matching blue ones when she spoke, and Florence nodded.

'Of course,' Florence chirped innocently, feeling a knot of guilt in her stomach and trying her best to hide it. Confident as she was in her ability to not judge others based on appearance and even some actions, she didn't quite feel as stellar in the keeping her mind open to all possibilities department. It had been five years since she had broken up with Ryan and she still could not find the confidence to join in with Olivia's enthusiasm when her friend came across possible suitors. Granted every time she had been tricked into going along, they had not gone very well as Friday could attest, but there was no denying that Florence predicted their demise before the date had even gotten off the ground. She really did try though; she dreamt of meet-cutes and she fell head over heels with the heroes in her books, but when it came to real life, the "L" word was not something she let herself believe she could have anymore. She had been burnt too many times in more ways than one and it downright terrified her. And anyway, she didn't need a man when books had proven far superior time and time again.

'Now, you must make sure to pack your bag. I want to see what your heart desires.' Her nanna spoke up after they had enjoyed their pancakes in a comfortable silence and were on their third pot of tea.

Florence's shoulders tensed. She had thought the game from earlier had been forgotten and that Margot had been joking. 'My heart desires an adventure with Meg, Jo, Beth and Amy today, Nanna. Can we play that another day?' Florence asked, hoping to put it to rest with a yawn and a stretch. She felt sleepy after her hearty breakfast and was ready to climb back into her dent on the settee, with nowhere else she or her nanna had to be today.

The elder of the two motioned for the living room, causing Florence to jump up and offer her hand. Once comfy in their rightful reading places, her nanna spoke again. 'Florence, you need a break and I will not take no for an answer. I cannot remember the last time you had a holiday and one should not go through life with all work and no play,' Margot noted.

Florence was listening but was determined to put Margot's thoughts to bed. 'You did not just quote my favourite book and use it against me?' Florence quirked an eyebrow. Her nanna smiled devilishly.

'You work far too hard Florence. You have been looking after me since you were a child and you have been working every day since it was legal for someone to hire you. I am putting my foot down this time, honey. I want you to take a holiday, like we used to, like we all used to.' Her nanna was tenacious, Florence knew that much but what concerned her was the note of desperation in her tone and her inviting a trip down memory lane. A trip that Florence did not wish to take. Florence didn't remember a great deal of her childhood before she turned five. She had a few golden nuggets she treasured and Margot ensured that Florence knew it was indeed a happy time where they had been like any other family, going on holidays, laughing and playing without a care in the world, but Florence's vision had become a touch blurry over the years.

Florence sat up, her feet on the giant rug. 'Nanna, please, I'm doing just fine. I don't need a holiday. I like work; I can't just take off. Now, can we please get back to our Saturday? I can stay right here on this couch and take as many holidays as I would like,' she said, waving her book at Margot, keeping her voice light, and turning away to indicate that the conversation was now over.

So, enamoured by the pages of her book, Florence paid no mind to her nanna watching her disappear into the pages of her treasured book. She was oblivious to the old lady's heart filling with a ferocious pride and a strong wave of protectiveness. Margot had tried over the years, but Florence's stubborn mind would not give in. Just a little push now – that is all she was going to give, and the rest would fall into place. For Margot was stubborn too and she was not about to give up where her granddaughter was concerned.

FOUR

'I'm sorry about Friday night,' Olivia said, passing a sneaky custard cream to Florence under their desktops. The look on Olivia's face the moment she had walked into the office this Monday morning told Florence that her friend had been riddled with guilt all weekend. Olivia looked at her with fluttery lashes and her chin tucked to her chest. When Florence accepted the biscuit her brows unfurrowed, and when Florence smiled and took a bite of the biscuit Olivia's shoulders relaxed from around her ears and her head tilted upwards more confidently. This was Olivia's sweet side, one that always gave Florence hope that one day she would listen to what she had to say and try to understand her a little more, but Florence had yet to see it last longer than any given week before Olivia was scheming again at the weekend.

Florence took a bite of the peace offering and immediately realised her mistake when her phone rang. With a mouthful of the crumbly crunchy delight, she picked up the receiver and choked out a hello, and in a very unladylike manner, sprayed a few crumbs over her desk as she did so. She was saved from spluttering over any more crumbs when whoever was on the other end of the line hung up.

Licking her sticky fingers and reaching for a tissue a sudden booming voice made Florence jump.

'Florence, can you come to my office please?' Charlie, their boss, announced from the other end of the room, causing a few heads to turn with curiosity. Olivia hastily shoved the custard cream packet into her drawer. They both knew eating wasn't allowed on the office floor, but for Florence the creamy biscuit had been too tempting to say no to. That and she had been touched that Olivia would risk breaking the rules just so she could make clear how sorry she had been about Friday and how much she cared. She could be a good friend, though now it seemed that Florence was going to be the one reprimanded.

'What does Charlie want with me?' Florence mouthed to Olivia as she stood up and brushed crumbs from her dusty pink dress with a pearl trim waist. Olivia sat up and made the gesture of clapping her hands but quietly to avoid making a scene. 'Maybe a promotion, or maybe he likes you,' Olivia whispered, making Florence sigh and her stomach gurgle with nerves. The apology had been going so well, but it seemed her friend could not help herself. If Florence had not been nervous a few seconds ago at the thought of stepping into Charlie's office, she was now. A promotion didn't bear thinking about because Olivia would be the deserving one of that accolade and therefore Florence would never be able to accept it. As for Olivia's latter theory, Florence would hear none of it: Charlie was her boss and she didn't think of him like that.

Charlie was handsome. Florence could admit that much. He was tall, rugged and broad and on the brief occasions that

Florence had met him – work meetings and Christmas parties – he had been kind and generous, but she had never once thought about her boss in the way Olivia had now just put into her mind. She did not concern herself with men liking her. Gone were the days where she allowed her brain to carry that sort of hope. Love had only ever left her in pain. Standing at the door she calmed her unease with a steady breath.

Inside the office, which was a deep red colour, with a big mahogany desk, Charlie rose and walked behind her to close the door. Gesturing for her to take a seat, he stood close enough that Florence could smell his aftershave. Calvin Klein, Florence registered having no idea how she knew that. She took a seat and as Charlie strode around her to get to his desk, he trailed his hand across the armrest of her chair and let his fingers graze her hand that lay upon it. An excited shiver ran down Florence's spine. She never thought Charlie had noticed her or would be interested in her in this way. She was beneath him, professionally speaking, and didn't care much for corporate ladders and his sophisticated world. Yet as he sat down, he looked at her, his eyes filled with unmistakable lust as he brushed a knuckle over his wet lips. Florence couldn't stop the urge that took over her and in a flash they both mounted the table and were...

'Are you coming in?' Charlie's voice sounded from inside his office. Florence's eyes bulged out of her head. Her mouth formed an "O" shape, clearly shocked by her own dirty thoughts. What was going on? She tugged at the bow on her dress, feeling hot and uncomfortable, then cleared her throat.

'Yes. I'm here, sir, I mean Charlie, I mean Mr Madden. I'm sorry, what do we call you?' she asked, incredibly annoyed with herself for sounding so flustered and feeling completely thrown off with where her thoughts had drifted. Florence didn't do frazzled, shy yes, but flushed and in a tizzy over a man? No.

'Charlie's fine, please do take a seat,' Charlie said, as he took her in with an amused look in his brown eyes. Florence sat hesitantly, then channelling Jo March, she straightened out her back, looked Charlie in the eye and focused.

'Florence, I'm sorry to inform you that I've got to let you go. I really hate to do this.' Which he did say with such sincerity that Florence believed him. 'I'm afraid numbers are down, and you've not been logging in as many calls as the others and as this is your third warning, I have to let you go. I hate to do it, Florence, I am sorry,' he added. The way he focused on her and didn't look away when he spoke made his words sound genuine, but Florence broke his gaze, looking to her hands as they shook in her lap. She wished computer programming and understanding never-ending changes to technology came naturally to her, but it simply didn't.

'Please, Charlie, I really need this job. I do try and I'm learning every day,' Florence voiced. She wanted to be brave and not weak but all she could think about was looking after her nanna. The lines between Charlie's brows deepened. He looked devastated with her plea.

'I'm sorry, Florence. I stuck up for you in the last two meetings, but I'm out of options,' he told her, his forearms now on the table. A few seconds passed in which Florence fought to compose herself.

She hated to challenge Charlie's sincerity, but her mind began concocting a speech. 'You're not out of options, Charlie, you could keep me on if you really wanted to. You could go to bat for me one more time, knowing how much I need this job. Am I really so bad that I've stopped you wearing fancy suits or caused the Christmas party to hold off on the champagne each year?' The speech never made it out of her mouth; instead, she rounded out her shoulders and forced a smile onto her face.

What she didn't know was that while her brain had begun to think the worst of Charlie, his was deliberating over reaching out his hand to comfort her. It wasn't something he could, would or should do, but in that moment, he wanted to. To him, Florence had always been an interesting character. He liked her sweet disposition, the wave in her hair and those eyes, though he could never quite understand her and how she often appeared dazed.

Empathy was visible in Charlie's face when she looked up. She admonished herself for her awful thoughts, but still his empathy was not going to help her pay the bills. Not knowing what more she could say, she simply stood to leave with a nod of her head and managed a quiet, 'Thank you, Charlie,' but as she twisted the door handle, she paused and looked back. 'Charlie, I may not be great at this job but one thing I do know is how incredibly hard Olivia works. She doesn't ask for much, but I'd say it was high time she was considered for a promotion,' she said, with a small nod before taking her leave. It might not have been her place to comment and so she didn't wait for Charlie's response. A seed was all she could plant in hopes that he would take note and water it.

Florence left the office after lunch and spent the afternoon in a state of bewilderment, wandering around Manchester, peeking at shop windows wondering if she would see any signs advertising jobs but it appeared people didn't do that anymore and it was all online advertisements. She felt too bruised to go inside and start making job enquiries just yet, wanting to avoid conversation with people. She was simply biding her time before getting the tram home and having to confess to her nanna that she was now jobless.

Only, when she got home, the house smelt like roast dinner and a suitcase sat at the foot of the stairs.

'Florence, is that you?' her nanna shouted from the kitchen.

'Nanna, what's going on?' Florence asked, rushing to the kitchen.

'Don't look so surprised, dear. I have made dinner. Sit please,' the cheerful lady practically sang. Florence narrowed her eyes suspiciously, her lashes pressing against her glasses.

'You are supposed to be resting, Nanna, you know this. You sit down; I can do the plates,' Florence offered; her voice came out like a whine. She could feel frustration bubbling. She needed her nanna to listen. She needed to take care of her. She could not fail her. She did not want to let her down. How was she supposed to tell her that she had lost her job?

'Florence, please do as you are told and sit down,' her nanna said again, while still gentle and cheery it packed a bit of oomph this time, the same oomph that told Florence she was about to say something Florence was not going to like and wasn't going to be able to escape. Florence sat. Her stomach deceived her and rumbled as her nanna placed a plate of roast potatoes, mashed carrots, thin slices of beef and broccoli in front of her. No one made a roast like her nanna nor did she think most people made a roast on a Monday evening, but here she was being spoilt, though it seemed because of an ulterior motive.

'My darling, will you indulge me for a moment?' Margot asked, taking her seat and gesturing for Florence to eat her dinner. Florence picked up her knife and fork slowly, not taking her eyes off her "up to no good" elder. However, the roast potatoes were exceptionally golden and crunchy and she couldn't resist them for too long and so began cutting into one crispy shell.

'I would like you to do this for me. You might think of me as selfish, but I fear I should have done this sooner. There are parts I know you remember and parts I know you have buried deep down, but for you, it is time, my dear. I have booked you a holiday.' Florence watched the pain on her nanna's face as she spoke. It was a pain Florence knew all too well. When Margot looked off to the side, Florence knew she was sifting through the memories in her mind. Painful memories that Florence had tried everything in her power as a child to expel, only ever wanting to see her nanna's eyes clear and happy. Florence would jump around performing monologues from her dearest nanna's favourite books, beg and beg to be read to at all times of the day and always had her coat ready to go to the theatre at a moment's notice. There were not many times that her nanna let her see her pain. She too upheld a smile, could recite paragraphs from Florence's favourite books at the drop of a hat and the theatre had been a lifeline in getting her granddaughter to see the beauty and magic the world still had to offer. But every now and again, smiles could crack.

As quick as the pain had come to her nanna's eyes, it was gone and replaced with a radiant beam that filled Florence with hope and excitement, with a tiny undercurrent of dread.

'Nanna, please, I told you I can't go on holiday and I would never think of you as selfish. You've been there for me, put me first my entire life,' Florence reminded her after swallowing a buttery mouthful of carrots. Her nanna simply waved off her words, steadying her hand to let Florence know that she did not want to hear such praise for taking care of her granddaughter. Growing up, if Florence had ever mentioned this, it would elicit the same reaction. Those moments when

Florence had succumbed to being a stroppy teenager, performing the occasional tantrum that unleashed such dialogue as: "I'm sorry I ruined your life," "You should have travelled the world and I ruined everything," were only met with her nanna's comforting hugs, a cup of tea and a story.

'Do you remember Camp Calla Lily?' Margot asked. There was no mistaking the touch of trepidation in her voice. Florence could see her hand shaking slightly as it held her fork.

A crunchy piece of roast potato caught in Florence's throat. Of course she remembered, but surely her nanna was not about to tell her that Camp Calla Lily was to be her holiday destination. Florence's palms began to heat. Returning to Camp Calla Lily was a conversation that Florence thought was deceased. The last time Margot had brought it up had been some five years ago now. It was a conversation that caused much friction between the two of them. However, this time there was something in her nanna's face that rendered Florence momentarily speechless.

'You know I used to frequent the camp in the summers with your grandad and your mum. Your mum then loved taking you there when you were little. It looks rather splendid at this time of year and they have these delightful huts that I feel you must see. Oh, when your grandad and I used to go, it was nothing more than a campsite and a cottage but yet it was still magical. Now, I will not say any more or ramble. It is one week, my Florence, you can please me for one week,' her nanna said, a tiny wobble in her voice. There was a look in Margot's eyes that belied their confident exterior. Something flickered behind them that spoke of their nerves, but her jaw remained set, stern this time, for Florence's sake.

Over the years, of course she had had her doubts about

how she had raised her granddaughter. Had she always done the right thing? But she believed that only natural and something all parents contended with; she had done it with her own daughter after all. Keeping Florence away from Camp Calla Lily because of her own fears, though, was a worry that wouldn't rest. Margot had enabled her granddaughter long enough, almost encouraging Florence's fear of the place so she didn't have to face her own. No matter how hypocritical of her it might be, she knew that this time she had to stand her ground and push Florence out of her comfort zone. She did not want her granddaughter to miss out because of her. What would her own daughter think of that? It was time now; Margot could feel it. She was not getting any younger. It was time for Florence to make peace with her past. As though all had been confirmed and consented to, Margot picked up her own knife and fork and tucked into the gorgeous feast.

Florence's mouth dropped open. She couldn't believe what her nanna had just asked of her, nor the way in which she causally began eating as if it was the end of the discussion and she had no say in the matter. Anger and fear bubbled in her gut, but it was mixed with a peculiar feeling of excitement that Florence was not used to. Had her nanna mentioned huts? Even Margot had sounded excited at the thought of the huts and her nanna had incredible taste for the whimsical, wonderful things in life. Florence's interest piqued as she looked away from her nanna and studied a roast potato.

The pain that had flashed across her nanna's eyes before had long since vanished and had been replaced by a glint of hope and a sparkle of joy. As Florence observed the gold crispy edges of her roast, she decided she couldn't bear to extinguish either. For a moment, Florence didn't speak, instead she got lost in thought. When she was a child, she noticed that her nanna didn't like to dwell on her losses, and she had taught Florence the same. Margot had elucidated that each night when one can dream and with each daybreak when one can think that nothing is lost. She went on to explain that a mind is not to be wasted when there were so many worlds to create and so many people to meet and talk to on any given day. Whenever Florence expressed her loneliness, Margot would simply tell her that those we love never leave our thoughts or disappear from our hearts; that they were always there.

However, that did not always quell the ache in Florence's soul. As a teen Florence had given up on these meets and greets, these meetings of the minds and trips down memory lane in her dreams. She had banished ideas and lost loved ones to the recesses of her brain and therefore any mention of Camp Calla Lily made her heart race at an uncomfortable speed. She was never prepared for the topic; it was too far gone in her memory bank. The only time she saw her parents now was when she looked at the photo frames that were dotted around the house. As her thoughts began to get carried away Florence could feel her brain spinning and suddenly her golden potatoes didn't seem so appetising.

'What about work?' she said, desperately, the spark and joy in her nanna's eyes being forgotten as fear took over. How could her nanna be so relaxed about work?

'Florence, people who work do take holidays, you know, and Olivia rang the house earlier to check on you. I would say what happened today at your office was perfect timing, would you not?' her nanna said, with a triumphant smile, though her left eye twitched. 'Your train leaves in an hour,' she added, causing Florence to nearly choke on a piece of broccoli she had tried to swallow.

'Nanna!' Florence cried, dabbing at her lips with her napkin.

'Yes, my dear,' her nanna replied nonchalantly, scooping carrots on to her fork. It would appear she had forgotten how to look people in the eye when talking. This only made Florence more irritated.

'Can you not come with me?' Florence tried, anxiety threatening to engulf her.

Her nanna raised her head for a second. 'I'm afraid I cannot. I have physio and appointments this week that cannot be changed. Besides, this is something I feel you must experience on your own, my treasure,' she answered, with a half-smile that didn't quite reach her eyes. Florence recognised the false bravery, which only cemented the difficulty in arguing with her nanna this time.

Florence sat back in her chair. Her nanna had never steered her wrong; she trusted her with every bone in her body. Deciding against another bite of broccoli, she pursed her lips and pushed her glasses up from the bridge of her nose. Florence's memories from under the age of five were but a few, therefore she couldn't remember much about Camp Calla Lily. She had in fact spent many of her early years trying to burn it from her mind, until it was just a mere smoky smudge. Occasionally, the ones that pierced through the smog were vague. Like now, a blurry vision of a lake came to her mind and colourful flowers blanketing acres of land. They spoke to her of happy times and great adventures but as quickly as they would appear, she would hastily shove them back to the depths of her brain. The colourful flowers lingered a little longer tonight, curiosity grabbing Florence and proving harder to dispel. After getting fired and with anxiety over getting a new job weighing heavy on her shoulders, she guessed she was all out of fight. If her nanna said that the time was now, clearly losing her job was some sort of sign, then Florence was struggling to come up with an excuse to doubt Margot. All out of arguments, she finished her dinner and sipped her tea.

'Do we have time for a chapter before I go?' Florence asked, looking over at her nanna, not wanting to miss their usual evening tradition and in need of a dose of comfort before embarking on an adventure she never thought she would take.

'There is always time for a chapter. How about Camp Laurence?' her nanna replied. Florence couldn't help the laughter that erupted from within her at Margot's pick of chapters, and because the day had been rather unexpected. She was free of Paperchains and she was going on holiday.

FIVE

The steam train whistled and chugged along the line. Children in their stockings and waistcoats ran side by side waving sticks and throwing stones, trying to keep up with the rickety-rackety beast. On the platform, flags and signs were being waved. Handsome men dressed in dapper suits and beautiful women in elegant dresses hopped from foot to foot, eager at the arrival of their beloved. Passengers leant out of windows too desperate to wait for that first touch, for it had been so long since they had held their loves. Cheers rang through the air in celebration and Florence herself punched the air with glee. She wanted to stand and rejoice with the others. Would her nanna be waiting for her on the platform? It had been months since she had seen her, the hospital having required her stay for longer than initially expected, but it was all over now. She was finally getting to go home and couldn't wait to...

'Excuse me, I need to get off,' a curt voice said sharply, suggesting that this request had been made more than once. Immediately Florence snapped right out of her thoughts, her cheeks flushed with embarrassment. This was why her nanna should have come with her and why, when she did venture out, Olivia was often by her side. At least when they were with her, she had support, another person at her side to indicate to the people around her that she wasn't totally cuckoo; she had friends.

'Oh, I'm sorry, where are we, if you don't mind?' Florence replied, a little dazed, as was the case when she visited such faraway times in her daydreams.

'We're at Rose Hill station,' the lady answered with a deep crease in her brow, clearly concerned for Florence who had been staring at the slim black tie of the man in front of her for the past twenty minutes, her orb-like blue eyes glazed over as trains whistled through her brain.

'Ooh this is me too,' Florence expressed, leaping out of her seat. She eagerly helped the lady with her bags to show she wasn't crazy, then she saw to her own. The lady smiled and nodded warmly yet wearily before disappearing into the crowd. Florence had not meant to drift off like that, but it was growing late, the sky a deep navy and the moon a pearly glow, an ambience that only enticed Florence to step into her dreams even more.

With her one small suitcase and backpack, Florence meandered through the station, smiling at everyone nervously. Most didn't smile back, for they had their heads down chatting on their phones. Florence simply couldn't keep up with their fast pace. Her walk was timid, a little more careful. Without her nanna or Olivia by her side, she felt quite isolated and alone when facing big crowds, not knowing how to fit in and wondering if people even made eye contact or said hello anymore. When she walked past the newsagent's near the exit, the hand that was holding her suitcase loosened its grip, so her nails were no longer digging into her palms and her breathing steadied. She caught glimpses of the books on the shelves, their covers crisp and bold, like beacons of light and hope. 'Hello,' Florence muttered as though she felt her friends were calling to her and encouraging her to go on with her journey and see her adventure through. She gave a small nod in their direction and continued.

Camp Calla Lily was situated a thirty-minute walk from the train station. Florence had brought a torch and had written down instructions from her nanna. She had been but a small child on their last outing so directions were not something she could remember clearly. The air was still quite warm, and Florence had no doubt the walk would soon make her sweat and keep her from getting cold. Walking was something she enjoyed, the fresh air always lending itself to inspiration, and so Florence set upon the path. Margot had told her the road did not bear a whole lot of traffic, for the camp was set back in its own rather grand spot of land. Florence didn't think she would come into any trouble. She certainly found more peace within the shadows than she did within the bustling train station.

It did not take long before the noise of the station was well out of earshot. The initial busy roads and roundabouts had surrendered to a narrow strip of concrete lined with blackberry hedges and fields and fields of green. Florence looked up as she walked, unable to keep her eyes off the glorious stars that burnt brighter without the pollution from the city. She only looked down or ahead when she heard rustling in the grass or noticed a change in the road in her peripheral vision. A sudden squeaking sound drew her attention to her right. Quickly illuminating the spot with her torch, she smiled at the sight of two tiny field mice scurrying between the brambles.

Taking her eyes off the happy pair enjoying a late-night snack she noticed the path ahead formed a particularly sharp bend.

Suddenly, beads of sweat began to form on her brow and she felt a shiver run down her spine.

'This was a stupid idea,' Florence mumbled to herself angrily. Her steps became tentative, but she had to keep going; it was too late to turn back now. She quickly looked around, across the fields either side of the dirt road, but her torch light came up empty of any suspicious figures and there was no other path she could take.

'I can't do this,' she protested.

Automatically her ears pricked up for any sound of cars. Her stomach somersaulted as she neared the sharp curve, and her mind was attacked by a loud screech and a blinding flash of light. Florence dropped her torch with a mighty crash and bent over to catch her racing breath.

'Stop. Stop. Stop.' She panted, her knees meeting the concrete as she braced herself in foetal position, curling in on herself. Oh, if the world could see her now, so weak and silly. Would it understand her resistance, or would it deem her the fool she believed she was? Normal people overcame such obstacles. Brave people built a successful life for themselves, but not her.

'Make it stop, Mum,' she whimpered, as sirens filled her head. Her knees began to ache against the hard surface, but she couldn't move, not yet.

It had been quite some time since her brain had conjured up images of that night. A night she wished she could take back; maybe even forget. It was hopeless of course. She knew she couldn't take it back just like she knew there was no forgetting it.

'Help me please, Dad, help me,' Florence cried softly

into the night. When Florence opened her eyes again, she was unsure how much time had passed. Her dress was damp with tears and she struggled to feel her legs from the numbness the cool concrete had provided. There had been no divine intervention, no moment of clarity, her heart simply felt heavier than before and all she wanted to do was turn back.

She had no hand reaching out to grab her and pull her off the ground and she couldn't hear any words of wisdom from her mum to encourage her to stand. Her only motivation was to get as far away from this spot and rid her brain of the painful images it held. Her legs shook violently, as though they were delicate branches caught in a fierce storm, as she forced herself to stand up straight. Wiping at her eyes, she took a deep breath in. Florence then tried, as she always did when this nightmare taunted her, to conjure up the laughter she could remember. She tried to envision a world more colourful than a rainbow and brighter than the sun to diminish the darkness that engulfed her, but tonight it was no use. There was no colour and no light, just emptiness. She set off on wobbly legs, this time with her head down following the beam of the torch and keeping her eyes to the ground, not wanting to see the path that had led her to such unbearable agony.

By the time the world had grown pitch black, Florence stood facing a large, mismatched stone building that was lit up faintly by old-fashioned lanterns. A wooden decking wrapped around the entire first floor and five windows displayed their own balconies on the second floor. The sky around it held stars that beamed bolder and brighter than the ones Florence had seen earlier, and so she stood transfixed. Only when she could feel the wearisome ache in the balls of her feet, now that she had stopped still to gander, did Florence close her mouth and make for the front door.

'Hello. Hello, George,' she called out to the empty reception area, using the name that Margot had told her. Her voice sounded hoarse from her earlier tears, so she coughed a little to clear it as she took in the room. The reception area housed a stone desk-like structure that was built atop a wooden floor. Florence could just about see the wood, for it was covered in ancient rugs. A mixture of old-fashioned rectangle lanterns and hanging flower baskets dangled from the stone walls. Florence smiled as she looked around.

Just then an elderly gentleman with a grey beard speckled with white strands and bushy drooping white eyebrows poked his head around a doorframe. There was no mistaking his annoyed expression, which Florence met with a bright smile, for she was engrossed by the charm of the room. She felt a tug of comfort in her heart that made her imagination stir in her brain. No more flashbacks attacked her; it felt like she was seeing the cottage with fresh eyes and her tears were kept at bay.

'Did you have any trouble finding the place? I take it your journey was OK?' the man asked, his voice a little rough around the edges as the well-rehearsed words left his lips.

'I do apologise that it's late, but my journey was indeed splendid, and I had no hiccups, for my magic carpet knew the way,' Florence said, her nerves getting the best of her. She hid her grimace behind a too bright smile, not wanting to think about her journey, though now the man probably thought her a crazy woman. Why did her imagination always have to get carried away? However, as her nostrils picked up on the smell of the potted calla lilies on the desk, the place only seemed to embolden her imagination. She couldn't help herself. Her tired eyes and heavy legs suddenly wanted to twirl around on the gorgeous flower-print rug that lay before the entrance to a lounge area and she imagined her ruffled Theo dress fanning out around her.

Shaking her head, Florence reduced her smile to a tight-lipped grin, not wanting to scare the man by showing too many teeth. He was giving her a look not unlike Olivia often gave her when she began to speak in gobbledygook. 'Sorry, I'm Florence. It's nice to meet you,' she added, her voice returning to a soft whisper as she tried to tone it down away from talk of magic carpets. Awkwardness was her expertise whenever she was nervous. The man looked her up and down for a moment. Something passed through his eyes that Florence could not place and when he spoke again, his words were slightly warmer.

'Please, follow me, Florence.' Florence watched his mouth move like it was attempting a smile, but it came off weak and resigned. She wondered if this was how he treated all his guests, whether they spoke of supernatural carpets or not.

It was a stark contrast to how Margot had described him, for she had said: 'Ask for the friendly gentleman by the name of George.' Florence didn't see how his attitude would be good for business; then again, she had checked in at just gone eleven p.m. The man was probably exhausted.

Florence decided against asking George any questions about the building. He was walking rather sprightly and speedily for an elderly gentleman, which suggested he didn't care to engage in conversation at such a late hour. He led the way past a staircase, through a magnificent room with a crystal chandelier and a beautiful stone fireplace where oohs and aahs slipped from between Florence's lips.

Each room she walked through warmed her skin from the

chill the cool night had coated her in. The gentle tremor in her hands from her nerves settled as the vintage feel of the building spoke to her and wrapped her in a welcoming embrace. Suddenly George stopped abruptly causing Florence to teeter on her tiptoes, so she didn't crash into his back. He fiddled around with a crowded key chain and unlocked a door at the back of the building. More old-fashioned lanterns hung from the stonework, casting a faint golden glow over the decking. What Florence could see in the dim light, she liked tremendously.

Down a few wooden steps, a short walk across a field of green, then just a little further on a dusty path, George stopped in front of what Florence assumed was to be her home for the week. She gazed at the oak hut that under the white glow of the moon looked to be painted a light pink shade. It looked like a hut out of a fairy tale. Florence almost hugged George but stopped herself when she looked over at him and saw that he stood tense and rigid with a sad look on his face. Florence wasn't quite sure if it was the hut or her that was making him sad.

'Thank you,' she said simply, as he handed her the key and promptly left with a muffled, 'Enjoy your stay.' Florence made a note to tell Margot about George to see if she knew any more about him. If her nanna had known George back in the day when they all used to visit and he had been the friendly man she had told Florence to ask for, something had certainly happened that her nanna must not be aware of. Florence watched him walk away for a moment and resigned herself to the thought that once the sun was out tomorrow, she would introduce herself again and maybe see if he was chirpier after some sleep.

Then she climbed the one little footstep and unlocked the

hut door. 'Oh, my goodness,' Florence gasped, a hand clasping over her mouth. The hut's interior was bright and snuggly hosting a double bed with a plush cream duvet in the middle. To the right side was a small counter area with cupboards and a tiny stove upon which a vintage teapot sat. At the back, an old-fashioned freestanding rose gold bath with the cutest little legs was tucked away amongst a few potted plants.

Florence kicked off her shoes, unable to believe how at home she felt as she popped her bags down. Her toes sunk into the fluffy cream rug and she felt as if she had entered an enchanted forest. The small hut was lit up by a honey-coloured lamp on the bedside table and a string of fairy lights above the bed. She couldn't wait to see the place in the daytime, though she was rather fond of the magic of the night. Retrieving her books from her suitcase, she immediately arranged them on the bedside table, and some on the floor by the bed, and felt the tension in her neck loosen. She then ran her hand along the cushy duvet before jumping atop it and sinking into the softness.

Lying back onto the inviting fluffy pillows, the business of the day catching up with her, Florence felt miles away from the trauma she had experienced earlier. She had thought coming here was a horrible idea and she had promised herself that when she arrived, she would get a little rest and return home tomorrow. Now, though, a small voice in the back of her mind was telling her to stay. The unexpected bursts of happiness she had experienced when the building had come into view and now as she looked around the darling hut were pleading with her to stay.

But with that came a spasm of guilt. How could she be so happy away from home, away from her nanna? How could she enjoy a vacation when she should be looking for work? The guilt gnawed at her. Her entire life she had told herself that she would never come back here, that she could never be happy here. Whenever her nanna had suggested she visit, fear had made her sink her heels in, not least because she could read the fear on Margot's face. If her nanna couldn't bring herself to come back, then she had no right to challenge Florence to. Oh, the arguments they had had.

The fairy lights over the bed cast tiny shadows onto the ceiling, Florence watched them, thinking about how something so delicate and pretty as the lights still created something so mysterious, foreboding even. But facing the shadows, looking at them with intent and not turning away, allowed her to see them for what they were: something not so scary after all. It was kind of how she felt about being here now. Though fear had engulfed her on her walk she had not run backwards; she had moved forwards with intent to get to her destination. Here she was, actually at Camp Calla Lily and her fears did not seem so terrifying.

Her nanna had so often told her that she had the power to control what she created, and that she could have a say in her visions. Control could sometimes be taken away – that was inevitable – but she should never let those struggles, surprises or bumps in the road rid her of her deepest wishes and her purest beliefs. The vision she had created of Camp Calla Lily was one of pain and suffering. Never did she imagine it could be beautiful again, but this hut alone proved otherwise. Reliving that horrendous night on the corner of the junction had been awful but now she was here in this gorgeous hut. She had overcome one obstacle she thought she never would, which only gave her further pause.

Florence tilted her head away from the fairy light shadows towards the tiny window to her left with its curtains still open.

More shadows lurked in the darkness, this time of the large trees out in the grounds. Her eyes threatened to glaze over as she thought about how her love of books and theatre had saved her from her deepest heartbreaks. They had saved her when she was five and then again five years ago when she split with her boyfriend, Ryan. With a book in her hand, she didn't have time to overthink her relationship and it had suited her just fine. Yet something niggled inside her. Five years had gone by. Five years of settling for a job that didn't light a fire in her soul. And five years where she had let each day pass without a fight. She had not stood up for the kids she left behind, or the theatre Ryan had taken from her and her nanna. Florence had run from it all and not looked back.

Swinging her legs off the bed, she didn't feel so sleepy anymore. She stood and wandered over to the kitchen area. Filling the teapot on the stovetop and lighting the happy flames, it occurred to Florence that these were thoughts she didn't stay with for long. Instead, she always chose to safely bury them in her heart's treasure chest, conveniently misplacing the key for months at a time. But with the twinkly lights glowing warmly at her and the stars so vivid and bold in the night sky outside her window, she ruminated on these ideas. She knew she didn't belong behind a desk; the theatre had been her entire life. The dreams she had been having of getting back into teaching drama classes were becoming more frequent as were the scenes that bounced around in her head.

For the first time in five years she felt the sudden urge to act on her visions and possibly come up with a plan. Maybe these daydreams were not meant to be left alone? Through the children, through her classes, from the pages of her books to the stage, she used to do just that. Maybe it was time to bring them to life once more and not be content with them simply playing out in her mind. Yes, that was it, those beautiful productions, the spectacles that took place in her mind, she would make them happen. For the future kids that she hoped to teach, she could make them a reality. At least on a stage no one could give her funny looks or scold her for her silly visions.

Maybe it was sheer exhaustion from the day's events, the fairy-tale-esque vibe of Camp Calla Lily in the dark of the night or the smell of the camomile tea that filled the room as it brewed, but Florence found herself feeling strangely determined. Cupping her mug, she walked back to her bed and settled on its edge. Could she find closure and solace in this holiday after all?

SIX

Florence woke with the sunrise the next morning feeling rested and refreshed. Her dreams had been as vivid as always, clearly depicting little ones running around in epic homemade costumes, laughing with pure glee as they acted out scenes – last night it had been scenes from *Peter Pan*, and it had been wonderful. She stretched her limbs like a starfish and made to open the cream curtains so she could watch the sun bloom into the sky.

As she moved across the hut, its full beauty became evident in the new light. The craftsmanship was stunning, no detail left unspoken for. The beams on the ceiling arched with smooth curves and were painted to match the outside of the tiny house. The knobs on the two kitchen cabinets and the small dresser were vintage and made of shiny ceramic and those too were painted a gorgeous pastel pink. Next to the potted calatheas and Boston ferns, a small pale pink, slightly rusty watering can rested on top of a stool. Florence walked slowly, pausing at each of the features, before filling the kettle on the stove to get the water boiling for tea. While she waited, she took great delight in feeding the plants from the cute watering can.

Whoever had designed these huts had thought of everything. If it had been the old man, she wondered why he had been so grumpy. He should be proud, Florence thought. Though no childhood memories had yet sprung to mind, Florence knew that these houses had not been here when she had visited before, not least because her nanna had told her they were new but because she didn't believe that she, her mum or her nanna would have ever wanted to leave if they had seen them. It was like every bookworm's dream, a tiny hut so peaceful and serene with the perfect amount of cosy to make you want to cuddle up inside. With a coffee table, or treat table as she liked to call them, stacked high with books, and the fact that the huts themselves looked so unassuming and rather cute, resembling garden sheds, no one would bother you for days.

The thought made her cheerful as she stirred a teaspoon of sugar in her tea and collected *Sense and Sensibility* from the pile of books she had set out on her bedside table. She'd needed to place some books on the floor, worried that the tiny table might topple over with the weight of them. She made her way to the light oak door. The door was like a piece of art with fine ridges and natural knots. Florence paused a minute before opening it just to admire the work.

With her book tucked under her arm and teacup aloft, Florence peered her head around the door to check for any signs of movement. She was conscious of not making too much noise. She didn't want to wake the old man or those staying in the distant huts. With the coast clear she crept out onto her decking and was immediately blown away by the vast land that spread out before her. Under the glow of the rising sun the deep green grass glistened with morning dew. The pink and white magnolia trees, of which there were many, gifted the breeze with a sweet aroma and she could just make out a lake that shimmered in the morning light hiding at the bottom of the rolling hills. Florence wished her nanna had come with her. She missed her so and it didn't seem fair that she was enjoying this view without her. Maybe once Florence explained how she had conquered a piece of her fear and how beautiful the camp was, her nanna might feel inspired to try and conquer hers too.

Taking a seat in the egg-shaped wicker chair that was canopied by the nearby pink Jane tree, Florence opened her book and read while the birds sang aloud.

The next time she looked up, the sun had made its full appearance and seemed set on providing another glorious summer day. Florence coloured for a moment, ashamed of the luxury that had been bestowed on her on a Tuesday morning, when she heard a voice from behind her.

'Hello,' the voice said softly, timid in its approach and sounding from a distance as though the person was opposed to scaring her or intruding on her reading.

Florence shot up from her seat and turned around, suddenly aware that she was in her strappy cotton nightdress that reached just above her knee, but the man did not survey her body, his eyes were trained on hers. Instinctively though, she clutched her book over her chest for comfort.

'Hello,' she replied, feeling apprehensive. The man was disarmingly handsome with curly brown hair and a heart-shaped face. He wore trousers, not jeans, and a white shirt that was crinkled, rolled up at the sleeves and seemed a little too big for his slim frame. He looked away to the Jane tree and when he returned his gaze, a smile spread across his features. It was kind, but his hazel eyes displayed a glint of mischief.

'I wondered if you needed storage for your magic carpet, ma lady.' He spoke with an Irish accent and a sudden confidence that made Florence's wall go up.

She clutched her book tighter, confused. She had not heard or seen anyone in the main cottage last night except the old man. Had George already warned the other guests of the strange new visitor?

'Don't tease me,' Florence said, boldly, the hurt and humiliation of Friday night at the bar still fresh in her mind. This time, however, she would have to stand up for herself – not having Olivia or Drew by her side.

'I would not tease,' the man said, stepping forward. He had his hands in his pockets and a smile still danced on his lips. Florence did not care for the smirk.

'Then don't mock me. I don't care to be mocked,' she countered, narrowing her eyes, her lips pressing together. Then she turned around. Florence felt a small rush of irritation with herself and with the man. She did not mean to be rude to the stranger, but nor did she want to engage in his playful banter. 'I don't desire a Mr Grey and I'm not going to be your Anastasia Steele,' she added, getting straight to the point. She kept her voice monotone and uninterested as she returned to her seat and opened her book, needing the comfort of its pages.

'I should think we would have to get to know each other better first, love.' No longer Irish, the man spoke with a thick Scottish accent as he stepped under the tree, a few feet away from her at the side of the decking. Florence looked up. Despite herself the change of accent gave her pause and she had to fight to keep her lips from curving. His words had come out so robust and full of alarming disgust at her insinuation. She had wanted to laugh. It was clear that he hadn't been thinking anything of the sort. When that thought registered in her mind, her cheeks coloured at having been the one to bring up Mr Grey.

Shaking away her awkwardness, she carefully placed her bookmark between the crease of her book and half closed it, keeping her fingers between the pages so she could return to it the minute she got rid of this annoying man.

She looked over to him. He stood tall under the pink flowers, one hand gently touching the branches, the sun highlighting his sharp cheekbones. He caught her watching him and their eyes met again.

'I take it you are on vacation, ma'am?' he asked, again with the Scottish accent that had Florence trying to decipher whether the man was really Irish or Scottish. The cheeky glint seemed to falter for a moment as he looked away from her and to the sky, like he too knew the question was a tad silly.

Florence turned back to her book. 'Whatever gave you that idea?' Again she forced the words out cold in hopes that he would take the hint and leave. The man shrugged and squinted his eyes across the fields. When he didn't move, Florence chanced a quick glance at him, her big Uranian blue eyes widening with curiosity at his calm stance and the way he stretched his long limbs to lean against the high branch of the tree; then she returned to her book. The atmosphere was restful. Being miles away from the city she could hear no cars, no people, just the peaceful chatter of the birds, but the man was disrupting her view.

'Have you taken up being a tree?' Florence said, without looking up but sensing the man had still not moved. She could feel him glance her way now, but she kept her head down. She wanted to get to the end of her chapter before going for breakfast.

The man ignored her comment.

'I think I shall join you, for you make such friendly conversation and are a delight to be around,' he said, now in a distinguished British accent. Florence had to fight harder this time to keep from looking at him. Who was this man?

When he sat down at the base of the beautiful magnolia tree and pulled out a battered copy of Charles Dickens's *Great Expectations*, Florence gasped. She hadn't even realised she had been looking but she had a sixth sense when it came to books and a desire to know what everyone was reading. Yes, that was what had made her look over at him for the third time.

'What on earth have you done to that precious book?' she demanded, her eyes bulging, forgetting for a moment her intention of being uninterested in anything to do with the man. He smiled. Florence quickly looked away. She didn't catch him looking at her with fascination. She could not know of the thoughts going through his head, for he did not share them with her. But there must be many thoughts racing through his head. For one, he could surely tell by the way in which she perched her book so gently on her knees and by how she delicately turned the pages that she might not care for his wayward ways.

'Books are to be loved,' he said, with no false bravado, as he looked the book over in his hands.

'You and I clearly have very different ideas of what love is,' Florence stated. She didn't miss that the man's voice came out calm, his accent southern with a gentle cockney lilt, making something inside her stir. Thinking it safe to glance at him again, with his nose buried in his book now, she looked over only to find him gazing at her. A moment passed between them before they quickly cast their eyes down to the pages before them.

Blinking away the world she had been immersed in, Florence looked up to find herself running along the lake. She had her imaginary horse beside her, and she was giggling with childlike glee. Wildflowers, daisies, and dandelions carpeted the field around her, and pebbles washed up along the grassy verges. She paused, stroking her horse's long mane before picking up a pebble and skimming it across the water. The pebble didn't ripple; it simply hit the water with a loud plop and sunk. Undeterred she ran along further in search of another stone. Catching the chatter up ahead after a few paces, she looked up to a bench that stood underneath a large oak tree. There sat her mum, dad and nanna and so she stopped and waved. Her mum blew a kiss making Florence laugh as she jumped to catch it. Her mum then rested her hand over her heart, smiling over at Florence, joy etched on her face from the pure happiness that could only be elicited by the sweet sounds of her baby girl's laughter. Filled with love, and content with her family watching over her, Florence stayed playing with her horse, finding a spot in the long grass. They sat down and plucked at the daisies, collecting them to make a crown. Suddenly a loud crash startled her...

Florence blinked again and shifted uncomfortably in her chair. When her vision became clear she realised there was a man kneeling in front of her, his hazel eyes flickering with concern beneath his dark curls and he was holding the teacup that she must have knocked to the floor.

'I'm so sorry,' she said, her voice trembling, a blush rising in her cheeks as her brows scrunched up in irritation. She had only just met the man and already he had witnessed her silly haze and clumsy actions. Why did her mind do this to her? 'I'm sorry,' she repeated. 'Just a silly dream – you should have woken me.' She was not altogether out of her stupor and looked around anxiously. He was too close. His eyes were too searching. Embarrassment washed over her. His eyes looked sad, like he was embarrassed for her. She cringed, wiping the sweat off her brow.

'I thought it would be rude to disturb you,' he said, placing the cup and saucer back on the armrest and standing. He didn't move away but Florence couldn't make eye contact. Why wasn't he moving away?

'I'm sorry, just a vivid dream – embarrassing I know. It wouldn't have disturbed me. You can go now,' she tried, still looking at the ground, her words coming out rushed.

'You could have been fighting off dragons for all I know and one distraction from me and one might have eaten you alive,' the man said, as he took a step back. With him not towering over her, her jaw relaxed.

The battle between Florence's stubborn heart and her lips was proving fierce. Her lips betrayed her and curved slightly as she looked up, a long way up from her sitting position. She squinted at him in the sunlight, touched by his words. Florence had spent her childhood being admonished by frustrated teachers whenever she disappeared into a daydream. Even now Olivia always seemed more worried than intrigued by them and like the lady on the train and George at the reception desk, people often thought of her as weird. No one other than her parents and her nanna ever asked about her dreams or cared to venture a guess as to what she could see.

The man stood patiently as Florence, with one eye closed and her lips pursed to one side, considered a bee that flew by. She had been rattled by her dream as it had all felt very real.

She had known it would happen given time; she simply hadn't quite been as prepared as she had hoped. Now her irritation had settled, she was grateful to the man for his distraction. A little hesitantly she stood, so they were mere inches apart, which made Florence laugh when she came level with his chest.

'Who are you?' she asked, tucking her book under her arm, and tilting her head skywards.

He took a step back, considered her for a moment, and bowed. 'The name's Jo – J, O.' He said, raking a hand though his hair to tame it as he returned to standing. Florence had the urge to reach out and mess it up again.

'Should you not be enjoying your holiday in your own hut or off bothering other holidaymakers?' Florence teased.

'I don't believe bothering others would be half as much fun as bothering you,' he replied, all side smirk and dimples.

Florence couldn't hold back; she swatted him and cracked a smile as she did so. Curiosity got the best of her and she let her guard down just a touch.

'Jo, as in Jo March?' she asked with a quirk of her brow.

'The very same.' He nodded, surprising Florence.

'Why Jo?' It intrigued her.

'My mum had high hopes for me.' He nodded, with a wrinkle of his nose and a casual shrug.

'As a writer?' Florence rocked forward on her bare toes.

'As a writer,' Jo confirmed leaning forward, hands in his pockets.

'Arrgh, so you are not to get caught up in the nonsense of men...' Florence started, finding her posh accent coming through as she relaxed in Jo's presence.

'Women,' Jo interrupted, with a boyish grin.

Florence continued, '...women then, and you should be off

in an attic alone somewhere scribbling away, not disturbing me.' She grinned back, a mischievous sparkle in her eyes.

'But where would the fun in that be?' They were both now grinning at each other, Florence looking up and Jo gazing down.

Florence gave a thoughtful, 'Hmm, so you are named after a girl?'

'One of the very best,' Jo contended.

'And that does not bother you?' Florence probed, rocking on to her tiptoes, for her neck was beginning to ache looking up at him.

'Not at all. Does it bother you?' Jo answered, curving his shoulders, and leaning down having noticed her standing on her tiptoes.

'Why would it? Jo March is my favourite.' Florence beamed.

They stood quite content in smiling at each other trying to figure the other out, until Florence's stomach drew their attention with a gurgle.

'You are hungry,' Jo commented.

'You are perceptive,' Florence teased, surprising herself. 'I am hungry, and I am also Florence,' she said, sticking out her hand for him to shake and smiling when he did so. Then she turned towards the door and disappeared inside her hut.

SEVEN

Jo was sat swinging on the bench that hung from a large thick branch of the magnolia tree when Florence returned from inside her hut after getting dressed. He looked up when he saw her, and Florence noticed that his eyes always went straight to hers rather than scanning her body. It made her instantly relax and feel like she could be herself around him.

'Are you ready for the best breakfast you've ever had?' Jo asked, giving his eyebrows a little wiggle. Florence's stomach gave another rumble as if to answer for her.

'I think that's a yes,' she said, Jo's smile rubbing off on her.

Jo led Florence up to the main cottage, which burst with colour in the daylight. They walked across the patio area where Florence had walked last night but instead of continuing in a straight line that would lead them to the reception area at the front, Jo turned right, which took them to a room with high ceilings and gorgeous large windows carved out of the stone that encouraged the sunlight to pour in and fill the room with its warm glow. The tables were mismatched, different colours of wood, shapes, and sizes. Plant pots that were home to pretty primulas and tulips created space between the variety of chairs and sofas. When the sun caught the petals, the prisms of light bounced from flower to flower almost as if they were saying hello.

The smell of bacon frying and crispy toast with melted butter made Florence's mouth water and pulled her attention to the corner of the room where a sign above the countertop read "Calla Lily Café". Behind the display of cakes Florence could see the chefs in the kitchen happily chatting as they prepared each breakfast. There were five tables occupied, each with couples who looked to be a little younger than Florence's nanna. Florence smiled at them all as some sat deep in conversation whilst others sat reading the newspaper, passing pages to their other half when they were done.

'Hi, Sal,' Jo said when they reached the breakfast bar. 'This is Florence,' he added leaning on the counter casually and smiling as he gestured at Florence.

'Nice to meet you, Sal,' Florence said, giving a small wave.

'Nice to meet you too, love. What can I get for you two this morning?' Sal replied in a jolly manner, which made Florence's grin broader.

'Please can I get a full English and a pot of tea,' Florence replied.

'I'll get a bacon butty please, Sal,' Jo said.

'Will that be to go again, Jo?' Sal enquired, giving Jo a narrow-eyed look like he was trying to read him.

'Please.' Jo nodded, before standing and looking around for a table. Florence followed his gaze and stopped upon a table by one of the large windows.

'I'll bring them over. Go take a seat,' Sal said, so Florence made her way over to the sunny spot and Jo followed. Florence felt silly at the touch of disappointment she felt in her stomach at Jo taking his breakfast to go. It conflicted with her earlier thoughts of wishing he would go away and leave her alone and so she really shouldn't be upset over getting her wish. Yet, she felt a tug of gloom at the thought of not being around him. Taking her seat, she focused on the smatter of clouds that filtered the sky, for she didn't want Jo to think she had gotten attached already, when she really hadn't. She barely knew him.

'I guess a writer never stops working, even when they're on holiday?' Florence questioned, turning her attention back to Jo, who had taken the seat opposite her, if just for a short while. For a moment, Florence thought she saw the brightness in Jo's eyes faulter. His brow knotted for a matter of seconds before his face bounced back to cheerful.

'Something like that,' he said, with a shrug and a wave of his hand.

'Do you holiday here often?' Florence asked, when Jo didn't offer further information about his work. But before he could answer Sal appeared with her breakfast and Jo's sandwich. Jo stood and bowed graciously to Sal before looking back at Florence.

He dipped into his regal accent and then took a bite out of his sandwich with an air of confidence that made her laugh. 'Might I suggest that the barn over the hill—' he pointed out of the window at the direction she should take '—is situated among pathways perfect for an afternoon stroll.' He raised his eyebrows and made his eyes wide before taking a few steps back and bidding her adieu.

Florence watched him leave, her elbow on the table, her lips resting against her fingers, as she did so. She wondered if he had a secret cave or den that he wrote in. The huts certainly seemed idyllic for a writer's retreat; maybe he came to Camp Calla Lily often to pen his novels. She suddenly felt a prickle of excitement that she must find a bookshop and search out Jo's name. Though she must enquire as to his last name or ask if he wrote under a pen name first. The thought that she could tell her nanna that she had met a writer made her grin.

There was not a single baked bean or crumb of toast left on Florence's plate some thirty minutes after Sal had placed it in front of her. She had taken her time savouring every bite and had enjoyed it immensely. It wasn't until the bacon was right under her nose that she realised she hadn't eaten since her nanna's roast dinner last night, and after her train journey and walk, she had been ravenous.

She thanked Sal and waved at the kitchen staff as she left and thought she would take a look at the lounge area and maybe try to catch the old man and make amends for having checked in so late. Maybe after a good night's sleep he would be in a better mood.

The bookshelves either side of the fireplace accommodated all the classics Florence had adored as a child. All were in beautiful condition, hardback and spellbinding. She absent-mindedly traced her fingers over them as she read their titles.

'You are more than welcome to help yourself to any of the books, my dear Florence.' The voice from behind startled her and she spun around, having to push her glasses back up her nose to see its owner.

'Thank you,' she said seeing George watching her from behind the reception desk, indeed bearing a kinder face than she had witnessed last night. 'Thank you,' she said again, not quite knowing what to say at his sudden brighter appearance. 'This place is beautiful, and I'm in love with my hut,' she told him when her brain clicked back into gear.

'I am glad you think so,' George offered with a warm smile as he continued writing in a book that he had out on the desk.

Taking *Alice in Wonderland* from the shelf, Florence stepped out of the room and closer to the desk with a question on her lips that she hoped the gentleman would not think her cheeky to ask, now that he was in a warmer mood.

'Sir, would it be possible for me to use your phone?' Florence asked, fiddling with the book in her hand. George looked up at her, the smile on his face being replaced by a sad expression, his fluffy brows covering his sorrow-filled eyes. Florence instantly regretted asking and worried that he had thought her request rude. Landlines could be expensive. 'I'm sorry, it's no trouble if not,' Florence started.

'Of course you can and please call me George,' he answered hastily as though forgetting himself for a moment, the smile now back on his face. Puzzled by his reaction, it took Florence a minute to take the phone he was holding out to her. She had to step closer, for it was a corded phone and didn't stretch far from the desk.

'Thank you,' she whispered, putting her book down so she could dial her nanna's number. George retreated into the back office, which Florence thought was sweet. She appreciated the gesture of privacy though aware she was standing in the main lobby and people were free to come and go as they pleased.

After three rings, her nanna's voice came down the line. 'Hello treasure, what are you doing calling me? I thought you would be off dancing with the wildflowers by now,' Margot said, securing a laugh from her granddaughter, which warmed her heart. Florence hated thinking of her nanna alone in an empty house. Margot had always encouraged Florence to get out and experience the world. She'd insisted she not lock herself away forever when the world had so many wonders to offer. They would dream big together, talk of the places Florence would visit, then they would get comfy on the couch with a book and the dream would be forgotten. With her nanna's vivid imagination, Florence felt like she had no need to actually visit another country, for it would appear so clearly in her mind. Quite to her satisfaction, she had vacationed in half of the globe by the time she was nine.

But here she was now at Camp Calla Lily when her nanna was home alone. She knew of course that this had been her nanna's choice, but still, doing things without her was new territory.

'I wanted to let you know I got here safe and, Nanna, there are flowers everywhere, they are gorgeous,' Florence told her, leaning on the desk, gazing at one such bunch of flowers that bloomed in a tall ceramic vase and filled the room with a heavenly perfume.

'That sounds lovely, my dear. Now all is fabulous here, so please do not worry yourself and go and enjoy your holiday,' her nanna said and it pleased Florence to hear that her voice was indeed chirpy and did not sound tired or troubled; maybe she didn't need to feel so guilty.

'OK, I will but if you need me or anything, I don't think George will mind if you ring the front desk and ask for me, OK?' Florence noted.

'I do not think he will either. I love you, my dear Florence, now go on.'

'I love you too,' Florence said, then she placed the phone back on the receiver, shouted another thank you through to George and headed out into the sunshine.

Florence couldn't bring herself to walk down to the lake just yet. The morning's daydream had left her with mixed feelings, and she wasn't quite sure how to deal with them yet.

On the one hand the memory had felt like a cuddle around her heart, like she could still feel the kiss in the palm of her hand that her mum had blown her way. And on the other it crushed her in ways she didn't know how to handle, other than to retreat into her books and watch the world go by.

She was not about to forget the lesson from her walk to Camp Calla Lily, of facing the painful bits to find the gold at the end, but she might need just a couple more days to face that memory. While the sad memories were indeed sad, sometimes the happy ones hurt more – only serving to remind her of the good that had been taken away. The wispy clouds from this morning had since dispersed to allow the pale blue of the sky to shine in all its glory as Florence shuffled along the dusty path in thought. Before Florence made her return to the camp just last night, after twenty-three years away, she had been trying so hard not to block everything out completely, to let people in and to face her torments. People like her friends at the theatre; the kids she had worked with; Ryan, Olivia and Drew had all been given access to her heart. Besides Drew and Olivia, when those at the theatre chose sides and Ryan showed his true colours, Florence concluded that letting people in only further damaged her heart. Since then, her daydreams had become grander and her heart more stubborn.

Cruelly, she knew she kept Olivia at arm's length. While her friend knew about Ryan, of the heartache he had caused, Florence had not mentioned the story of her parents. No one but her nanna and her school teachers knew. Some stories felt real when you read them aloud and this was one Florence wished with all her heart was nothing more than a twisted, dark fantasy that ended the moment she closed the book.

Instead of the lake, Florence found herself walking in the direction Jo had pointed out earlier. The path was lined with bright pink magnolia trees and the occasional English oak and London plane. All were in full bloom, the pink of the blossoms popping out with the backdrop of the vibrant greens. Everywhere Florence looked there were dog roses, begonias, honeysuckles, periwinkles, lavender and of course calla lilies. She also noticed the benches hiding in the shade and the hammocks swinging in the sun and decided she would stop for a while and soak up some sunshine and read a chapter or two of her new book. It had been a while since she had read *Alice in Wonderland* and after her big breakfast she felt deserving of curling up in the sunshine with a good book.

EIGHT

Sometime later, when the pages of the book illuminated a little too bright as the sun moved higher into the sky and made Florence's eyes sting, she stopped the hammock from swinging with her heels against the grass, and went in search of the barn that Jo had told her about. It was a pleasant walk with the summer breeze guiding her along the path.

When Florence came to a gap in the clearing, she couldn't believe her eyes. For there nestled behind two large common beech trees was a grand structure. With two turrets on either side waving flags at passers-by, a window on the second floor with a balcony and two gorgeous windows on the first floor either side of a great double barn door. The panels were painted a sunflower yellow with white and mint accents and old-fashioned lanterns hung above the doorway. Inside there seemed to be some kind of gala going on with the music that streamed from the windows. Florence couldn't possibly enter, for she was not dressed for a ball. She wouldn't go inside but she most certainly had to peek. Crouching down so she would not be seen, Florence took a step closer when something flew at her and hit her on the forehead...

Florence jumped backwards fearing she had walked into a spiderweb but when she looked down a paper aeroplane lay at her feet. When she looked up to find its pilot, the grand structure was gone, and she saw Jo standing atop a hay bale on the second-floor balcony that was dressed in scaffolding and did not look safe.

Florence reached down, picked up the dusty aeroplane and unfolded it to see words hastily scrawled on it.

"How did you see it?" they read, making Florence smile. She looked up using her hand to shield her eyes from the sun. Jo was leaning against a haggard window frame wearing loose-fitting jeans, a white T-shirt, thick boots and gloves. It was a more barbarian kind of look in contrast to how he was dressed this morning, but it suited him all the same.

'Less crumbly,' Florence shouted up playfully, grinning at him and seeing the barn for what it really was – a little on the run-down side. After Jo's mention of dragons this morning, she found herself spilling her vision to him with no hesitation.

'Colourful panels, sunflower yellow with mint ice-cream green accents. Flags waving welcomingly in the wind. A sturdy brass knocker on a big double front door. Lanterns outside every window and fairy lights...' Florence paused for effect and stretched out her arms '...everywhere. This entire space, the whole barn, covered in them.' She laughed, a laugh that sounded alien to her own ears. It erupted from the depth of her belly and felt freeing as it sounded out through the forest. When she looked back to Jo, he was smiling, his head tilted as if he were trying to picture what she saw. He probably thought her naïve. It would take a lot of work. For starters, the splintered beams had to go, as did the broken panels, the moss and dust and general debris. There was so much to do, and Florence didn't have the first clue about renovating a barn. For all she knew, one swipe of paint on these panels and the whole thing would tumble to the ground.

'Should you really be up there?' she asked. Her laugh lines had been replaced with worried creases as she skipped a little closer to the barn and out of the sun so she could see Jo without squinting.

'I like the view,' Jo voiced. Florence laughed again and looked around. The clearing was certainly spectacular. She didn't doubt that from his viewpoint, looking down on the smaller trees, being closer to the canopies of leaves and getting a bird's eye view of every colourful flower, was entrancing.

'It certainly is beautiful out here,' Florence replied, looking around then turning her attention back to the barn when she heard creaks and thuds. Suddenly, Jo appeared at the spot where Florence assumed the barn door used to be. 'What happened to this place?' she asked, moving closer still and pulling a piece of moss off the window ledge.

'Unfortunately, it's not been able to compete with the big theme parks, adventure centres, even iPads. Each year we've been getting fewer visitors and so this place was of no use anymore,' Jo explained, gathering up broken pieces of wood and adding them to his bonfire-like pile. A shadow of sadness crossed his features. Florence absentmindedly began passing him bits of rubble and splintered wood.

'We?' she questioned.

'My grandparents own this place. The old fella who checked you in is my grandad,' Jo informed her. Florence noticed the same flicker of darkness pass through his eyes, like it had done earlier when he spoke of work.

'He seems troubled. Is he OK?' Florence asked, genuinely

concerned for George. She had much preferred seeing him happy this morning rather than grumpy as he had been the night before.

'Yes, he just doesn't like to hear of change. Since my grandma died, he's not been the same. This place is not the same. He can't keep up and doesn't like to hear of help,' Jo said, throwing a larger plank of wood a bit harder at the pile, his frustration evident to Florence.

'I'm sorry about your grandma,' Florence said. 'And I'm sorry about this place. It's stunning. I used to come here when I was very little but then we stopped coming and I don't remember too much about it to be honest,' Florence confessed, feeling a touch guilty that her family had been one to desert the place too, though not because they had given their business to another place and certainly not because of iPads.

Moving her hands to her hips, she looked over Jo, his attire and the loose curls that kept falling into his eyes and said, 'So, writer Jo, do you work here?'

He stopped what he was doing and placed a long leg on a smaller pile of wood. Florence watched as he leant forward to rest his hands on his knee. 'Not exactly. I don't remember much of this barn either to tell you the truth. Up in the cottage there are pictures of this place bustling with people on the walls. I think they used to hold dances and parties here,' he told her in a tone that graduated from solemn with a hint of heartache to enthusiastic and hopeful that one day it could be restored to its former splendour.

'And so, the writer thought to swap his pen for a hammer?' Florence asked dubiously. She had to ask, for when she looked around there was a lot of work to do and an awful lot of heavy lifting. Jo was slim and his arms were not much bigger than hers, though she could see the muscles in his biceps twitch as he moved the panels, showing he clearly did not lack strength. Catching her looking at him, Jo smiled mischievously at her. Her cheeks heated. He clearly read her lack of confidence in him and for a moment she felt ashamed for judging.

'I read about it in a book somewhere. How hard can it be?' Jo retorted, his voice light and playful, as he looked up at her under hooded eyes from his bent-over position. Florence was unable to resist laughing. She bit her lip and scrunched up her nose.

'Would you like some help?' she found herself asking.

'I wouldn't want to keep you from your books or your holiday,' Jo said with so much sincerity she was taken aback. She was not used to that genuine tone when most people begged her to remove her nose from her books. She was a little shocked at herself too, when it dawned on her that she wanted to do something other than read.

'I would like to help,' she told him sweetly, walking around to collect more fallen branches lying in the barn's doorway.

'Take these please,' Jo said, stopping her with a gentle touch to her elbow and passing her the thick garden gloves he had just been wearing. Florence smiled at his generosity and thoughtfulness.

'Do you not need them?' she said, worried that his hands would now get all torn up.

'Aye, but I'm a brute of a man and I must look out for the lady,' he said, his Scottish accent back, which took away any urge she had to argue with him on being sexist when he looked at her and bowed dramatically. She liked his old-fashioned manner and the fact that he too had a plethora of accents up his sleeves.

In a comfortable silence Florence and Jo cleared debris

from around the barn, creating a small mountain of fractured logs and panels that had fallen off their hinges in the clearing.

'What is it you do, Florence?' Jo asked a little while later as they shuffled more rubbish onto their pile.

Florence stood up, stretching out her back and wiping at her brow with the back of her gloves.

'I actually just got fired from my job. I worked at Paper-chains Office Supplies. It was nothing glamorous, but it looked after my nanna and me,' she told Jo, feeling more at ease in his company as the minutes went by, which made her chest rattle a touch with nervous energy.

'Is that what you've always done?' he enquired. 'Forgive me for judging, but you don't seem like you belong in an office.'

Florence considered Jo, unsure of how much of herself to give away. Yes, he was judging but it unnerved her slightly that he had judged her so well. Her past experiences had made her weary, yet that feeling of ease came again, slowly pushing her anxiety out of the way. There was a calmness to Jo's voice that lent itself to genuine interest and his judgement had not been rude or wrong for that matter.

'I was there for five years. Before that I worked at Old Maude's Theatre in Manchester. I had worked there since I was seventeen doing everything from cleaning to stagehand to props, then I started teaching children's classes. We did plays and productions – oh I loved it. I loved putting the sets together. The kids helped of course, but seeing their faces when it all came together, watching their eyes light up, it was a dream. The way they pranced, danced and performed on the stage uninhibited, it was a joy,' she expressed, her voice having grown wistful at the memories. It had been a long time since she had spoken of the theatre or spoken so freely around anyone but her nanna.

She could feel her cheeks ache as her smile grew with her words, then she caught Jo looking at her and quickly turned away. She shook her head and saw to an old mouldy chair leg, throwing it onto the pile.

'What happened, if you don't mind me asking?' His tone was gentle, which felt like an invite for more honesty from Florence than she wanted to give. She suddenly felt like a weight had been lifted off her chest in sharing her memories of her old job. A desire to talk openly grew but so did the familiar fearful tremor in her chest.

'I stupidly,' she began in her most practised and posh British accent, 'fell in love with the art director. You see he was not the art director at the beginning of our courtship, just a young boy who loved the theatre as much as I...' She was moving between the dirty debris now, almost like she was floating across a stage, with a cheeky smile on her face that appeared between the acting mournful and sad faces when she spoke. 'Everyone encouraged our relationship. They so wanted it to be, for it would be good for me.' Her arms went up beside her as she spun around on the spot, her dress twirling at her feet.

Florence clutched her chest, her hair blowing in the breeze, some strands sticking to the sweat on her cheeks as she sung out in a very Pinocchio-like voice, 'A girl like me must not live on books alone, for a girl needs a real man. I had to get myself a real boy.' Her eyes met Jo's when she finished – they were clear and happy – then she tilted her head back and laughed.

When her face met his again, she puckered her lips in thought and a slight flush crept into her cheeks. Then, surprising herself, her voice returned to normal and she continued opening up as if out here in the depths of the forest her secrets would be safe.

'I was nineteen, we'd spent lots of time together at the theatre and knew each other as kids. I was comfortable around him, so it had all been wonderful and exciting at first, especially with the support of everyone around me. But your twenties are supposed to be a time for fun and experiences and our ideas of fun ended up being completely different. I can't blame him really, liking different things is not a crime, but he just didn't end up being who I thought he was. I became a bit of a joke, a prude in his eyes and I guess he felt a need to keep up appearances with everyone at the theatre. His mum and dad being the owners and all, he thought he could sort of separate the two worlds without telling me. I was his girlfriend at work and then he would cheat on me and ignore me in the real world, so to speak. It went on for a while until the girls started showing up to plays and I cottoned on. I think he feared I would make a scene or ruin his reputation within the theatre or his chances with the girls and so I conveniently got fired,' she said blowing out a breath and flopping onto the hay bale beside Jo.

'Love doesn't happen the way it does in our books, Jo,' she said softly, looking up at him, from her lying position, her words coming out almost as if she were saying them to herself.

Dramatically Jo flew to his feet. 'Who on earth told you that?' he asked incredulously.

'Take that back at once, Florence,' he said, as he climbed to the top of their mountain of logs and debris.

'Here I stand on top of the world.' The planks wobbled precariously, Jo balancing on one of them like a seesaw. 'And if I should not find a love to take my hand, I shall fall off the ends of the earth and it will be my demise.'

Florence didn't move. She started at him, her lips trembling with suppressed laughter. Jo edged closer to one side of the plank, making it wobble more violently now. His arms spread out like an eagle to steady himself.

'One lover's grasp is all I need – that magic touch will save me,' he called out making Florence sit up. She held his gaze and held her tongue in her cheek, but still did not move. She had only just met this man. Her body and mind felt torn. She couldn't take his hand. She hesitated, suddenly feeling silly and confused by how he made her feel, how she had opened up so brazenly and told him all about Ryan and the theatre. He must think her an idiot for not realising sooner that Ryan was cheating on her, or worse he could think her naïve and that he could get anything he wanted from her, for she had just bared her soul so easily. The tremor in her chest grew stronger.

'One more step and I will never know love's...' Jo took another step making the plank lift. Unexpectantly and by the look on his face, Florence thought unintentionally too, the logs rolled away underneath him and down he went, landing with a thud on the mud.

Florence shouted and jumped up, running over to the rubble. Leaning over the scattered debris she saw Jo lying on the ground and winced.

'You fell,' she stated.

'You were supposed to take my hand,' he choked out, sounding a tad winded.

'I've only just met you. I am not your lover, Jo,' she replied with a small smirk. He looked so helpless and not at all conniving lying there in a heap.

'And nor do I think I will ever take one again,' he sputtered pushing away the logs that had landed low on his stomach and high on his thighs. Florence let out a bark of laughter then quickly covered her mouth. She helped him relieve himself of the logs but stepped back leaving him to get to his feet by himself. She didn't make eye contact, instead returning to the task of collecting debris. Somehow this action cleared her mind as she concentrated on the lines in the bark and bugs that clung to the mossy planks.

All went quiet until she heard rustling and a few bangs behind her. She assumed Jo was back to concentrating on his clean-up mission too. Neither of them said a word and Florence daren't glance at him. Minutes passed and her back grew warm under the heat of the sun. Her skin prickled as she sensed Jo's eyes were watching her, but she didn't turn around. Had she been a fool to give Jo that piece of her? There was no way Jo – with his charm, his quirks and his accents – could possibly be real because she'd never met anyone like him before.

NINE

The sun had sunk behind the trees by the time Florence and Jo decided to call it a day and leave further cleaning until tomorrow. After clearing the space around the barn, they had moved indoors and managed to tidy away a good portion of the rubble to the point where they could now see half of the barn floor. Their work had been done in a mix of comfortable silence and book chatter. Florence had felt safe talking about books. However, by the time the conversation turned to lunch, she wasn't one hundred per cent certain that book club had been so safe after all, for she was pleasantly surprised with how well read Jo was, which endeared him to her a teeny bit more. Her mind was saved from overthinking by the fact that they had both skipped lunch, having lost track of time, and were now racing back to the cottage feeling famished. The summer breeze getting caught in her hair was as refreshing as the shade the rising moon was providing.

Florence's muscles ached and her hair was damp with sweat, but she forced herself to keep up with Jo and his long strides with the incentive that once she stopped running, the best fish and chips she had ever tasted would be her reward at the finish line; so Jo had told her. The other guests must have retired to their bedrooms, for when they reached the back patio and made their way through the cottage there was no one about.

'Sal, kind sir, can me and ma lady here trouble you for your finest fish and chips at this late hour?' Jo panted when they reached the café. Florence was two steps behind him. Both looked dishevelled with dirt on their noses and twigs in their hair.

'If it is not too much trouble, Sal,' Florence piped up, wiping at her glasses that were speckled with dust.

Sal looked up from cleaning the cake counter. His grey eyes moved from Jo to Florence and back again. Then he let out a hearty guffaw with one hand on his belly. His eyes returned to Jo with a roll. 'What on earth have you two been up to? And not at all, ma lady,' Sal said, with a small nod of his head in Florence's direction. This eased her guilt on bursting in on him and the kitchen staff when they were probably getting ready to close. She smiled. 'This kitchen is always open. Whatever it is you want, I'll make it,' Sal told her, flipping his tea towel over his shoulder and sending a wink her way.

'Thank you,' Florence replied, nodding with gratitude. She wiped at her nose with her sleeve, having noticed Sal's eyes wander over her face in amused confusion. 'We've been cleaning up the old barn. It's such a beautiful structure. Jo plans on restoring it,' she added, feeling rather accomplished and part of something. However, that feeling quickly evaporated when Sal's face immediately turned to stone and he gave Jo a less than favourable look.

'I'll bring your food to you,' Sal said, with not a word about the barn. When he looked at Florence his features had sprung back to warm and friendly. It was almost as if Florence had imagined the anger in his eyes mere seconds ago. When she gulped and looked to Jo, she knew she had not imagined it, for his face was creased with shame and sorrow. He looked down at the counter before swiping his hand over his face, hiding his eyes for a moment. Had she said something wrong?

'I'll be over in a minute,' Jo said, with a smile Florence knew now was very much forced. His eyes did not wrinkle, and his cheek did not make a dimple.

With her head down, Florence wandered over to the same spot she had sat in that morning. She could see the night's beauty – the moon filling the sky with it lustrous glow, but she could not enjoy it. She had spent one day making friends in the real world, chatting with real people – George, Sal and Jo – and she had already ruined it, said something she shouldn't have and messed it all up. When she looked up, she saw Jo leaning on the counter. His face looked angry but there was desperation in his eyes as he spoke. Florence couldn't make out what he was saying from where she sat, but whatever it was, it didn't seem like Sal agreed. When Sal threw his cloth down on the counter and walked away from Jo, she jumped and looked away feeling guilty for prying.

'Sorry about that.' Jo's voice made her jump again. She pulled her eyes away from the window as Jo sat down. His flamboyant demeanour had vanished and Florence hated the way he looked so vulnerable, his arms crossed over his chest, his eyelids drooping. She had seen that closed off body language many times before in her own mirror and it broke her heart to see it in someone like Jo.

Too exhausted to speak and for fear of saying something wrong, they both sat in a self-conscious silence and watched the shadows creep over the enchanter's nightshade. It wasn't long before Sal appeared with two thickly battered fish, freshly fried chips, and a healthy blob of delicious-looking mushy peas.

Jo nodded his thanks while Florence thanked Sal profusely, hoping to make up for whatever she had said wrong earlier, and dived in. The batter melted on Florence's tongue and the fish was meaty and tender. The chips were perfectly crunchy on the outside and fluffy in the centre and she had half a mind to jump into the muddle of mushy peas; they were so full of flavour she ate them in just a few forkfuls.

Sitting back in her chair, her hunger now satisfied, Florence wasn't sure if it was the happiness from the mushy peas that had given her a boost of bravery. Fighting her eyelids that were growing heavy and sitting up straighter despite the reluctance from her thighs, which had started to seize up, she cleared her throat.

'Are you OK, Jo?' she asked gently.

From under heavy lids, she watched Jo's eyes narrow and look over her features before he sat up and said, 'Shall I walk you back lass, or shall I fetch you ya flyin' carpet?' His Scottish accent once again scored a laugh from her. However, Florence didn't miss the fact that Jo had resorted to an accent rather than an answer. She knew that game too well and it was for that reason she chose not to push her question or enquire further about what Sal and Jo's disagreement was all about.

'I wish I could fly,' she said wistfully instead, as Jo stood up and reached out his hand. Florence hesitated for a second. Jo's hazel eyes shone with a need that Florence felt to her core. She knew that look. Did he need a friend as much as she did? She took his hand and allowed him to pull her up.

When they reached Florence's hut, Florence went straight

for the wicker chair on her deck, collapsed into it and tucked her feet up under her to get comfy. Jo went to his position by the tree, the same one he had taken up that morning. Just as he had done then, he pulled out his book. While Florence gazed up at the sparkling stars, Jo read aloud. He finished the chapter while Florence still inspected the stars. She had a dreamy smile on her face and didn't see Jo lift his eyes off the book to look at her. Then quietly without looking at Jo she said, 'Do not worry, little book, I will get him a bookmark and you will not have to suffer any more creases or dog ears.'

Florence heard a faint chuckle from by the tree. Only then did she turn to see Jo looking at her as he stood. 'Night, Florence,' he said, tipping his book like a hat.

'Night, Jo,' Florence replied and when she could no longer see him in her peripheral vision, something inside her made her turn around to watch him. When he disappeared into the neighbouring hut a couple of yards away, Florence found herself smiling a contented smile as she forced herself up and into her own hut, in need of a hot bath.

* * *

The next morning Florence set about her usual routine of waking up just before sunrise and sneaking on to her deck with a cup of tea and her copy of *Sense and Sensibility*. She wanted to get a few chapters in before the sun came up; finding that she was hoping Jo would come along, for she was looking forward to another day of helping with the barn. Last night she had slept like a log after a thoroughly busy day. Adventure had exhausted her, and she had felt a rocket ship away from being sat behind a desk for eight hours a day. She'd been reminded more of her old job – running around, and performing with the children – and it further cemented her determination to seek out a job in that field when she got back to Manchester after her holiday.

Jo had made for wonderful company and she couldn't believe how free she had felt when moving around the barn and focusing on the simple task of picking up branches and adding them to a neat pile. After the initial tension she had felt following Jo's fall from the logs, her mind had not raced or overthought as they spent the afternoon decluttering. She appreciated the respite. However, as she settled into her wicker chair, her mind replayed the looks on both Jo's and Sal's faces last night at dinner. Sal had been angry, disappointment evident in his eyes, while Jo had looked exhausted and helpless. Her mind stayed on Jo for a little longer. Here was this handsome man who, when he stood tall and spoke in his silvery voice, looked and acted sophisticated and dapper. But the next minute he would splash on a devilishly charming smile, put on an accent, and be overcome with such enthusiasm and imagination. He didn't seem to have any regard for society's rule book for what a man should be, which caused Florence's stomach to flutter. She felt drawn to him. He was like a character from one of her novels, not unlike his namesake or his namesake's best friend for that matter, but that thought made her a tad nervous.

As the sun gave life to the fields before her, the emerald blades of grass bold and beautiful with the morning dew, Florence nipped back into her hut. She deposited her book on her bed and raced off to the café in search of her new friend. With it still being early she didn't bump into Jo on her run or see him in the café. Rather than knock on his door – she didn't want to disturb him after yesterday's tiresome work – she thought she would head to the barn and wait for him there.

When she got to the café, the spring in her step became a stumble. She stepped inside tentatively. Sal was at the counter serving a slice of cake and a cappuccino to an elderly gentleman and seeing that he looked jovial, Florence decided to take her chances and act casual.

'Good morning, Sal, how are you today?' she asked merrily. Sal smiled when he saw her, all tension from last night forgotten.

'I'm well thank you, love. And you?' he returned, plating up a croissant and adding it to a tray holding two cups and a teapot.

'Just fine, thank you. Could I place an order for two bacon butties to go please?'

'You're not eating with us this morning?' Sal questioned, busying himself by waving at one of his waiting staff. He motioned for them to take the tray to an elderly couple who were sat on a couch doing a puzzle together. He did not meet Florence's eyes.

'Erm, no. I'm heading to the barn,' Florence said, her voice a little less chirpy than before.

This time Sal met her gaze. Florence felt like she was thrust into an impromptu no-blinking contest, until Sal shook his head and said, 'Of course and that's no trouble. No trouble at all.' Florence didn't miss the resigned way in which his words came out. She bit her lip in thought.

'Sal, I don't mean to impose but are you mad at Jo? I mentioned the barn and it seemed to cause friction between the two of you and I never meant for that to happen,' Florence said, resting her interlocked hands on the counter. Sal looked to the floor and then back to Florence, his grey eyes turned from sad to happy and his lips curved into a smile.

'Pay no attention to me, Florence. All is well and you did nothing of the sort. I knew that kid when he was in nappies. That's how long I've been here.' His words began to trail off like he was telling someone else and not Florence, then he seemed to catch himself. 'I won't be a moment with your breakfast,' he said, with a wave of his hand as he disappeared to the fryer.

Sal had wished her a productive day when he handed over her breakfast and she left the café feeling positive with a hint of curiosity as to why Sal sounded so disorientated. But she could not pry anymore; it was not her business. Unable to resist the freshly fried bacon, Florence ate her butty while taking in the scenery on her route to the barn. The trail filled with a scrumptious smell of crispy bacon and hot buttered bread.

Having already devoured her breakfast when she reached the barn, Florence got to work removing the remaining mess from the back of the large open space. Her hot bath had loosened up her tight limbs as had the walk this morning, so she made quick work of a rather tangled set of branches. As she pulled them up from the ground, she suddenly noticed something in the floorboards. A patch stood out unlike the rest. It was glistening gold with not a spec of dirt and there in the middle was a lock. She leant over closer to inspect it. Its obscure shape and rustic appearance made her wonder how long it had been hidden. Was it a trapdoor to another world or a hiding place for someone's treasure? Should she investigate? Well, that was a silly question; of course she had to investigate. She had to know what was below it. But wait, where was the key? She took a step forward; maybe it had fallen under the debris. Without warning, she felt a pain shoot up her ankle, her foot was caught in a trio of knotted branches and she could feel herself falling.

Bracing herself to hit the floor, a cry escaped Florence's lips as two arms wrapped around her tight, stopping her from hitting the ground and shocking her out of her daydream.

Peeling open her eyes she came face to face with Jo, who had caught her in a dipped position almost like they had been dancing.

'Well at least we know one of us will be there to catch the other when they fall,' Jo remarked with a friendly smile.

'I got you breakfast,' Florence retorted as if it was consolation for not taking his hand yesterday and letting him fall into the mud.

Jo tilted his head from side to side, exaggerating his thinking over Florence's apology. 'You're forgiven,' he said, pulling her upright, with a chuckle.

'Thank you,' she said, 'for saving me and for forgiving me,' she added, shoving him in his bicep.

The sun's rays were already beaming through the cracks, making Florence glad of her lighter outfit. Today she wore a dusty brown playsuit with white polka dots that allowed her to move a little smoother and not trip up over a long skirt, there were enough things to trip over as the branches just proved. Jo wore a grey T-shirt that was baggy on his frame but suited him with his worn jeans.

'I don't think it will take too long today. The floor should be free of debris in another hour or so. We could get a few cleaning products, give it a mop and a polish. I can nip into the village when we're done here and pick up a few things. I mean, if that's what you think we should do – you can clean it however you'd like,' Florence said, telling her thoughts to Jo and suddenly panicking that she was intruding on his project. She hadn't mean to come across so bold but something about the barn lit a spark inside her and she couldn't contain the inspiration or excitement. Having found his bacon butty that Florence had perched on a relatively dust-free rock by the door, Jo was munching away at it thoughtfully, while listening to Florence.

'I'll go with you; we can drive in as it is a fair walk,' Jo said after finishing another bite. Florence's worry that she had overstepped instantly went away with Jo's calm response, but her pulse spiked at his suggestion of driving. 'And I'm grateful for your enthusiasm,' he added with a smile.

'No, I mean great but honestly it's fine. You don't have to drive,' Florence said, aiming for her voice to sound casual, like she didn't want to be a bother, but she could hear the higher pitch the words came out in.

Jo stopped eating his sandwich. 'How do you plan on getting there when there are no buses around here?' he asked, tilting his head. His face was a picture of puzzlement. 'It's a thirty-minute walk or do you really own a magic carpet?' He raised his eyebrows with great curiosity.

Florence would have laughed if her palms weren't sweating. With her words lodged in her throat, she looked down at her feet and gave her legs a wiggle. This was one area she didn't feel ready to unload on Jo, but Jo was being frustratingly kind. 'I'm not having you carry heavy cleaning supplies back on your own, nor am I having you doing a job that is mine to do. I can go and get supplies and you can come if you'd like,' he said, resting a hand on his hip.

'I'd very much like to come but I'd like to walk please,' she said. Her voice shook when she spoke. Then she quickly turned away, going at the branches with a vengeance, aware that her stance was now closed off. She just had to steady her pulse and cool down. It helped that Jo didn't question why she didn't want to drive. Instead, he started eating his butty again and gave her space.

As she gathered some of the smaller branches by the window, Florence's mind caught up on the overthinking she had been having some success avoiding. She hadn't meant to shut Jo out. Yesterday, he had proven to be a good listener when she had spoken of her theatre days. But the fact remained that she had only known him for one day. There were moments where she felt like she knew him and saw a caring soul but then there was the argument with Sal. Could she really trust Jo completely?

Besides, some memories were too hard to share. Some memories couldn't be made less painful by putting on an accent. In addition to her having a break and taking some time for herself, she knew that was part of the reason for her nanna sending her here; so she could create new memories and not see this place as the horror movie she had built up in her head. Though Margot hadn't voiced it, Florence knew she didn't want Florence ending up like her and hating this place forever. Being at the camp, Florence felt that the scary movie posters she had pinned up for Camp Calla Lily were starting to peel away, but she couldn't bring herself to acknowledge or talk about the reason for them having gone up in the first place, at least not yet.

The images she had seen on the road to the camp were not images she wanted to revisit anytime soon. The barn was a helpful distraction and Jo could be too if she just kept him at arm's length. She would address her lessons on her own and in her own time but for now she wanted to focus on the fresh air and breathing new life into this old barn.

A little time had passed rather peacefully. Just the birds singing in the trees and the shuffle and thud of debris being thrown onto a pile could be heard.

'Did you have a nice lie-in this morning?' Florence asked, breaking the silence, and wanting to show Jo that she was fine. 'I never lie in, but even I snuck in a couple extra minutes,' she added, chuckling to herself.

Jo looked up and cleared his throat. 'Erm, yes. Thank you, I did,' he said, uncertainly. Florence watched as he raked a hand through his hair and closed his eyes when he thought she wasn't looking. It hadn't been a difficult question. Her brows knitted, causing her glasses to dig into the ridge of her nose.

Florence didn't miss his sudden shiftiness, she waited for a moment to see if he would elaborate on his answer or give her a clue as to why a lie-in had made him seem so nervous, but in a flash his body language became buoyant again and a bright smile appeared on his lips.

'Florence?' he said, once but a few spindling twigs were left on the large-planked floor.

'Yes,' she replied, straightening out her back, wiping her brow with the back of her hand and adjusting her glasses to relieve the throb in her nose.

'Before I came in here, what were you dreaming about?' he asked casually and merrily.

Her lips gave a shy smile, her nose wrinkled and with her chin tilted towards the floor, she looked up at Jo from under her long lashes, her stomach prickled with a trace of nerves. This time she wasn't quite as shocked by Jo's enquiry but in the same respect she still wasn't all that used to sharing her dreams with others. She had grown accustomed to them being received with laughs whenever she let them slip. School had been difficult in that regard. She had learnt quickly that the girls were only looking for ammunition when they urged her to share her thoughts. She had fallen for it a few times but by the fifth time, when she was part way through introducing her pet unicorn at ten years old, and the girls had burst into fits of giggles, shoved her and ran off, she realised her mistake and another brick had been added to her wall.

Florence threw the last of her twigs out onto the rubbish mound and looked over at Jo. His hazel eyes didn't show signs of judgement but genuine warmth and interest, yet she was rattled by the fact that there was definitely something he wasn't telling her. However, maybe if she let him in just a little, he would offer her that same trust in return and she could help fix things with Sal – not that she should be thinking about helping them fix things. It was after all, she reminded herself, none of her business. With Sal having known Jo for as long as he had, Florence imagined him watching out for Jo as a boy growing up on this land. She hated that they were at odds, but had to assume bickering was only natural when you had known someone that long. At least, that is what she told her nosy brain. So, Florence pointed to the spot on the floor that had distracted her earlier. In reality it was no different to the rest, but of course her mind liked to play tricks on her.

'I saw a trapdoor,' she explained.

Jo closed one eye, crossed one arm over his chest, the other stroking his chin like he was Sherlock Holmes. Then in one sudden movement he became animated, his curls bouncing around as he took two strides to where she was pointing and bent over to examine the floor. Florence startled.

'A trapdoor, you say – no way. Over here, did you say? I

see,' Jo said, moving in a circle, still hunched over, now pretending to smoke a pipe.

Florence held on to her stomach as laughter bubbled inside her.

'Then please tell me what you are doing over there. We must investigate at once,' Jo said gesturing to Florence and making her spring forward mirroring his stance, looking down at the imaginary trapdoor.

'No, no, not here, the key, dear, we need to find the key,' Jo said, now standing tall and waving her away making the laughter erupt from inside her. He flailed his arms. 'Look around, look around, bring the key to me.' Florence shoved him in his side before complying with his instructions. She began running around in search of the key and so the next half hour unfolded with both Florence and Jo scrambling around the old barn, laughing until their sides hurt in search of a long-lost key. When they were all out of energy and breath and couldn't possibly laugh or run anymore, they flopped onto a lonely hay bale at the front of the barn.

'Miss Florence, can I interest you in an ice-cream and a bucket and a mop?' Jo asked, staring up at the roof before turning to look at Florence, the hay tickling his cheek.

'What more could a woman ask for?' Florence replied with a smirk. She then swiped at a touch of dust on his cheek and made herself laugh in the process. 'I may have just made that worse.' Their eyes locked for a fleeting moment, causing Florence to snap her hand away. What was she doing? Why had she just touched a stranger's cheek? That wasn't something normal people did.

'How about we freshen up and meet at the main desk?' Jo suggested. His voice came out a touch croaky. His eyes had become ardently interested in the ceiling as had Florence's.

A few silent minutes passed before they both cleared their throats and stood up. Looking anywhere but at each other they stepped back, hands on hips, to admire their morning's accomplishment and nodded.

'Break,' they said in unison before retreating from the barn and making their way back to their respective huts.

TEN

Florence made quick work of getting ready. She ran the bath while scrubbing her face in the small ceramic sink to wash away her sweaty make-up. When the bath was full enough to where she could splash water over herself and scrub the dirt and grime off her body, she jumped in and out in timely fashion and threw on her yellow ruffled summer dress. After dabbing some fresh cream onto her face along with a touch of blush, she headed to the lobby. She wanted to check in with her nanna before she and Jo were to walk to the village. As she swung open the door of the main cottage, she heard a voice that sounded a lot like Jo's. Florence's brow knitted, for it wasn't a tone that she had grown accustomed to from Jo. He sounded angry.

Not wanting to eavesdrop, Florence slowed her pace towards the front desk, for the noise was coming from George's office. She looked around the reception desk wondering if anyone else was around when Jo's voice grew loud.

'What exactly would you have us do, Grandad? Our

hands are tied – surely you see that?' he shouted, frustration clear in his voice.

Suddenly, George came out of his office, causing Florence to spin around on the spot making a dramatic attempt at looking like she had just come from the lounge. She was about to greet George cheerfully, to not let on that she had heard a snippet of his conversation with his grandson but stopped when she saw this his face looked crumpled and old. Florence much preferred when he smiled. Could she ask him what the matter was or was that too nosy? The urge to help was becoming keener. But before she could say a word, George waved in the direction of the phone, barely looking up. 'The phone is there, my dear. Use it as you need,' he said before shuffling back into his office, clearly not wanting to talk.

Florence turned and twiddled the phone's cord between her fingers as it rang, feeling a little rattled over seeing George's defeated face and hearing such an angry tone in Jo's voice moments ago. A further flash of worry zipped through her brain as she waited for her nanna to answer. By the sixth ring her hands started to grow clammy. Panic made her fear her nanna had fallen or that something else was horribly wrong and she couldn't get to the phone. She gripped the desk when just before the seventh ring her nanna's voice came through.

'Hello, petal,' Margot sang merrily. Florence sank against the desk letting out a relieved sigh. 'You just caught me and Olivia in the middle of a good chat,' her nanna explained, the delight in her voice making Florence beam. Olivia had only been to their house on a few occasions, so it meant an awful lot that she had popped in to check on Margot without being asked. Florence had spoken to Olivia on the phone before she had left on Monday night to tell her of her travel plans and

Olivia had assured her she would ring her nanna every day to
see how she was getting on and to see if she needed anything.
Olivia had also been ecstatic that Florence was going on holiday. It was incredibly heart-warming that her friend had paid
a visit to Margot to keep her company. The action made
Florence feel understood, something she didn't always feel
with Olivia.

'That's lovely, Nanna. Hi, Liv, how are you both?'
Florence asked, perking up, her clammy hands drying up now
that she knew Margot was more than OK.

'We are fine here. How are you, treasure?' her nanna
asked.

'Have you met any dishy country men?' Olivia shouted
from the background. And there was the Olivia Florence
knew.

'It's wonderful, Nanna, and no, Olivia,' Florence said,
firmly. Movement behind her made Florence turn around. It
was Jo coming out of his grandad's office with his grandad
following him with his head down.

Both grandad and grandson looked withdrawn and
forlorn. Was Jo the reason for George's grumpiness? The
question zoomed around Florence's brain. She couldn't see
how Jo could make anyone miserable, yet after Florence had
mentioned the barn and helping Jo yesterday, Sal had given
him daggers. She swallowed down the nervous lump in her
throat, wondering if she had read Jo all wrong. Was his kindness a façade? Besides the odd time when she was a
teenager, she could never imagine shouting at her nanna.
What could have made Jo so mad that he would treat his
grandad like that? Florence narrowed her eyes as if that
would help her figure out what was causing the friction
between the two men, but then Jo caught her eye and his

face transformed with a dazzling smile that made his eyes sparkle.

Florence seemed to lose herself for a moment, forgetting she was on the phone and that she needed to keep her guard up. But Jo was no longer wearing his baggy jeans and grey T-shirt; they had been replaced by cream trousers and a billowy checked shirt, with the sleeves rolled up and the sight of him made something stir in the pit of her stomach. 'Right, I've got to go. Jo and I are going into the village. You two be good,' Florence announced to her nanna, suddenly wanting to get off the phone before Olivia read her mind through the airwaves and called her out for her out-of-character thoughts. She snapped her eyes away from Jo, who stood with his hands behind his back patiently waiting for her to finish her phone call. He made no gesture for her to rush, which caused havoc to Florence's current conflicting thoughts.

'Who's Jo?' Florence heard from the other end of the phone; making her jump and remember what she was doing. The voice of course belonged to Olivia.

'I'm going to go now. I love you, Nanna, and thank you, Liv, bye,' Florence said, ignoring Olivia's question and nosy mind.

'I love you too, petal,' her nanna returned.

'Is Jo a man or a woman?' Olivia questioned faintly in the background.

Florence hastily put the phone down but not before she heard Margot faintly say, 'Now, now.'

When Florence placed down the receiver, she looked around for George to offer her thanks, but he was no longer standing in the reception area and his office door was closed. Seemingly reading her mind as she glanced at the closed door, Jo said, 'I can thank him later for you. Shall we get going?' His words came out soft and the smile he wore was nothing short of caring. Florence considered him for a second, then nodded. Jo held the door open but as she walked past him, she didn't miss him hesitate slightly as he looked back in the direction of his grandad's office before following her outside. When he thought she wasn't looking his lips pressed together and his hazel eyes turned a little murky, but they cleared as soon as they landed back on Florence.

'Is everything OK?' Florence couldn't help but query as they began walking down the path.

'Yes, yes, I'm sure it will be, in time,' Jo replied softly, raking a hand through his hair before pulling out a book from his back pocket. It was not *Great Expectations* but it was very much worn and as badly dog-eared. He brought the book up to his face, covering his nose, and gave Florence a pointed stare as if to say: "I will hear none of your lectures on how to look after books" and so Florence merely opened her eyes wide and made the action of zipping her lips.

At first, it was tough for Florence to concentrate on the story as Jo read aloud. The niggle in the back of her mind that he was doing something that was causing great distress to his grandad troubled her. But what could she do about it? She was simply a visitor of Camp Calla Lily and could she really call Jo a friend after two days? She was more of an acquaintance. Whatever was going on was nothing to do with her.

By the time they reached the small village Jo had read three chapters from *Little Men* and they had discussed each chapter in great detail, which had permitted Florence's nerves to take a back seat. The sun was still shining and lit up the cobbled streets and buildings with a beautiful happy glow. The old-fashioned ice-cream shop was tucked into the wall and for a minute Florence could remember gazing up at its multi-coloured bunting and glittery sign as a little girl. But before she could walk any further down memory lane, the shop next to it pulled her attention. She crossed the road and stared through the window of The Vintage Bookshop. The owner had created a gorgeous display of classic novels that sat under a wooden tree. Baubles of books dangled from the pink blossom branches and children's books lay under vibrant orange sunflowers.

Florence automatically reached out to touch the glass, wanting to stroke the bindings and feel the cloth of the hard-back books. As she did so her hand slipped through the pane. She found herself in the middle of the tiny shop. Books were flying around her, pages fluttering in the air saying, "Pick me, pick me." Characters leapt from book to book as she stared up in awe. Was that Huckleberry Finn chasing after Tom Sawyer? A splash from the floor made her whip her head towards the ground. Oh no, was that Captain Hook thrashing around in his boat, the crocodile licking its lips awaiting his dinner?

A rustle behind the bookshelf made Florence spin around on the spot. 'Aww,' she gasped as she saw a woman peering around a bookcase timidly gazing at a man who was staring longingly back at her. Was a meet-cute about to happen? The man and the woman started walking towards each other, but wait, why was Jo in the way? He had to move. If he didn't move the star-crossed lovers were bound to kiss him on each cheek and he would scupper their first kiss. Florence lifted her hand, waving to get Jo's attention to tell him to move but he hadn't seen her.

'Jo, move!!' Florence said out loud, pushing Jo in the chest and startling when his willowy frame rocked into her.

He shouted, 'Oh God, what is it? Is it pirates making me

walk the plank? Or is a witch trying to cast a spell on me?' He spun in a circle, clumsily bumping into Florence again, shocking her back to the present.

Drawn into his questioning and very much liking having someone to share her visions with now, Florence didn't hesitate to answer him this time. Jo had proved himself to be a trusty companion, where her visions were concerned, like this morning with the trapdoor. She was already giggling at his dramatic reaction and at her own self for having shouted out into the real world.

'Neither – you were about to ruin the most magical first kiss for a beautiful couple and I couldn't let that happen,' Florence told him, as a couple walked by and gave them an odd glare. Florence's hand was still resting on Jo's chest, having put it there to steady him when he had bumped into her. She smiled shyly at the couple. She was far more used to their rather unkind reaction than to Jo's nurturing one. Heat prickled in the apples of her cheeks with humiliation, but Jo didn't pay the couple any attention.

'Oh, I would have never forgiven myself,' Jo said, placing a hand on top of Florence's where she had it pressed against his chest. Florence felt contented with the softness of his skin on hers. 'Are you telling me there is a romantic in there after all?' he added, before Florence took her hand away smoothly in the act of pushing her glasses up her nose. Jo matched her faux casualness and flipped back the curls that had fallen in his face. Gazing back at the books in the window, Florence squinted at the gold-embossed titles and the special edition leather-bound classics as though she were squashing out all thoughts of Jo and guiding her brain back to safer territory. She knew she shouldn't seek that sort of contentedness from Jo and so she would talk about books.

'Oh, romances are my favourite. They are beautiful when they are tucked between the pages of a book and are happening to someone who's not me,' Florence said, instantly regretting her words. She hadn't meant to say that last part out loud. She avoided Jo's gaze as he stepped in line for ice-cream. The bookshop would have to wait, for the walk had made them both desperately hungry for creamy gelato and so she joined him, keeping her lips tightly closed for fear of exposing herself even more. Jo didn't reply straight away. He seemed to be lost in examining the menu, which suited Florence simply fine. Why did she always have to make things awkward?

A few moments passed where Florence too took great interest in all the ice-creams on offer. The menu was rather spectacular, offering a range of simple classic scoops and fresh modern twists. So intrigued by the concoction that was a Unicorn Sherbet Bomb Supreme was she, that it took her a second to tune in to Jo's voice when he started talking.

'We mustn't let our heartaches distort our visions. Learn from them, yes, but we can't let them ruin us,' he said slowly, as if reciting something he had been told many times before and was still trying to believe in too. Florence tore her eyes away from the menu and tilted her head to look at him. His heart-shaped jaw was set, and there was that sadness that passed through his eyes for a split second that he never seemed to let stick around for long. Without meeting her gaze, he added, 'If you can believe it in the pages of a book, you can believe in it in real life.' He then pursed his lips as though challenging that comment in his own mind.

Florence contemplated this for a minute. 'Yes, that might be true, but my own story hasn't quite ended up like the great classics or gorgeous rom-coms, as I told you, and I'm learning to be OK with that,' she said, finding herself opening up once more today before she could stop herself.

'Ahh, but Florence, don't you see? You have closed those books. Their stories have come to an end so of course they ended happily, but yours has not ended yet. You're still writing the chapters and I shall call this chapter "Underneath the Ice-Cream Stand",' Jo noted with a charming smirk, the sadness in his eyes vanishing when Florence let out a hearty laugh.

'You might be right, but I believe books provide me with that joy, for love is not to happen in my life. The same way I don't own a magic carpet, nor can I ride a unicorn, to know that those people get to have a happy ending and that the special few in real life do too, makes me happy. I find comfort in knowing that they are happy,' Florence said, her voice light and joyful in thinking about all the fairy-tale endings she had read, and real-life stories she had heard. She didn't want to see herself as missing out or hard done by; the knowledge that others got to experience that magic was enough for her. She hoped Jo would understand that.

There was a touch of sadness in her admission, of course, for she hadn't come to this conclusion on love easily. Pain had been her guide but as she had grown older, she had become more accepting of it. There were times she still wished she believed in her own happy ever after, but her nightmares would only serve to knock some sense into her. A look of understanding passed across Jo's face. Florence took in his smile, the one he gave that she had now classed as his false grin of merriment. It was far too thin with none of his pearly whites on show and it did nothing to create crinkles around his eyes.

'Is your theory drawn from experience, Jo?' Florence

asked, intrigued as to why Jo sounded as though he had had this conversation before. With such deep thought behind his eyes, making the hazel turn a hazy green-grey, Florence speculated if the conversations had been with himself or if his writer mother had imparted such beautiful words of wisdom on her son. Florence would have to speculate a while longer as the couple in front joyfully collected their delicious-looking ice-cream and moved away to enjoy it at one of the picnic benches across the road.

'Florence, I have an important question,' Jo announced smoothly changing the subject, which again didn't go unnoticed by Florence.

'Go on,' she said. Not forgetting her questions, she stored them at the forefront of her brain for safekeeping and easy access.

'One scoop or two?' Jo asked with a smile that now lit up his whole face. Florence marvelled at the joy ice-cream could elicit for grown-ups as well as children and let out a chuckle.

'Definitely three,' she answered, scoring a laugh from Jo. A warm feeling settled in her bones when she did this, a feeling she was simply going to attribute to a sense of pleasure in making other people happy. It had nothing to do with Jo specifically, she told herself.

And so, they ordered their ice-creams of sherbet, candy floss and vanilla with all the sprinkles for Florence and chocolate brownie, cookie dough and cheesecake for Jo and indulged in their delights as they walked along the river that ran through the village. Florence enjoyed the moments of pure contented bliss walking side by side with Jo, not having to say a word, just appreciating each other's company and the creamy delicate flavours that ignited their taste buds. She had never walked side by side with a man before and felt this ordinary, but in a totally unordinary kind of way.

After her last bite of the crunchy waffle cone, Florence asked, 'How come you're so patient with me and don't find me and my daydreams strange?'

Jo swallowed his last bite and placed his hands in the loops of his trouser pockets. 'Oh, I find you plenty strange,' he said, leaning into her with a playful smile that was infectious and caused Florence to roll her eyes at him. 'I don't know,' he said after a few moments.

'That was incredibly profound for a writer,' she teased back. Jo looked at her staring up at him and Florence found she could not pull her eyes away from his. The haziness had cleared to make room for a hypnotic hazel with flecks of green that gleamed in the light of the sun. Never had she experienced banter so easy. It was something she was starting to treasure, though the niggle of doubt remained at the back of her mind whether she should fully trust him. Along with that niggle came another voice, but this voice wasn't backing her up. This one was telling her that she was making excuses. Families argued sometimes; that didn't make Jo a terrible person. She was just afraid of the feelings that he was beginning to stir up within her.

'I grew up around books. I lived with my mum in a tiny studio apartment that had more books in it than furniture. My mum was driven and intent on writing a classic novel, always had a nose in a book, always studying. So, I guess, imaginatively and physically speaking, I've always seen stories everywhere. A book is more than just a bunch of paper sewn, glued or stapled together; it's a whole other world. We can look at things as they are or as we wish and dream them to be. We see sugar, flour and eggs and we create a cake – just like that I believe the world has potential,' he finished, his cheeks flushed, and he looked away as if he had just said something wrong, making the new feelings in Florence's stomach whizz around at a terrifying rate, for he hadn't said anything wrong at all.

Florence smiled at the ground. Jo's words wrapped like a hug around her heart. She too often questioned why she was to simply accept the world for what it was and stop dreaming the older she got. It was rather heart-warming to share that with another soul.

'Did she? Did your mum write her classic?' Florence asked, fascination rising in her tone.

'I don't know,' Jo admitted, turning back to her slowly. There was a hesitation in his movement, but Florence smiled encouragingly, as the desire to learn more about him built. 'She had me when she was sixteen, which I've been told was a shock to everyone. She was all about her studies and so I kind of interrupted her plans of college and university. She tried for a few years, but I was too much of a distraction. I was six when I was put into foster care.' His words came out in one long breath, which made Florence think it wasn't a story he cared to tell often. She was familiar with those sorts of stories and felt touched that Jo had shared his with her.

'I'm so sorry, Jo,' she offered, gently touching his forearm in pause. Jo shrugged. 'What about your grandparents?' Florence couldn't help asking. She had built up this idea in her mind that Jo had grown up at the camp and had had the most wonderful childhood within its grounds. The camp seemed like the most idyllic place for a child to grow up and Jo looked incredibly content moving around the place. Could his grandparents not have stopped him going into the care system? Is that why they were still arguing, were things between him and his Grandad strained because George had failed to look after him?

'She didn't tell them. Like I said, they were never close. And they had the camp to run and my grandma was sick for a long time. I think I would have been too much for them,' Jo explained as they walked along the riverside. Florence didn't reply straight away, allowing for Jo to continue if he wished to. It sounded like there was more to that part of the story. He looked to his feet for a moment before running a hand through his hair. 'It was a bit of a shock when I turned up at my grandma's funeral, a year ago. Grandad cried a lot, said he thought he'd never see me again. My mum kind of went off the grid and I was six; there was nothing I could do about it.'

A few moments passed before Florence thought it safe to ask a question and she wouldn't be interrupting. Her heart was beating a little harder after hearing Jo's tale; her hand stayed on his forearm as they walked.

'You said you've been back a little over a year. How come you didn't seek out this place sooner?' Florence queried, finding that she wanted to know more about the man before her, now that her assumptions had been wrong. Jo gazed down at her for a moment before turning his attention to the road. 'I'm sorry. I didn't mean to be nosy. You don't have too...' Florence started anxiously, worrying that she had overstepped and knowing how much she disliked it when people asked her questions about her life that she didn't want to answer.

'It's OK,' Jo interrupted gently, smiling at her with a warmth in his eyes that made the hasty knot in her stomach unravel. Jo then fiddled with a piece of cotton on the seam of his shirt. 'I remembered bits of it. I remembered my grandparents, but I would beg my mum to bring me back here all the time. The day I watched her pack her bags, I mistakenly and excitedly assumed we were coming here, that we were going on holiday. She got mad and told me to forget about this place and that my grandparents were busy and didn't want to be bothered and then she dropped me off with social services. I was angry for a long time,' Jo explained.

Sometime during Jo's explanation, they had stopped walking and fallen side by side, looking out across the river with Jo holding on to the railing tightly. Florence recognised the wobble and need of support. She looked across the shimmering water, the glistening sunlight warming her skin. She didn't want to stare at Jo; she wanted to give him space to tell his story. 'As I got older and once it dawned on me that my mum wasn't coming back, I angrily vowed to start afresh. If my family didn't want anything to do with me, then I didn't want anything to do with them,' Jo continued. 'My grandma had left me a little spends when she passed and that's how I found this place again,' he added, putting the pieces of the puzzle together for Florence, who wiped at her eyes and then turned to him.

Looking at the shadows floating behind Jo's eyes as he went silent, Florence felt the sudden urge to help him as he had helped her these past two days. There was nothing she could say to take away his pain but there was much she could do to bring some light and fun to his heart. She grabbed his wrist and ran back in the direction of the bookshop.

'You, sir, are in need of a bookmark,' she proclaimed, skipping along and revelling in the sound of Jo's laughter as it filled the air. She knew too well that opening up could be exhausting and that sometimes people need to get things off their chest without having to then discuss further their emotions or hear someone else's opinion. It was simply nice to be heard and with the way Jo leapt and ran behind her, she had been right.

They spent the afternoon with Ella, the owner of The Vintage Bookshop, who Florence learnt had become well acquainted with Jo since he had been back at the camp and popped in whenever he had a spare minute. She was a lovely woman, with mystic brown eyes, tight black curls, which were styled into two bunches atop her head, and a cheerful disposition. She wore a stylish tea dress with a hummingbird print and the coffee mug that was glued to her hands read: "professional bookworm". Florence and Ella became fast friends and Ella didn't bat an eyelid when after sitting peacefully reading for an hour, Jo and Florence stood up to act out a scene from *Pride and Prejudice*, dancing in and out of the bookshelves. By the time the clock struck five, Ella was shooing Florence and Jo out the door while insisting they return the next day to provide her with more entertainment.

They both promised they would as Jo bowed while Florence curtsied out the door.

'Oh no,' Florence gasped after Ella had locked the door. 'We need cleaning supplies and food, but cleaning supplies should probably come first.' She held her finger in the air to articulate her thought. Jo grabbed at it playfully before pulling her along. They quick-marched to the corner shop, making it just in time before their five-thirty close, to pick up what they needed.

With mops and buckets in tow, they then retreated to the Crown Vic Pub to refuel before their trek back to camp. Florence hadn't been able to resist the smell of Yorkshire puddings and crispy golden potatoes wafting through the pub's garden. It turned out Jo too was a fan of a mouth-watering roast.

ELEVEN

It was Florence's third day of her week-long vacation and what a surprisingly lovely time she was having. At first, she hadn't thought it was possible. With the worry over leaving her nanna and the stress of finding a new job, among other things, she didn't think she could or should enjoy her stay, but many of her woes had been alleviated with every conversation she had with Jo, every game they played together and the cleaner they got the old barn. There remained a slight niggle of guilt over the fact that she wasn't actually all that upset about not having to return to sitting behind a desk all day, but that guilt was lessened by her determination to seek more joyful employment in a field that she enjoyed once she returned home.

There was also the matter of the two voices battling in her head over trusting Jo. One was telling her that she couldn't trust him, not when she had known him a mere forty-eight hours. There was the shouting at his grandad, the daggers from Sal and oddly the evil glares aimed in his direction she had witnessed from some of the villagers yesterday. She had been having such a wonderful time that she tried to pay no mind and brush it off, for she was accustomed to the snide looks from others, but her mind had taken note all the same. Then there was the other voice telling her that there was nothing wrong with Jo. It scolded her for trying to sabotage her new friendship on the premise that it was terrified. The latter was currently gaining momentum after Jo had opened up about his mum yesterday. Initially after spending those first few hours with Jo upon her arrival to the camp, she had assumed him to have had a magical, creative upbringing surrounded by these lush fields and an overflowing bookshelf with parents who loved him, like most of the kids she had grown up with. She had never expected the story that he disclosed. On hearing it she felt that tug of a kindred spirit and encouraged her brain not to overthink. She was on holiday after all.

'Jo, what does your castle in the sky look like?' Florence asked, as she swept the floor while Jo prepared a soapy bucket of water on the other side of the window where there was an outdoor tap.

'Ahh, the brilliant mind of Louisa May Alcott,' Jo replied in an inspired tone, taking his eyes off the bucket, and glancing up at the clouds. Florence smiled down at her brush. 'I would propose a pirate ship so I could sail through the sky and roam as I do now, and in my roaming, I will find my great novel,' he added quietly, getting back to the bucket, and turning off the tap.

'You wouldn't settle?' Florence queried feeling something inside her shift. It wasn't something she could place quite yet, though she did worry about Jo and believed that he wasn't answering all that truthfully. For someone who had spent his life in foster care, Florence had imagined his castle to be one filled with consistent love and family, a place that provided him what his mum never could, but then maybe she was projecting her ideals on to him. But there was just something about his distracted eyes that suggested otherwise.

'Me? No,' came Jo's short and mumbled reply. This only confirmed to Florence that she might not be projecting after all. As she sensed from Jo's eyes, he was keeping his castle locked and guarded.

'I would own a theatre and I would teach little kids, and my nanna would be healthy and live forever in my castle,' Florence professed. The words seemingly finding their way out into the open without fear. Sometimes she couldn't quite tell if it was Jo or Camp Calla Lily that was helping her find her voice. Florence studied the tiny specs of debris she had collected into a pile with the brush and bit her lip. A little voice in the back of her mind spoke up of a love and family of her own but she quickly shushed that voice, much preferring the safety net of the castle she had shared with Jo, for teaching children was much more achievable than finding love.

'What about your parents? What about a family?' Jo asked, coming to stand by the window. Florence couldn't fault Jo's questioning or be insulted that he was insinuating all women wanted a family, when she had asked him the very same thing.

Florence found herself frozen for a moment. She stared at Jo contemplating the pieces of him that hid behind the fog in his eyes. Her skin shivered with goose bumps as she felt a sort of kinship pass between them, like maybe the something he wasn't saying was very much the same as the something she didn't know quite how to express or deal with herself. That the idea of love and of having a family of her own one day seemed not just impossible but downright terrifying. Florence could understand how Jo growing up in foster care and his mum doing what she had done could cause his mind to be wary of love, but she wondered if there was more. He was handsome and kind. Did he have someone like Olivia pushing him to date all the time with no luck, it only causing more harm than good? Did he have a temper like she had heard from George's office? Florence stayed with that thought for minute, then shook it away. She didn't feel Jo to be mean, even with his eyes currently hazy and not their usual clearness, they appeared kind and inviting. As she looked to his lips, she was reminded of the question he had innocently asked moments ago. 'What about your parents?'

Florence felt exposed at Jo's questioning, almost like he could read the deepest depths of her mind that she tried so hard to bury, but that was silly, for he did not know anything of her past; innocence was all it was. Brushing the dirt onto the dustpan she tipped it into a bin bag they had tied around one of the window ledges before moving to sweep a different spot. Her conversation with Jo from yesterday drifted through her mind. He had been so open about his mum when talking to her in the village and the barn felt like a safe space where she didn't feel pressure to give all herself away but little bits each day felt comfortable and right, and so Florence took a deep breath and spoke.

'My parents died when I was five. We were driving back from our holiday here, coming around one of the country bends when another driver hit the passenger's side, spinning us off the road. He was exceeding the speed limit, not paying attention to the road because he was talking on his phone.' She paused, her voice trembling, but she held it steady, finding that now she had started talking she needed to get it all out. My mum died instantly, and my dad ended up in hospital with a concussion, two broken collarbones and a broken leg. He could have pulled through and he would have pulled through if it hadn't been for his broken heart. He overdosed on morphine two weeks after he came home, unable to cope with the loss of my mum.'

Florence had not seen Jo jump through the window, for her vision was blurry and her cheeks soaked with tears. It took her a moment to realise that Jo's arms were wrapped around her shoulders and she was resting her head against his chest as she heaved loud, heavy, and painful sobs. These were the tears of someone who had held this secret in since the day she had watched her dad's coffin being lowered into the ground next to her mum's. She had been just a small child who wouldn't leave her nanna's side and so not attending the funerals had not been a choice. She had nobody else to look after her. She hadn't quite understood what was going on, but she could feel the pain in her chest where it had felt as if she had a giant hole. The world seemed black, dull, and dreary. Where once the world around her was full of people laughing and talking, on this day everywhere she looked people had their heads down, tears fell down their cheeks and she couldn't find a single smile.

It was like the world had fallen into silence when Florence stopped sniffing, except for a slight beating sound. As her cries quietened and her shoulders stopped shaking, her ears pricked up to the peace that engulfed her, and from where her head lay, she recognised the small sound to be the beat of Jo's heart. For a moment she allowed herself to feel comfort in this intimate embrace, but a moment is fleeting and was all she could manage. She stepped back and removed her glasses to wipe down the lenses, before she looked up at Jo with puffy eyes. 'I feel like a theatre production of *Annie* wouldn't go amiss right now.' She smirked, wiping at her nose, and shaking her head to dispel the vulnerability she had just bared. Jo hastily wiped at his eyes and looked away up at the sky through the cracks in the wood. Besides her nanna, Florence had never cried in front of anyone before, let alone with someone. The tears in Jo's eyes made her feel less fragile.

Then without warning, Jo picked up his mop and burst into a rendition of "It's a Hard-Knock Life" while prancing around the barn and covering the floor with soapy bubbles. Laughter exploded from Florence with the same enthusiasm that the tears moments ago had; causing her to double over in stitches. After a second or two of enjoying Jo's performance she collected her own mop and joined in, not wanting Jo to have all the fun. She felt there had been an unspoken under-standing between them or at least she hoped that was the case and Jo didn't think her bonkers, happy one minute, hysterical the next. Though the look on his face had certainly made her feel far from bonkers and more accurately, safe.

It didn't take long before the cleaning had turned into a water fight and the mops were replaced by their cleaning starfish, which consisted of them lying on their backs moving their arms and legs up and down in the soap suds. Florence hadn't laughed this hard in a very long time; in fact she couldn't remember a time past the age of five where she had laughed so hard, she snorted. For it had been her dad, always on his hands and knees pretending to be one animal or another – a grizzly beast or a dazzling kind unicorn, crawling around the living room of their tiny family flat, that made her giggle with glee as a child. There was no voice he couldn't mimic, no animal he couldn't perform and no hour of the day where he wasn't invested in his little girl, unless he was away for work. Florence's snorts bounced off the barn walls as Jo hollered and pranced around as she tried to keep up with him, him on his stallion, her on her unicorn. When their buckets were empty of water and every inch of the barn was soaked, Florence and Jo returned to the floor where they lay staring up at the ceiling watching the glorious sun through the cracks in the roof.

'My mum and dad loved this place. We lived in a tiny flat that was littered with canvases and scripts. It was cosy and filled with love, like I could feel it in every nook and cranny of the house. But I can see why my parents liked coming here. The open space, the fresh air, the inspiration. But I just couldn't do it, Jo. My nanna, she loved it here too but the last memory I have that is linked to this place is losing my mum and my dad saying, "We should never have gone," over and over, saying he needed to turn back the clock. Every time my nanna suggested I come back, that it might do me a world of good, I shouted, I rebelled and wouldn't hear a word about it. I would chastise her for being a hypocrite, encouraging me but unable to face it herself. I was so cruel. I didn't want to remember the beauty; I was so angry, but there's so much beauty,' Florence said softly. She could feel the droplets of tears on her eyelashes and pinched her eyes closed. In her mind she saw her dad galloping along the lake with her, her mum with a sketchbook cross-legged by the water, their faces beaming with joy and for a moment in time it felt like they were right beside her again. Florence hadn't realised just how much she had needed that; how much Margot had been right in not being afraid to visit them in her mind. In baring her soul to Jo, it felt as though all the memories she had tried to burn from her brain had come roaring back and she found that she had missed them terribly.

Next to her Florence could feel the warmth of Jo's body

heating her skin, though the sun was burning through the ragged roof of the barn, the water from their cleaning expedition was beginning to chill her clothes. When she turned to look at him, he was already looking at her through glistening eyes.

'I'm glad you came,' Jo whispered.

'Me too,' Florence whispered back. 'Do you let yourself think about your mum?' she asked softly. Jo's chest rose and fell with a heavy sigh.

'Naturally, my mind sometimes wanders to where she ended up, if she had ever found her great novel. I used to type her name into Google,' he said, a small chuckle falling from his lips. 'I guess a part of me hoped that she had succeeded, for it had been the one thing she had wanted most in life, more than her own son. A big part of me wanted to see that giving me up had been worth it, but for all I know she could have changed her name, got married, started a new family and so I've never had much luck with my searches, not that I've cared to look for a long time.'

Florence wasn't sure how to respond, how she could take away Jo's pain. It had hurt losing her mum, she still felt the jagged shards of her shattered heart poking at her chest, but losing her dad, knowing that she had not been enough to keep him alive, it had crushed her, making it feel as though every bone in her body had crumpled with no chance of repair. She felt for Jo living with the knowledge that his mum chose to walk away from him, for she knew that pain agonisingly well.

'I'm sorry, Jo,' she whispered after a few moments.

'Me too,' Jo returned. Florence then turned towards the sun as its light beamed through the cracks in the roof and bounced off the wet floor creating rainbows in the bubbles. A little time passed and her thoughts drifted from her parents to

121

faraway lands and scenic images. Her eyelids began to flutter, her tense muscles relaxing in the peaceful surroundings. She felt as if she were floating on the water.

'Don't disappear, tell me,' Jo said, disrupting the quiet, though his voice was gentle and calm. He turned his head to the side watching as Florence's eyes fluttered open and she bit her lip in thought.

Florence smiled at his request. Feeling the water underneath her soaking her dress and cooling her body, the chill now gone, she breathed out a delicate breath.

'Right now, I'm in the ocean, in a tropical paradise somewhere. The sea is warm, yet soothing and refreshing and it's lapping around me, the waves calming my thoughts. The clouds are smiling down at me and they are sparkling as though made of glitter. Each is a different colour – indigo, turquoise, silver – for Care Bears live up there you know?' she told Jo, who closed his eyes tight. Florence hoped he could picture what she was describing. 'Arrrgh, ooouch, oh my God, there's a shark and it just bit my leg,' Florence screamed suddenly sitting up and grabbing Jo, tickling his stomach and jolting him from the restful daydream and scaring the living daylights out of him. His face was a picture of fright, his mouth wide open, his breathing heavy as he tried to bat away her tickles.

'Florence,' he protested, but Florence was rolling around laughing, screaming, and holding her faux bitten leg not paying any attention to his pleas. With a look of revenge on his face, Jo splashed at the water on the ground, eliciting more screams from Florence as she tried to crawl away, the water dripping off her glasses.

When they had both exhausted themselves with laughter and Jo resorted to being a gentleman and letting up on his revenge, Florence flopped back down on the barn floor. Jo leant back next to her, propping himself up on his elbow, while Florence let her hair fan out around her. Her glasses were a little foggy and her dress clung to her body, but she was content.

'That was not funny. That was mean,' Jo said once their breathing had returned to normal. He gave her a mock scolding.

'It was a little funny,' she replied, holding her thumb and forefinger inches apart when she said "little". Jo batted away one of his curls and pouted playfully but then his eyes turned serious and his lips curved into a small smile. 'I'm sorry about your mum and dad,' he said, his voice sweet and consoling.

'Me too,' Florence said, with no tears sprouting in her eyes. A small smile crept onto her face as she looked at him. She felt different somehow, happy and relaxed in a way that she had never felt before. 'We used to come here in the summer holidays, just for a few days. I would play by the lake and they would sit under the blossoms reading to each other or joining in with my escapades. Nanna would come too sometimes. I'm lucky in that she didn't come that year because she was working. I don't know what I would have done if she had been in the car and gotten injured too. I was fortunate that my car seat provided such protection, had I not been so tightly strapped in with all that padding around me, well..." Florence trailed off. "She won't come back; my nanna I mean. I think I absorbed her fear and I know she carries guilt for that. I used to get mad at her for suggesting I come on my own. I'd shout and make a fuss over her thinking if it was so easy for me to do, then why couldn't she. But she lost her daughter and son-in-law. I can't imagine losing a daughter, I wouldn't want to,' Florence confessed, feeling strangely at ease in talking about her past now. Jo or this place somehow made it easy.

'I'm sure she understood, and you're here now. Grandparents sometimes have a funny way of expressing their love,' Jo said in a way that felt to Florence like he was saying that last part more to himself than to her. Then he stood up and reached out his hand to help her up. Florence smiled and took his hand, jumping to her feet as he pulled.

'Now, stop being lazy when we have work to do,' he said, grabbing his mop and catching her forehead clumsily with the handle. 'Oh God, I'm so sorry.' He took a step towards her as she rubbed at her head.

'No, stop! Don't come too close, Jo!' Florence shouted. Jo froze. Then a smirk lit up Florence's face. 'I might just have to get you back for that one,' she said, holding one arm between them in warning.

A couple of hours passed as they saw to washing down the walls and scraping moss from the window ledges when Jo announced he had an idea for dinner. It was getting late and they had spent another full day at the barn, having brought sandwiches with them for lunch. Florence was intrigued, though she would also be perfectly happy with Sal's fish and chips.

'I say we call it a night,' Jo said, propping the mop carefully against the wall and gesturing for Florence to take off her gloves to which she obliged, arching her back and stretching out. The day's work was catching up with her.

'Can you wait until eight o'clockish to have dinner?' Jo asked, as they walked down the path towards the cottage and the huts.

'Ooh I don't know about that,' Florence said playfully, but truthfully. They had eaten lunch around one o'clock and it was currently half past five. She would be in need of a snack or two before eight.

'Trust me? It will be worth it,' Jo said, a questioning infliction in his voice when he said trust me, causing Florence to glance sideways at him.

'If I must,' she teased, with a shrug while stifling a yawn. Trusting him with dinner was one thing, but could she fairly say she trusted him as a friend completely?

'OK, great. See you later,' Jo said and then he ran off towards the cottage leaving Florence to spend a few hours relaxing and attending to her books in her hut.

TWELVE

It truly was a gorgeous little hut with all the amenities one could ever need. With her hair starting to dry matted and feeling a little shiver in her damp clothes, Florence went over to the tub and began running herself a bath. Drawing the pretty cream curtain over the small window, she stepped out of her summer dress and placed it by the door to hang outside once she was ready to go meet Jo. She then spent ten minutes deciding which book would accompany her in the old-fashioned bathtub.

The twinkling lights gave the room a warm and cosy ambience and with a touch of extra light from the lamp, her eyes were not in danger of straining when reading. The room was a bookworm's haven; it even had a shelf over the bath to prop up books. Whoever built these huts sure was a genius. Florence hoped that maybe with Jo around and with the resurrection of the barn, Camp Calla Lily would start to gain some recognition as being a totally luxurious holiday destination. The endless fields, wonderful food and now the addition of these huts, it was the perfect place for adults to relax and for children to let their imaginations loose. Adults too for that matter could come and unwind and get lost in wonderful dreams, for they often more than children needed to allow their imaginations to guide them sometimes. As Florence waited for the bath to fill, a memory came to mind of when she had visited Camp Calla Lily as a five-year-old. She accepted the reminiscence as it came. She remembered staying in one of the rooms up at the main cottage, jumping in the big bed with her parents while her nanna stayed in the room next door. Sometimes she would sneak out in the middle of the night and knock on her nanna's door, not wanting Margot to be lonely, and climb in bed with her. Thinking over the memory as it came flooding back sent goose bumps over her skin, but a smile found its way to her lips.

Once the tub had been filled and the bubble bath had saturated the room with a rose-scented perfume, Florence climbed into the water and sank into the bubbles.

It didn't take long before she was running alongside Meg, Jo, Beth and Amy, joining them in their Pickwick productions, storming about the attic and laughing until tears sprung to their eyes. With every chapter of *Little Women* Florence's nanna had read to her when she was a little girl she had wished for a sister or a neighbour like Laurie, but having her guard up all the time and disappearing into her own faraway lands meant that she struggled to get close to people. Not even Ryan had been able to pass the guards. Only Jo. In thinking of her Jo, suddenly there he was, her Jo dancing merrily with the sisters, a flower in his hair and a broad smile on his face. He saw her watching him and made his way over to her holding out his hand. 'May I have this dance?' he asked mischievously, and Florence accepted. They danced through the fields long after Marmee had called the little women in for supper, their dance moves outrageous, their hollers and laughter scaring the birds. They were free and racing down the hill when something smacked Florence in the head causing her to jump in shock. Her bottom slipped on the base of the tub and her head sunk into the water. She let out a shriek and promptly swallowed a gulp of soapy water.

Her eyes stung from the bubble bath as she flailed desperately in search of her towel. When she found it, she grasped on tight, holding it high so as to not get it wet and dabbed at her face. Feeling a little breathless, she carefully opened her eyes, fearing a spider and was relieved to find a packet of yoghurt-covered raisins floating a top the water. Noticing a shadow, she looked up and let out another frightful cry when she saw Jo was stood with his back to the bath but twisting a hand behind his back holding out her towel for her.

'Jo!!' she yelled, though a small wash of relief fell over her that he wasn't an axe-wielding murderer.

'I didn't look, I promise,' Jo stammered, his head fixed on the headboard above the bed. 'I threw them over from the door but then I missed, and you panicked,' he added. Florence listened and as she did her heart rate slowly went back to normal and she could feel a little laughter bubbling in her belly.

'You, sir, have a very bad habit of hitting me in the head with things,' she mused, calming her breathing, and feeling thankful for his assistance with her towel, lest she drown in the bathtub alone.

'I was at the door; I couldn't see a thing and I was aiming for the bath shelf,' he said, innocence in his tone as he hastily tried to explain himself. But Florence was certain he was muffling a laugh. She had to believe him, for he was standing truly rigid respectfully keeping his eyes trained on the bed in the middle of the room. The laughter crept higher in her belly; she'd never seen Jo's limbs so wooden.

'Well, you have exceptionally bad aim,' Florence said, looking down at the snack bobbing about in the water and smiling.

Jo chuckled, his shoulders moving up and down while his head remained still.

'You can let go of the towel now and please promise me you won't turn around?' Florence asked, feeling strangely warm and at ease with Jo's proximity but also a little chilly with the drop in temperature of the bath water.

'You have my word; I have to be off now anyway,' he said, sounding slightly flustered as he let go of the towel and shoved his hands into his pockets nervously. Jo took a few strides forward, while Florence tried not to slip in the bathtub. The soapy bubbles made her movements squeaky and slightly perilous, but she made it onto the fluffy bathmat unharmed.

'Jo,' she said, her voice sweet and melodic, causing him to stop in his tracks.

She adjusted her towel, tightening it around herself as Jo turned around slowly. The look on his face, the flush in his cheeks and the brightness of his hazel eyes when he did so, caught her off guard and nerves fluttered in her stomach. Did she look a mess? For the first time since she had met Jo, she cared about what she looked like and it didn't bear thinking about. Her wavy wet hair was probably fuzzy from where she had manically patted her face with the towel. Her lips were most likely pruney from staying in the bath so long. She was grateful for the dim light of the lamp and the twinkling lights that caught the water droplets on her shoulders and hopefully gave her a little healthy glow while her brain tried to figure if Jo's look was scrutinising in a good or bad way. Deciding

LUCY KNOTT

lasted mere seconds before she cleared her throat and pushed those thoughts away, for the room was beginning to heat dangerously. She waved the bag of raisins at Jo with a big smile on her face. 'Thank you for my raisins; they're one of my favourites.'

When Jo didn't speak, it only allowed Florence's brain to happily take over again. This moment felt like every meet-cute ever written in any book. Jo hadn't taken his eyes off her, but that was only because she had just made a fool of herself and probably looked like one of those tiny dogs whose hair flattens and sticks to their faces when they get wet.

Her looks aside, there was something about Jo looking so innocent, his lips slightly parted, his hazel eyes sparkling behind his curly locks and his cheeks flushing a rosy hue that made Florence not want to look away from him either or want him to leave.

But she couldn't confuse their friendship. She didn't do love and relationships; she would only mess it up. And what was she even thinking? Jo didn't see her like that. He'd just admitted he wasn't the settling type. They got on so well because, though Jo talked in pretty poetry about her story not having ended yet and her finding her happy ever after, Florence wasn't silly enough to miss that when Jo had made this grand speech at the ice-cream shop, it was aimed at her, not himself. She had felt that connection, where just like her he believed that everyone else could have love but not himself. And so, she let out a heavy sigh and smirked, rubbing at her forehead where the bag of raisins had hit her, breaking whatever spell had been momentarily cast over her.

Her smirk seemed to bring life back to Jo and he rolled his eyes with a laugh. Giving her a quick nod, he ruffled his unruly hair, turned on his heels and left. When he did so,

Florence's chest deflated. She rubbed a hand over one shoulder, trying to ease the tension there. Her chest felt tight with a pain she could not place. Anticipation? Want? Need? She climbed onto her bed, the fluffy duvet snuggly against her bare skin, and opened her snack. She chewed on each raisin one at a time slowly and thoughtfully, trying to decipher the feelings fluttering around in her stomach. Was she really craving more than a friendship with Jo? After a good ten minutes, she decided that it was best to deem those feelings as hunger pains and got herself dressed.

* * *

When Florence stepped out of her hut at ten minutes to eight, she delighted to find a trail of sprinkles, like tiny stepping stones for a fairy, positioned along the path. She hungrily followed the colourful strands and what she saw at the end of the trail as she rounded the back of the main cottage was a rather spectacular site. Though not a scrumptious candy-coated house made of liquorice and strawberry laces like the Hansel-and-Gretel-esque trail might have suggested, the roaring campfire surrounded by lanterns, deck chairs and a table that sported an array of tasty-looking dinner options was, in her opinion, far greater. She stood and gawped taking in the woodsy smell of the burning wood in the firepit, her eyes following the wispy smoke as it ascended into the air.

'Ma lady, your dinner awaits,' came Jo's voice from behind the flames. He was dressed in a baggy navy jumper and loose-fitting khaki trousers and his hair seemed to bounce a little extra after his shower. Florence smiled when she saw him, her awkward feelings from earlier vanishing with the distraction of the ashes and embers.

'This is amazing,' Florence breathed as she skipped around the fire, her long flowy baby pink dress swishing as she did so. She cast a look up to the dark sky that was littered with golden stars that were so fluorescent out here in the country it was like someone had painted them individually sparing no expense on their detail. The she tuned in to the calming crackle of the fire. 'I can't believe this,' she said when she stopped and stood by Jo, surveying the options he had prepared for dinner. He had thought of it all: sausages, hot dog buns, burgers, and baked beans. There was even Snickers and marshmallows and fruit to dip in the fondue for dessert. 'I can't believe you did this,' she added, nibbling a pickle Jo had garnished their plates with.

'I remember the boys used to talk about camping at school and how they would tell ghost stories and melt Snickers and you must remember when Tom Sawyer went camping?' Jo told her with an enthused smile. Florence nodded. She too had heard the girls talking about campfires and s'mores when she was growing up, but she was far too shy to join them at Brownies.

'Sausages or burgers first?' Jo asked, holding out a silver dish and his cooking tongs in the air.

'Ooh sausages,' Florence replied, helping Jo unwrap the juicy sausages and popping them in the metal dish. He then put it on the small metal shelf, almost like a cooling rack, he had made over the fire. 'There's a lot of food here, Jo,' Florence noted as she helped herself to another pickle, her stomach growling, seemingly telling her to be quiet as all the food looked delicious and she could no doubt eat it all.

'I mentioned the campfire to Sal when I was picking up the food from the village and I bumped into Mr and Mrs Phillips earlier. To my knowledge they come here every year.

They are a sweet elderly couple – you'll have seen them at breakfast. I told them that they are welcome to join us, and they said they would consider it if they didn't fall asleep,' Jo said, with a soft shrug, which made something inside Florence's stomach somersault. *No,* she told her mind and popped a slice of tomato in her mouth to quench the troublesome hunger, which she was stubbornly ascribing these unusual feelings to. 'If I make extra and they don't make it, I'm sure Sal will rustle up something incredible for breakfast with the leftovers,' Jo added, keeping an eye on the sausages while opening a big bag of Kettle Chips and placing them in a bowl by two of the deck chairs near the fire.

Florence took a seat and when she was comfortable, she pulled out her book. With Jo being otherwise occupied with dinner, she felt it was her turn to read tonight. Currently she had three books on the go: *Sense and Sensibility*, *Alice in Wonderland* and *Little Women*, always *Little Women*. She had been dipping in and out of that book since she was small, her nanna having read chapters to her most evenings, but tonight she had chosen *Wind in the Willows* from her bedside pile.

Florence read a few chapters while Jo saw to the food and when the sausages were ready, they made up their plates and sat side by side in front of the fire, savouring the flavours of the scrummy sausages with ketchup and mustard.

'I thought a place like this would never go out of style,' Florence said after she had finished her first hot dog. She had understood their earlier conversation when Jo had told her that Camp Calla Lily hadn't been able to compete with the parks offering so many activities. Sitting by the fire, it was an experience so magical that she felt created endless possibilities for kids and adults alike. Imagine stories around the flames while the children made fondue and roasted marshmallows or evenings where adults got to sit and talk under the stars with a glass of wine. It was like heaven to her, and not to mention the huts.

'Do you think if you rebuild the barn, you can resurrect this place, Jo?' Florence asked, as her mind danced with possibilities. Jo seemed to shuffle uncomfortably on his spot. He looked away into the flames, that flash of worry flitting through his eyes.

'Erm, yes. I think with some new offerings and a little advertising, I believe it could stand a chance. The huts haven't been here long – that was a start, a step in the right direction – so yeah, I think they can save it,' Jo said. Then he tucked into his second hot dog, with a mixture of determination and uncertainty behind his eyes. Something gave Florence the impression that he didn't wish to continue with this topic but then he spoke again. 'Looking through the photo albums Grandad has, they used to have a campsite, allow people to pitch tents but the washrooms grew too dirty and hazardous and got knocked down some time ago. It looked incredible, a true way to connect with nature, but people don't want to pitch tents anymore; they want to experience the outdoors with all the luxury and amenities of the indoors,' Jo explained while Florence ate.

Florence's eyes lit up at the idea of camping and pitching a tent, but she didn't argue that case with Jo, for it seemed as if he was trying to justify these words to himself, like the more times he repeated 'people don't want to pitch tents anymore,' the more chance he had of believing it himself. She wondered why he was going against his own beliefs and who 'they' were.

'So, do you plan on sticking around here?' Florence enquired, not wanting to press the matter of the tents, which seemed to spark struggle behind Jo's eyes, as she pinched a few crisps from the bowl. Armed now with the knowledge that Jo hadn't grown up on the camp, she wondered about his life before finding his grandad again. 'I imagine it's a great place for a writer, so peaceful and tranquil. Where did you live before?'

'No, this isn't my home and my grandad isn't my biggest fan right now,' Jo replied sounding a little defeated. The hesitation was back in his voice when he spoke of the camp and George. Florence forced her Uranian blue eyes to remain bright and free of judgement. Did she tell him she had overheard them arguing the other day? Did she ask why George wasn't happy? But before she could ask any questions Jo continued. 'I live in London and you're right, this place is heaven for a writer,' he added dreamily, though his eyes drooped with sadness. He didn't offer more information about London and so Florence decided a change of topic might help.

'You know, it has been three days and you haven't shown me any of your work,' she said, nudging him gently, hoping that talking about writing would lift his spirits. He always wore a smile when they talked about books.

'That's because I'm yet to have anything published. I've been working on a novel, but I can't seem to finish it,' he confessed, not looking at her but into the flames. 'I'm sorry, I seem to have turned this evening to doom and gloom.'

Florence placed her plate on the ground and sat up straighter in her chair. 'Nonsense,' she said, no judgement coming from her lips. When she had worked at the theatre, she used to do an activity with the children when they put on plays. She would go around the circle asking them to each give her a sentence and together they would create a story. It helped her whenever she got writer's block and it helped bring the shyer children out of their shells as no sentence was wrong and they would all work together and marvel in what they had created together. 'Tell me the last sentence you wrote,' she said with great enthusiasm, her heart warming thinking back to her theatre groups.

Her excitement had the desired effect as after a brief pause where Jo eyed her curiously, he took a deep breath, turned towards her so their knees were touching and told her. Except once the sentence was out of his mouth Jo didn't stop. Words flew out of his mouth as he unwrapped his novel in fine detail. Florence occasionally reached down and picked up a crisp, chewing it ever so slowly and thoughtfully as she hung on his every word, not wanting to miss the action as Jo spoke theatrically and passionately. Minutes passed. Jo stood, then sat, stood again, then sat again and when he finished Florence demanded, 'Then what? Don't stop. What happens next?'

'Well, I guess that would be the end. It would be a cliff hanger,' he said with a chuckle.

'So then, pray tell, Mr Hadlee, when exactly were you stuck? I think this is more a serious case of procrastination, not writer's block. Just pick up your pen and write all that down,' she said waving her hands in the direction of his animated performance that contained all the words for his novel. Jo let out a light and hearty laugh that made Florence beam.

'Well, I don't know. I think you might be right, Miss Danver,' he exclaimed.

'I want to know what happens next, Jo. That poor man, you can't leave him in despair; he needs you. You have not one great novel but two and they must be written,' Florence said. She didn't like the thought of characters being left in limbo. It was ever so hard for her to stop reading if one of the characters was in trouble. She felt she was doing them a great disservice to not continue reading and see them out of it before she got on with her day. Jo smiled and this time his eyes twinkled.

'Can I interest you in dessert?' he asked. Florence could almost see the thoughts whizzing through his brain through the twinkles.

'Yes, please,' she said, her own eyes glistening under the moonlight and the low flames. 'Jo, will you promise me one thing?' Florence felt a rumble of excitement in her veins, but also a touch cheeky asking this question of a writer, knowing that his story was entirely up to him.

'What's that?' Jo asked, collecting all the things they needed for their fondue from the table behind where they sat.

'That you give the man a happily ever after,' she said. Jo considered her a moment and Florence held his gaze. Then he simply nodded casually, a small smile at his lips, as he saw to unwrapping the Snickers. Florence turned away, her own lips curving into a satisfied grin.

'This is the fun bit,' Jo then announced, handing a Snickers bar to her. They both knelt closer to the fire, stirring the chocolatey treats in the pan until they became a gooey, sweet mixture.

'You should advertise campfires here, Jo. Families would love this,' Florence noted, reaching for the strawberries and a stick.

'I like the way you think,' Jo replied, spearing a marshmallow on the end of his stick. Florence hoped that whatever it was Jo and George were arguing about would be resolved soon. From what she could gather, Jo cared about Camp Calla Lily and wanted to see it thrive and George had certainly held on to the place even when it wasn't profitable and had fallen into disarray. She believed that together they could bring it back to life. In that moment she certainly felt as if it had brought so much life back to her.

It was there by the fire they sat chatting and quoting their favourite lines from books until the fire had burnt out and every trace of chocolate had been scooped out of the pot by eager fingers.

Once they had tidied away and cleaned the pots and pans in the cottage kitchen, they made their way back to their huts, Jo dropping Florence off outside hers first. In saying good-night, Jo casually leant in and kissed Florence's cheek. The spark that sizzled as his lips grazed her skin meant he lingered longer than necessary but neither of them pulled away and Florence found that her eyes closed, savouring his touch.

'Night, Jo,' she whispered, her eyes still closed unaware that Jo stood watching her, his feet not functioning properly.

'Night, Florence,' he said just as she opened her eyes. Florence felt her cheeks flush and she took a step back feeling embarrassed. Her feet became rather interesting as she reached out for the door handle. She could feel Jo's gaze on the back of her neck. Had she just made a fool of herself again?

'Thank you for a lovely evening,' she croaked, with a brazen nod as if shaking herself from her thoughts. 'Tomorrow, I'm going to paint the barn and you are going to write. And that is an order,' she stated, reverting to her clear and playful tone before slipping inside her hut.

Jo bowed with a cute smirk, which she caught as she turned to close her door. When he smiled like that she so wished life came with a narrator so she could hear the thoughts going on in his head.

THIRTEEN

For the first time in a long time Florence had missed the sunrise and had had to skip out on reading her book, for when she woke her clock had informed her that it was already past nine a.m. and she had a lot of work to do today. She had thrown on her puff-sleeve flower-patterned dress and made her way hastily to the café to pick up two butties and then galloped to the barn. Jo was nowhere to be found and she found herself smiling at the memory of last night, staying up late reading under the stars and enjoying his company. He had put a lot of work into dinner. She felt he too deserved a lie-in, what with all the stress and pressure he was under to help his grandad and get this place up and running while finding time to write his great novels. A shadow always crept over his face whenever he discussed his grandad and it worried Florence. Maybe George was worried that Jo was spending too much of his energy on the barn when he needed to concentrate on his job as a writer and getting published. Florence wondered for the first time what Jo did to keep himself afloat; maybe George was struggling to pay him, and it was causing a rift between the two of them? With his grandad being all the family Jo had left, it pained her to think they didn't see eye to eye, when it was clear Jo loved this place just as much as George did and was only trying to do what he thought best.

After their thorough soak of the barn, as well as themselves, yesterday, the wooden floor was looking exceptionally sparkly and the place looked a far cry from the depleted shack it had resembled only a few days earlier. But they still needed to sand down the good panels before they could be painted, and they could breathe some life back into the walls and make them shiny again. Jo's butty had gone cold by the time Florence had sanded down the barn doors and the two panels either side, as there was still no sign of him. He must have needed the rest, Florence thought. However, as lunchtime rolled around worry had crept to the forefront of her mind, so much so that she ventured back to the huts to check on him.

She knocked lightly on his hut door but received no answer and so she walked a little around the back and peeked through the tiny window, where she saw him sat at his desk looking exasperated, his hands in his hair and talking to a woman who was perched on the edge of his bed. Florence's stomach performed an uncomfortable lurch, her eyes grew misty and she darted as quick as she could away from the window and up to the cottage. Collecting herself on the patio, she took in a few deep breaths of the glorious fresh air and shook her head. There had been no need for such a ridiculous reaction to seeing Jo, otherwise occupied with a woman other than her. He was a companion, a friend, an acting partner; he was allowed to have a girlfriend. At the mere thought of the word *girlfriend*, a wave of queasiness hit Florence hard. She was not girlfriend material; she knew that, and it was clear Jo didn't see her that way either. Had she wanted him to? The thought made her clutch her stomach and her eyes sting. These were not feelings she was used to.

A shuffle of feet behind her made Florence jump. She turned to find George walking on to the patio with a newspaper in hand.

'Is everything OK, my dear?' George asked, sounding sprightlier today than when she had seen him last.

Florence raised her head with confidence, thrilled to see the old man out of his office and enjoying the sunshine and also feeling grateful for the distractions he gave her from her silly thoughts of wondering who the woman had been in Jo's hut and how it made insecurity swamp her.

'It most certainly is, George. It's stunning out here,' she answered clearing her wobbly throat and forcing her words to sound merry. George had problems of his own; she didn't want to burden him. The fact that the scenery was indeed stunning, and the leafy green trees were swaying in the warm breeze, the birds singing upon their branches, helped with Florence's merriness. She didn't have to try too hard to smile. 'How are you today?' she asked, her discomfort from mere moments ago dissolving the wider George's grin grew as he matched her gaze in looking across the fields. Love for the land was evident in his green eyes, the trees reflecting in their hazel hue.

'I'm well thank you, Florence,' he said, sounding a little unsure of that statement but not expanding on this fact. 'What have you been up to this morning? I see you dancing around the grounds just as you did when you were a girl,' he added, glancing over to her this time. 'Those crystal blue eyes of yours are full of just as much magic as they held when you were tiny,' he added, with a look that told Florence this pleased him greatly. It was a shift from the night she had checked in when she thought he must think of her a prize idiot talking of magic carpets. 'I hope I didn't embarrass you the night of your arrival, my dear. That was never my intention,' George said as if reading her mind. 'I'm afraid the day had been rather challenging, and I took that out on you; for that I am most sorry.'

Florence was taken aback by the words that came out of George's mouth. How had she not remembered him when he remembered her? Of course, he would have been here when she was a girl. The camp had been in the Hadlee name since long before she came along.

'Forgive me for not remembering you, George. My memories of this place have been under lock and key for quite some time and if ever one did escape, I have to admit they were never very fond,' she told him truthfully, her hands intertwined nervously fidgeting on her lap.

'I know, dear, and that is quite all right,' he returned, placing a caring hand on top of her hands and giving them a squeeze. With this action, Florence didn't feel the need to explain herself, like somehow, she knew George understood her reasons. 'Your nanna told me as much. Now, do tell me of where your dances have been taking you these days,' he said, his eyes crinkling when he smiled at her.

Florence looked up feeling overwhelmed by his warmth and his revelation of knowing her and her family. She didn't mean to ignore his question, but she backtracked on his mention of her nanna.

'You have spoken with my nanna.' It came out more like a statement, but she had meant it as a question.

'Ah yes, Margot is a dear friend,' he said, wistfully, making Florence smile with the fondness in his face when he said her nanna's name. 'We have never lost touch all these years. That is why you must forgive me, dear girl. I was anticipating your arrival and promised Margot I would look after you, but I have not been myself.' He looked down to where his hands lay over hers, the shame rising on his features.

'Don't be silly. I understand. It was late; we all have those moments. It brings me so much happiness that you know my nanna. I apologise we've not been back here for some time,' Florence started but her words trailed off, for she didn't know how to finish that sentence. With George being so kind she felt guilty for having hated the place and sad that her nanna had feared it so much that she had stayed away from her friend.

'Oh, I will hear none of it. Life happens. I talk to her most every day. I believe she will come back here in her own time. I will not push her,' he said, raising his hands. With a small shrug, he smiled cheekily. 'Though I know she does a lot of pushing. I do hope that her pushing has served you well, for it brings me great joy to see you exploring this land again. I have not quite made my mind up on your spending time with my charming grandson admittedly,' he said, his bushy brows raised with his playful tone, making Florence laugh, but something else fluttered in her stomach. Why had Margot never told her about George? They had been friends all these years and her nanna had never cared to mention him. Florence felt the urge to enquire about their secret friendship but the cheeky look on George's face squashed down any demands she had to know why her nanna had been hiding it from her.

'Is that what you call him? I would call him trouble,' she teased back. Their banter and understanding of each other comforted Florence and allowed her to slip back into easy conversation rather than get caught up in secrets.

'Yes, I have called him that before too,' George said and

though he smiled a flash of sadness passed over him when he spoke of his grandson.

'He has a beautiful imagination,' Florence said, hoping to keep the conversation fun and thinking that maybe George just needed to be told how wonderful his grandson was and then he might not be so mad at him for whatever it was he was mad at him for.

'Arrgh, yes, that imagination of his. Where has it taken the two of you this week?' he enquired making Florence smile. How nice it was to be surrounded by people who encouraged imagining. At the same time, a flash of guilt washed over her that she had spent her life living with her nanna, who never made her feel silly for her wild ways, while Jo had been in foster care, his grandparents unaware of his whereabouts and Jo missing out on their love and encouragement as a result. She pushed her glasses up her nose, collecting her thoughts, not wanting to upset George with them. 'We've been out by the old barn,' she answered. It seemed that Florence could upset George even when not talking about Jo's upbringing, because at the mention of the barn, his face fell and hurt clouded his eyes.

'Ah, the old barn. Don't you be getting lost in that barn now, Florence. There's plenty of other things to see and do,' he said, putting on a cheery smile.

'But Jo says that he's doing it up to help this place. If we revive it to be like the good old days, then maybe business will pick up,' Florence said, unable to hide the glee in her voice and really wanting George to be on board with Jo's great idea. Is that why Jo had been getting so frustrated with his grandad? Because George didn't believe in his vision?

Before Florence could stand up for Jo and explain how if the barn were up and running, they could hold dances and events and entice a new generation of families, George spoke. 'Is that what he said?' Though it came out more like a disbelieving whisper more to himself than Florence; then he shook his head.

'Don't you be worrying about the camp, my dear. That's my job. Now, do you not have other places to be than sitting here chatting to an old man?' he said with a chuckle, letting Florence know that he didn't want to discuss that topic further and leaving her to wonder what on earth he meant by: "Is that what he said?"

'It's been lovely chatting with you, George, but yes, I'd best be off. Can I get you anything from the village?' she asked, standing up and feeling a fresh wave of determination to complete all the jobs on hers and Jo's to-do list. With or without Jo, she wanted George to have his lively camp back and to rid himself of worry. And maybe, just maybe, if they could bring the good old days back to the barn, Florence could get her nanna to come back too, which she had a feeling would make George see that it was all worth it.

'No, I don't think I do, sweetheart. Have a pleasant walk dear and do be safe,' he said. Florence could feel her cheeks burn with a slight flush at the warmth in George's voice in knowing and not judging her walking habits. She curtseyed, feeling free to be herself before heading in the direction of the road.

The walk to the village felt a little longer without Jo by her side reading and entertaining her but it was beautiful nonetheless. It also gave Florence time to think and calm the emotions that ambushed her earlier. She wasn't one to get attached so easily and Jo had come out of nowhere on her holiday and made for such great company that she had unmistakably become a tiny bit attached. Once she reached the village, she had settled her mind on being slightly jealous over seeing him with another woman who may or may not be his girlfriend because she had gotten so used to having him all to herself. And she admitted that him not turning up at the barn had upset her; leaving her to all the jobs that morning had been somewhat disappointing. She had thought him more thoughtful than that – that was all.

But it was no bother. Florence had invested herself in the barn and wanted to do her bit in the renovations before it was time for her to leave on Saturday morning. It felt extra special now that she knew George and her nanna were good friends. It gave her a new goal of getting her nanna back here again and securing George's future. Those thoughts kept her mind focused on the task at hand.

Jo had told her the day before that the paint order was going to be available to pick up from the corner shop today, so after popping in to say a quick hello to Ella at The Vintage Bookshop, she called in to check if it was ready. Expecting to find maybe two to three cans of paint, Florence was shocked to see there were six rather large cans. She had clearly underestimated the size of the barn and had maybe been a tad overzealous in her plan of carrying the paint back to the camp. She stood for a few moments, lips pursed, hands on her hips as she tried to come up with a plan to get the paint back to the barn in one smooth run.

'Let me load them into my truck, Florence. I can close up for a minute and take you back,' Roman said from behind the register. Florence appreciated his kind gesture greatly but that didn't stop her palms clamming up.

'No, it's OK, thank you, Roman. I have an idea. I'll be back in a few minutes. Is it OK if I leave them here?' she asked.

'Sure,' Roman replied, in his laid-back manner. Florence liked the village. In contrast to Manchester where everyone was in a rush with their heads down or eyes glued to their phones, here in Lily Pines everyone made eye contact and treated you as though they had all the time in the world to chat to you; she was really going to miss it.

Florence nodded her thanks, headed out the door and dashed over the road to the small fruit, vegetable and plant shop that had trolleys.

'Hi, would it be possible for me to use one of your trolleys to deliver some paint to Camp Calla Lily? I promise I will bring it back,' Florence asked. The woman looked Florence up and down – something she was not used to in this village. Everyone had been super friendly all week, at least to her. She remained suspicious about the looks they had been giving Jo. But when the woman opened her mouth, the reason behind her judging eyes became clear.

'Are you Jo's girlfriend?' she asked causing Florence to let out a nervous chuckle as she stood fiddling with the strap of her shoulder bag. Oh boy, did she have to wait for an answer? Could she not just get the trolley and leave now?

'N-no, I'm just staying at the camp,' Florence stammered, looking over at the trolleys to encourage the conversation back on topic and so her mind did not wander back to Jo's hut and the woman sitting on his bed.

'Do you know if he has one?' The woman was not done with her interrogation of Jo.

'I think he might,' Florence said, softly, not wanting to upset the woman. She seemed keen on Jo; maybe they knew each other from when Jo was a boy. Maybe they played together at the camp or maybe they had gotten to know each other since Jo had come back to Camp Calla Lily over the last year?

'Are the rumours true?' came the lady's next question. Florence deepened her already pensive brow, puzzled by such a bold question.

'What rumours? I'm afraid I'm only here on holiday for the week. I'm not aware of any rumours,' she politely told the woman.

The woman slowly gave her the once-over again and seemingly deciding that Florence was no longer threatening, she smiled and leant forward.

'I've seen you two popping into the village. I thought with you staying at the camp you might know something, or you might be one of them.' She spoke in a hushed tone now.

'One of who?' Florence enquired, matching the woman's quieter tone.

'One of those big-shot architects in London. All we've heard is that Jo's come back here with plans to buy out his grandad and sell off the land to one of those glamping traders. Poor George is beside himself. Jo has been in and out of the place for the past year. First those huts popped up and I've seen the occasional suit nosing about the village. I thought you might have been one of them, but I should have realised you weren't. I love your dress by the way.' The lady finished with a warm if not conflicted smile. The passion for the village was evident in all the shop owners here and by the swirling anger and hurt twisting around in Florence's gut, she could understand the women's inquisition. She too felt protective of the village, after just three days, and even more so of Camp Calla Lily. These rumours surely had to be false. She didn't want to believe she had read Jo all wrong, but then again, she knew she shouldn't have been reading him at all and should have stuck to her books, for reasons exactly like this. She had let her guard down and look what good it had done her. No wonder George had been sad, and Sal had been angry when she had mentioned the barn. Jo was doing it up to sell it off. He was going to sell their livelihood. How could he?

'I'm not a big-shot architect and I don't believe that that is Jo's intention with the place,' Florence managed, feeling a little shell-shocked. Why was she still sticking up for Jo? Maybe a part of her thought that if she did, if she believed with all her heart and said it out loud it would make it true. But she couldn't silence the warning bells in her ears: how George was always so edgy and disgruntled whenever he spent time with his grandson. The sadness in his eyes whenever he spoke of Jo. The renovation of the barn. Jo knowing exactly what to do when building. Jo not having completed any books and the lady in his hut this morning. It all made sense now. How could Florence have been so foolish? The first day they had met he had said he needed to go to work. He wasn't a writer, he was working on the barn. He was an architect, a builder. Florence could feel the blood pulsing uncomfortably around her head making her feel dizzy.

'I hope so,' the woman said with a gentle sigh. 'Help yourself to a trolley. I trust you,' the woman added making Florence blink and shake her head from her stupor. Realising there was a customer behind her, Florence nodded at the woman in thanks and left, her brain ticking over with how she was going to face Jo when she got back to the camp.

As Roman helped her load the cans into the trolley with an amused look on his face at Florence's idea, Florence felt miles away. It was probably just small-village gossip and nothing more. Jo would not do that to his grandad, not when he knew how much the camp meant to him, the history his family had there. He couldn't possibly; it would be cruel. Upon heading into the village Florence had had the intention of grabbing a bite to eat, having not had lunch yet, but now she didn't feel so hungry. She thanked Roman and rolled her trolley past the pub, the smell of delicious everyday roasts not quite having their usual inviting effect, and trudged on in the direction of the camp.

FOURTEEN

Florence rubbed her thumbs over the handle of the trolley feeling irritated. Her brow was sweating in the summer sun, which was blazing down on her from another cloudless sky. The camp was quiet with no one about, but she spotted him straight away. Sitting on the deck chair with his hands behind his head lounging with his feet up. Jo had a strange smirk on his face, one that severely lacked its mischievous and sweet charm. Without hesitation, Florence marched up to him.

She cast a shadow over his slim frame, blocking out the rays making Jo sit up and acknowledge her. He didn't greet her with his normal playful accent or kind grin, but with a look of annoyance.

'Are you going to sell this land? Are you really a writer or was that story yesterday all a ruse? What are you doing here, Jo? Tell me the truth!' Her voice came out strong and forceful as she held her head high, not wanting him to see the sadness this was causing her. Jo flew out of his chair with a menacing look on his face. His eyes were icy and cold, making Florence's lips tremble and then he tilted his head back and laughed, an evil laugh that...

Suddenly a car horn blared, and Florence caught herself just before the trolley made contact with the car's headlights. Lost in her own head she had swerved onto the road. She stopped still for a moment to calm her heavy breathing and catch her breath, then scolded her brain for thinking such vile thoughts of Jo. She shouldn't overthink or jump to conclusions; she simply had to find him and talk to him.

When she arrived back on the campgrounds, she headed straight to the barn to drop off the paint and not finding Jo there, she then went in search of him. Florence wasn't sure what she would do if she found him with the woman again or if they were still occupied in his cabin. Did she have a right to knock; to burst in and demand the truth? But what if the smartly dressed suit was his girlfriend and not just a big-shot architect? Florence couldn't be so rude as to intrude on their time together.

Florence need not have worried about the woman in the suit, for when she got closer to the cottage, she saw Jo walking towards her, his hair dishevelled and grey shadows under his hooded eyes. Her anger shifted for a few seconds as his tired state drew concern from her.

'Florence, there you are. I have been looking all over for you. Are you OK?' Jo asked, his voice sounding desperate, lacking any of its usual confidence. 'Grandad said you had gone to the village; you shouldn't have walked all that way on your own.'

'I'm not some damsel in distress, Jo. I am quite capable of walking by myself,' she snapped, quite surprised by her boldness. She narrowed her eyes at him, but when she looked at him, his warm hazel eyes and rosy cheeks disarmed her, causing her not to feel quite as brave as she had felt in her daydream. But when she thought of George, anger rose in her chest and she stepped forward. 'Why do you not listen to your grandad? Do his feelings not matter to you?' she asked. She had thought Jo cared about him and after all he had told her about his mum, she would have thought that he would take care of his grandad, him being the only family he had left.

'I listen to him all the time,' Jo answered with a smile. Could he not see she was upset? His smile threw her off. Was this funny to him?

Florence stepped forward, stabbing Jo in his chest with her finger, not wishing to be lied to anymore. Emotion swelled in her chest making it rise nervously. 'No, you don't. Why do you not do as he asks of you and respect his wishes?'

'I'm confused. What's going on, Florence?' Jo asked, not stepping back, or cowering at her touch. He reached out like he wanted to comfort her, put an arm around her shoulder, but she shrugged him off. At least now he showed some empathy.

'Who was that lady in your hut this morning? Why did you leave me to the barn all by myself? And why, Jo, have you been lying to me all week?' she further probed, walking forward, giving Jo no choice now but to step back. She'd never spoken to anyone like this before, but all her worries were spilling out. She didn't like the idea of her and Jo keeping secrets. Then suddenly her eyes grew misty.

'Are you a writer, Jo?' Florence asked, her voice returning to its regular soft tone, but replacing its usual lilt of wonderment was vulnerability.

'Yes,' Jo said.

'And?' Florence urged.

'And I'm an architect,' Jo went on with a sigh, placing his

hands on Florence's shoulders, and bending down so he was eye to eye with her. Though the movement stopped her having to crane her neck into the sunlight, she did not wish to make eye contact or for Jo to touch her. Again, Florence shrugged him off and took a few strides away from him. 'I'm sorry I didn't tell you, Florence. It was stupid of me, I know. I just...' Florence didn't want to hear excuses; she cut him off.

'Are you buying this land off your grandad?' she asked. He took a step closer to her, but she turned her back. She didn't want comfort, she wanted answers.

'No, but I want to...' Jo tried to answer.

'So, I've been helping you with your evil plan all along and you didn't tell me? You're not rebuilding the barn for your grandad, you're doing it for you so you can flip the place, sell it and take it away from him. I can't believe I fell for your whole act,' Florence said, pacing now, her lips wobbling but an underlying note of anger carried in her tone. Florence wasn't sure who she was angrier with, Jo or herself for believing him.

'Fell for what exactly? What evil plan? Florence, would you let me explain and not just take the village gossip as the whole truth for just a minute?' Jo asked, walking over to her now, determination in his strides. But Florence's stubbornness was not to be messed with. She continued to pace and not look at him.

'Your plan to rid your grandad from this property and sell it just to make money. You were just indulging me in my madness so I wouldn't tell him or maybe you had a shred of sympathy for me and wanted to let me enjoy going down memory lane while I still had the chance before architects come in here and modernise this place, destroy its charm and its legacy,' Florence said, turning to look at him now with a defeated shrug, her eyes wet. After having avoided this place for the past twenty-three years, she couldn't quite believe how much this whole debacle was upsetting her. But in the last five days the place had sunk into her skin and she'd felt more alive and contented here than anywhere else. Even the occasional flicker of her parents' faces in her mind when she looked out to the lake or wandered by the benches under the blossom trees were now bringing her more peace than grief. It was the last place her family had all been together. She needed Camp Calla Lily.

'Florence, is this the part in the story where the two leading characters have a big misunderstanding and either never speak again or kiss and make up after realising their mistakes?' Jo asked, when she finally gave up to his gaze.

'Do not do that. Don't make fun of me, Jo,' Florence said. Her voice came out so small and quiet that Jo scrunched his nose and bowed his head seemingly understanding the gravity of her hurt now. But then how could Florence be sure he understood her at all anymore?

'Florence, you know in your heart that I would never make fun of you. I'm an architect and I have been for the last nine years. For the last few years, I had been getting caught up in these massive projects, modern glamorous affairs, high-rise buildings and such. I didn't start out with those projects but once I'd done one and experienced how lucrative it could be, I'm ashamed to admit, I got sucked in. The project had gone well, and I was proud to be sought after. I felt like I'd made something of myself.' Jo's words came out fast, he was barely taking a breath.

'I've dreamt of being a writer my whole life – I guess the apple doesn't fall far from the tree – but I was terrified. I didn't want to become like my mum and so I buried the desire to write and focused on other things. The creative in me turned

155

to drawing and then a need to build what I drew grew and so that is how I became an architect and somewhat of a builder. Small projects I can build. I don't actually get to work on any of the high-end projects, but maybe one day. I came back here for my grandma's funeral and it gave me a little respite from my life in London. When I saw the camp in such a shambles, I thought I could help, take a year to build and create, maybe have more time to write, and help my grandad. The minute I heard you talk of magic carpets you inspired me and when I saw you, I felt like I didn't have to hide who I wanted to be, who I saw myself as. Then when I introduced myself and you assumed I was a writer because of my mum's choice of name, I just went with it. I'm sorry I kept a part of me from you,' Jo told her, his eyes never straying from her face. When he paused, he stood a little taller and Florence simply watched him breathe air into his lungs not quite knowing how to respond.

She drew her brows, trying to process what he was telling her.

'I'm not buying the land from my grandad. I wanted to give him money to help with his debts, but he refused to take it. The other option was to sell it on. Kirsty, the lady you saw this morning, gave him a great deal. She owns Luxury Acres, a hotel and spa chain and glamping company. Look, this place has been in disarray for quite some time now; the glamping trade would give it a new lease of life. He's mad at me all the time because he is stubborn and doesn't want my help but if we don't do something now, he will fall further into debt and the campgrounds further into ruin. I wish we didn't have to sell it but it's an amazing deal. Her company have been looking to expand their sites and think this would be a perfect spot. I've been working on the modernising as much as I can myself with the huts, wanting to renovate the barn to keep the Hadlee legacy on the grounds and she said Grandad can still work here and live here, that not much will change bar the management and hopefully a rise in customers,' he added, panting a little when he stopped as he had been following in her pacing.

Florence rubbed the back of her neck; it felt a tad sore from looking up and over at Jo for so long, then she looked at the grass and then over to the magnolia trees to bide her time before she spoke. She felt dumbfounded by all this news and rather regretful that she had jumped to conclusions and had been so hard on Jo. Her nanna would have been disappointed in her for not having kept an open mind and for holding such judgement against the friend she had come to know. She didn't like what he had told her about having to sell the land, but at least now she knew why.

'I'm sorry for being mean and for judging you, Jo. Please forgive me,' she said, her voice coming out slowly as she broke the silence and returned her eyes to his gaze. Then she closed her eyes and let out a breath, holding a hand to her chest where her heart was pounding. Her emotions were running high today and she wasn't sure what to do with herself. 'Though, I wish you would have told me that you are an architect.' She pushed her glasses up on to the bridge of her nose and looked at him. 'As well as a writer,' she added with a small smile.

At first, Jo didn't return her smile. 'I don't think it's you that should be saying sorry. I should have told you. I've just felt so far away from that world since being back here, I kind of liked it,' he confessed. Florence couldn't argue with that, for she too felt miles away from the shy, quirky Florence who skirted around Manchester skittishly, afraid of everything and everyone. She liked who she was at Camp Calla Lily.

'So, you really have to sell it?' she asked, her shoulders sagging.

'I don't have a choice. The upkeep of the land costs too much. We can't afford to pay anyone to run it and Grandad's getting old. Sal tries his best but it's too much,' Jo replied with a heavy sigh.

Florence looked out across the rolling green fields. It had not occurred to her how expensive the land's upkeep would be or the cost of keeping it afloat and in the Hadlee name. With no customers, how could one man keep the flowers blooming and the gardens maintained year-round? The thought saddened her.

Suddenly, Florence felt Jo's finger under her chin as he gently tilted her head up. His cheeky smile was back on his face causing Florence's stomach to flip.

'Should we kiss and make up now?' he said, mischief in his tone. Florence ignored the butterflies that joined in with the somersaults in her belly and punched Jo in the arm.

'No, I'm going to go and dunk my head into the lake for humiliating myself and for being so mad at you. Gosh I was so mad at you,' she said, almost to herself as she moved a hand over her forehead, her eyes wide, astonished at herself for her own behaviour. OK, the rumours had been half true – the land was being sold - but now she had the whole story she was heartbroken more than angry at Jo.

Jo laughed. 'You really were. I was terrified for a minute,' he joked. 'Forgive me, for keeping that part of me a secret, Florence?' he added, raking a hand through his curly locks, the humour in his face turning serious for a second.

'Maybe we both need to walk the plank,' Florence

commented, before turning on her sandals and racing towards the lake. It was only when she reached the edge of the water that Florence realised it was the first time she had felt inclined to visit the lake since she had been back at Camp Calla Lily. Her vision of seeing her parents sat under the nearby blossom tree when she was a girl, on her first day, had at first unsettled her. Yet now, with her body full of emotions that she'd not felt in a long time due to her not letting anyone get close to her, she felt comforted by the water and drawn to it. It felt even more right with Jo by her side and as she paused on the grassy verge, her toes tickling the water, she glanced over to the bench and could see her parents waving happily over at her and Jo with beaming grins on their faces and love in their eyes.

As Jo came up beside her, Florence reached out her hand. Caught up in the moment she didn't stop to think of the magnitude of her actions. She had been the one to reach out her hand to him and Jo took it in his without hesitation. Nodding at each other they waded into the water, gasping over its coldness before quickly getting over that fact and proceeding to splash each other, laughing with delight. All trace of their argument having been forgotten.

FIFTEEN

After swimming in the lake and trying to dunk each other's heads into the water time and time again, Florence and Jo lay on the grass watching the clouds shape-shift and glide across the sky, as they dried off their soggy clothes. When Florence's stomach rumbled it was once again their cue to make a move. Now that they had communicated and got to the bottom of the rumours, Florence was feeling a lot better, though she still felt a pang of sadness when she thought of going home on Saturday morning knowing that Camp Calla Lily was going to be sold to a popular hotel and glamping trader. Seeing Jo with that woman this morning had thrown her and now she wasn't sure if she felt better about the fact that the woman was an investor and not his girlfriend or worse.

Her brain decided to examine the girlfriend theory first. Just because that lady wasn't his girlfriend, it didn't mean Jo didn't have one. It wasn't something she could bring herself to ask him. He would then wonder why she cared to know and that was not something she had quite figured out herself yet. But that was the trouble wasn't it? That she did indeed care enough that she was thinking about it. Jo was bound to meet more women when she was gone. He would meet stylish, sophisticated women back in London and they would replace her. He might even bring them to Camp Calla Lily and read to them and frolic around the campsite with them and that would be that. She really shouldn't be bothered by it, she told herself as she watched one very fluffy cloud form the shape of a bear. It was ridiculous for her mind to even be examining it. She liked Jo but they could never be more than friends.

Florence was the oddball, the prude, the woman with one toe dipped into reality while the rest of her lived in the land of misfit bookworms and if by chance someone did not see her as all those things, there was that small matter of her being petrified of love. Like all children she had loved her mum with her entire being and her mum had been brutally snatched from her. Her dad had been the apple of her eye, but love had damaged his mind and led him astray. She had loved Ryan and that love had hoodwinked her and turned her into a fool. Where the road forked bearing one signpost for love, the other for safety, Florence would always choose safety.

Plus, even Jo had mentioned that he wasn't the settling type. That didn't bode well for a relationship and therefore their simple companionship should remain just that. Yes, a simple companionship suited them.

With that settled in her brain, she breathed in the buttercups and the crispy grass and jumped up. She hadn't addressed the other tribulation in her mind yet, but if she was going to think of ways where Jo didn't have to sell the land, she was going to need fuel.

'I'm famished,' she announced, her appetite coming back now that she had her emotions in check.

'Well, let's get you some food,' Jo said, taking her outstretched hand as she pulled him up.

In the café, they chatted to Sal and said hello to the other guests while enjoying a late lunch of ham and cheese toasties. Sal was much sprightlier when they avoided talk of the barn. Once refuelled it was time to get back to their day's work and get the barn painted. Florence felt a certain ominous feeling now that she knew the real reason behind the barn's makeover, but she also couldn't shake the excitement of saving it from a trip to the tip. There was too much history inside it.

Jo laughed with great affection when he saw the trolley full of paint cans and commended Florence for her brilliant initiative. He also promised that he would be the one to return the trolley and put the rumours straight when he did so. Florence knew it wasn't going to be straightforward and she shuddered at the thought of confrontation. Poor Jo. She imagined that the villagers, like her, wouldn't be totally convinced that the land being taken over by a hotel and glamping trader would be the right move, but only time would tell. If it saved George from debt, allowed him to keep his house and it preserved the land, then it couldn't be all bad.

Reading over the paint labels with great focus, Jo revealed to Florence why there were so many cans- three were for the interior and three were for the exterior of the barn and he couldn't mistake them. They were working on the indoor today. Satisfied he knew which was which, Jo cranked open two of the paint cans, revealing a pearly deep red-brown shade of paint. Florence couldn't help but think that her sunflower yellow and mint paint job would have brought a whole new lease of life to the barn and made it pop against the green and brown of the wilderness, but this was Jo's project; he could paint it in the colours he liked best.

'You don't like the colour, do you?' Jo asked, breaking into her thoughts with a small side smile. Florence's eyebrows shot up. She hadn't meant for Jo to see her disappointment; now she felt rude.

'Of course, no it's beautiful. It's the perfect barn shade,' she said quickly, cringing slightly. Did B and Q do a "perfect barn shade" collection?

Jo shook his head and chuckled. Florence sensed he could see right through her white lie. 'How about you get to painting the barn doors and I'll get more of the sanding done,' he suggested. Her face lit up as she yielded the brush excitely over the tins. It might not be her colour of choice, but Florence loved to paint. 'We can at least get that side painted today and leave this side to rest overnight before it's painted.'

Both Jo and Florence fell to work in the comfortable routine they had created over the past week. Side by side they got on quite contentedly in each other's company, doing their work with great passion and enthusiasm. Florence was mesmerised by every swipe of paint she swished onto the barn door. Though not quite as happy and vibrant as a yellow, the pearly sheen of the brown made her smile as she covered the sandy beige panel with a new life that emitted cheer and possibilities. Jo sanded down each panel with determined vigour and Florence could feel that pull to him once more. He wasn't afraid of hard work and it was something she admired. Speaking of hard work, she had a question.

'So, tell me more about being an architect,' Florence said, glancing back at Jo as she moved into position to paint the second barn door. Jo's curls were speckled with dust from the panels, the muscles in his arms flexing as he scrubbed. Florence enjoyed watching him at work.

'I started out drawing the scenery in my head that I had

for different novel ideas. The places where the characters lived, the haunted houses, the castles, anything far-fetched. Through fear of putting pen to paper and following through with any of those stories, I decided I wanted to build the structures. I put myself through school, working any odd job, and then eventually constructed sheds and playhouses for kids. It was just me at first, freelance. I had the network of foster carers and did custom orders and I loved it. Those were the projects that truly set my soul on fire,' Jo told her, smiling at the memories.

'What happened? Why did you stop doing that type of work? Which sounds rather wonderful,' Florence asked, averting her eyes back to the barn door she was painting, a small smile curving at her lips when she thought of Jo making playhouses for children. Then she turned back to look at Jo when he spoke.

Jo stopped sanding and rested his elbows on his knees in his squatting position. He turned the sandpaper over in his hands. His lips were pursed in thought. 'I made a princess hut for a client who was a well-respected lawyer. He later started up his own company and enlisted me to design his new building and oversee the project. I was twenty-seven at the time, fresh out of years of taxing schooling. The lifestyle appealed to me and I felt I deserved the recognition and the rewards,' he told her. 'It skyrocketed me from the nerdy outcast kid who had bounced around from foster home to foster home until I settled with my long term foster family when I was nine, to making something of myself and becoming a distinguished architect. It felt good, really good.' He shrugged with a faraway look in his eyes, the last words coming out in a sigh.

'I don't think you should be ashamed of wanting recognition Jo, or money and stability,' Florence said.

'I guess so,' Jo stated, but he didn't look convinced by Florence's words. So, she continued. 'Seven years is a long time to be in school. That's an amazing accomplishment,' she noted, encouragingly. Though she loved her books and had done well, getting exceptional grades throughout high school, she had never gone to college. With her job at the theatre having been secured at an early age and it being a place she felt safe and happy, she hadn't thought much into further education. That and college had too many people who she didn't know, and her fear of that new social environment kept her from pursuing it. In hindsight, Florence knew she should have gone and got a qualification in something, but she had been comfortable within the theatre.

'I like books.' Jo shrugged, looking over at her from under a curly lock, which had fallen in front of his eyes, but Florence was pleased to see a grin spread across his features. Then he stood up to stretch his legs and continue sanding. 'What are you going to do when you get back home?' Jo then asked, curiosity in his tone. 'You have such a special imagination, Florence; you must do something with it. You shouldn't settle for an office job, if you don't enjoy it,' he added, giving her a meaningful look that caused a family of butterflies to hatch in her belly.

She turned away, carefully painting the panels, her eyes narrowed in concentration as she made sure not to paint over the accent beams that were to be white. That was one of the nicest things anyone had ever said to her. How was she supposed to respond? Weirdly for her, her mind went with honesty and openness. Jo made it easy and after their fight earlier; she much preferred when they had no secrets.

LUCY KNOTT

'I'd love to find work in a theatre again or maybe a class where I can teach kids. I don't have any qualifications, just experience so we will see. I'll do anything to keep nanna and I afloat. Maybe I'll even try and find work in a bookshop – that would be lovely. I ended up at Paperchains when I was fired from the theatre because it was good money and they were the first people to say yes, so you shouldn't feel bad about having had the money entice you, Jo.

I imagine becoming an architect wasn't easy and after everything you've been through, you made something of yourself. You should be proud. I think I'd like to do that, you know, have the confidence to go back and maybe even take a course. I was just always so scared of everything before. This place has truly opened me up to possibilities and allowed me to let go a little bit. I think I needed that,' Florence expressed, still concentrating on the door while she mulled over her decision in her mind.

Being at the camp and overcoming her fear of talking about her parents had released a huge weight from her chest, albeit even if it were only Jo in whom she felt she could confide. Furthermore, Camp Calla Lily itself and getting to focus her mind on the rebuild of the barn had been a wonderful source of inspiration in giving Florence that extra dose of determination to set about doing something she loved when she returned home. It wouldn't be easy not seeing Olivia every day and having to introduce herself to a new crowd, but Jo had given her faith that meeting new people didn't always turn out so bad.

As Florence spoke, she could feel her cheeks reddening under Jo's piercing gaze. He had stopped sanding to listen to her and she suddenly felt conscious, more aware of herself. Today she was wearing her golden waves in a loose high pony and another long-ruffled dress that reached a little higher than her ankles. Her fashion inspiration growing up had been her nanna. Margot always looked other-worldly with an old-fashioned elegance that Florence adapted with a modern flair. Her round clear frames didn't take over her face and accentuated her blue eyes. Margot had told her this when she helped her pick them out. The bohemian, baggy style, she knew was not everyone's cup of tea. Ryan had mentioned on a few occasions that being a grown-up meant that you could show off more skin, but she loved the feel of the silky gowns and high collars against her skin.

'I think the kids would be lucky to have you teach them. I imagine you are a rather splendid teacher, Miss Danver,' he said, clearing his throat when they broke eye contact. Florence did not do smug, but for a brief moment she felt herself soar with Jo's compliment and for a flash of a second she floated on self-assurance and a confidence she never knew she could have. She chuckled to herself, feeling slightly ashamed, but then in her moment of confidence she let an idea slip.

'This place would make for a beautiful theatre and art space,' she mused. She then stuck out her tongue, careful not to get paint on the accent beams. Her brows drew together in great concentration, as she brought herself down from her perch and focused on the work she was supposed to be doing. A clatter from behind her distracted her once more and she turned to see Jo stand tall, with great confidence. He paused for a split second, a look passing over his face that Florence could not pinpoint. His brows knotted, then rose, knotted, then rose before a smile took over his face. Florence could have sworn she heard him squeal.

'Is everything OK, Jo?' she asked softly, not seeing Jo dip his finger into the brown paint before he stepped closer to her.

Then with a flick of his wrist and as quick as a flash, Jo swiped paint across Florence's nose, with a joyful smirk. Florence stood dumbfounded, her mouth making a perfect "O" shape. 'Yes, everything's fine,' he replied before he turned to walk away.

He hadn't made it back to his sanding spot before Florence launched a flick of paint at him that hit the back of his neck and dripped off his curly brown locks. She gasped at her braveness. He scrunched his shoulders up to his ears, trying to halt the running paint from going further down his back, but Florence watched it trickle past the neck of his tee. When he turned around to face the culprit, his eyes sparkled with mischief, a mischief that Florence's crystal blue eyes matched. For she was far more advantaged now, armed with a paintbrush and an open can of paint next to her. Where Jo now stood, he had nothing but sandpaper and dust at his feet.

'Jo, did you really think that through?' Florence asked from across the barn. There was a cheeky threat in her tone. He held his hands up as though surrendering and let out a laugh.

'No, I don't believe I did,' he confessed with another chuckle. Then his eyes grew wide and pleading. His hands drew together in prayer. 'But surely a kind lass like you would not attack an unarmed fellow?' he added, in a thick country accent.

Florence held in her laughter, waving the paintbrush around in her hand, one arm crossed over her chest. She pressed her lips together in a tight pout, pretending to consider his plea, before taking a slow step closer to where Jo stood. 'Around these parts we have to look out for ourselves. Ain't no telling the kinds of folks that pass through this here

Wild West,' Florence informed Jo, swinging her paintbrush a little wilder now, her accent matching his.

'It ain't like you cowgirls to draw on a man without a fair and even draw,' Jo tried again, knocking his knees together as if quivering in his boots. He too was keeping his face serious, which accentuated his distinguished heart-shaped jaw. Florence stopped in her tracks, her eyes narrowing, a finger tracing over her lips in thought.

'So what, sir, are you suggesting? A shootout?' she asked, quirking a brow.

At this question, Jo stood up straighter and placed his hands in his pockets as though they were a holster and said, with a shrug, 'You're damn right. It's only fair – you don't wanna be giving cowgirls this side o' town a bad reputation, not playin' by the Wild West laws, now would ya?'

Florence tilted her head and took a few steps back without taking her eyes off Jo. She reached around for another paint-brush and threw it at Jo. He caught it and made a show of locking and loading it and placing it in his holster.

'There ya go, cowboy, let's see if you're all talk,' Florence said, copying Jo in holstering her own weapon. They then counted out three paces backwards and turned so their backs were to each other. 'Are ya ready?' Florence then asked.

Each took a deep breath in and yelled, 'Draw,' before making a dash to the paint tin. Cackles of laughter blared from the barn and continued into the evening. Had the paint been glow in the dark, they both would have been lighting up the path back to their huts.

'Jo, I think the barn is going to look fantastic and I think George is going to love it. You are going to get this place back up and running, I know you will – and even with new management, the Hadlee name will be clearly on display with your beautiful huts and the cottage. I'm sure George will come around in time once he sees this place full of people,' Florence said, smiling up at Jo as they trudged back to the huts, the paint on their skin beginning to harden, making them walk like robots.

'Thank you, Florence,' Jo started, softly, smiling down at her. 'I'm starting to believe that we can make it into something special again too.'

'Now, speaking of huts, please tell me about them,' Florence requested.

'What about them?' Jo returned.

'What inspired you to design and make them?' Florence looked at him with a sparkle in her eyes, a dimple popping in her right cheek from the smirk on her face. Jo chuckled.

'When I came back here for my grandma's funeral, it was the only way I could think to help. As I mentioned, I was struggling to find the joy in my work in London and when I found out how badly the camp was struggling to survive, I did my research on other holiday sites and came across all sorts of huts. It seemed like the perfect opportunity for me to create something homey and simple, nothing high-tech and flashy like I had been doing for years whilst also appealing to investors,' Jo explained, the moon highlighting his high cheekbones and the brown specks that sat upon them. 'A few traders said they would only invest if they would be making money right away and so that's been my project and my reason for staying this past year.'

'Would you not consider staying and running the place with your grandad?' Florence queried.

'I've thought about it but it's a huge risk, Florence. Doing all this has been a welcome break. It's made me see that I have a little more freedom and choice of what jobs I agree to now in

London, but I need to go back. The money is good; it's stable. I'm not sure I'm ready to give it all up entirely yet,' Jo explained. It was a reasonable answer, Florence thought, but she couldn't help the sadness that weighed down her heart. She believed Jo could do magical things with this land, but it had to be his dream and if it wasn't, there wasn't much she could do about it.

'Well, I for one think you've created a bookworm's haven. I truly hope that the new investors will make the most of that. I can see book clubs and writers' retreats. Just think of all the bestsellers that could be penned inside your huts, with no distractions and such peace and tranquillity around them, this place could be a writer's paradise. Oh, speaking of writing, you were supposed to write today,' Florence said, raising a hand to her forehead. 'I'm so sorry;

I completely forgot my deal.' She sighed, as they reached her hut first.

'It's no problem, Florence,' Jo said. The same look from earlier passed over his face, the rise and fall of his brow, like his brain was processing something, something he wasn't sharing. But Florence attributed it to tiredness, for she herself felt weary.

She smiled a sad smile, feeling bad about forgetting her plan. 'Tomorrow, you can write tomorrow,' she said, through a yawn.

'I have other plans for tomorrow. I think you deserve a day off from the barn; the new panels and window fittings need to be fitted before we can do much more anyway, and you are supposed to be on holiday,' Jo noted, rocking back and forth on his feet.

Florence felt her stomach sink at the thought of Jo having made plans without her but she guessed he was right: they had been working awfully hard on the barn and there was more she had to see and experience at the camp before her train home on Saturday morning. She hadn't meant to take up all of Jo's time this week, but she couldn't say she hadn't enjoyed his company.

'Yes, of course. We should have a break and you probably have so much to do around here that I've kept you from,' she replied, scratching at her forearm where the paint had set and was beginning to itch her skin.

'Don't be daft, ma lady, tomorrow I shall pick you up for brunch at half ten on the dot. But now what do you say to a hasty change and a stroll up to the café to see what dinner special Sal has on tonight?' Jo asked in his regal tone, with a gesture towards the main cottage.

'I say that sounds like a grand idea,' Florence replied, matching Jo's accent. They nodded at each other as Jo departed for his hut and before long were walking the grounds once more, lanterns now lighting up their path in the dark of the night, owls hooting in the distance and both Jo and Florence hungrily anticipating tonight's feast – the barn work proving to make ravenous wolves out of the two of them.

SIXTEEN

With Jo planning on meeting Florence at her hut at half ten, Florence had indulged in a slow-moving morning of relaxing on her deck in her nightdress, dipping in and out of the books she had brought with her while sipping on copious amounts of tea from her small china teacup. Earlier the sun had been a spectacular sight to behold as it appeared to rise out of the lake, making the water dance as it did so. The birds as always were right on time with their morning's gleeful chorus. As the gentle summer breeze blew, the smell of the sweet calla lilies perfumed the air, lending itself to the magical atmosphere and making every word Florence read pop off their pages. The characters came alive right before her eyes, more prominently than ever before.

Now though, she threw on her vintage playsuit, the one with the collar and pearl buttons and wandered up to the cottage, wanting to check in on her nanna. George greeted her in a friendly manner and with a bright smile that made Florence wonder if things had settled between him and Jo. She desperately wanted to tell George not to worry and that

Jo had a plan. Granted it was not the most perfect plan in the world, to Florence that would consist of the land staying in the Hadlee name, but it was a plan that at least would see the land taken care of and Camp Calla Lily thriving once more, but she wasn't sure it was her place.

'Morning, George,' she said brightly instead.

'Morning, my dear,' George returned. 'The phone is all yours. Please do say hello to Margot for me and that I look forward to speaking to her again this afternoon,' he added, his cheeks flushing a rosy hue with his request. It felt as if lots of secrets had been unravelled in the last few days and it seemed to be doing everyone the world of good.

Florence beamed but decided against putting George on the spot. He looked happy and she didn't want to spoil that with an inquest into just how friendly he and her nanna were. That inquest would be saved for her nanna when she returned home. 'Thank you and of course,' she said simply. 'How are you today, George?' Florence then asked, resting her hands on the desk, and wanting to check in with him before checking in on her nanna.

George looked up. 'Better thank you, Florence,' is all he said, not giving away his personal qualms with his grandson and therefore Florence did not let on that she knew anything.

'That's wonderful to hear,' Florence said with a smile as George nodded and backed away to his office, giving her some privacy to talk with her nanna.

After two rings, Margot picked up the phone, always somehow knowing it was Florence calling. 'Hello, treasure,' she said as Florence curled the cord around her finger. 'What are you up to today, dear?'

'Hi, Nanna, I'm just waiting for Jo, then we're going to

have brunch,' Florence told her nanna. 'How are you? Is everything OK there?'

'Brunch sounds lovely and yes, nothing to worry about here, Florence. This spring chicken is just wonderful,' her nanna informed her, with cheer in her voice. Florence chuckled, wondering if it had everything to do with her afternoon phone calls with George. It made Florence happy that they both had each other and that her nanna was able to bring some happiness into George's day. She wondered if Margot knew about the troubles with the camp and made a mental note to ask her when she got home.

'I'm glad. I can't wait to see you tomorrow. I have so much to tell you,' Florence said gleefully.

'I'm looking forward to seeing you too, my love. Now, you go and enjoy your last day,' Margot replied, her voice sounding even more cheerful than seconds ago. Florence's heart skipped a beat at the thought of hugging her nanna tomorrow. She hoped with all her might that telling Margot of her adventures would ease her nanna's fear of Camp Calla Lily and inspire her to come back too.

'OK, I'd best get back to my hut. Jo said he would meet me there,' Florence replied. 'Oh and George says hello,' she added ensuring a cheekiness to her tone that her nanna would not miss. Florence then spun around on her toes, feeling a little floaty and unable to wipe the grin that came to her face when she thought of how George had blushed upon saying her nanna's name. The romantic in Florence was ever present when it came to others.

'Please tell George that I hope he is keeping well. Now run along, treasure, you do not want to miss brunch.' There was no mistaking the delight in her nanna's voice at the mention of George. Florence could picture the blush on Margot's cheek too when she said his name.

'Why don't you check in on his wellness yourself when you rendezvous with him later? I love you, Nanna,' Florence said, through a chuckle. She got karma for her cheek when she realised she had tangled herself around the phone's cord when she went to return it to its receiver. Glancing around to see if anyone was bearing witness to her fumbling, she bent low and pulled the cord over her head, the curliness of it getting stuck in her hair. 'Ouch,' she whimpered, not sure whether it was a saving grace no one was around or more of a hindrance. It took two more twirls and a pivot before the phone was safely back on its perch. Florence straightened her glasses and patted herself down before heading to meet Jo. On her way she thought about her nanna and George. Florence could only assume their relationship was purely platonic. At the time Florence's family used to vacation here Margot was still married and George had been too. But it had been such a long time now since Margot's husband had passed. Florence didn't remember much about her grandad as he died a few short months after she was born, and she never did know her grandparents on her dad's side, for they had both died young. Since George's wife had passed a little over a year ago, Florence wondered if he was lonely and that this might be a wonderful time for him and her nanna to be reacquainted.

Florence practically skipped back to her hut where she found Jo in his spot under the magnolia tree wearing a loose white shirt, necktie and black trousers with sandals. Florence admired his style, for it was one she felt couldn't be categorised; Jo wore what he wanted, and he suited everything he wore. She picked up her pace when the field dipped towards her hut, running towards Jo.

'Did you know that your grandad knew my nanna?' she said, a little loudly, startling Jo, who snapped his book shut and stood up to greet her.

'He mentioned it just this morning, but it would explain why he has asked about you every day, making sure that I'm being kind to you and treating you well,' Jo said, with a cheeky smirk. 'I didn't tell him that I dunked your head in to the lake yesterday.'

Florence laughed, feeling that today was going to be a good day. Then with one hand on her back, Jo gestured in the direction of the barn and they walked along the field side by side.

'Do you think they like each other? When I spoke to him the other day, he seemed to know lots about me, stuff that no one knows, only you and my nanna, so they must be close. He said that he talks to her most days,' Florence told Jo, continuing the topic of their grandparents as they walked their familiar route.

'I would say so. He spoke of Margot with great admiration and said she had been a dear friend for many years, and I've no doubt of her awesomeness if you are her granddaughter. I'm glad they've stayed in contact all these years. He certainly looked happy when saying her name.' He then paused before adding, 'I think it would be a shame to give up a friend like that.' The words formed a pleasant stir in Florence's belly. Was Jo attesting to their own friendship and that he might want to stay in contact with her when she left? She knew that she was going to miss him terribly, feeling that he was a part of her now, for he saw her and accepted her in ways that not many people did.

Instead of ruminating on the question, she came straight out with it and asked, 'Will you write to me, Jo?'

Jo smiled a confident smile. The smile got broader with each new step they took in front of them. 'Of course, you would do well to look out of your windows and keep an eye out for my owl,' Jo replied, making Florence chuckle. She shoved him playfully, loving the way he blended the real world with books just as she did.

'Why are we going to the barn? Did your order come in? Should we get on with the work? I think we should while I can still help you,' Florence said, firing off her questions as she looked around the path at the primulas and daisies that lay beneath the trees on the trail towards the barn.

'No, there's no work to be done, though it seems fairies have been busy at work all night and I needed you to come and see what they have constructed. I was too scared to nosy alone,' Jo said, sparking curiosity in Florence who glanced at him sideways, trying to figure out what he had been up to, to cause the mischief in his dimple.

When they came to the clearing by the barn, Florence let out a gasp, her hands shot to her mouth in shock. String had been tied from one corner of the outside of the barn across to one of the giant oak trees that stood tall by its side. Sticks and thick branches had been dug into the ground to support a plethora of blankets to make a canopy and a small tepee. On the floor were more colourful blankets and a cosy-looking pink rug that cushions nestled atop, making the whole thing even more inviting. In the middle of the rug there was a picnic basket, but that was not the most marvellous thing of all, nor were the strings of lantern-shaped fairy lights or the candles dotted about, for when it got dark, it was the stacks of books that inhabited the tepee. Florence wouldn't be surprised if Jo was solely keeping The Vintage Bookshop afloat with his purchases in the tiny village. The thought curved her lips into a bold grin as she took her hands away from her mouth.

She glanced at Jo as if to receive the go-ahead to run and explore. He nodded and Florence dashed over to the blankets and kicked off her shoes before ducking her head inside the tepee and caressing every blanket that made up the canopy. Florence's enchanted eyes lit up with a magical glow.

'If you do excuse me, sir, I am now going to live here forever. I shall never leave,' Florence announced, parking her bottom on the sun-drenched pink rug.

'You know, that sounds like a marvellous idea,' Jo replied in a wistful manner that caused Florence to tilt her head skywards to look at him. His face wore a smile so gentle and sweet that again she found herself wishing she had the power to somehow read his mind to know exactly what he was thinking at such precise moments as these. Of course, she could simply ask him but that would in turn require a reply and would distract from the way in which his lips curved softly, with a slight and perfect pout to them. When he realised she was looking at him, he winked, which sent that familiar swirl around her stomach.

Before she could look away, he spoke. 'No one back in London ever dares talk of fairies.'

'That seems such a waste,' Florence tried, though her mouth had gone oddly dry. She needed to look away from him. But there was something in his eyes, a flicker, a want, a plea to be seen.

'I agree, but fairies are not manly. Going to the gym and lifting weights is manly,' Jo continued, as if reciting someone else's words. He was still looking at her, though his eyes now were far away, which at least gave her a little respite from his piercing gaze.

'Sure, that's manly for some men, Jo, but fairies can be manly for others,' Florence noted, getting the feeling that Jo was lost in personal memories and very much wanting to be there for him.

'Florence?' he said, stepping forward like he had been jolted back to the present. His voice this time sounded chirpier and more hopeful.

'Yes,' Florence answered, stretching over to grab the pile of books from inside the tepee.

'What do you say of people who wear trousers with sandals and who quote books daily?' he asked, taking a seat beside her on the rug. Florence shifted a couple of books slightly to accommodate him.

'I'd say that those were the best kinds of people. Why, Jo?' she asked thoughtfully, as Jo turned a book over in his hands.

'I just wondered, is all,' he said nonchalantly. Florence didn't believe it was mere wonderment. It was an awfully specific question and one that evidenced experience. Had Jo been bullied for his peculiar ways? Though they were not odd to Florence, she too knew what it was like not fitting in, not conforming to what was referred to as the real world. Her heart gave a tug of understanding as she watched Jo kick off his shoes and lie on his front. He pulled out his notebook and pen, which made Florence squeal. 'Are you writing the end of your great novel?' she asked, resting her hand on the copy of *Jo's Boys* she had picked up out of the pile.

'I'm going to try,' he told her, returning her smile.

'I suppose I should stop talking then,' Florence considered, giving Jo a playful wink, then she took a deep breath in as she looked over her surroundings once more. *There was every chance fairies could live here,* she thought.

Suddenly, Jo pushed himself up to sitting position and

pulled the picnic hamper closer to him. 'I suppose you should – it would be impolite for me to respond with a mouthful of chocolate cake,' he stated, opening the basket to reveal all sorts of wondrous treats.

Florence let out a giggle. 'I like your take on brunch,' she said, her eyes wandering over the chocolate cake and doughnuts, the strawberries, the cheese and cucumber sandwiches and the ice-cream that was tucked into a small, cooler compartment. Jo gave her a little wink and passed her a pretty pastel yellow knife and fork set. That reminded Florence of the huts and how each one was a different pastel shade. She imagined the others also had their matching kettle and watering can and teacups inside too, like hers did. With so much swirling through her mind over the last twenty-five hours, finding out Jo was an architect and their argument, Florence couldn't bring herself to disappear into her new book just yet.

'Why did you choose pastel colours for the huts?' she asked, lifting her head up and looking at Jo.

'Pastel colours, they make me think of new beginnings. They're fresh and happy and bring clarity to the mind,' Jo answered quietly, handing her a plate with a chunky slice of cake on it, which was covered in multi-coloured sprinkles.

'Do you think when you go back to London you'll get back to the smaller projects you love, like making children's dens?' Florence questioned, nodding her gratitude as she carefully put her book on the cushion next to her and took the cake Jo was offering.

Jo nodded, modestly, and took a bite of his cake. He didn't jump to speak right away and so Florence took delicate nibbles of her cake as she savoured its gooey texture and rich chocolatey goodness while she surveyed him. Then she smiled and nudged him playfully. 'Jo, you can talk about your work you know. I'm not going to think you are showing off or you're being egotistical. I want to hear about them. You've done a magical job and I can only imagine the beauty of the play-houses you made,' she said, her eyes encouraging and warm. Jo returned her smile and gave a look that suggested to Florence she had just read his mind.

He took another bite of chocolate cake, thoughtfully before, hesitantly, he began to speak. 'If you would have met me in London, I don't think you would have liked me much, Miss Danver,' he said with a shake of his head.

'Whatever gives you the impression that I like you now, Mr Hadlee?' Florence teased and giggled into her cake. Jo bowed his head and licked his lips, hiding his smirk behind his fork. 'Sorry, do continue,' she said, forcing her face straight and her tone serious.

Jo rolled his eyes playfully.

'London is incredibly fast-paced. In my world it can be competitive, driven by materialism. There's something tran-quil about the pastel shades, something innocent and childlike that filled my mind with possibilities. I wanted to create castles and princess houses for adults.' Jo told her all the while Florence sat up straight, her legs crossed, taking in every word as she munched on cake and felt Jo's passion in her own veins.

'Oh, Jo, that's amazing. They're the finest and most darling huts and I dare say they are simply capital,' Florence gushed, with a wink that made Jo blush, but then her face fell sombre. 'You're really going to give all this up, hand it over and go back to London? What will become of your novels when you're thrown into the rat race once more?' she enquired, thinking that his life in London sounded very unlike him and full of people who didn't quite understand how his mind worked or appreciated his fashion choices. People Florence was all too accustomed to herself.

'Even if I finished my novels, Florence, who's to say they would get published right away, if at all? I have to make money. This place isn't making money, I can't support my grandad with no money. And I have a life in London, a life I should get back to,' Jo said, pushing a bite of cake around his plate. As Florence took in Jo's drooping eyes and solemn features, she felt it best not to debate Jo's decision. She could feel a tension in the air, how when talking about the future of the camp, it seemed the life was sucked out of the trees as well as Jo. The summer breeze stilled, and the birds paused their chirping. It was as if the grounds were in limbo, not quite sure of the next move and when they could breathe again. He was right, he had a life he had to get back to just like she did, however that didn't stop her brain from running away with her and dipping into her imagination, hoping to smooth out the worried creases in Jo's forehead and maybe, just maybe give him some ideas that would make him rethink Camp Calla Lily's destiny.

'Can you imagine...' Florence started, her voice soft and airy; a few sprinkles scattered over the rug as she disappeared for a moment, her eyes glazed over, her plate tilted, '...a story trail around the grounds? Imagine taking the little ones on a bear hunt or roaming the fields with the one you love in search of love letters stored in mini post boxes hidden in the trees.' Goose bumps rose on Florence's arms at what she thought a rather brilliant idea. Passion filled her voice, and she was sure Jo rubbed at his forearm too. Was there hope left yet?

'I love that idea, Florence,' he stated, finishing his last bite of cake and shaking his head. His eyes were large with a mixture of amazement and disbelief.

'What?' Florence questioned.

'I think you'd be better running this place,' he said giving her a meaningful look before retrieving two small bottles of milk from the hamper and passing one over to her. Suddenly, Florence could feel the weight of Jo's worries. She couldn't possibly run the camp; she would be terrified of running it further into the ground. No, she would have to trust Jo. The new owners would look after it and restore it to its former glory. She would visit and everything would work out. She gave a wry smile. 'Hmm, you should pass that idea on to the new owners. Tell that lady about the huts. They could be used for "The Three Little Pigs".'

'I will,' Jo noted, clinking his bottle against hers in a melancholy cheers.

Florence looked around at the quilted tent, in between the thick tree stumps, over at the pretty flowers and up at the canopies of leaves and blossoms, letting out a sigh and breathing in the fresh air as she did so. She felt it best to change the subject before both she and Jo were lost in the depths of despair of not quite being able to save Camp Calla Lily the way they would have liked. But Jo was doing his best and Florence had no doubt that all his efforts would pay off and that Kirsty would help restore the camp to the quaint, quirky, and enchanting place it once was.

'You should be writing,' she quipped.

'You should be reading,' he retorted.

Their stomachs now full of chocolate cake with little room for much else just now, Jo turned over to lie on his stomach, scribbling away in his notebook, and Florence retired to her book. They indulged in the quiet for a long while until Florence's eyes grew sleepy from focusing so diligently on the tiny words and she thought it would be nice to rest her head on the cushions inside the tepee. Closing her book, she crawled along the rug and into the quaint enclosure and lay back, delighting in the shadows of the trees and blowing leaves she could see on the canvas. It was a few moments before Jo joined her, having had to wait for his pen to pull away from the paper, for his words had been flowing.

They lay side by side. Just their breathing and birdsong could be heard when Jo glanced at Florence and noticed her eyelids begin to flutter. He reached out and held her hand.

'What can you see?' Jo whispered.

Florence squeezed his hand and after a brief pause wistfully expressed that she could see: 'This, exactly this. Blankets, cushions, forts and lessons in the forest.'

SEVENTEEN

The hours ticked by in a pleasant daydream of reading chapters aloud from every book, some of which they even acted out. Logs became shipwrecks, carriages, and caves. The tepee became the rabbit hole where they found the Mad Hatter and offered him a sprinkle-covered doughnut. The forest floor became an elegant ballroom with all the space in the world to dance until their feet grew sore. And when finally, the sun began to set, the candles and fairy lights lit up the night sky as if the princess had found her way home and was where she was meant to be.

Florence helped Jo tidy away the rest of their picnic, which had all been perfect and delicious, and they sat back on the cushions to watch the flames flicker and enjoy what the night now had to offer; the creamy moon, the mass of glittering stars and the hoots of the owls in the trees.

'I feel Manchester is going to be appear noisier now than before,' Florence said with a small chuckle, her chest deflating slightly at the thought of leaving the camp behind. She was ridiculously excited and ready to see her nanna, but she wasn't all that thrilled about her forthcoming job hunt and the inter-view processes. She would do it though. She would always do what was necessary to look after her nanna, no matter how much meeting new people terrified her. Those formal inter-views always made her sweat. They felt so forced and like everyone was just trying to say the right thing and Florence never knew what the right thing to say was. Maybe this time luck would be on her side and she would find something that she was actually good at and enjoyed. Being around Jo and talking about her love of theatre and working with children had certainly given her a small confidence boost to at least look for work in that field.

'Aye,' Jo replied, with an Irish lilt, making her giggle and distracting her from her worrisome thoughts. 'Don't you settle, miss, you make sure ya follow your rainbow – it'll lead ya to your pot of gold,' Jo added, with a flash of his cheeky grin.

'Do you think we could actually sleep out here? Or will bears eat us in our sleep?' Florence asked when her laughter died down.

'Bears for sure will eat us, especially if they know we're full of cake and doughnuts,' Jo replied casually, ensuring further laughter.

'I think we should be fearless like Belle and brave the beasts,' she said with a grin as she curled herself up on the blankets and rested her head back on a blue and gold patterned cushion. 'You never know, the bear could like books and simply just want to sit and read.' Her eyelids flickered as Jo propped himself up on his elbow, seemingly studying her with his piercing hazel eyes that dazzled like emeralds under the candlelight. Heat ignited in her stomach.

'What are you doing?' she asked, her voice a touch hoarse.

'Just looking at you,' Jo said innocently, wearing a soft smile.

'Well don't,' Florence said, forcing a little chuckle, but his gaze was doing something to her.

'Wait, so you can look at me, but I can't look at you?' Jo harrumphed with laughter in his tone, but there was a serious flicker behind his eyes. 'But what if you're rather beautiful to look at?' he added, filling the atmosphere with a static-like charge.

Bells chimed in Florence's head, though not the wondrous melody of wedding bells, or a clock at midnight ringing in the New Year, more like alarm bells and those of a screeching fire drill.

'Florence,' Jo said, his voice now a little raspy. Florence's pulse quickened. A loose curl fell over one of his eyes and she had to resist the urge to want to tuck it behind his ear, for her hand would be too close to his flushed cheek, and she knew in her gut that to touch him would be dangerous.

'Yes,' she replied, her voice matching his.

'I would really like to kiss you.' The words hung thick in the atmosphere. Florence's breath caught; their eyes remained locked. Did he just say he wanted to kiss her? Surely not. She wasn't someone men wanted to kiss. But Jo wanted to kiss her. He had asked so eloquently and gently that her heart had skipped at least two beats. She wasn't in some dream. He had actually said it, but did she want to kiss him? Did she want to be kissed by Jo? Abruptly, Florence sat up making Jo wobble on his elbow. When he steadied himself, he sat up so that their faces were mere inches apart.

'We can't,' she whispered, her eyes drawing to his plump bottom lip as her mind wandered with great curiosity over what it would feel like pressed against hers.

'We can't,' Jo repeated. Then his eyes narrowed in confusion.

'No, we mustn't,' Florence agreed, with herself, despite the flutter low in her belly and the lump in her throat telling her otherwise.

'We mustn't,' Jo again echoed. This time he gave his head a small shake making his curls flop across his face. 'I like you, Florence, and I know that I'm not a physical specimen of a man with a six-pack and bulging muscles or a stylish suit-wearing lawyer or fearless knight or powerful king.'

'Jo, stop, please,' Florence said, taken aback by the insecurities that fell from Jo's lips. To her Jo was beauty and brains and everything she would want in a man. Sitting up straighter and putting a hand on his chest, where his heart was beating erratically, she cried and shook her head. 'Stop being silly, Jo – those things, you think you have to be those things. You're being ridiculous.'

'But I'm not. I'm not like those men, Florence,' he started.

'Of course, you're not, Jo; you're you as you should be,' Florence interrupted, sounding maddened.

'Then what is it?' Jo asked. 'Am I an idiot? I'm so stupid. You don't like me in that way? I'm so sorry, Florence. Forget I said anything.' Jo raked a hand through his hair and looked away embarrassed. Florence was having a hard time keeping up with his questions as her brain tried to decipher what her heightened pulse and her hammering heart were trying to tell her. She didn't care for Jo thinking so little of himself, but words were failing her miserably.

She took her hand away from Jo's chest, hoping that would make her think straight and looked around at the cushions to buy herself more time. 'Jo, please don't. Look it's not you, it's me,' she stammered softly when her mouth finally decided to move. Of all the clichés in all the world – she cringed inwardly.

Jo rubbed the back of his head as he looked around the tepee. Then he nudged Florence with a playful smirk on his face. 'You really just fed me a line from a movie,' he said, teasing.

Florence pushed up her glasses, grateful to hear the laughter in Jo's voice though her chest was still rattling, her hands clammy. 'But it's true, Jo. For me, love belongs in books, where it is safe and stable and where it can't hurt me.'

'But maybe that's why we should try, Florence, because I believed that too until you came along. I've been more myself with you in a week than I have ever been around anyone else in my entire life. Maybe me and you together can work,' Jo urged, his voice losing its lightness from moments ago.

'But it can't, Jo, and it won't because fairy tales don't exist in real life. You don't need muscles or to change who you are; you will find someone who loves all of you. But this – you and me – I can't have it. Who you are, the things you do, the things you say, it's all in my head. It's like I'm dreaming. You can't possibly be real,' Florence expressed, her lips now trembling.

'But I am real, Florence. I'm right here, and you know that. You know it deep down fairy tales do exist, I know you do. Your fairy tale is real too, you just have to believe in it,' Jo pleaded but a tenderness to his voice remained. He swiped a hand through his curls and ducked his head to search for Florence's eyes, but she could not bring herself to look at him.

'I don't, and I can't. This happens in books; it doesn't happen to me,' she said, scooting out of the tepee and stretching her legs as she stood on the rug and collected her shoes.

'Of course, it can happen to you. Florence, those things I

just told you, not being flashy enough, not being muscly enough, those things are real, those are things I've been told time and time again. If that's real, then why can't love be real? Why can't we dream and make the beautiful and good things true? You're telling me you want to live in a world where we don't try and change that?' Jo asked, begging with her now, his voice growing firmer, his hands drawn together. He took a step towards her, having followed her out of the tepee.

'What do you want me to say, Jo? The real world is not the kindest of places. Bad stuff happens. This is not real. I made you up,' Florence said, feeling flustered, her chest rising and falling painfully as she held on to her shoes and started walking out of the clearing and back towards her hut. She didn't want to be doing this now, to be arguing with Jo. He shouldn't have spoilt what they had, but hadn't she too been curious? Hadn't her brain imagined what it would be like to kiss him? Had she not allowed her heart over the past few days to care more than she should have?

'Stop saying that. I'm here. Look at me, Florence, please. This is real,' he said, the tremble in his voice making him sound desperate, water filling up his eyes. Florence stopped walking and turned to look at him. Her usual welcoming pools of blue had been replaced with anger.

'You stop it. Don't you see? I live through my books. I visit these worlds to give me a break, Jo. But my life is not some romance novel. I'm not a strong, empowered heroine. This has been a wonderful holiday, a little break from reality but tomorrow I wake up and I go home. I go back to worrying about bills, worrying about my nanna's health and I go back to being the girl who saw her mother die and was not good enough for her dad to stick around. I'm not strong, Jo. I miss them every single day. I don't come out of this on the other side. I just don't. Love for me, Jo, is pain. Please, let me be grateful for this story and tomorrow we close the book. We can stay in touch; we can be friends but please don't make this into something it can't be,' Florence told Jo, her face damp now with tears that had fallen while she spoke.

Jo stood stock-still staring at the muddy earth beneath his bare feet. He held a hand to his chest, looking the picture of a man who had just had the wind knocked out of him. His breathing was ragged like he was struggling to get air into his lungs.

'So that's it, this is all our lives will ever be huh? The book is finished, done. My mum didn't love me. I have never fit in. I've been made fun of my whole life. And now the one person who I thought might just get me, who might just accept me for who I am, is telling me that the life I keep hoping for, the life that this week I felt I might actually be deserving of, is not meant for people like me. That my book has already been written and I don't get the fairy tale because it's not real for people like us. I get it, Florence; I may have thought that before too, but I don't believe that anymore,' Jo said, tears streaming down his own cheeks now. Tears that Florence had put there. Her heart ached. He rubbed at his face harshly. Florence watched the water drip over his lips and Jo shudder at the salty taste of them.

Florence went to step forward, wanting to comfort him, to hug him, to touch him, to stop the hurt she saw in his eyes, but she couldn't do it, not after what she had just said. What was wrong with her? She retreated. What had she done?

'Oh, Jo. You know I didn't mean you. You are brave, you are brilliant, and you are every bit the hero and leading man. And you are a writer, I know you will have the life you dream of; you will create it and you more than deserve it, just not with me,' Florence said, her head bowed, her hands shaking. After the uncomfortable ache of jealously she had felt seeing a woman on Jo's bed only yesterday, her mind really was becoming rather masterful at turning a blind eye to her feelings. Now, she was telling Jo he would find happiness, find love with someone else. This beautiful man whom she cared deeply about had simply asked to kiss her. How had she turned it into this? Right now, Florence didn't want to be in her own head, neither in reality nor in a daydream; she was far too angry with herself. Her fingernails dug into her palms as she clenched her fists together and closed her eyes, wanting just once to be normal.

'You deserve it too, Florence. You are still brave, even when you miss them and even when you're scared. That doesn't make you any less brave,' Jo noted, his hands in his pockets now for comfort.

'I'm sorry, Jo,' she mumbled, fidgeting with the fabric of her dress. 'I can't lose you too.' Her words were barely audible, so much so that Jo took a step forward to hear her and while he took her hands in his to steady them. His touch made Florence's whole body fizz. *It's easy, just hold on tighter, embrace him, let him in.* Her heart fought but her body was paralysed, overcome with fear. She couldn't do it.

'Florence, you can't fight your heart, fighting with your heart is the only way you lose.' Jo spoke gently, his words soft but matter-of-fact. Then ever so slowly he released her hands and wrapped his arms around her neck, pulling her to his chest. His hug felt safe, like she was wrapped up tight in protective body armour. Feeling the warmth and affection in his embrace, Florence briefly laid her head against his chest until the anxiety in her chest began to slowly trickle away.

'It's hard to stop fighting when you've been doing it your whole life,' she replied with a heavy head.

'Let's get you back to your hut,' Jo whispered, dropping a heartfelt kiss on to the top of her head.

Abandoning the tepee and Jo's magical setup, they walked the familiar path back to her pink pastel hut. Camp Calla Lily, though normally peaceful under the moon's watchful eye, now felt eerie. In the warm night Florence felt ill at ease; her bones felt cold and frail.

Neither of them said a word until they reached the hut's pink door.

'I'm so sorry, Jo. I hope you don't hate me and that you will still be my friend,' Florence mumbled; her blue eyes glassy. Jo gently rubbed a hand over her bicep and bent his knees to look her in the eyes. He gave her a kind, crooked smile and tilted his head.

'I don't believe I could ever dislike you, Miss Danver. Now, get some rest,' he said before bowing slowly and turning away.

Florence watched Jo fade away into the night before she fell onto her bed fully clothed. Her limbs felt stiff and hard from the tension that zipped through her body and her mind felt somewhere between numb and exhausted. Too tired to change into her pyjamas, she rustled into the duvet and pulled it over her head. Soon her tears were falling as if the dam had been broken and no cement would ever be strong enough to fix it.

When Ryan had left her, she had not felt this distraught. When the many dates that Olivia had set her up on had not quite panned out, she had not felt this empty. But the sadness behind Jo's usually bright and happy eyes flashed through her mind, it was all she could see. It was a look she had seen many times growing up, when she would look in the mirror after school. Trying to hide her tears from her nanna, she would splash water on her face and close her eyes to fill her brain with good thoughts, so that the sadness would go away. There had been weeks and months where this had been an everyday occurrence, when Florence still had the ability to have hope that the children at school would let her join in, only to then have them shut her out and call her names, until finally she got the hint that she was different. Jo had given her the very same look. The look of someone who had been robbed of hope, of someone who had thought for once he was about to fit in, only to have the very idea snatched away from him within minutes. She had just done to Jo what the children at school had done to her, what the many dates had done to her over the years and the worst part about it was that she hadn't meant it, any of it.

EIGHTEEN

Florence saw Jo standing on a thick branch high up in the apple tree, not far from the barn. When he saw her, he smiled brightly and waved her over enthusiastically. She picked up speed, skipping along, the sweet perfume of the apples propelling her forward. As she took in the glorious summer's day, she hummed a merry tune feeling lucky that she had found a friend in Jo. His abundance of energy and penchant for playing along made each day she had spent with him fun and unique. When she reached the tree, she noticed the grooves Jo had used to climb and began scaling the same path. Just a little further and Jo reached out his hand. Looking behind her to see how far she had climbed, her forehead began to sweat. Nothing but clouds swam beneath her and where she was expecting to see the luscious lawn below, it was grey and gloomy. She blinked. Suddenly the air felt thin and she found herself gasping for breath. She hastily turned her attention back to Jo for guidance. He was still reaching for her, but his face was no longer cheerful.

'Take my hand,' he urged.

Florence stretched further but her foot slipped and before she knew it Jo's fingertips were getting further and further away as she hurtled towards the ground.

A loud cry jolted Florence awake. She was sitting in bed, her hair sticking to her sweaty cheeks and forehead, with a mouth as dry as sawdust. It took her a few moments to realise that the scream had come from her own vocal cords. She held her chest hoping to calm her unpredictable heart. It had not been a restful night, but now the sun beamed through the open curtains indicating the start of a new morning, her last morning at Camp Calla Lily.

Slowly and unsteadily, she climbed out of bed and set about making a cup of tea. All the while her brain thought of Jo. She had tossed and turned all night thinking about what she was going to say to him today, how she was going to make it up to him, before she had to leave to catch her train, but she hadn't come up with anything that she felt was good enough. Sorry was the only word that kept popping up. After a quick change, a quick packing job and an even quicker cup of tea, Florence bid farewell to her hut and dragged her suitcase out in search of Jo.

When he didn't appear to be in his hut, she headed for the main cottage. No one was about except George who was stood behind the reception desk with his head down and brows furrowed. He was tapping his pen against the desk calendar with a look of deep concentration.

'Hello, George,' Florence said, feeling a little guilty for disturbing him but knowing she needed to get on her way and say her goodbyes.

'Oh, hello dear,' George said, smiling when he saw her. He then placed his pen down and gave her his full attention. It reminded Florence so much of Jo and how whenever she spoke, he gave her his undivided concentration, never making her feel rushed or uninteresting. 'Are you all set to leave? Is there anything else I can do for you?' George added.

'I am yes. I very much wish I didn't have to leave; I have loved it here, George. The camp is beautiful. I hope to come back with my nanna,' she replied, smiling when she saw George's own smile broaden at the mention of Margot.

'As long as there is something here for you to come back to, it would be my pleasure to see you both again,' George said, causing Florence's brow to raise with curiosity at such an odd choice of phrasing. Whatever did he mean by if there was something for them to come back to? Conscious of the time, she stored those words at the forefront of her brain to go over later.

'Erm, thank you, George. I don't suppose you have seen Jo around?' she enquired.

'I'm afraid he had to leave early this morning, my dear, but that reminds me, he did tell me to give you this,' George said, stepping out from around the desk and handing her a folded piece of paper. Florence felt her stomach sink, like she'd just hit the dip on a rollercoaster. She wasn't a fan of rollercoasters. She and Margot had been to Blackpool only once and it was enough times for her to figure out that rollercoasters were not for her. She had too little control over the metal beasts and the twists and turns. 'Now, you get home safe, Florence, and please give Margot my regards.' Before George could walk away, Florence collected herself and let go of her suitcase to embrace him in a grateful hug.

'Thank you,' she whispered before stepping back. 'And I will. Erm, I'll just pop into the café and say bye to Sal but thank you again, George,' she added, suddenly feeling a little discombobulated as she held on to Jo's letter, tried to push her glasses back up her nose and grab her suitcase at the same time. Jo was not here; she couldn't say bye to Jo. Was he mad at her? She didn't have time to stand there and bombard George with questions on whether Jo had been happy when he left or if the letter held good news or bad. She was stumbling over the words in her brain, wanting to ask but scared to face those realities. 'OK. Bye, George,' she mumbled instead, knocking over her suitcase.

'Are you all right, Florence?' George asked.

'Yes, yes, I'm fine,' she said, forcing a smile that bared no teeth. Then she bent down hurriedly, gripped her suitcase tight and nodded another thank you to George before walking through the cottage to the café.

There was a lot of noise coming from the kitchen when she entered the conservatory. A few of the regulars she had become accustomed to greeting were sat enjoying a lazy breakfast, seemingly not paying any mind to the clatter and crashes. Florence edged closer to the counter. 'Sal, is everything OK?' she called out. A few moments passed before Sal appeared, not looking at all like his cheerful, bubbly self. Though he pasted on a smile when he saw her.

'Everything is fine thank you, love. Though I will certainly miss seeing your face around here,' he said, disappearing again for a moment and then re-emerging through a side door next to the cake counter to give her a hug. Florence was taken aback by his friendly action. She had only been here for one week. Of course she was going to miss Sal, but she didn't think he would miss her as much. He saw people come and go all the time.

She returned his squeeze and replied, 'I'm going to miss you too, Sal, but I hope to be back with my nanna next time.'

'Oh, now that would be a treat, if this place is still standing,' he said when he released her. Then he retreated back behind the counter before she could get a good look at his eyes. People were speaking rather oddly this morning, she thought. Why would this place not be standing? Just as she was about to ask that very question, Mr and Mrs Phillips shuffled up behind her to place their breakfast order.

'OK, right,' Florence started, a little flustered. 'Bye, Sal; bye, Mr and Mrs Phillips,' she said with a nod. Grabbing her suitcase, she made her way back through the cottage and took one last glance at the living room with its grand fireplace and enticing bookshelves and sighed. She truly was going to miss this place and couldn't believe that after putting up such a fuss all these years about coming here she had actually enjoyed her stay and wished it could be longer. But the real world beckoned.

The sun began to rise higher now as the morning drifted on, warming her bare shoulders with its orange Calippo-coloured rays as she walked the country roads in the direction of the train station. Her long tea dress swished around her ankles while Jo's letter burnt a hole in her pocket. A slight tremble in her fingers and a tightness in her chest signalled that she was coming up to the bend where one week ago she had crumbled to her knees on the concrete as the painful memories of her mother's death haunted her. Today, Florence held her head high and when she came to the sharp turn, she looked around for a safe spot in the grass, a few metres from the road, and sat down.

Florence gently traced her fingers over the sprinkle of daisies that were scattered about the grass and breathed in deeply through her nose. The road was quiet with no screeching cars or grunting engines to disturb her. As she let out her breath she spoke. 'Hi, Mum.' Saying the words out loud that she had been unable to voice since she was just five years old, was both painful and freeing. She could feel her bottom lip begin to wobble and so she pushed on. 'I finally went back, Mum. The camp was beautiful just like you always said when we visited. I know I was only five, but I can still hear you. You laughed so much at the lake and everything you saw – the water, the flowers, the stones and bricks that made up the cottage – you said it was all beautiful. But you used to tell me that I was the most beautiful thing of all.' Florence chuckled at that memory just as she did when she was five and her mum said it while tickling her belly.

'It was like I fitted in there, Mum. I'm not sure if you can see me from up there but I've not quite mastered the art of belonging in the real world. Some people make it look so easy, but for me it's one of the hardest things. You know what nanna's like – she's all about me embracing who I am. I imagine you would have been the same, but just once I'd like to be good at blending in.' Florence paused to look up at the sky where the plumes of white clouds had dispersed so that the sun beamed directly over where she was sitting. As the heat hit her cheeks, she smiled. 'I met a man. He didn't make me feel like I was so peculiar, but I wish you were here to guide me in matters of the heart. I know he's special, but I can't let him in.' As she spoke those last few words, her nose became damp from a trickle of tears as the weight of what she was saying hit her. Was she truly happy to resign herself to a life without a true love or more specifically was she truly happy to resign herself to a life with Jo as her companion and nothing more? 'I miss you, Mum; I miss Dad. Why does love have to be so tricky and painful?' she said, squinting into the sunlight and then bowing her head. A low and warm breeze made the grass sway and Florence's pocket rustle. She wiped at her fallen tears with the back of one hand and tentatively reached into her pocket to retrieve Jo's letter with the other.

Unfolding the paper, her heart gave a gentle spasm at Jo's scrawl, as the soft breeze blew around her encouragingly once more.

Florence,

I apologise for my hasty departure, but I have urgent business to attend to back home in London.

Meeting you this past week has been nothing short of serendipitous.

Take care of yourself, Miss Danver, and do not forget: "Everything that is real was imagined first."

Yours, Jo

Upon reading Jo's note, Florence felt a flurry of confused emotions. There was a tiny hint of sadness that he had called London home, which was rather silly of her if she was honest because though he may have looked content and at home at Camp Calla Lily, he did not live there. A slight fear weaved its way in next in thinking of what urgent business Jo had to attend to. Did it have something to do with George and Sal's disgruntlement when she left the camp earlier this morning? Then came hope, for he had called their meeting serendipitous. Then anxiety came to say hello. He had not expressed a desire for further interaction or divulged a way of getting hold of him. A wave of happiness came after, for she was grateful for Jo's graciousness, that his words read with the same kindness he had displayed to her last night, walking her back to her hut and not belittling the magnitude of emotions that had poured out of her, even when they were not the emotions that he had been hoping for. Lastly, a smile tugged at her lips at his words of wisdom. In all her complex emotions she rose to her feet. It wasn't by any means a mean letter, which she half thought she deserved.

'Thank you, Mum, I love you and I love you too, Dad,' she said looking up to the sky and hugging Jo's letter tight to her chest. She took a few steadying breaths, tucked the note safely away and continued on her way. A new voice was calling her name and it was telling her she had work to do.

As Florence neared the train station, the world seemed to pick up speed. Car horns beeped, traffic lights hummed, people shuffled about with their heads down and she found herself turning around to look back down the path she had just walked, all the commotion threatening to take away her newly acquired determination and confidence. It was hard to believe that only a few miles down the road she had found a place where she had felt like she belonged, almost like she'd stepped into one of her books and disappeared for a week into another world, a world where her wildest dreams became reality and no amount of fairy talk made you immature. Where there was no limit on ice-cream scoops or books that one could read and where people made eye contact and spent hours in nature talking and playing. But she could not let this other world scare her anymore.

* * *

When Florence arrived home around Saturday lunchtime, she was overcome with emotion upon wrapping her arms around her nanna. A week might only seem a short time, but Florence had missed Margot dearly, having never left her for that long before. People came and went from Florence's life, she knew that much. It was one of the reasons she struggled to get attached to people and let them in. But her nanna, her nanna had been her angel since she was a baby. She was the only person Florence could trust and the only person she could not bear to part with for too long. She released her nanna and they both sunk into their dining room chairs where Margot had prepared a lovely lunch of tea and sandwiches. Having skipped breakfast, she dove into a delicious roast beef butty while Margot sipped on her tea and surveyed her granddaughter. There was something different about her that pleased the old lady.

'How is George, treasure?' Margot asked, with a warm smile from over her teacup.

Florence took off her glasses and rubbed at her tired eyes. Travelling and the walk in the sticky summer heat had exhausted her, but the thought of George made her smile.

'I think it's me who should be asking you that question, Nanna,' Florence said with a grin. 'How long have you two been enjoying your afternoon chats and why did you never tell me about him?'

Margot placed her teacup on the table, taking a moment to gather her thoughts. 'I suppose I should have told you. We have been friends for an awfully long time, but in the last few months our fondness for each other has grown and I could not bring myself to tell you. I was fearful, my dear; I have been for too long. If you knew about George, I feared you would push me to visit the camp and that I was setting a bad example to you of keeping people you love at arm's length,' Margot said, uncharacteristically fiddling with the teaspoon that lay against her teacup.

'Nanna, you have never been a bad example. My fear was my own, not yours. If you would have told me about him, I don't know what I would have said. Maybe I would have told you to forget about him along with the camp, but I suppose your pushing me did a bit of good. Meeting George, seeing how you both light up when you speak of each other, well now it just seems preposterous that you have not been to visit,' Florence said, placing a hand over her nanna's arm to calm her fidgeting. She gave Margot an understanding smile. Though she tried to keep her tone light and playful, she knew all too well that her nanna could not simply snap out of her fear. It was going to take a little more gentle convincing.

'I was mad at you on my walk there. The accident, the aftermath, it all came flooding back in fresh waves. I was angry that you made me do it alone, but now I see why. I needed the push. I needed to be free of cloaks and cover pages, no protective shields, just me. The happy memories paid me a visit too, our days spent by the lake, dancing under the magnolia trees.

I had buried them so deep and didn't dare let myself enjoy them for fear that I'd only miss them more,' Florence said, her words quiet, her hands trembling slightly as they lay over the top of Margot's, not doing much good to steady hers. 'That fear is real but I allowed myself to see them. I even spoke to Mum today and it hurts, it does. I do miss them more. I get frustrated that they were taken from me so soon but then it feels like my heart is expanding, like Mum is filling it with so much love, like she is reminding me she was there, Dad was there, for a reason. Those five years mattered, they do matter, and I should not try to forget that,' Florence finished and though there was still a touch of tightness in her chest, she could feel the love that she was talking about filling up her heart and realised that she had been looking at things all wrong.

Margot had tried to encourage her to speak of them, but in the same regard Margot spoke of them very little and Florence worried it would hurt her nanna too much and so they had both merely gotten on with life without them. Florence squeezed her nanna's hands and gently nudged at her teacup, urging her to take a sip to bring some colour back into her cheeks. Margot, for once, did as she was told. When she placed her teacup down, she twisted slightly in her seat so that she was facing Florence. Her bright blue eyes peered directly into her granddaughter's.

'You were five when your parents died. You went through a traumatic experience, one that I was never quite sure how to handle, and I do not know if keeping you inside with your books was best, but seeing you curled up safe, I may have been selfish but it was my way of protecting you. I should have done more. The hospital had suggested a children's grief counsellor, but you cried when I took you. You clung on to me so hard and I panicked, hearing you scream like that. I could not do it. I had not seen what you had, and I felt by taking you there I was forcing you to talk about your pain and to relive it. You were five. I was an adult, I couldn't bear to imagine it, yet you had witnessed it all.' Margot's eyes glistened with tears, but Florence could see that she was trying to hold it together. She squeezed her nanna's hands tighter for support, until she said everything she needed to say. Then Florence tucked her legs up underneath herself for her own comfort.

'When you had a book in your hand, and eventually, when we would go out to the theatre, you were happy. The smile on your face, the worlds you would talk about seeing in your head, I felt it far better for you to fill your mind with such lovely visions. You had, and still have, the most wonderful imagination, treasure. I did not wish to hinder that. You have such a beautiful soul and, my dear, I didn't want to destroy it by getting you to remember that dark time. Selfishly, I struggled to talk about Darcy because the pain was intolerable, but that was not fair on you. I felt one day you would need to go back to Calla Lily, that maybe you might feel her presence and it would bring you closure, but the thought of going myself, well I'm not as brave as you. I could not bear to walk the path where my daughter had been taken from me and what caused my darling son-in-law to leave me too.' As the words fell from Margot's lips, so did the tears fall from her eyes. Florence calmly stood and wrapped her arms around her nanna's shoulders, resting her head against hers.

'You must think me awful, for sending you back on your own, but George had told me of the huts and of Jo and you had been fading a little as of late, my Florence. Sitting behind that desk was doing you no good and though dear Olivia's heart is often in the right place it pained me to see you come home after these encounters with men looking so forlorn and disheartened.' A blush grew on Margot's cheeks and the tears were replaced by a mischievous glint in her eyes. Florence kissed her nanna playfully on the cheek, quickly wiped at her own wet cheeks and took her seat.

'Nanna, did you send me to the camp to try and set me up with a man?' Florence gave her nanna a pointed stare, making Margot purse her lips in innocence.

'Not just any man, dear. I hear that Jo is quite the writer. George tells me he is working on a novel.' Margot raised her brow with a grin.

Florence tried to defer chatter of being set up with a man and instead confided in Margot the worries she felt for George and Jo's relationship. 'I think he and Jo butt heads sometimes. George never seems happy when Jo is around, and his face is always frowning whenever Jo leaves his office. Jo came to help him save the camp. I know selling it is not in anyone's interest, but Jo's plan isn't a bad one if everyone would trust him,' Florence noted.

'George is simply wary, my dear. He's been around the moon a fair few times now; he's worried that Jo has put his trust in the wrong people.' She tilted her head from side to side. 'Then there is simply that stubborn heart of his that finds it impossible to give up the land that he has loved and lived on for his whole life. My heart is heavy for him, for one's home is one's home and you will find when you get to my age, it is extremely difficult to break old habits and routines.' Margot's eyes reflected her own fight but just as her nanna had not given up on her, Florence would not give up on her nanna. Margot needed the camp and Florence was determined to get her back there. Maybe her nanna could work her magic on George and Jo's relationship? Before Florence could make this suggestion, her nanna continued. 'I believe George carries a lot of guilt over not being around for Jo and so he struggles to accept the help when he was not there for his grandson when he needed him most and yes, it's not quite the help he had in mind either,' Margot added with a small smile and a wave of her hand. Florence refilled their teacups from the teapot and had a nibble of her sandwich while she mulled over her nanna's words. They made sense.

'But I don't believe Jo holds any anger towards his grandad for not being in his life. He has so much love for the place and wants to see it succeed. And being a successful businessman and architect, I'm sure he knows all the right people and George is in safe hands,' Florence said, in between chewing on her sandwich thoughtfully.

'Oh, I do not doubt Jo for a second. I believe he is quite handsome too,' Margot said with a twinkle in her eye.

'I can't believe you. Do not for a second think I am not

mad at you for sending me there with no warning about this man.' Florence gasped, playfully, enjoying the light in Margot's eyes. A large part of her was happy to play along, but a small piece of her felt perturbed that her nanna had felt the need to set her up. 'Besides, you know I don't need a man,' Florence added indignantly, returning the two bites she had left of her sandwich to the plate.

'Oh, behave. I didn't send you there to meet a man. That was simply a happy coincidence, my treasure. If I had warned you, you would have fussed and meet-cutes do not come with warnings,' Margot informed her with a nod of her head. At the mention of meet-cutes, Florence's mind drifted back over her initial encounter with Jo, how he had stood regal under the magnolia tree, his floppy curls dangling in front of his face but unable to hide the piercing emeralds that were his eyes. There was a shyness in the flush of his cheeks yet a confidence in how he held his heart-shaped jaw when he dipped into his accents. It certainly had all the makings of a memorable meet-cute. The voice from earlier that told her she had work to do piped up again. This time it told her that she might not need a man, but she might like a Jo. The clink of her nanna's teacup blinked Florence back to the table where Margot was looking at her expectantly.

'Jo is a marvellous creature, Nanna; I think you'd like him. He doesn't think of me as odd or weird but runs with the thoughts in my head,' Florence said, unaware that her tone had turned wistful, though this did not go unnoticed by Margot. Then her face turned sombre as she stared at the delicate pattern on her china teacup.

'Nanna?' she said softly, raising her head to meet her nanna's warm gaze.

'Yes, dear,' Margot replied.

'Do you believe George to be your true love?' The question had been formulating in Florence's brain during their conversation. Not until Margot had spoken so hopefully of Jo had Florence decided to pay attention to it, but now it gave her pause. Her nanna looked at her and Florence could see a tiny hint of a smirk appearing at the corner of her mouth. Was it obvious to Margot what Florence was thinking?

'When your grandad died, I did not believe I could ever find another Prince Charming so to speak, nor like you, did I want one. I was absolutely terrified of the thought. Then when Darcy died and Henry too, the only thing I could think about was you. I loved my daughter, I loved my husband, but to give up everything in a way I had never known, to put every ounce of thought, worry, joy, care, attention, and love into one being, to create a bond like one I have never known... You, my darling, have been my life's truest love. Do not let your books confuse you. Do I believe George to be my Prince Charming?' She returned the question with an airy shrug. 'If I would like him to be and of course if he would so choose to be, then yes I can believe it.'

Feeling a little thrown by the magnitude of her nanna's answer, having not expected the depth in which it made her both feel and think, Florence sat back in her chair and pondered Margot's words. She already knew true love in her nanna and their life had been one full of heartbreak and magic. They had created a beautiful world from the ashes of a crumbled past that threatened every day to bring them pain. Yet they had laughed, adventured, explored, and built their life together and while of course Florence would give anything to have her parents be in her life, she wouldn't change what she and Margot had for the world. It wasn't that she wasn't capable of love, that she couldn't have the love that Jo had offered, it was the fact that she was choosing not to.

'When one puts limits on what life can be or thinks they are too old to imagine, it is such an awful shame, a waste of a magical mind and all the love the heart has to give,' Margot said in a soothing tone, breaking Florence's trance. She had been limiting her life because she was scared, running away from things that could be good because of all the things that had been bad before. She had built a wall separating the real world from her dream world, simply accepting the fact that she was a little different, that she was a little bruised and would never be able to have what other people had because she wasn't a part of their world. If Jo was going to choose her and she wanted to choose Jo, then she was going to have to work a little harder to break through her fears and find a way to blend her two worlds into one.

Smiling at her nanna's advice, and feeling slightly queasy about it too, Florence sat up straighter in her chair and took a refreshing sip of tea.

'Nanna, I'd like to take you back to Camp Calla Lily soon and I will not take no for an answer. I understand your fears, for I had them too, but you ain't getting any younger and we have spent too long letting the world write our story for us,' Florence announced, getting up from her chair and refilling the kettle. That last sip of tea had not been quite as refreshing as she had hoped, for it had gone cold. She looked out of the window, across the narrow, cobbled road, at the recycle bins that lined the street and smiled a wobbly smile. Her heart thumped against her chest, adrenaline made her legs feel like jelly, but she could feel in her bones that she was not simply about to write a new chapter; the next page would be more like a part two.

NINETEEN

Florence found herself shivering under her duvet. As her eyes flickered open she saw the sheer white curtains blowing violently in the wind, her window wide open. Hesitantly she crept out of her bed, scurrying as quickly as she could across the stone floor and over to the castle ledge. There wasn't much she could do about the draught. The rickety frail wooden frame wasn't strong enough to hold off the chill but still she attempted to push the window to. She had only made it halfway back to her bed when a loud slam from behind her indicated that the window had once again been forced open by the gale. The rain was getting louder, the storm more aggressive, there wasn't much she could do to keep the window shut. She would simply have to pull her duvet tighter around herself and wait for the storm to pass. As she turned to return to her bed, her feet going numb on the icy stone, a clap of thunder and a flash of lightning illuminated the sky. When it did so, Florence noticed a figure in the field below. A white stallion, almost glowing under the yellow streak of the lightning, rose on its hind legs, knocking off the figure atop it.

Florence gasped and without thinking grabbed her dressing gown off its hook and bolted to the door.

She had to get to the rider, to help him or her up and get them out of the storm. It was far too dreadful outside to be horseback riding. Whatever were they doing out so late at night?

'Hello. Hello,' Florence bellowed through the pouring rain. 'Hello, can you hear me? I have shelter. You must follow me,' she shouted, but there was no movement in the fog, causing Florence's heart rate to pick up. Had the rider hurt themselves? What would she do then? Would she be able to carry them back to the castle and into the warmth?

'Hello,' she tried again until she could make out a dark silhouette lying in a heap on the ground. She ran towards the figure and threw herself into the mud, kneeling close to check for signs of life. When she touched the figure's shoulder, a loud grunt emitted from somewhere deep in the mud and it started to stir. Florence sat back on her heels not wanting to crowd what she now presumed to be a man. When he rolled over onto his back, his face was covered in dirt and the gooey mud that had softened his fall, it was hard to make out all his features except for his piercing hazel eyes that lit up when they fell upon their rescuer. In that moment, another clap of thunder shook the night sky and...

Florence sat up in her bed, panting and sweating and feeling around her pyjamas for signs of mud. Coming up mud-less and clean, she patted her sweaty forehead. It had only been a dream. She rolled her eyes at her heart just as her alarm clock decided to ring out and she sprung out of bed as fast as she could, grabbing her glasses off her bedside table so she could focus on the day ahead.

* * *

The first thing on Florence's Monday morning agenda was to return to the job section of the newspaper and ring up the potential places that she had spent Saturday afternoon and Sunday highlighting. After a quick shower and throwing on her long polka dot shift dress, she made herself and her nanna a pot of tea and some toast and sat at the kitchen table.

'Morning, treasure,' her nanna said upon finding Florence in the kitchen looking fresh-faced and determined, her cheeks still rosy from the hot shower.

'Morning, Nanna. I made you tea. I'm just going to see if I can get hold of some of these places and then I'll nip out and let you have some peace and quiet so you can ring George in private,' Florence said, wiggling her eyebrows and taking a bite of her toast. She could only assume that her nanna spent her days on the phone to George when she was at work and though Florence was extremely curious about their conversations, she also didn't wish to intrude on their time and eavesdrop now that she wasn't currently working. Plus, she hoped that she would have a productive morning and get some interviews lined up that would mean making a trip out anyway.

Her nanna grinned as she eased herself into her chair and stirred a teaspoon of sugar into her tea.

'Right, wish me luck. I'll be in the front room,' she added, picking up the paper and heading for the armchair by the corded phone.

'Good luck, my Florence, if you need anything I am always here,' her nanna replied. Florence paused before leaving the kitchen and turned around to give her nanna a cuddle and a kiss before going on her way.

After getting comfortable in the armchair, which meant

THE LITTLE BARN OF DREAMS

placing cushions on her lap to fiddle with as she dialled each phone number nervously, Florence spent the morning answering many of the same questions over again and hearing the same patronising advice numerous times. By the time the clock ticked over to eleven a.m., she was feeling wholly disheartened and defeated. Blending into the real world was not easy. There were only so many times one could hear:

'And what qualifications do you have?'

'Can you email us over a copy of your résumé? No, well, this position is highly sought after. It would be advised that you get it over to us as soon as possible.'

'What is your mobile number? Sorry, did you say you don't have one? How do you expect people to contact you? A landline?'

'How much experience do you have working with computers?'

'One job in a theatre does not qualify you to teach drama, I'm afraid.'

And so many times one could doubt themselves:

'Maybe I could apply for this one, but I don't have two years' experience.'

'That one looks interesting, oh but what is Pinterest?'

'I can plan activities. I'd love that. No, I need an early years diploma.'

When the clock indicated it was lunchtime, Florence felt utterly miserable and the tears she was trying to keep in were beginning to sting her eyes. She took off her glasses and massaged her temples while trying to steady her breathing.

Maybe she was simply going about this the wrong way. If she was determined to find a job in a field she loved, the first thing she needed to do was research courses and see if she could acquire a qualification. That would mean a trip to the library to use one of their computers. Florence was aware that technology had advanced since she was a little girl. She wasn't stupid when it came to understanding mobile phones and the usefulness of the internet. She had had to learn IT skills at school, and they had served her well during her time at Paperchains. Olivia would tell her about apps and had spent many hours encouraging her to purchase a phone so they could text, but Florence happened to like their phone calls from the landline. She rather enjoyed sitting in her cosy armchair and speaking with Olivia. She simply had no desire to stare at a screen the way she saw others do. That little portable device had been the reason she had lost her mum and it was not something she thought she needed in her life, but she had been doing a lot of rethinking over the past two days.

Moving her cushions to one side, she made her way down the small corridor, absentmindedly tracing her fingers over the books as she walked past them and into the kitchen where her nanna was rustling up some lunch.

'I can finish that, Nanna. You sit down please,' Florence said, gently touching her nanna's elbows and trying to edge her towards her chair, but the old lady stiffened.

'Florence, I do not need to sit down. You can help me, but I will hear none of your worrying,' her nanna said, shaking a wooden spoon that she was using to stir vegetables in a frying pan, at Florence. 'Whatever is wrong, dear?' Margot asked, noticing the redness around Florence's eyes.

Florence moved away to fill the kettle up to boil some water for the rice. 'Nothing. I'm fine. Job hunting is just a touch daunting. I think I might need to get a qualification if I want to pursue a career in teaching children drama or assisting in drama classes. I have the experience with the theatre, but it's not enough.'

'Oh, my dear, I believe in you. I think you can do anything if you put your mind to it,' her nanna said with a warm smile that crinkled her eyes.

'Being at the camp made me realise how much I loved working with children. I miss my job at the theatre, and I don't want to let what Ryan did stop me from getting back into it. I have spent five years behind a desk and whilst I'm not complaining – it put food on the table and paid our bills – I think I would like to look at other drama groups and classes. I let Ryan take that away from me and I can see that now, but I want to spend my days being creative again,' Florence said with a determined nod. Saying her dream out loud to her nanna suddenly made her feel both invigorated and petrified. She didn't want to fail. Her nanna had been an assistant at the local newspaper office, then when she had Florence's mum, she became a stay-at-home mum while her husband worked. Margot had doted on her daughter but when Florence's mum was all grown up, Margot had gone to work at a children's bookshop. When Florence's grandad had fallen ill before Florence was born, Margot had taken to being his full-time carer at home. One thing Florence remembered growing up was hearing her nanna's stories about the jobs she had so loved. She had loved being around the news, seeing words come to life in print and had adored reading storybooks to kids at the bookshop. Florence wanted to have that same passion for her work once more.

'I think that is a marvellous idea, honey. I know you will find your place,' her nanna told her.

Their lunch of a vegetable stir-fry was delicious and Florence took a moment to appreciate being able to enjoy a Monday lunchtime with her nanna before gathering up a few old printed résumés and a notebook and setting off to the library. It was quiet out in the early August sun and the roads looked beautiful lined with vibrant green conker trees. They reminded Florence of her days spent listening to Jo reading to her in his favourite spot under the particularly stunning magnolia tree, with its bountiful full leaves, by her pastel pink hut. She wondered how he was getting on with the barn, if he had completed it, if George and he were getting on any better. Without thinking she glanced up to the cloudless blue sky just in case any owls came swooping by and a chuckle escaped her lips when she realised what she was doing.

She entered the library and found herself a quiet spot at the computer near the window and got to work making notes on all that she could find about theatre schools, kids' classes and day and night courses for getting a teaching qualification. Thankfully all her GSCE grades had been high passes and so she didn't need to retake any exams, which gave Florence a confidence boost. However, the courses would all cost money and they weren't exactly cheap. She would be able to use a little of her savings to take the first leap if she ran it by her nanna, but she would have to find work to ensure the bills were paid.

Satisfied that she had collected enough information, Florence packed up her notebook and returned home, where she spent the afternoon telling her nanna of all she had found out and ringing around the colleges to see if they had spaces available. As the summer sun drifted in and out of the evening clouds Florence sipped on her tenth cup of tea of the day and let out a sigh, causing her nanna to lift her head from the books she was reading.

'I can do this, can't I, Nanna? It all seems daunting going back to school now. What if I'm the oldest there?' Florence asked, her stomach a twisted knot of nerves just thinking about classrooms and lots of new faces and people.

'I believe that you already took the first steps in profoundly moving forward by going back to Camp Calla Lily. I believe that while it was scary, you did it and you are much brighter for it. A lesson you have now passed on to your ancient nanna. I believe, dear Florence, that doing something new will always be frightening. It does not mean we should not pursue it. Though my fears are still there, I feel inspired by you and so, my treasure, I believe you are more than capable of getting a degree and stepping into a world of learning and new people, when you are quite capable of stepping into worlds of dragons and goblins and often come out without a scratch,' her nanna finished with a wink.

Florence chuckled. 'If the world of résumés and job interviews is anything to go by, I think dragons and goblins are much tamer.'

TWENTY

Florence had spent the week organising her funds with her nanna and writing out a plan for her new start. She had been back to the library a couple more times to go over her options and had settled on acquiring an Associate Diploma in Teaching the Performing Arts with a renowned drama company that had schools all over the UK. She had been drawn to the website and had kept revisiting it in between her searches, for she loved the idea of holiday camps and weekend workshops for kids and how this specific school emphasised fun and creativity and setting her up for those kinds of events.

Florence had put aside some money to ensure that the next two months of bills were covered and so she could see how much she had saved that could go towards her deposit while she sought out a new job. Money had always been tight for her and Margot and so Florence had become quite adept at saving. With her mum being a painter and her dad being an actor they had lived a modest life. Her mum's paintings had been exquisite. If she thought hard Florence could remember watching her mum at work in the living room painting whatever came to mind. Margot still had one of her paintings hung up in her bedroom, but Florence had found it difficult to look at growing up. It was just another reminder of the incredible woman she had lost. Her mum's paintings quickly sold to art collectors not long after they were put up in the local art galleries. This money kept her small family fed and looked after for months at a time.

Florence's dad would act and do his best but acting was tough. He made a pretty penny working on one of his proudest achievements: a long-running British TV show that was wildly popular and for which he appeared on three seasons, but much of his work came through being an extra or doing commercials here and there, in addition to his two runs on London's West End. The humble savings that Florence's parents had put aside for their little girl's future had been needed for a much sadder occasion. Funerals were not cheap, and Margot had used her funds to bury her husband, only a few years before she had needed to dip into it again to cover what she could for her daughter and son-in-law too. It had been a trying and tragic time.

Margot had done what she could, working in the local produce shop while Florence was at school, but she retired at sixty-five due to niggling health issues and also because by the time Florence started working at the theatre, Florence was insistent that her nanna rest and let her look after them. Florence had stuck to her word, putting all her money into bills and anything that needed doing around the house. Between her job at the theatre and her nanna's pension, they had been living comfortably but frugally.

Now, Florence felt grateful for her own small nest egg she had been saving, for she found that she was able to pay for a little less than half of her school tuition but would need to seek out a loan and hurry up in getting herself a new job to pay the complete fee and if she was to acquire a laptop. It was a lot to take on but surprisingly she felt inspired and capable after her time spent at Camp Calla Lily and after her talk with Margot.

Now, Florence entered the living room with a tray of chocolate biscuits, a fresh pot of tea and a smile upon her face. Though the job hunt wasn't moving quite as quickly as she would have liked or going quite as well as she had hoped – just yesterday when asked about a live stream, Florence had confidently babbled about a brook and given an answer she felt made her sound like an expert, only to find that a body of water was not quite what the lady had been asking about – she had been enjoying the extra hours in the day that she got to spend with her nanna. As she refilled her nanna's teacup, she asked in her sprightly tone, 'How is George? Have you spoken to him this week?'

Margot's brow furrowed, which made Florence freeze on the spot and her stomach sink. Her nanna's face usually glowed at the mere mention of George's name.

'Is everything OK?' Florence urged, setting the biscuits on the tea table.

'Yes, yes, sorry, dear. I cannot help the thought that he is deeply troubled, for he has been rather quiet this week. I'm afraid Jo has not returned from London and rumours are rife in the village. I fear he regrets signing over the land. I do think I would like to visit him sooner rather than later, if that is possible,' Margot said. 'But let us not worry,' she added as Florence took to her spot on the couch.

Her chocolate biscuit hovered inches from her lips. She had written two letters to Jo, which she had sent to the camp asking George to pass them on if he could, but she was yet to hear back from either Hadlee. Suddenly the idea of a mobile phone didn't seem so terrifying but rather handy. 'What rumours?' Florence mumbled.

'You know I do not care for rumours, Florence. It is probably mere waffle. People becoming on edge over seeing more men and woman in suits floating about. Do they not know suits are all the fashion these days?' Margot laughed, making light of the situation. Florence gave a gentle chuckle and shook her head, trying to shake away her nerves. If there were businessmen and women in the village, they were no doubt just making acquaintance with the people of Lily Pines for when they took over the camp and helped George run things. It was most likely nothing to worry about and she did so love hearing her nanna talk excitedly about going back to Calla Lily.

'I know why Mum and Dad loved the camp so much,' she said, focusing on the more positive side to the conversation as she stared over at the bookshelf, her eyes glazing over. 'The fields and the flowers lend themselves to the imagination so beautifully. There's space to think and dream without so much traffic clogging the brain and you feel like you can do and be anything out there,' Florence finished. Margot smiled and took a sip of her tea.

'I believe it is inhabited by fairies,' Margot noted with a wink that made Florence chuckle. Distracting herself from thoughts of what Jo was doing in London and if he was ever going to return to the camp or reply to her, she picked up her copy of *Little Women* and opened it to a random page. She had read the book so many times now that she could pick up from anywhere and still get lost in the story. However, while Beth played the piano in the depths of Florence's mind, at the forefront she went over her plan for tomorrow, for her plan now had to move quicker so she could ensure funds for Margot and her to take a little holiday.

'Nanna, I'll be out most of the day tomorrow. I've got to go to the bank and continue my job search and Olivia rang earlier asking about going for a coffee when she finishes work. Will you be OK?' Florence asked, looking over at her nanna who was sipping her tea thoughtfully, her book resting closed on her lap.

'I will be fine, dear; you do not need to be fussing over me,' Margot said, with a warm smile and a twinkle in her eye.

'If you speak to George, will you tell him that I was asking after him and that I send my love and maybe ask if he was able to pass my letters on to Jo?' Florence added, returning her eyes to her book.

Margot's smile widened as her eyes surveyed her grand-daughter. 'Of course I will, my treasure.'

TWENTY-ONE

The music thumped around the grand hall, the laughter and chatter of the guests competing with the merry rhythm. The chandeliers sparkled from the ceiling where they hung, and wine spilled over glasses as people cheered and accidently jostled one another in their jolly states. Florence had been wandering the quiet halls, choosing to occupy her time studying the larger-than-life paintings on the walls than mingling with the wild dancers. A particular painting had caught her eye and in front of it is where she now stood, staring into the thick brushstrokes and paint that twisted and curled off the page.

It was growing late. The moon shone through the high stained-glass window and cast a creamy glow upon the art that made it difficult for Florence to pry her gaze away. The balls of her feet felt the late hour, wanting to find themselves relieved of the stone floor and pressed against the soft sheets of her bed, but the party was not over and it would be rude to leave early. Though Florence sincerely doubted anyone would know she had departed, for here she stood quite alone and content away from the masquerade, or so she thought.

A small cough to the right of her made her jump. She turned her head and startled again as the culprit behind the cough looked at her from behind his gold-rimmed, white, black, and beaked mask. Florence's pink feathered disguise dangled from her fingertips in her left hand.

'Can I join you?' the man asked, with a gentle bow, his hands behind his back. Florence recognised the voice, but it was hard to tell who the tall presence was and if she had met him before due to his cover. She hoped he would take it off, for it was tricky to see the full beauty of the painting through tiny eyeholes and sparkly decorative clay obstructing one's view.

Florence nodded and the gentleman took a step closer making her breath catch, for when he did so, the moon's luminosity lit up his eyes and there was no mistaking the fellow. His eyes were a vibrant hazel with mischievous turquoise flecks that Florence had seen many a time in her dreams, since that day she had rescued him from the storm. When the man caught her staring at him, her lips parted, his own lips curved to one side in a disarming and rather cheeky smile, almost like he could sense Florence's desire. The spark between them tickled her skin and when the man lifted his hand to remove his mask, Florence feared he would be able to see the pounding in her chest as her heartbeat sped up and a moan escaped her lips. Suddenly a loud knock from somewhere in the distance made her spin on her heels and as she turned, she became entangled in her soft, fluffy duvet whose fresh linen scent awoke her from her dream. 'Florence dear, breakfast is ready,' her nanna called out, alerting her that she had missed her alarm rather uncharacteristically.

It took Florence a moment to collect herself. She didn't

quite feel ready to depart from her fantasy land, having been enjoying the rather vivid encounters she had been having recently. Not being around Jo seemed to be making her dreams more intense, like a longing to see him manifested at night when there were no distractions from the world around her. Based on his abrupt departure after she caused him pain and only the short note he left, she wasn't sure if allowing her brain to enjoy these dreams was wise or she needed to nip them in the bud somehow. Through her sheer cream curtains, the bright orange sun was already high in the sky, beckoning for her to get a move on. It was to be another glorious summer day and she had plenty to do that meant she couldn't dilly-dally and lie in bed thinking about Jo all day, though that idea was surprisingly very tempting.

* * *

The woman, Jackie, at the bank had been lovely and it hadn't taken too long for Florence to discuss her schooling plans or for Jackie to run through important information and logistics with her. Thanks to the woman's kind demeanour, Florence didn't get a headache. Her nanna and herself had always been on time with bills and with Florence only recently having been let go from her job, and with her assuring Jackie that she was actively looking for another one, Florence had been instructed to ring back within the week when she had found a job. Then Jackie could happily provide the loan no problem. Florence felt in a buoyant mood when she left the bank, but it faded quickly after her next job interview.

All had been going so well until when asked what she would do if a tick-tock failed to load, she had answered change the battery. How was she to know the young man had not been referring to a clock?

Six shops later and Florence was dragging her feet along the cobbles. She had been job hunting for most of the afternoon now and was becoming weary. Her smile was slowly fading, and she was beginning to hear the whispers of her books making her want to retreat home. She had been turned down based on not having qualifications nor a phone by five places and told to apply online by the other two, even when she had her résumé on hand.

As the city centre began filling up with people coming out of work, she veered away from the main path and down a side street. It was void of people and so she took a deep breath and closed her eyes for a count of five. When she opened them, she looked up past the dark, grey buildings to the clouds.

'Mum, Dad, if you can hear me, please give me a sign. I'm not having much luck here,' she whispered to the heavens. Returning her gaze to the bricks and mortar of an office block in front of her, Florence narrowed her eyes at it to look for a clue, as if her parents were going to appear inside waving her in. But the building looked cold and too modern for her liking and the people going inside surely knew how to fix a tick-tock, but she was getting desperate. When her parents didn't encourage her in, she walked a few steps to her left stumbling upon a café she hadn't seen before.

Her mouth dropped open as she read the swirly quirky writing displayed over the window that said, "Caffeine Heights". A group of teenagers ran past her, their loud chants and conversation making her aware that she was stood gaping at the quaint café with the appealing name. Florence quickly moved out of the middle of the path and rustled inside her bag to pull out the piece of paper where she had written down the directions for the coffee shop Olivia had told her to meet her at. She looked across the signposts and the street name to find that she was indeed in the right place. Excitement bubbled in her stomach. How did Olivia come across this place?

As Florence pushed open the glass door, she noticed a sign on the window informing her the coffee shop was hiring. A squeal very nearly slipped from her lips. She dipped back into her bag and pulled out the neatest-looking CV while briefly closing her eyes and sending up a thank you to her mum and dad. Then she crossed her fingers that the manager would accept it and her. Joining the line of three people, she scanned the cosy coffee shop. It wasn't exactly a drama school or buzzing with kids and rainbows, but it was decorated with classic book posters and there were bookshelves placed between the coffee tables. The place was almost like a library but with a sweeter more delicious scent in the air. This felt like a dream within a dream – the idea of not sitting behind a desk all day and working in a place surrounded by books and tea while she worked on bringing her other dream to life seemed too good to be true. She crossed her fingers, gripping on tight to her CV.

In the line, Florence glanced up at the menu above the counter. "The Great Espresso," "To Kill a Macchiato" – the menu was outstanding. When she reached the counter, she was greeted by a girl who wore a bright smile on her rosy-cheeked face. The bags under the girl's eyes suggested she was exhausted, and Florence wondered about her story.

'Hi, what can I get for you today?' the girl asked, her eyes wandering over Florence and to the door. Florence followed the girl's gaze and turned her head, curious to see what the girl was looking at but there was no one there. 'I'd like to apply for the job vacancy please. I have my CV here,' Florence said, turning back around and holding up the paper in her hand and silently praying the girl would take it and not suggest she apply online.

'Oh, that's fantastic. I'll take it,' the girl replied, leaning forward on the counter, and resting on her elbows. Then the girl's eyes scanned Florence from top to bottom and her brow knitted with curiosity.

'Why do you want a job here?' the girl asked, leaning a little closer and lowering her voice. Florence took a small step nearer.

'Because this place is fantastic. It's a bookworm's dream. And I got let go from my last job and I really need a new job to get myself through school,' Florence admitted, her own voice coming out a little rambling and hushed, though there was something about the girl that made her feel like she could be honest and not put on pretence, like she had felt at the other job interviews.

'Why ever would you get fired? You look so elegant and chic and I can already tell you're smart – there's an aura about you,' the girl said, taking in Florence in her long cotton mauve polka dot dress, loose sandy curls, and clear frames. Florence had never met anyone whose blunt words and immediate judgement were so kind and favourable.

Florence felt her cheeks heat as she let out a chuckle. She wasn't used to getting compliments from strangers, odd looks yes and the occasional once-overs and chat-up lines from men, but never something so innocently sweet. There was something about this girl and her large brown eyes and long lashes that Florence liked. 'I wasn't very good at it,' Florence told her with a shy shrug. 'I struggled to sit behind a desk and look at a computer all day. I tend to drift off,' Florence added and instantly panicked at her truth. 'But I think I'll be good here; I like to be on my feet,' she hastily said, but the girl was smiling a warm smile and seemed to have perked up a little extra. She stood up straight and reached out to take Florence's CV.

'I will see what I can do. My name is Bronte, by the way. My best friend owns this place,' Bronte said, sticking out her hand. Florence shook it and beamed at the girl's name.

'As in Charlotte Brontë?' Florence could not help but ask. Bronte's face lit up and she nodded. 'I'm Florence.'

'And I'm in need of a coffee,' came a curt voice behind Florence.

'Oh, I'm so sorry,' Florence said, moving out of the way of an older woman in a sharp grey suit who was giving her a stern glare. Florence waved at Bronte, who gave her an apologetic look in return. Florence went to find a table. The minute she sat down her stomach grumbled reminding her that she had forgotten to order any food while it was her turn, but she would let the intimidating woman get her coffee before heading back to the queue and placing her order. And besides, she felt happy that her encounter with Bronte had gone well, now she just had to cross her fingers that Bronte's best friend wouldn't be put off by her lack of qualifications or coffee knowledge and then hopefully she could get approved for this school loan and get it paid off quickly and smoothly.

The coffee shop grew busier and so Florence stayed tucked away in the shadows at a table towards the back of the shop, looking through the stack of books on the tiny table next to hers, too nervous to get back in line after the encounter with the rude lady, so when Olivia spotted her just after five, Florence was exceptionally hungry. At the same time her stomach swam with added nerves upon seeing a tall man emerge from the back office and take her CV from Bronte.

'Hi, Flo, is everything all right?' Olivia asked striding over to the table and placing her purse on the chair opposite Florence. Florence shook her head and pulled her attention towards her friend.

'Yes, sorry. I've not eaten in a while and I handed in my CV here. I think that man is looking at it,' Florence responded, pointing at the man, and then smiling up at Olivia. 'How are you, Liv? It's good to see you.' And it really was. Besides her nanna, Florence hadn't spoken to many people since getting back from camp, bar Felicity at the library, the cashiers at her usual weekly shopping spots, and the people at the school she was enrolling in. Actually, she had spoken to quite a few people over the last week if she thought about it. There had been Jackie at the bank and all the shop assistants and managers she had reached out to and then today Bronte. She had been a better social butterfly this past week than she had been the last five years since getting fired from the theatre and starting work at Paperchains. The thought intrigued her. She had never thought about being a social butterfly before.

Her lack of interaction with others was not something she often thought about due to her books. Every single day she felt like she met new people and caught up with old friends as she dived between the pages. However, after a week with Jo and his bubbly companionship, and thinking over her bravery this past week, she didn't think it would be so terrible to meet others and find her people as she had done at the theatre for all those years. If she allowed herself to admit it, she missed the people there and the laughter, chatter, and camaraderie between them all. She hoped she would be able to find that again at college and maybe here at the coffee shop if she got the job. She liked Bronte.

'That's great, Florence. What would you like? You keep the table; I'll go and get it,' Olivia said, with a beaming smile.

Florence placed her order with Olivia and returned her gaze to the tall man. He had chocolate brown eyes, broad shoulders, a gorgeous smile and was chatting animatedly with Bronte as he turned over Florence's CV in his hands. When they stopped talking Bronte turned to Olivia.

'Did you hear him say anything about me?' Florence asked, her elbows on the table, hands clasped together, when Olivia came back to their table with a pot of tea and a panini for Florence, a coffee and muffin for herself.

She wiggled her eyes at Florence suggestively as she took her seat. 'I like this new you. He's cute,' Olivia teased before taking a bite out of her chocolate muffin.

'Liv,' Florence protested, raising her eyebrow as she poured her tea. 'I just told you I handed in my CV.'

'You're no fun.' Olivia smirked. 'No, he was asking that girl about her writing classes and something about acting.'

'That's Bronte. I just met her,' Florence said through a big bite of mozzarella and tomato. She liked Bronte even more now upon hearing the words *writing classes* and *acting*. Florence hoped she would be able to speak with her more. It also made her feel that somewhere deep in her gut she was meant to work at this beautiful bookworms' coffee shop and, that there were more people out there like her and Jo.

'How come you chose this place to meet?' Florence enquired after swallowing her tasty bite.

Olivia smiled softly, picking at her muffin. 'If ever there was a coffee shop that screamed your name, it would be this one. I thought you'd like it in here.' She shrugged casually but Florence's heart filled at her friend's thoughtfulness. She did like it, very much so.

'So, tell me more about your holiday. How are you feeling? Who's Jo?' Olivia asked, nudging Florence's hand and grinning. It was hard for Florence to open up when Olivia was more the dust yourself off and try again type. When a man wasn't worth it, it was no big deal as there were plenty more fish in the sea. Florence didn't share that same mentality and it seemed no matter how many bad set-ups and disastrous double dates Olivia caused, she only became more determined to continue the search on Florence's behalf. Florence appreciated that her friend cared to a degree and didn't want to fault her for that and the fact that she had been so sweet to bring Florence to Caffeine Heights, Florence thought to let her cheeky grin go this time.

'It was wonderful, thank you and I feel good. I mentioned it on the phone, but it inspired me to look for a job that I feel passionately about, so I'm going to be starting school in September. That is if I can secure this job to cover a loan and stay on top of things,' Florence told Olivia with a smile to encourage her positive vibes to fill the space around her and find their way over to Bronte and her best friend, who were back to chatting animatedly behind the counter. Florence chuckled at them, feeling that tug of belonging again before turning her attention back to Olivia.

'I'm proud of you, Flo. That's amazing news. And go on, do tell of your holiday romance,' Olivia urged, leaning in with excitement etched on her face.

'Thank you and there was no holiday romance,' Florence started, absentmindedly sipping her tea, and holding her cup with both hands. 'I simply spent the week rebuilding an old barn with Jo.'

The way Olivia's face crumpled, and brows furrowed in confusion made Florence laugh. 'Is Jo hot?' Olivia asked after a moment's pause. Florence instantly felt her face flush and burnt the back of her throat on a rather large gulp of hot tea.

At the mention of "Jo" and "hot", her mind suddenly drifted to the night Jo had come to save her in the bathtub after he had accidently thrown a bag of raisins at her head. Goose bumps had prickled her wet skin, with Jo's proximity, his mischievous yet shy smile and his awkwardness, in her dimly lit hut. He had looked positively gorgeous. She hadn't let herself acknowledge the fuzzy feeling that had presented itself in her belly then, but it was getting harder to ignore now. Jo certainly had those handsome features, that heart-shaped jawline, mystic hazel eyes and that bouncy dark hair. He towered over her and made her feel protected and safe. If she were a writer, he was the kind of leading man she would want to write.

'I'm going to take that silence as a yes,' Olivia noted, her voice coming out in a higher pitch than before as she beamed at Florence. Florence jumped having gotten lost in an image of Jo in her mind. Ever since her talk with her nanna, it was true that both her heart and her brain had started to see Jo in a different light. Little by little she was letting him in, but then she supposed that was easy when he wasn't right in front of her; it was almost like he was some fictional character in another world. Would she be able to let him in when she returned to the camp? A small voice in the back of her mind reminded her that Jo was in London and not Lily Pines. What happened if he had already moved on? It unhelpfully questioned.

'How is Drew? How are things at the office?' Florence asked, quickly changing the subject, which earned her an eye roll from her friend.

'I'm up for a promotion next week and Drew is as lovely as ever,' Olivia said, with a dreamy look on her face.

Florence sat up straighter in her chair. 'That's fantastic, Liv. You work so hard; you deserve a promotion. I will keep everything crossed for you,' she said with a smile. 'And please say hi to Drew for me. I'm happy to hear things are going so well,' she added before finishing her panini. Olivia picked at the crumbs on her muffin wrapper.

'One day we will have a double date you know, and it will be, as you would say, magical,' Olivia said with a wink. The friends talked until the crowd in the coffee shop dispersed. Olivia listened to Florence talk of the books she had read recently and what the teaching course offered, and Florence listened to Olivia talk of possibly moving in with Drew and what the promotion would mean for her. As they gathered their things to leave, Bronte skipped over.

'Florence, hey. Can you come back tomorrow for an interview?' Bronte enquired with excitement in her tone.

'Hi, yes, yes, I can do that,' Florence stammered, getting caught putting her bag over her head and knocking her glasses. She pushed them back up her nose and smiled at Bronte. 'Thank you.'

'No problem. See you tomorrow,' Bronte said and galloped away, her silver hair tumbling down her back and glistening under the bright lights of Caffeine Heights.

TWENTY-TWO

It was now Friday afternoon and inside the coffee shop was quiet, for most people were sitting at the tables outside enjoying another beautiful afternoon of the summer sunshine. Nearly all of today's orders had been for iced coffees and flavoured frappuccinos, which Florence found to be the easiest to make. Since she had gotten the job on Tuesday, she hadn't quite got the hang of the milk frother or giant espresso machine just yet.

Speaking of getting the job, Florence's interview on Tuesday had gone swimmingly thanks to Bronte and her best friend Langston's love of books and the arts. Florence had found out that Bronte was currently taking acting classes and working on an English degree and Langston was an aspiring poet who had opened the coffee shop because for him writing and coffee went hand in hand and he had always felt inspired when working with the smell of coffee in the air. The two of them together, Bronte and Langston, were a dream. Passion poured out of them when they spoke and Florence adored talking to them, finding that she herself loosened up and let go. She was able to tell them her own tale of how she loved to teach and work with children but at the time that had been by pure luck and chance, more of a "it's who you know" situation as she had grown up around the theatre. When she had been fired she hadn't quite known what to do and that's why she had ended up at Paperchains for so long.

Bronte had shown great sympathy for her as well as using some rather colourful language to express what she thought of Florence's ex-boyfriend Ryan, and though Bronte was a few years younger than Florence, the two got on like a house on fire. Each day this week, Bronte had gushed over Florence's outfits and greeted her with a line from Shakespeare as they got ready to open the café each day. Florence had felt inspired by Bronte's confidence and ability to be herself no matter who came in the café. Bronte shouted out orders with quotes from the books that matched the drinks and wasn't deterred by the odd looks she received from some of the customers for her dramatics.

With her shy nature the busier hours in the café had been a shock to Florence's system at first and she had become frazzled on more than one occasion. However, with the drinks being named after many of her beloved stories it certainly made them hard to forget, that and with Bronte never being far from her side and always offering words of encouragement had slowly eased Florence's nerves.

'So, do you have a partner?' Bronte asked when there was a lull in customers. She was leaning on the counter while Florence cleaned the espresso machine.

Florence put down one of the stainless-steel jugs and looked over at Bronte, a smile curving up at her lips. 'It depends, if you're talking about fictional characters, I have many. In real life, no, no I don't. I'm not the real-life boyfriend type.'

Bronte let out a laugh and played with the paper straws that stuck out of a mug on the countertop. 'You can't have all the fictional characters; you can only choose one,' Bronte asked, dreamily. The statement made Florence's smile grow wider. She liked the way Bronte's mind worked.

She placed her cleaning rag next to the espresso machine and joined Bronte near the cake counter. This was a serious question and one that needed to be thoroughly thought about. She glanced over the apple and cherry pies and made "hmm" noises, while Bronte gazed at the ceiling.

'If you'd have asked me this question in the interview, I don't think I would have passed,' Florence noted with a chuckle.

'I believe it's impossible to answer. Think of all the books – there are far too many,' Bronte replied, turning her attention to Florence.

'Maybe but I have one name that is at the forefront of my mind and it has been there since I was a little girl. No matter who I've met over the years, all the book boyfriends I've said hello and goodbye to, there is one that will not move on,' Florence told Bronte as she bit her bottom lip and narrowed her eyes at her friend. Bronte smiled a cheeky smile and sighed.

'Laurie,' the girls said in unison before falling into giggles.

'He's timeless,' Bronte noted once their giggles had subsided.

'He's elegant and gentlemanly but fun and mischievous,' Florence added, her hands clasped over her chest, an away-with-the-fairies look on her face.

'He was always there for the March sisters and did the

most thoughtful things,' said Bronte through another deep sigh.

'He made life exciting and dreams seem possible,' Florence said, her voice coming out airily, her mind filling with images of Jo. She shook her head quickly and cleared her throat. 'How about you? Do you have a significant other?' Florence asked to distract herself from her wayward misbehaving mind.

Bronte's eyes narrowed, she looked over her shoulder to see who was around before she turned back and gave her answer. 'I don't have a boyfriend no. Though there are a lot of beautiful boys in acting class, but... I don't know,' she said, slowly, her eyes shifting around again. 'You know when you meet someone and no matter what you do you simply can't get them out of your head? Kind of like Laurie, there's something about them that stays with you?' Bronte queried.

Florence nodded, her thoughts drifting to Jo again, her eyes threatening to glaze over.

'Well, what do you do when you can't be with them?' Bronte spoke casually, her question making Florence tilt her head towards the window in the swinging door where she could just make out Langston's head as he moved about the kitchen. Bronte followed her gaze with a nervous smile twitching at her lips. Florence felt for her new friend. What made Bronte think that she couldn't be with her person? Or was it simply something she had put into her own head, like Florence had done with Jo? 'Who can't you get out of your head?' Bronte asked, her brows furrowed, her lips pursed. Apparently, Florence's acting skills needed work, for Bronte hadn't quite accepted her earlier answer.

Florence matched Bronte's deepened brow, feeling amused by the kinship she felt having only known Bronte a few days. Then bravely she said, 'On three, one, two, three...'

'Langston,' Bronte said before her hands shot to her mouth as if she couldn't believe she said it.

'Jo,' Florence said at the same time before she could catch herself or hide behind her wall. Her eyes had closed and when she opened them Bronte was grinning at her, which made her cheeks flush and giggles slip from her lips too. 'You're in love with your best friend?' Florence swooned, registering the name that came from Bronte's lips, but Bronte waved away her comment.

'Never mind me, I knew there was someone behind those eyes. I don't believe for a second, Miss Florence, that you don't do real-life boyfriends. I understand you have been hurt but that is only because Ryan was not your Laurie. Who is this Jo?' Bronte stated with a confident nod as she served a customer, who had just walked in, a Scarlett Latte.

'You don't know Jo; how can you say he is my Laurie?' Florence found herself asking. There was something about Bronte that made her feel safe and free to talk about her feelings. Olivia, though her heart was always in the right place, never quite understood Florence's vulnerability and inability to date and date until one guy stuck. Whereas when Bronte spoke, she spoke like a true romantic. She spoke to Florence's heart.

When the customer left and took their Scarlett Latte to go, Bronte spun around to face Florence and took her hands in hers.

'I have a hunch.' Bronte shrugged. 'But look, no one can ever be one thousand per cent certain but when we meet that guy in the first chapter we get that feeling, that feeling that no matter the obstacles and ups and downs that are to come, we want to know more about the guy and we want to see him with the girl. We stick around, we invest in the story, we read on until the very end. We take a chance on him, willing him to be the good guy we believe him to be deep down or hoping that he wins the girl because he is an utter sweetheart and deserves it. There is always that hope. Can you honestly tell me that you don't want to see your Jo in any more chapters and that you have lost all hope forever?' Bronte asked, still holding on to Florence's hands, and looking at her with such care and warmth.

'Spoken like a true bookworm,' Florence said, pursing her lips to one side. 'It's far easier to have hope in books,' Florence noted as a slew of customers came through the door, pressing pause on their conversation and giving Florence chance to mull over Bronte's words and think of a good answer.

'You do realise that books hurt us too. You're stronger than you think, Floss,' Bronte leant over and whispered as she blended a berry Pride and Pre-juice. Florence's brows furrowed and she turned to Bronte with a quizzical look.

'How long did it take you to move on from Ryan?' Bronte asked while handing over the drinks and taking another order.

Florence handed back some change to a customer and thought about it for a moment. 'Maybe a month. Though he left plenty emotional scars, I was very much over thinking about him, loving him and missing him in about a month,' Florence answered with a nod.

'How long did it take you to get over Jo and Laurie not getting together?' Bronte then asked after waving bye and quoting Maya Angelou to the last customer.

Florence looked at the floor and gasped. 'Oh my gosh, I still don't think I'm over it.'

'Exactly. Those fictional characters are people too and

they teach us every day. You have put yourself in many people's shoes and experienced people's pain alongside them and you are stronger for it. The fictional world and the real world are not entirely separate when you really think about it,' Bronte said, scooting around the counter.

'Oh, and Floss, you're like me – you read with your heart not your head. Maybe try that in real life and listen to your heart a little more. I'm going to tidy up outside if you could see to in here,' she added as the clock moved closer to closing time. Florence thought about Bronte's insightful words while she cleaned the tables and wiped down the counters. She thought about Bronte's words as she hopped on the tram and walked home. She did not stop thinking about those words until she sat down at the dinner table with her nanna and came face to face with a too-flashy leaflet that made her stomach turn unpleasantly.

TWENTY-THREE

Florence was a tea person. She had always preferred a pot of tea to a coffee, and not fancy teas but just your simple, everyday breakfast tea, with a splash of milk and a sprinkle of sugar. When she was growing up, tea parties were a regular occurrence between her and Margot. They would sit around the dining table or on a picnic blanket in the garden and talk about the latest book they had read, or Margot would read stories or make up her own. Florence treasured those memories and tea had become her favourite drink. At Caffeine Heights, they served many kinds of tea, but the coffee was exceedingly popular. Florence could understand what Langston had said about the aromas in the air and though Florence was becoming partial to the smell of the lemon and honey tea when it brewed, the rich perfume of robust coffee bubbling up in the espresso machine had a magic to it that wrapped her in a warm hug and filled her brain with possibilities.

Now though, that cosy hug was making her feel claustrophobic and uncomfortable. She was too tightly wound. Her eyelids were growing heavy as she wavered on her feet after serving the last customer in a line that had been consistent for the past two hours. It was the midday rush and having not slept last night she felt exhausted.

'Something on your mind?' Bronte questioned, while refilling the cake counter with some Bakewell tarts, that Langston had just brought out to the front. Not only was Langston a poet but he baked most of the scrumptious treats they served at Caffeine Heights.

'Huh.' Florence made a soft noise as she picked up a clean cloth from the sink and wiped down the milk frother.

'Yesterday you were all smiles, today not so much,' Bronte noted as she filled up the napkin dispenser.

Florence placed the cloth in the sink and looked over at Bronte from under her heavy eyelashes. She pushed her glasses up her nose and pursed her lips. There was something about Bronte that made her want to talk. Bronte's open mind and view of the world tugged at Florence's heartstrings. Her comments yesterday about books and real life not being so separate had truly struck a chord with Florence and if anyone were to understand her confusion it would be Bronte.

'I met Jo...' Florence started slowly, leaning against the counter, and fiddling with the bracelet on her wrist. For the next five minutes Florence told Bronte the story of meeting Jo, her realising how much she loved and needed Camp Calla Lily, how new investors were coming to take over the land and help George restore it to its former glory, but George didn't want that. She explained about the rumours in the village and the mix-up when she had gotten angry at Jo for wanting to destroy his grandad's legacy and how Jo had promised that wasn't the case. Florence noted how much Jo loved the camp and seemed so content there, how he dreamt of being a writer but couldn't risk leaving his architect life behind even though he didn't enjoy it all that much. She then went on to say that Jo had expressed he had feelings for her, which she had been unable to reciprocate and that Jo had returned to London without saying bye, though he had left her a lovely, if not short, note, but he still hadn't returned to the camp or reached out to her.

It felt like the customers of Caffeine Heights understood the importance of her getting this all off her chest, for the café remained quiet and free of new customers while Bronte's expressions weaved in and out of joyful, hopeful, and intrigued as Florence poured her heart out.

'Hmm, I see,' Bronte noted, sounding very much like Watson, finger on her lip and all. Florence mused that she could certainly do with a helping hand to decipher Jo's grand plan and all the mixed-up feelings in her mind right now. 'So, you think he lied?' Bronte asked.

Florence let out a sigh. Hearing it out loud made her feel sick. Her heart thudded in protest, but she simply could not make sense of the leaflet. Jo had given up on his grandad. He'd given up on Camp Calla Lily. He'd given up on her. At least Jo walking away from her could be somewhat understandable. Maybe he realised that he had everything he needed back in London and had found someone who could love him back. However, giving up on his grandad, allowing Luxury Acres to do what he had promised to George they wouldn't do didn't seem like the Jo she knew at all. And maybe that was it, maybe she didn't know him at all.

'Look,' Florence said, pulling the leaflet from her apron pocket. In a too neat and modern bright white font were the words "Coming Soon to Lily Pines and Under Construction", around which were pictures depicting a bold white brick spa, a large conservatory that held a swimming pool and a three-storey luxury hotel. A map on the back detailed the route to the village and tourist attractions close by. There was no mistaking which plot of land this monstrosity was going to devastate. 'He promised this was not going to happen. He promised he was going to take care of George, that he was going to ensure the land was looked after. He knew of its importance to me, to my nanna, so how do you explain this?' Florence asked, feeling as if all the positive steps she had taken over the last two weeks had been for nothing and that once again, letting her guard down had only allowed pain to wreak havoc on her heart. Her heart that was currently palpitating in short painful bursts.

'You said yourself George was in terrible debt, maybe this really was the only way out? Maybe Jo is just as devastated as you,' Bronte tried, but Florence could see her face was scrunched up in search of a decent explanation. George's home, the original cottage, was nowhere to be seen on the photos. Debt was bad but making his grandad homeless didn't sound like a solution to her at all.

'Then why would he up and leave? Why leave his grandad to deal with all the village rumours and businessmen and women and head back to London when his grandad needs him? What if he got some form of commission for getting his grandad to sell and now, he's taken the money and ran? What if he and Kirsty were in cahoots the whole time?' The words came out small as Florence couldn't believe she was saying them or that her brain had even come to such a conclusion. Her heart ached. She had promised to take her nanna back to the camp to see George, but would George still be there when everything was torn down? Or had that been a lie too? She wasn't sure she could stomach a visit to this new resort, not when she knew the beauty that it had demolished.

Before Bronte could further speculate, the coffee shop door opened, and a barrel of people walked in ready for refills and their afternoon pick-me-up.

* * *

The fire crackled and coyotes howled as Florence lay back in her deck chair staring up at the pitch-black sky that glimmered with thousands of tiny stars. The flames, which were still burning tall and bright from that evening's dinner, warmed her body in the night's breeze. She had no need for a blanket or a jumper, for the crisp air on her skin felt perfect.

'What can you see?' asked a voice from the deck chair next to hers. Florence squinted, not taking her eyes off the heavens.

'I see a bear, a big grizzly bear with her cub walking alongside her,' she said, after a few moments. She stretched out her arm, pointing her finger to draw out the figure, connecting the stars together.

'She's looking for food – look there's a fish,' the voice replied, copying Florence's motion, and drawing a fish in the sky next to the bear. Florence laughed and turned her head, her cheek squishing against the frame of the chair. In that same moment, he too turned his head, but the hazel eyes she had come to expect did not meet hers. Instead there were inky black holes that made Florence shriek...

'Hey, watch it,' came an angry voice. Florence jolted, hot coffee spilling over the takeaway cup she was currently squeezing a lid onto. The coffee burned the back of her hand but not as bad as the scold she was getting from the customer before her.

'Oh, gosh, I'm so sorry. Let me make you another one,' Florence said hastily, quickly carrying the soggy paper cup over to the sink and grabbing a fresh one. She shook her head and poured the fresh liquid into the cup, thankful that the man had not asked for a fancy coffee that would have had him glaring at her disapprovingly for longer. She put the lid on, carefully this time, focusing on the small task and handed the man his coffee, receiving no thanks in return.

When he left, Florence let out a sigh and wiped her brow. She had not meant to drift off like that. Working amongst the bookish crowd at Caffeine Heights had given her a sense of belonging. She loved that customers were accustomed to the flair and drama that Bronte delivered daily with her affinity to quote the greats expressively, but Bronte never nearly burnt customers with her quirkiness. Florence had to pull herself together. Since the leaflet had crossed her line of vision, however, it was proving incredibly difficult to keep it together.

'Here,' Bronte said, walking over to her with a cool cloth in her hand. 'Put it on your hand.'

Florence took it. 'I'm so sorry. I don't know what happened. Are you going to fire me?'

To Florence's surprise Bronte laughed. 'You drifted off; it happens,' she said with a shrug. 'Though I'm glad you spilled the coffee on you and not him. Now, where did you go?' Bronte added with a clap of her hands.

As she dabbed the cool cloth over her hand, Florence saw the black holes in her mind's eye and her body shuddered. Not only had Jo disappeared in real life, but he was also starting to disappear in her dreams too.

'Bronte, what do I do? Mere days ago, my nanna was full of excitement talking about taking a trip back to Calla Lily. I can't take her to a building site. I can barely look her in the eye. She told me George was wary and I defended Jo. I stood by him,' Florence said, not missing the wobble in her voice. Was this all her fault? Had Jo left because of her, because of the things she had said about fairy tales and them being out of reach for people like them? But she had made it clear to him that he could have it all, that he deserved it all, that he deserved to live among the lilies and write his great novels with someone who loved him. Was he angry that Florence had turned down his love and now this was his revenge? *OK, stop it, Florence, you have read one too many thriller novels,* she told herself. She hardly thought Jo the revengeful type. If not that, then had this been his plan all along?

'You should speak to your nanna. See if she's heard from George, make sure he's OK in all of this, that he has a place to live and then the two of you can decide about visiting,' Bronte suggested, giving Florence's mind a brief respite from its overly dramatic thoughts. She then nodded her thanks to Bronte as a group of people came in carrying a copy of Dr Jekyll and Mr Hyde for their afternoon book club. Florence gulped.

TWENTY-FOUR

Fairy lights swirled around every tree trunk, like a twister ice lolly Florence used to eat as a kid and still enjoyed to this day. The horizon looked like a masterpiece, the trees like dark silhouettes against the fiery pumpkin-orange sky that blended into an autumn-leaf red. In the distance a shadow moved up ahead causing Florence to take a step closer. As the figure became smaller and smaller Florence found herself running. Her feet were leading the way, for they knew she had to get to the figure before it disappeared.

A loud crash snapped Florence back into the low light of her kitchen. A plate lay shattered at her feet. She grunted, annoyed with herself and went to retrieve the dustpan and brush from the cupboard underneath the sink. Her dreams had steadily been getting worse. No longer was she having pleasant dreams of a tall stranger with fetching hazel eyes that made her feel safe and valid, no they had been replaced by a stranger with soulless eyes who was getting further and further out of reach. Tonight, she had tossed and turned unable to stand the images for much longer only to find herself getting lost in her mind as she filled the kettle gone midnight.

She had to do something. Not hearing from Jo and not being able to speak to him was driving her crazy. She wasn't sure if he would listen to her or if her opinion on Camp Calla Lily would matter that much to him now, but deep in her bones she knew she needed to fight for it. She couldn't sit back and just let these new investors rip it apart. All the ideas she had shared with Jo – the book trails, the campfires – all the ideas Jo had shared with her – dances at the barn, writers' retreats – could they let all that slip away with the swing of one giant wrecking ball? Florence didn't believe she could.

'Is everything all right in here, my love?' Her nanna's voice startled her as she tipped the broken pieces that lay on the dustpan into the bin.

'Yes, sorry, Nanna. I didn't mean to wake you. Would you like some tea while you are up?' Florence offered, pulling out one of the kitchen chairs so Margot could sit.

'I suppose I will.' Margot chuckled. 'What has you up at this hour?'

Florence busied herself pulling teacups from the cupboard and with prepping the teapot.

'I was just thinking about George and everything that's going on at the camp. I'm sorry I trusted Jo and not you or George, Nanna,' Florence said, flopping down onto the chair and ignoring the click of the kettle. She laid her head in her palm. 'We just got the camp and all its beautiful memories back into our lives and now it's going to be taken from us again,' Florence cried. Her nanna reached out and stroked her hair.

'Treasure, I don't believe your trust in Jo was misplaced; maybe Jo's trust in others was unfortunate, but that is just my opinion. Only time will tell. The last I heard from George was that all was as good as it could be and that he needed a few days.'

'What if we go on strike? Hold up signs or I can chain myself to Mum's favourite magnolia tree. We can pitch a tent like you used to do and refuse to move,' Florence said, perking up at her ideas. Surely one of them would work.

Margot chuckled. 'I love when you are passionate,' she said, getting up to fill the teapot with the recently boiled water while Florence was running through ideas in her head of how to raise money to save Camp Calla Lily, while simultaneously getting mad at herself for not thinking of the idea sooner. Would Jo care for ideas now if they hadn't been enough to stop him selling it then?

'If Jo did finish renovating the barn, we could hold a fundraising event, just to get George back on his feet. With advertising, I'm sure the little huts would attract travellers and then we'd just have to keep them interested all year round, just think of the fairs and the festivals. Jo got this far, why would he just give up now and let the people trample all over his hard work? I thought he had a vision, Nanna,' Florence noted, helping herself to a custard cream from the biscuit tin Margot had just placed on the table.

'I'm sure he did but I don't suppose it would be quite as lucrative as the investors would like. Fairs and festivals sound wonderful, Florence, but George is but one man and an old one at that. Maybe Jo was right to persuade him to sell. Maybe this is what is to become of Camp Calla Lily.'

'Nanna.' Florence gasped in shock. 'Don't say that. I can help – you and I can help. We must do something.' Florence felt a stir of adrenaline course through her veins. Since she had faced her past by holidaying at Camp Calla Lily, she had got herself a job she enjoyed at Caffeine Heights, made new friends, and had applied for school – all things she had previously been fearful of. Adding Save Camp Calla Lily to her list now didn't seem so daunting.

She looked to her nanna with a new determination on her face, to find Margot looking at her, her blue eyes considerate. 'Is there more to this than just saving the camp, my dear?' she asked gently.

Florence bit her lip and played with the lid of the biscuit tin. She let the question linger in the air while she gathered her thoughts. 'If I can save the camp, if I can show Jo that it doesn't deserve to be given up on, then maybe he will feel the same about me and not give up on me,' she confessed with a shake in her voice. Margot patted her softly on the hand and then pushed another custard cream in front of her with a sweet smile. Florence picked it up and nibbled at its creamy corners.

'I will pack my bags,' Margot then announced to Florence's great surprise. She had been happy to hear her nanna talk so joyfully of visiting the camp and seeing George again over these past two weeks but hearing her announcement so bold and so confident bowled Florence over. Though the saying often went "diving into a book", Florence felt that she and her nanna were taking great strides of late – leaping out of their books and grabbing the real world by the horns.

* * *

It wasn't like Florence was able to pack her bags right away and leave on the dot with Margot. After putting a plan together, Florence decided that she would need to give Bronte and Langston enough time to think over her holiday. After all she had only been working at Caffeine Heights for coming up to three weeks and she didn't want to lose her job. On the Monday she had helped Langston unload a tray of wonderland brownies into the cake counter and put in her request for the weekend off. Florence had spoken quickly, her nerves getting the best of her, but Langston had been incredibly kind about the whole thing, Bronte having filled him in on the situation.

The week had gone by with Florence gaining more confidence and easing into a rhythm at the delightful coffee shop. There had been no more accidents or disapproving customers, for which she was thankful, and her nightmares had been replaced by thoughts of Camp Calla Lily buzzing with people enjoying picnics and the great outdoors and only the occasionally one of a tall stranger falling down a well.

Friday afternoon soon rolled around. Florence and Bronte were getting ready to close up the café for the night, seeing to their usual routine of organising the counter before splitting up and seeing to the patio and the café floor. Florence looked around to see if Langston was out of earshot and occupied in the kitchen. When the coast was clear, she spoke.

'Have you spoken to him about how you feel?' Florence asked quietly as they jumped into action sterilising the machines.

'There's never a good time. He's always so busy with this place and back at the flat is the only chance he has to get some writing in. I never want to disturb him,' Bronte said with a shrug.

'But your feelings are important; he'll want to know. I know it's scary. If I can do anything let me know. I can be someone else's wing woman for a change,' Florence noted, trying to keep the conversation light for the sake of her friend.

She saw the way Langston looked at Bronte, how his eyes were always so focused on her when they spoke, taking in her every word. They were so at ease in each other's company, but Florence understood Bronte's fears and didn't want to force her to speak up when she wasn't ready. They had something beautiful. She could see why Bronte was showing trepidation about change. She of all people knew how scary opening up your heart was.

'Thanks.' Bronte laughed. 'I should probably be taking my own advice really, huh?' she added with a wink.

The nerves in Florence's stomach danced and twirled for her friend. It was refreshing to talk about someone else's love life and slightly comforting to know that she wasn't the only one who struggled in matters of the heart. By the same token, she didn't wish for Bronte to go through the same tribulations that she constantly put herself through with her brain forever battling her heart. It was exhausting. As, the minutes ticked down for Saturday, the time drew nearer to when Florence would be putting her words to the test. She did not know what lay ahead at Camp Calla Lily, whether Jo would be there. What she did know was that Jo being present or not, she was going to help George and do her utmost to rally the village and do her best to save the camp. She would let her emotions do the talking and show the big-time investors that what they were doing to the precious land was a travesty and she would not stand for it.

Once all the customers had left and Bronte had flipped over the sign to closed, Florence took a deep breath, breathing in the last lingering smells of the Mansfield Tarts and Huckleberry muffins from the day's menu.

'You, you are going to be just fine,' Bronte said, coming to stand next to Florence and reaching out to rub her forearm softly, as if sensing Florence's brain noise. Florence opened her eyes and smiled gratefully. 'Take it at your own pace and I know it's scary but listen to that heart of yours. I think we've been tricked to believe that our hearts steer us wrong and get us in to trouble, but really the trouble, the doubts, they only seep in and make things messy when we mistake our mind for our heart. If you start to feel overwhelmed, just stop, close your eyes, breathe and really listen,' Bronte said, with a bright smile. Then she wrapped her arms around Florence and squeezed her tight in a giant hug. 'Those investors won't know what hit 'em,' she added making Florence chuckle. A few weeks ago, she would not have imagined that sentence to be used when talking about her. It sounded so brave, so feisty.

'I wish you were coming with me,' Florence said when Bronte released her. It was true. In just a few short weeks Bronte had become the closest thing to a sister that Florence had ever felt. Florence envisioned the two of them on the hill-top, looking out across the land, bulldozers, and diggers opposite them preparing for battle as she and Bronte held their thickest hardback books aloft and made to charge.

'Me too,' Bronte added, dreamily. Florence wondered for a moment if her friend was picturing the same thing. 'But this time it's your adventure. I will come along for the next one,' she added with a smile.

'Deal,' Florence replied, matching Bronte's grin.

'Oh, and if Jo is there, don't be afraid. You are a mighty warrior,' Bronte said, squeezing Florence's shoulders.

'OK, well from one mighty warrior to another, maybe talk to Langston while I'm gone,' Florence returned.

'Hmm, deal,' Bronte replied with a nod and a warrior stance, making Florence laugh.

* * *

No dreams filled Florence's head Friday night; instead she tossed and turned, got out of bed and back in bed numerous times and eventually stayed out of bed and started packing at five a.m. As quietly as she could, not wanting to wake Margot, she chose her outfits for the weekend. She fingered the soft flowing fabric of her vintage maxi dresses and neatly folded her collared playsuits and lace blouses into her small suitcase and when the clock struck six, she tiptoed into the kitchen to make the morning's first pot of tea.

She would not have to sit around and fester in her nerves for too long as they had an early train to catch at nine a.m. Margot joined Florence in the kitchen, as the kettle finished its boil and the toast popped up from the toaster, and she took her seat at the table.

'Morning treasure,' she said, sounding sprightly.

'Morning, Nanna,' Florence returned, placing her tea in front of her nanna at the table.

'Thank you, dear. I do not suppose your stomach is aflutter with nerves like this old lady's?' Margot asked, leaning back in her chair, and shakily picking up her teacup. Florence stopped buttering the toast and turned to look at her nanna. In her own distracted state this morning, she hadn't noticed the wrinkles around her nanna's eyes that contradicted the cheerful tone of her voice. Her face looked faintly white and she looked tired – all signs that Margot hadn't slept much either last night.

'Oh, Nanna, are you nervous about seeing George again?' Florence asked, rushing to Margot's side, and squatting down in front of her, her own anxiety forgotten for a short time. She held her nanna's delicate hands in her own, after taking the wobbly teacup from her.

'I have not felt these dastardly things in quite some time. They are mighty uncomfortable,' Margot said with a look of playful annoyance. She looked young when she pouted. Florence let out a chuckle.

'That they are,' she commented, squeezing Margot's hands. 'I've no doubt that they will turn into happy flutters once you set eyes on George again,' Florence reassured her.

'Ahh the happy wings, those are the welcome ones. Your grandad gave me those happy wings every day you know,' Margot noted, her eyes gazing off across the kitchen table. Florence gave her a moment, knowing that look and letting her nanna wander in her thoughts to say hello to her husband, to see him again in her mind. A smile spread across her face and her eyes shone with tears. Florence was patient and still and after a few moments her nanna was back in the room and tapping Florence's hands, then waving her off to see to the toast.

'I think Grandad would be happy that you're going back to Camp Calla Lily and to see George,' Florence said casually, sensing that her nanna was feeling some guilt over her excitement in reuniting with George after all these years, even if it was just in friendship.

'Oh yes, dear, I know he is,' Margot replied with a smile and a more confident sip of tea.

'I know Mum and Dad are too,' Florence added gently. She had been speaking to them a lot more in recent days and it had been a great comfort to involve them in her life and imagine what they would do or say. Of course, she couldn't quite know for certain but there were times when she felt that warmth in her heart or a light breeze around her and she felt they were with her, watching her and guiding her. Her nanna smiled a small smile, her eyes glistening. Florence took the seat next to her and buttered her some toast before helping herself to some, hoping that the butterflies in her own stomach liked toast and that they would settle once they were fed.

'When she was a girl, Darcy would lie at the top of the steepest hill and roll down all the way to the bottom, shrieking. She always looked a mixture of terrified and exhilarated when she reached the bottom, then she'd do it again.' Margot chuckled. 'Ned and I used to watch in amazement and wonder how we had created such a fearless little creature. Then you came along. Henry suggested we make the camp a family tradition, knowing how special it was to your mother.' Margot paused and Florence stopped chewing, listening to her nanna intently. It had been a long time since Margot had shared a memory of her daughter, Florence's mum. 'You were coming up to three, confident on your feet, always twirling and dancing. During one afternoon stroll, you spontaneously dropped to the ground and flew down that very same hill. You about gave me a heart attack until Darcy gave me a knowing look before both her and your dad rolled after you. By the time I safely walked to the bottom, you were all huddled together, giggling. It was music to my ears.' When Margot finished, they both reached for a tissue to dab at the tears that had sprung to their eyes.

'Maybe you can show me the places Mum used to play and where she and Dad used to adventure. You and Grandad too,' Florence suggested through her sniffles.

'I'd like that,' her nanna replied. Florence sent a little prayer up to her parents that she wasn't too late and that she could salvage any damage that had already been done to their treasured camp.

TWENTY-FIVE

The ladies made quick work of getting dressed and gathering their belongings. With the sun already warming up the day the short walk to the train station around the corner from their house was a pleasant one. They made their train and with Margot by her side, Florence stayed present for the journey as she chatted with her nanna about the scenic views beyond the windows and the books that they should look for in The Vintage Bookshop.

It wasn't until they arrived at the train station in Lily Pines that Florence came to a bump in their smooth trip thus far. Looking in the direction of the taxi rank, her nanna paused, seemingly sensing the tension in Florence behind her.

'My sweetheart, I know this is quite the big task and I do not wish to frighten you but dare I ask that you do this for me?' Margot said, as a taxi man walked over to help her with her things.

Florence was glued to the spot. She knew that her nanna couldn't possibly walk the miles to Camp Calla Lily, and she couldn't bear to leave her in the taxi alone. She wasn't sure which was causing her more anxiety at this point, her having to get in a car or her nanna going in one alone while she walked. She didn't know what to do. Her legs stiffened, and she couldn't move. The taxi man was looking at her with an odd expression as she felt the blood leave her head and plummet to her toes. Her nanna came and stood next to her, taking a clammy hand in hers.

'Take your time, my treasure,' Margot whispered, holding her tight.

'Ma'am, there are other people waiting. Are you getting in the taxi or not?' came the taxi man's gruff voice, said not nearly as patiently as her nanna's words.

Florence had got by over the years with trains and trams and she loved to walk, but cars she hadn't been able to manage. She tried to act nonchalant, shrugging her shoulders and encouraging her legs to put one foot in front of the other but it was not happening. Margot raised her palm at the taxi man, kindly asking for a few minutes.

Closing her eyes, Florence heard a small voice in the back of her mind, her dad's voice: *'My brave girl,'* he said. She saw him then, sat in between the book stacks on their living room floor, clasping her hand and raising it in the air as they both stared down at the cuddly toy dragon that had a paper sword they had made, tucked under its wing. A smile teased her lips and nudged her forwards.

'Sorry, sir. Yes, thank you for waiting,' she said to the taxi man as she helped her nanna into the vehicle. The man took their bags while Florence played her dad's words on repeat in her mind to drown out the thumping in her ears and the heavy thud of her pulse as she fastened her seatbelt.

Margot told the taxi driver of their destination while Florence took steadying breaths. The journey was a quiet one, neither woman saying a word as the car drove down the winding country lanes. When they came to the site of the accident, Florence reached out and took her nanna's hand while Margot looked out of the window towards the heavens. Florence allowed her nanna that moment of what she hoped was closure after all this time. She hoped Margot could hear Darcy and Henry too and that she knew how thankful they were to her for raising their little girl. Florence felt her mum encouraging that thought.

'Mum's proud of you. She is thankful for you. She says I turned out pretty wonderful.' Florence spoke quietly at first, then let out a small laugh, causing Margot to turn and face her. Her bright blue eyes beamed.

'I am thankful for her too and I could not agree more,' her nanna noted, giving her hand a squeeze.

The knots in Florence's stomach loosened as the roads became familiar and she sensed they were only a few minutes away from the camp, but that feeling didn't last long, for when they descended the hill where the camp came into view, all the eye could see was trucks and machinery. Florence's heart sunk quicker than a lead balloon. She was too late.

The taxi hadn't come to complete stop before Florence was unbuckling and pulling at the door handle. The gravel crunched under the wheels and when the man did stop just inside the gates, Florence flung open her car door. The normally fragrant air, perfumed with peonies and blossom, smelt metallic and stale. The symphonic sounds of the birds chirping had been replaced with a dull hum of foreboding.

Almost forgetting herself for a moment, the close of another car door whipped Florence's attention back around to her nanna getting out of the car. This wasn't the picture-perfect moment she had dreamt this of being for her nanna.

The lush, vibrant and stunning views of the land had been disrupted by the ugly, cold metal of the looming beasts. Florence rushed around the car to help Margot, who waved her away.

'Do not fuss, Florence, I'm fine,' she said, though Florence could hear the strain in her voice. This time she didn't believe it had anything to do with her nanna's physical pain. Assured that her nanna was indeed capable of standing on her own two feet, Florence hastily grabbed her bag and paid the driver after he saw to collecting their luggage from the boot. He gave her a confused look as he looked over what now appeared to be a construction site and not exactly an ideal holiday destination. Florence returned a tight smile. She couldn't blame him; it looked dangerous.

Securing the handle of the two suitcases after a brief protest from her nanna, Florence began walking the gravel path up to the main cottage. Margot walked by her side. Once they passed the machine graveyard and the cottage could be seen up ahead, Florence's shoulders relaxed ever so slightly, and she heard a gasp escape her nanna's lips. She slowed her pace, allowing Margot to take it all in.

As her nanna's eyes danced over the charming stone structure, Florence heard the gravel crunch with footsteps coming from around the back. The footsteps grew louder until George appeared. He walked towards their party with intent, his arms outstretched and a smile all over his face. Florence glanced at her nanna whose eyes were now glistening with unshed tears. When George reached her, there was no hesitation as Margot fit nicely into his embrace. Florence choked back her own sobs at seeing the two of them together after all this time. Love broke through the musty air, giving Florence hope.

'Margot, my dear, you're here,' George said, after breaking

their hug. He held Margot at arm's length, drinking her in. 'You have not aged. Look at those crystal blue eyes, so alive and sparkling, as bright as I remembered,' he gushed, making her nanna blush. Florence stood quietly for a moment not wanting to interrupt their moment.

'Oh, George, you were always such a charmer. You still look as dapper as you did back then,' Margot replied, making Florence think that the apple didn't fall far from the tree. Jo had that charm about him too and that old-fashioned vibe to him, which one could only attribute to his grandad, Jo having never known his dad.

The thought of Jo caused Florence to pipe up. 'I'm sorry to interrupt, but George, what is going on? Whatever you need, we're here to help. I have a plan,' she said desperately. George placed a hand on her shoulder and smiled gratefully before gesturing that they continue into the cottage. Florence let the two friends lead the way as she pulled the suitcases behind her.

She supposed in all the madness, it was rather lovely hearing her nanna and George talk in hushed tones, their hands clasped together, leaning into each other as they walked, as though they were catching up on all the gossip they had missed. Stepping inside the building, George settled Margot on the bench by the reception desk as Florence busied herself pulling out her notes and paperwork from her bag and placing them on the desktop, feeling like there was no time to lose.

'George, look, we can't let them do this to your land. If it's money you need then we simply raise the funds. We hold an event, raise enough to get them off your back and get those awful machines off your property and then we regroup. I'm sorry that Jo left you. He might not believe in the huts anymore, but the point is that they are here. We advertise, we showcase them, we won't fear social media, we will use it to get those huts a million hearts.' Florence's own heart was racing. She had never talked with so much gusto in all her life. 'We can get the village involved, hold a summer fair and bring in vendors. You don't have to do it on your own, George, we can help you. Sal will help you.' Florence was confident that Sal would back up her idea when she told him. His face that day she had spoken of the barn made sense the moment she had laid eyes on the leaflet. How had she been the only one to naively fall for Jo's plan? Everyone knew it was a bad idea to sell to Luxury Acres but her. But had Jo's heart really been in the wrong place? Why would he have spent time building the huts and renovating the barn if he knew it was all going to be destroyed? Hadn't he just been trying to help? But if that was the case and he hadn't simply wanted to make a commission then where was he now?

George stepped behind the desk and looked over the sheets of paper Florence had put down.

'You've been working hard. How do you suppose helping me will fit into your busy schedule once school starts?' he asked, looking at her with a warm smile. Florence could not understand how he was being so calm after everything she had just said.

'I will manage it, George. You have Nanna too. Her brain has many more years of imagineering experience than mine. There are endless possibilities of how you can keep this place afloat without careless investors taking over and obliterating it,' she pleaded; her face serious though she heard Margot snort through a stifled chuckle. She wasn't calling her nanna old, merely experienced.

'You are both incredibly kind and I am sincerely grateful

that you care so deeply as to come here and help, but I am afraid that my time has run out,' George explained, looking slightly forlorn as he rustled Florence's papers. 'It's all a bit of a mess. One I must take blame for too. I let it come to this,' he added with a sorrowful sigh.

'Is there nothing we can do?' Margot asked, sympathetically. George wandered over to the bench to sit with her as Florence paced the beautiful, patterned rug. George took Margot's hands in his and gave a small, defeated shrug. Florence felt her skin prickle and anger bubble in her stomach.

'We need to get Jo on the phone now. We need him here. Be it by accident or on purpose, this whole thing was his doing; he needs to fix it. He should not have just left. You need to speak to him, George, demand that he return and sort this out,' Florence stated, her voice rising as her anger built. There was still that tiny sliver of hope in her heart that this whole thing had been some misunderstanding but at this point that sliver could not allow her to step back and rest. There was no time. 'I don't care that he is a grown man, you are still his grandad and he should be held accountable for what he has done. We need him here,' Florence finished, aware that her voice had come out with more desperation than she had intended it to at the end. Selfishly, she needed to know if the Jo she couldn't stop thinking about was real or if it had in fact all just been a figment of her imagination.

As if someone had just turned the page in a romance novel at the moment when all hope is lost and the heroine is about to give up on the hero, the cottage door creaked open and a tall silhouette appeared in the doorway. The sun cast a shadow on the heart-shaped jaw and the floppy curls were wilder than usual. When he stepped out of the glare of the sun, Florence's heart about leapt from its cage, traitorously. Jo's piercing hazel eyes were as vivid and enchanting as she remembered but the bags underneath them were new.

'Grandad,' he shouted, then he froze on the spot upon catching sight of Florence. Florence's body too stiffened and though aware that her mouth was open, she couldn't get the signal to her brain to close it. In that moment, it felt like there was a tornado of feelings causing havoc in her mind. Tears sprung to her eyes as she studied his face, his high cheekbones, his expressive brows, and lips that could curve into the most handsome smile and recite the most beautiful words. She had missed him so much, yet at the same time the anger still fizzed over all the trouble he had caused for George.

George got to his feet causing both Florence and Jo to pry their eyes off each other and turn to him. Margot stood too.

'Jo, what's going on? Where have you been?' George asked, walking over to his grandson, worry etched on his face, but there was a deep love in his eyes. He reached out and put a hand on Jo's shoulder. Jo stepped forward and dropped a kiss on his grandad's head before turning to look at Florence. He then raked a hand through his unruly hair, his brows furrowing as he surveyed her.

'Are you angry with me?' he asked. George chuckled. Florence couldn't believe Jo's attention was on her, when his grandad had just asked two very important questions.

'Jo, your grandad just asked you a question. Stop looking at me,' she said, his intense eyes making her pulse quicken.

'I know but are you mad?' he asked again.

Florence narrowed her eyes. 'I think that very much depends on how you are going to answer your grandad's questions,' she said. Jo nodded and that's when Florence noticed he was holding a piece of paper. She thought herself a patient person but in that moment her hands prickled with anticipation. What was written on that paper?

Florence looked at Jo expectantly, but he wasn't looking at her, for he had noticed her nanna stood over by the bench. He took two strides towards her and bowed with his hand out. 'Hello, Mrs Margot, I'm Jo,' he said, as Margot shook his hand. Florence had to suppress a smile at Jo's need to be polite in the middle of a crisis.

'Hello, dear boy,' Margot replied. 'While I appreciate your politeness, I do believe you have some explaining to do,' she added, with an earnest glare.

'Shall we go to the café and get some tea?' Jo suggested, holding out his arm for Margot to take and gesturing in the direction of the café to Florence.

'Jo, there are bulldozers parked outside this building ready to demolish this place. What on earth is going on?' Florence snapped. It seemed adrenaline and passion did not make for a patient concoction.

'I promise I'm going to explain.' Jo said calmly but Florence gave him a suspicious look. He had promised that the camp was in safe hands before but the diggers out front begged otherwise. However, as he started to walk, she didn't have a choice whether or not to follow.

They were all sat around a large wooden table with mismatched chairs, except Jo who was pacing the floor with a knuckle hovering at his lips. Sal had brought out tea and coffees and was now sitting with them too. There were no guests to see to and so the kitchen kept quiet and still.

'I had thought the transaction final. We signed the land over to Luxury Acres and that was that. I thought the camp would be in safe hands as that is what they had promised but when Kirsty visited that week you were here, Florence, I started to have my doubts. Everyone was angry with me, speculating that I had made a mistake to trust them, to believe that humble huts and barns would be their vision for this land, but I didn't see a way out of the debt, a way to keep this place running without significant help. I wanted to believe that Kirsty cared about my family's history but then I recalled her mentioning something about a pool and a vague question about water mains for the old shower unit, but I wasn't paying much attention as I was late for meeting Florence. When Florence mentioned book trails to me, something triggered in my brain about an email I had received about a new road, a trail that cut across the land for easier access from the motorway. I panicked and knew I had to go back to London and speak to Kirsty to find out what was really going on,' Jo told the group, who all sat in stunned silence. Florence felt a pang of empathy for Jo. He had simply wanted to put his faith in another human being and Kirsty had betrayed him. Then a spasm of guilt made her heart twitch uncomfortably. Had she done the same?

If she was truly honest with herself, after their time together, she had felt their chemistry had been undeniable and their bond unquestionable, then he had trusted her with his heart, put faith in her that she might look after it and she had let him down. The worst part was she had felt all the things Jo had felt, but had made him believe she did not, all because she had been scared. She swallowed down the lump in her throat and tuned in to what Jo was now saying.

'You were all right. Sal, Grandad, please forgive me. When I went to Kirsty and asked to see the plans for the land, she first tried to tell me that they weren't ready yet, that they would email me. Then she made a comment about how the land was not mine anymore and so I shouldn't worry so much about it, that I could relax and get back to my life in London, that everything was taken care of. That's when I said to her that I wouldn't leave until she showed me,' Jo said and Florence could picture him as a pirate standing on the bows of his ship holding on to the sail, refusing to give up his captaincy no matter that the ship was sinking.

'Jo, it's clear that their plans were not the same as yours, the heavy machinery out front told us that, but what are we going to do about it?' Sal asked, which was the question on everyone's mind. Florence appreciated Jo's story, but he needed to skip two steps ahead and tell them what they were to do now that the land was sold.

'Sorry, yes, yes,' Jo acknowledged waving the paper he still had in his hand. 'When she showed me the plans, I could have cried but I couldn't let her see me like that.' Florence's heartstrings gave a strum at Jo's words. She hated that he struggled so much to be himself in the world sometimes too.

'I left her office feeling defeated. I had encouraged Grandad to sell the land, I had made him sign the papers, for of course the owner of the land needed to sign on the dotted line. In thinking of the ownership, something propelled me into looking over the deeds and that's when I found it.' With this Jo's voice grew more triumphant and everyone sat up a little straighter, nodding their heads. Jo still had not told them any new information or given them the solution, but the relief that Jo's intentions had been pure made Florence relax ever so slightly. She glanced around the table, studying the looks on everyone's faces to see if anyone knew where Jo was taking this story. She was at a loss and couldn't understand why he was smiling. Then slowly George's lips began to turn up with a grin.

'God bless her – Audrey,' George said, shaking his head

and then wiping a hand across his face as tears wet his cheeks. 'How could I have forgotten?'

Jo stepped forward and wrapped his arms around his grandad's shoulders, then placed the paper in his hands.

'My nanna had a covenant placed on this land that states no large hotels, nor malls, nor industrial buildings nor motorways can be built upon it or through it, and that it is to remain a recreational park, in all its natural beauty, for the community of Lily Pines to enjoy,' Jo announced causing a cheer to erupt from around the table. Florence felt her whole body shake with elation. She wanted to get up and hug Jo, but Sal had beat her to it and was patting him on the back. When Sal returned to his seat, Florence tentatively stood and hovered for a moment suddenly feeling nervous. Jo saw her and took a step towards her, brushing a curl out of his face.

'It seems that somehow my nanna is still looking out for me. I imagine dealing with my mum growing up wasn't easy; no doubt she knew I was bound to make a few mistakes here and there,' Jo said, with a small side smirk. He looked at her from under his hooded lids, his face flushed. He looked embarrassed.

'We all make mistakes, Jo,' Florence started, but before she could finish, Sal interrupted with questions.

'What does Kirsty make of all this? Do I still have to answer to her?'

Jo gave Florence a longing look before turning his attention back to the group. 'Ah, well Kirsty and I had words after my findings. It scuppered their plans, but she was somewhat grateful that I had brought it to her attention before those bulldozers were called to action or she could have been facing legal action or hefty fees. I told her we would give her the money from the sale back immediately if she would so kindly give my grandad his land back,' Jo told them.

'And she agreed?' Florence asked, surprised that it could have been that straightforward.

Jo scrunched up his nose and pouted. 'Yes,' he said, lingering a little too long on the "s".

'But?' George urged, his brow raised, a flash of worry zipping through his eyes.

'She wants a pirate ship hut for her kids by Christmas.' Jo shrugged and Florence couldn't help herself, a giggle erupted from within her. Poor Jo, he certainly had made an awful lot of work for himself, yet she was relieved by the fact that he was still smiling.

'I think this calls for fish and chips for everyone, celebratory lunch,' Sal announced, standing up. 'Jo, do you mind giving me a hand in the kitchen?'

'Not at all,' Jo replied, catching Florence's eye before he followed Sal.

Florence then sat down opposite her nanna. Margot smiled at her with a twinkle in her eye.

'Your first visit back to Camp Calla Lily in quite some time has certainly been eventful,' Florence said with a casual shrug.

'I like him,' Margot replied, her blue eyes gazing at Florence intently.

'Did you hear that, George? She likes you,' Florence said with a cheeky smile, turning to George who sat next to Margot. They were holding hands Florence noticed. George's shoulders moved up and down as an easy laughter barrelled out of him. How nice it was to see him so cheerful, the bags under his eyes slowly brightening.

'Oh, I don't believe she was talking about me, my dear,'

George said baring a grin. Florence knew she wasn't either, but it was worth a shot trying to distract them both. And it worked, for their laughter brought with it memories from before Florence was born and so she got up to leave them to their reminiscing.

Florence wandered through to the living room and seated herself in the nook of the window ledge. She stared out through the glass at the brilliant rolling meadows that looked ever brighter now that they were safe and found herself reminiscing.

When she had listened to her heart, it had allowed her to take part in performances of *Annie* and shoot-outs with Jo. When she had stopped fighting it, she had relaxed by his side lying in the grass and splashing about in the lake. When her mind had interrupted that play, she had acted not out of instinct but with fear and she had misjudged him. She had hoped and prayed that Jo had not given up on her, yet she had given up on Jo before ever giving him a real chance. Seeing him again had made that clearer than ever. The way he hugged his grandad, the way he had fought for this place, the way he had introduced himself to her nanna, Jo was unapologetically Jo and she loved him.

The smell of freshly fried chips drifted through the cottage and snapped Florence out of her gazing. Hearing the chatter and the clatter from the café, she got to her feet and made to join the party once more. The meal, as she had come to expect from Sal, was hearty and filled both her mind and her stomach with joy. The same could be said for the conversation that saw Sal and George talk of a festival they had run on the grounds that left them picking up rubbish for a whole week afterwards and George having to explain to Audrey why all her beloved trees had carvings in them. Jo had had to leave the table a few times due to phone calls but as he was organising the people to come and collect their equipment, no one thought him rude for having to do so. Florence pondered more than once whether to follow him and sort of hover until he had finished his call so she could speak to him but finding the nerve to do that grew increasingly difficult.

The next time Jo re-entered the café after taking a call, he looked a little downtrodden and Florence felt herself grow clammy. Had something gone wrong? Had Kirsty changed her mind? He caught her looking at him and stopped for a moment, just smiling at her. Florence felt her cheeks heat.

'I've got to get back to London, but this time I won't be long,' he added at the table's groans in protest. Then he turned his attention to Florence. 'Will you come back next weekend?' he asked.

'Is everything OK?' Florence questioned, not meaning to ignore his question but worry bubbling in her gut. Jo squatted down next to her chair.

'It's fine, everything's fine. Trust me. I have one last thing to see to in London, OK?' he said, his eyes growing wide, almost puppy dog like. Florence nodded. She did trust him. She trusted him with her whole heart and as he looked at her with those soulful eyes, she found that she wasn't so scared of that feeling anymore.

* * *

Bronte oohed and aahed as she broke tiny pieces off a cupcake and nibbled on them absentmindedly while not taking her eyes off Florence. This was the fifth time Florence had retold the story of what had happened five days ago at Camp Calla Lily to Bronte and each time Bronte had looked just as riveted.

She made for a supportive audience. Florence smiled at her friend as she took a healthy bite out of a vanilla slice.

It was gone five o'clock and Caffeine Heights was closed. Just the two women sat at a table discussing the week's events. Florence had spent Sunday at Camp Calla Lily walking arm in arm with her nanna around the grounds, listening to her nanna tell stories of vacations gone by. It had been closure for them both. On Sunday evening she had left Jo a note with George that simply said, she hoped everything in London had gone well and that she would see him the following week and that she was looking forward to it. She had then left George all her ideas for the camp and said she would ring him during the week to see what ideas he liked and what they could put in place that was doable and profitable. Now that the land was George's once more and after Margot had given him a stern talking-to, he knew he had to accept help if he was to avoid risking the camp again.

Settling back into the routine at Caffeine Heights had been comforting and with her mind so focused on the weekend in anticipation of seeing Jo again, the hours had flown by. She was having fun and had even started quoting her favourite lines from books to customers just as Bronte did and had acquired some regulars and tips because of it. She really felt like she was finding her footing in the real world.

'You know, you not having a phone is quite romantic. It's rather quaint having to schedule times to call each other and wait to see each other,' Bronte noted after Florence had told her the part where Jo had given her his contact details before he had left this time, after he had explained that he hadn't seen her letters due to his mind being a flutter over the land, then apologising profusely. He had phoned her on Wednesday night telling her that he had got back to the camp on Monday and all had been going well. He had also mentioned that he and George loved her ideas, and she was to look forward to their first Summer Spectacle on Saturday. Florence had no clue how he was going to manage pulling an event together in a week but she had faith.

'I like it too. It keeps the relationship interesting,' Florence said, sipping on her rose tea to wash down her flaky vanilla slice. Bronte's eyebrows shot through her hairline and her mouth twisted into a satisfied smirk. 'Why are you looking at me like that?' Florence asked innocently.

'You just used the word *relationship* when talking about Jo,' Bronte informed her.

Florence waited for the fear to grip her, but instead a band of merry butterflies danced around with hope in her stomach and her lips pursed trying to fight a too-big smile at the idea of being in a relationship with Jo, but had the damage already been done? She tried to push the negative thought away.

'Maybe I need to go on vacation so that Langston can miss me,' Bronte thought out loud, making Florence giggle. Her friend hadn't had much luck in telling Langston how she felt this week and so Florence didn't think that such a bad idea. Bronte deserved a rest. She and Langston had been working around the clock over the last ten months getting this place off the ground; she could do with a bit of adventure and Florence knew just the place.

'You should come with me tomorrow,' Florence stated causing Bronte's eyes to light up.

'You know what, I should.' She gasped, the excitement in her tone palpable. Bronte then shot up from her chair calling Langston's name as she ran into the kitchen. Florence sat back in her chair sipping on her tea, thinking about how much her life had changed in the last five weeks. Her workplace was no longer dull, nor did it fill her with the anxiety that Paper-chains had. She had made new friends in Bronte and Langston and received daily smiles and conversation from regular customers. Her parents now felt very much a part of her life and she thought about them every day. And daydreams of Laurie had somehow been replaced by a real-life man who she had to admit made her swoon as much if not more than her fictional favourite.

TWENTY-SIX

If Bronte had energy inside the four walls of Caffeine Heights, it was nothing compared to the energy she had with the smell of adventure in the air at nine in the morning. Florence couldn't stop grinning though, like her, Bronte was most certainly a morning person and had met them at the train station with to-go paper cups from Caffeine Heights and a box that made everyone on the platform look their way with jealous expressions. Langston had been happy for her to accompany Florence, as he had a friend who owed him a favour who had agreed to help him out over the weekend, but Bronte had carried out her usual tasks helping him in the kitchen and setting up shop before she had had to head to the station. Which meant breakfast was exceptionally scrumptious this morning.

The train journey had been one filled with joyous conversation as Bronte got to know Margot by asking a plethora of questions about her favourite books and plays. She only paused for breath to listen to Margot's answers but even then, she was dancing on the edge of her seat. Margot looked at

Bronte with great affection and so Florence had relaxed into her seat, very much awake and unable to drift off for the fear that she would wake up and find this all to be a dream.

'Is that him?' Bronte had asked when they had disembarked the train. Jo stood by the station's bookshop leaning against the frame with one ankle crossed over the other. In his hand was a book, just as battered and well-loved as his other books, and he was reading fervently. Jo looked every part the odd man out while to Florence he was every bit the perfect fit.

'That would be him, yes,' Florence answered. When Jo spotted them walking towards him, he immediately shoved the book in his back pocket and rushed towards them to help with their bags. Bronte's initial look of approval flickered, and Florence saw her eye him threateningly, as if she was letting him know that she was protecting Florence. Even with all the romanticising her friend did, she was still looking out for her, which comforted Florence a great deal. The evil glances didn't last all that long though, for once Jo opened his mouth and the conversation began flowing, Bronte was back to her chatty self and kept mouthing "oh my goodness" at Florence, causing Florence to suppress her laughter. The drive to Camp Calla Lily this time went by in a safe and contented blur.

* * *

The path was lined with pastel-coloured balloons, a large banner blew in the breeze between the two giant oak trees at the entrance way, and the parking lot was full of cars. There were more flowers of every kind and colour, some in pots, some in new flower beds that had appeared in the grass, and strings of twinkling lights hung around the porch of the main cottage. The place looked even more magical than before and it was busy, very busy. There were people milling around the grounds as far as the eye could see. Florence's pulse quickened as Jo pulled the truck into a spot near the building and turned off the engine.

'Jo!!' Florence gasped but then paused, for she had no idea what to say. Her eyes were darting from the side windows to the windscreen so they could take everything in. Jo smiled and climbed out of the truck so he could help Margot with the small step down and out of the vehicle. Florence practically dived out after her, breathing in the air and twirling around on the spot, her pastel yellow polka dot dress fanning out at her ankles. Bronte stood gaping like a fish.

George came rushing to greet them. 'Hello, my dears,' he said, giving Florence a quick hug and introducing himself to Bronte, before embracing Margot in a much longer and tighter embrace. Florence chuckled. She could feel the happiness and excitement bounce off him. 'Can I take your nanna with me?' he asked Florence politely.

'Of course,' Florence told him, as he collected Margot's bag, then took her hand and guided her up the path towards the cottage. That left Florence and Jo stood in silence looking at each other and Bronte looking back and forth between the two of them with an intrigued expression on her face.

'I smell books,' Bronte then announced. 'I will catch up with you both later. Jo, this place is magic,' she added; then she looked at Florence with an encouraging nod and back to Jo with a more serious expression, like she was warning him to look after Florence, before skipping away.

Florence spoke up first after a few moments had passed. 'I missed you.' The warm wind caressed her exposed skin and the fresh air gave her mind even more clarity over the feelings she was harbouring for Jo. If only she had listened to them before.

'I missed you too.' Jo replied, gathering up her belongings with a shy, but somewhat cheeky smile on his face. 'Come on, let's drop these off at your hut and then I can show you around,' Jo added. Florence smiled, liking the sound of "her hut".

The chatter grew louder as they rounded the back of the main cottage and another gasp of glee escaped Florence's lips. The decking was strung with yet more fairy lights, more pastel balloons decorated the fencing and there were long tables lined up on the grass. Pretty plant pots bearing daisies, forget-me-nots and calla lilies made up the centrepieces and a couple of yards to the left wooden chairs sat around a white stone pit that was to be the campfire later that evening.

'You sure know how to throw a party,' Florence complimented Jo as her eyes surveyed the tables full of delicious-looking and wonderfully aromatic foods. Sal had done an amazing job with the food and Florence had no doubt that he had been waiting for an event like this for some time, so he could really get stuck into the kitchen and show what he was capable of. The thought made her ridiculously happy.

'I can't take the credit. Ella has been amazing getting the village involved with such short notice. I'm just happy people seem to be enjoying it. It's great to see this place so busy again,' Jo noted, his eyes wandering over to the fields where children ran around playing tig, young ones and older ones, laughing and playing together. It was beautiful and all he had dreamt of for this place. 'I'm doing a book trail at three, if you would be interested in joining in,' he added, walking down the steps, and nodding at people as he moved along. Florence followed as they made their way along the familiar route towards the huts.

'Oh of course, I'd love to.' She gasped, merrily, breaking into a skip when her pink pastel hut came into view. Jo unlocked the door while Florence busied herself caressing the wicker chair she loved to sit in each morning, and then she traced her hand over the window ledge that now held a small tray of daisies. When the hairs on her neck prickled, she looked up to see that Jo was watching her movements. 'What?' she asked, her voice coming out raspy.

'Nothing, I just love that you notice all the small delicate touches,' he replied, running his eyes over the strap of her yellow polka dot dress and down her arm to where her finger gently played with the petals of the sweet plant. Florence bit her lip as the butterflies in her stomach performed a loop-de-loop. Jo hastily rubbed at the back of his neck and looked out across to the magnolia tree. Florence noticed his cheeks bloom a rosy red.

Florence could sense that Jo's brain was working a mile a minute as he looked at her. She suddenly felt the urge to reach out and hug him, but right now there was a lot going on and she didn't feel it was the right time to discuss her feelings when Jo had so much on his plate with today's event. If Jo had moved on, she feared it would make the day awkward and she didn't want to be the cause of that when Jo had worked so hard to make this event happen. So instead, she took a few giddy steps forward, ruffling Jo's hair to keep things light between them and stepped into her hut. With her arms open wide, she spun round on the spot, breathed in the woodsy, flowery perfumed scent of the cosy quarters and relieved Jo of her bags. She then pulled out her books from her small backpack, five books in total, and placed them on her bedside table before announcing that she was ready to explore.

Jo chuckled and Florence grinned. They stood beaming at each other as the sun streamed through the open curtains and after a minute Jo declared, 'Race you to the lake,' and ran outside. Florence followed suit, shouting after him.

'Do you not need to be up at the main building with the guests?' she enquired.

'Sal is seeing to all the food and Grandad has that under control. Besides the lake is where our book trail begins,' Jo explained, running at full speed towards the lake at the edge of the camp lines, the warm wind zipping through his hair. Florence loved the feel of the grass between her toes, she was wearing her open-toe sandals and could feel the shorts blades tickling her feet. All the worries and stress over wanting to talk to Jo, of her feelings, over money, school and looking after her nanna, melted away as she chased Jo towards to the lake, contentment filling her lungs.

They reached the lake and Jo made his way over to the bench under the glorious magnolia tree. Upon the bench lay pencils and clipboards with sheets attached that asked various bookish questions that made Florence's face crease into a broad smile.

'Hey, don't look. You must wait for the others; I can't have you getting a head start on the questions. I believe showing favouritism would not make me a very fair host,' Jo said with a playful wink. Florence tiptoed as Jo picked up the clipboards so she could read over his shoulder, but he gave her a mock stern glare and so she retreated to the water, sticking out her tongue as she frolicked away. Jo laughed, squinting his eyes at her, while giving her one of his charming side smiles. She looked away, not wanting to get distracted by the fluttering that stirred in her stomach.

'Did you manage to finish the barn, Jo?' Florence queried as the water crept up to her toes. She momentarily felt a little jealous that she hadn't been able to aid him in the rest of the renovating. It had been incredibly therapeutic for her.

'Maybe,' Jo said with a teasing grin.

'I don't suppose that I get a sneak peek at the barn then either, if you can't be seen to be showing favouritism to your guests?' Florence asked, as she paddled through the water, having thrown her sandals in the grass. She hitched up her dress allowing the cool water to calm her.

'Ma lady, how dare you even consider such a proposition,' Jo said, raising a hand to his chest mock aghast. 'I would not dream of spoiling such a surprise for the sky shall be just right and the atmosphere perfect later this evening so you, especially you, will have to wait,' he said, in his royal British accent.

'I do apologise for askin', sir, but forgive a lass for her curiosity. She is so desperate to see the fine job you have done,' Florence replied in a sweet southern drawl, that drew Jo towards the water. He placed the clipboards down and waded into the lake.

'Well, how would you know if a fine job has been done?' Jo teased. He was now a cowboy, taking on the southern accent too.

'You look like the kinda man who does a job right,' Florence answered, her cheeks flushing when she heard what she said. Jo's eyes sparkled with amusement.

'Damn right,' he noted, pretending to tip his cowboy hat, and propping his foot up on the bank so he could rest his elbow on his knee and strike a pose. With the sun highlighting his cheekbones and catching the mischief in his hazel eyes, it was hard for Florence to peel her eyes away from him. Her heart was in a tizzy. Allowing herself to listen to it and unlock the guard she had built up around it and see Jo in this new light of desire was all kinds of fun but incredibly terrifying at the same time. She didn't know that her pulse could beat so fast. She laughed nonchalantly and forced her eyes to the rocks at the bottom of the lake, wanting to keep it together and rid her mind of the image it had now conjured up of Jo dressed as a cowboy and riding a horse. She just had to get through the rest of the afternoon and the fundraising party and then she would speak to him and tell him how she felt.

Saving Florence from further blushing were a group of guests, both adults, and children, making their way towards the lake with bright smiles on their faces, chatting to one another and looking around taking in the scenery. Many jaws dropped when they saw the lake and the giant trees, and all but two of the fifteen kids ran into the water and began splashing around before anyone could stop them, not that anyone wanted to.

Florence allowed the children to get all their splashing out of their systems while Jo dried off in the sun and mingled with the adults. She loved overseeing the mayhem in the water, learning the children's names and ensuring their safety. They had a blast collecting a couple of rocks before she gently encouraged them to get back to dry land so they could begin the book trail. She began reciting "The Bear Hunt" and acting it out as she waded through the water. At this the younger children in the pack cheered with excitement and dashed to the grass, shaking off their wet feet and running over to their parents eagerly. The older ones smiled at her and enthusiastically walked towards Jo. Their smiles warmed Florence's heart and made her feel more confident in her school plans for September, plans that she couldn't wait to tell Jo about. There were a lot of things she wanted to share with him and again she found herself hoping that the time would come later to do so, and that Jo would be happy to hear them.

Jo explained the rules and instructions of the book trail to the large group before him. Florence could see the joy written all over his face at the turnout and she was pleased that the adults looked just as excited as the children for this event. After handing everyone a clipboard, some people had decided to group up, parents with their kids, even a few different parents teamed up while their kids giddily announced that they were going to beat them, Jo handed a clipboard to Florence who took it with a playful curtsey.

'The first instruction will take you to the first clue. Look out for the characters lurking in the grounds and answer the questions they are holding and that will give you the next clue,' Jo informed the teams. Then with his arms in the air, he shouted, 'Good luck,' and the groups eagerly mumbled the first instruction to each other, some darting off quicker than others. For a moment Florence got lost in seeing the children's faces light up as they shouted out the answers. The adults too were alight with wonder as the answer of *Matilda* took them back to their childhoods. It was truly a beautiful sight to behold, watching the magic of books connect people and bring smiles to people's faces.

'I don't believe it. Have you never read *Matilda*?' Jo said, his boyish grin back on his face as Florence stood there. 'The answer to the first question is *Matilda*, which will take you to the library,' Jo said, shaking his head, in playful disbelief. 'But shhh, don't tell anyone I helped you and don't think I am going to help you with the next one,' he continued, laughter in his tone.

Florence pulled her attention away from the guests to whack Jo in his bicep. 'I thought you weren't supposed to help me, and of course I knew the answer. *Matilda* is a rite of passage for any bookworm. Now please, sir, do not insult me and stop trying to sabotage my chances of winning this book trail by distracting me with your conversation.' She gave him a side smile and small nod and ran ahead.

'I would do no such thing,' Jo shouted after her.

Florence wandered the grounds, occasionally getting lost simply observing the other contestants. Her competitive spirit wasn't very bold. She watched as Jo walked around ensuring everyone was playing by the rules. Of course, it was all for fun and everyone was good-natured but it amused her and the guests when he occasionally popped up and stated that the book fairies who lived in the trees would not take kindly to the use of mobile phones or peeking at other teams' answers. The kids giggled and ran among each other, whispering to get a rise out of Jo. He would chase after them and claim he was the fairy police patrol and they would squeal and sprint away from him promising they were not cheating only to repeat the same actions again when they found the next clue. It was even funnier when they unintentionally gave away the answers by shouting them out for all around them to hear when they got so excited that they knew one. The whole thing was highly entertaining.

Florence took her time strolling from clue to clue. She was very much enjoying all Jo's questions and the thought that he had put into each one. The cardboard characters were an absolute delight and finding "The Hungry Caterpillar" on a low branch of a giant oak tree, "Winnie-the-Pooh" eating honey in the forest area where the trees were more dense – not too far from the barn, and "James and the Giant Peach" nestled by the peach tree had been a pure joy. Jo had made these characters a part of the real world and it was incredibly moving for someone like her.

She was the last one to reach the end of the trail, which came to completion back at the main cottage. Jo had set up tepees on the other side of the campfire, which contained stacks of books, colouring sheets, snacks for the children and Ella.

'Ella,' Florence shouted, grinning broadly as Ella ducked out of one of the tepees, wearing long denim dungarees, with one strap hung loose displaying a tee that read: "So many books, so little time". Her beautiful hair was in braids and bouncing around as she dashed over to Florence to give her a friendly hug. 'How are you?' Florence asked, as Bronte bounced out of the same tepee.

'I'm doing great thank you. It's so good to see you again. I've missed you at the shop. Jo's one-man performances just aren't the same without you,' Ella noted making Florence laugh. 'And Bronte here is wonderful,' she added to which Bronte curtsied.

'Florence, I never want to leave this place. I'll let you break the news to Langston,' Bronte informed her. Florence chuckled, the apples of her cheeks aching with how big she was smiling.

'I've missed you too. This is amazing – what you've done,' Florence told Ella, gesturing over the books and the tepees. 'And you'd break the poor man's heart,' she added, winking at Bronte.

'Thanks, but I believe it was your idea. Jo said something about you mentioning a book trail and then he just ran with it and put together all this. I only helped with the pictures for the trail and provided the books of course, but I think it's wonderful. Parents have been asking after the shop, so I'm grateful to be here. I think it will help the village too,' Ella said, and with that a parent wandered over to ask questions about children's books as a child tugged on Bronte's jeans asking about a story, so Florence bowed away happily allowing her friends to hopefully drum up some business and indulge the child in a fantastical adventure.

The scene truly took Florence's breath away. Every stop on the book trail had been more enchanting than the last and now this was the cherry on top of the cake; this patch of land that Jo and Ella had turned into a bookworm's paradise.

'You have outdone yourself, Mr Hadlee,' Florence noted as Jo came to stand by her on the decking, having disappeared to change out of his more scruffy and wet clothes.

'I may have called in a few favours from some architect types in London, who prefer this kind of thing to the high-profile jobs. We're not all bad. And you've not seen the barn yet,' he said softly, handing her a glass of lemonade.

'There you two are,' came Margot's voice from behind them. Both Florence and Jo turned around to see George and Margot walking towards them. Florence noticed that her nanna's eyes were glistening, and she looked like she had been crying.

'Are you all right, Nanna?' Florence asked, more than a hint of concern in her tone.

Her nanna reached out and placed a hand on Florence's forearm and the other took Jo's hand. 'Jo, this place is utterly splendid. It pained me over the years to hear George talk about how quiet and unloved this place had become, but now it is alive again, as it should be. You should be proud,' Margot said, squeezing Florence's forearm and Jo's hand.

Jo took a step forward and wrapped his arms around Margot. 'I'm glad you think so and this weekend wouldn't have been possible without Florence and all her ideas. I didn't think any of this was possible and nearly got this place demolished, so I by no means can take any of the credit,' he said modestly, making Florence look to her feet with embarrassment.

'You brought all my ideas to life Jo; in ways I wouldn't have known how to. I honestly believe events like this will keep Camp Calla Lily afloat,' Florence said quietly.

George stepped forward and shook his grandson's hand, then winked at Florence. 'You make a great team,' he said to them both. Margot nodded her agreement. Both Florence and Jo caught each other's side glance and gave each other a shy half-smile. George then checked his watch and clinked his glass, drawing their attention and the crowd's to him. The sun was slowly beginning to set on the horizon, lending a stunning orange and yellow glow to the already beautiful outdoor décor, so much so that Florence hoped her red cheeks wouldn't be so obvious.

'Ladies and gentlemen,' George started, making Florence's stomach flutter with excited anticipation. 'Thank you all for joining us here today. My grandson Jo and I hope that you have been enjoying the festivities. For those of you who have visited before, we hope that you like the new additions to the grounds in addition to the new activities we have on offer. For those of you who are seeing Camp Calla Lily for the first time, we hope it has captured your hearts and that you will return.' There were many cheers and claps with this notion. George nodded his head graciously and continued, 'This is where I believe I am to pass you on to my grandson, for he has been planning something I have not been allowed to set my eyes on. To say I am slightly anxious would be an understatement.' Cue laughter from the guests and a chuckle from Jo. 'But if this event so far today has taught me anything it is that even us old folk are always learning and I have learnt that I must have more faith and trust in my dear boy, for what he has done thus far has been truly outstanding, lifting up not only the camp but also my spirit.'

Jo stepped forward and hugged his grandad, causing Florence to search out a napkin to wipe her damp eyes. 'If I can draw your attention to the golf carts,' Jo said, pointing towards the path that led further into the forest, in the opposite direction of the huts, where five golf carts lined the dirt. 'It's not a long walk so for those of you that are able, I ask that you kindly give your seats to those who might need them and follow behind. It's time for the grand opening of the Wild Lily barn,' Jo finished, to a round of applause.

The guests started making their way over to the carts, kids and adults helping the elderly guests. Florence went to step forward, but Jo reached out, gently catching her shoulder and saying, 'Ma lady, you are coming with me. You require a blindfold,' he said, holding them both back a little until the guests had begun their walk and Sal and the kitchen staff had driven away on the golf carts.

'I told you before, I am no Ana Steele,' Florence said, surprised by the flirtatious way those words had come out. Where normally they would have come out hard and stern, now they left her lips with more than a hint of teasing. She could feel the heat rise in her cheeks.

'And I am no Christian Grey, unless you like that sort of thing,' Jo whispered, close to Florence's ear as his fingers gently brushed over them while he tied the bandana around her head. Florence could almost feel the vibrations of Jo's heart and as he took a deep breath when he moved his fingers away, she found herself hoping that his feelings for her hadn't changed and that she wasn't too late.

'Jo!!' Florence expressed, trying to smack him playfully but missing as now she couldn't see.

'You started it,' Jo said, his voice returning to its normal octave. 'Are you ready?' he added.

'Lead the way, Captain,' Florence said, with a salute.

TWENTY-SEVEN

Even with her blindfold on Florence could feel they were getting closer to the barn. The shadows of the giant trees gave way to a soft and cooler breeze. The canopy of oaks and English planes blocked the fading sun and the fragrant smell of a trifle of flowers filled the air. The noise picked up telling her that they had reached the clearing where everyone had gathered. There were lots of gasps and 'wow', 'it's so pretty'. Florence even heard a tiny voice asking, 'Do princesses live here?' Her stomach twisted into knots. When was Jo going to let her see it?

Gradually her ears pricked up to the hum of music that sang out around the forest and she felt Jo's hands near the back of her neck. Her skin tingled as he untied the knot in the bandana. Then he leant in close again and with a whisper said, 'I could not have done it without you,' before letting the blindfold drop away.

Florence had to blink a few times to unblur her vision and the minute it was clear, it went blurry again through a flurry of tears. She had to pinch herself to be sure she hadn't just disappeared into one of her vivid daydreams.

Bulb-shaped lights were draped from tree to tree creating a giant circle around the barn. Rope lights spiralled around thick tree trunks for as far as the eye could see. Old-fashioned square lanterns hung from the barn windows and lit up the barn walls. And the walls, the walls, they were not the brown barn shade she had painted with Jo. They were a vibrant, happy sunflower yellow, with turquoise accents. A flower print flag blew in the breeze from a top the small apex at the front of the second floor of the barn, that also displayed a circle-shaped stained window, which the dipping sunlight was bouncing off. It was the barn from her dream, the very barn she had described to Jo upon first seeing the dilapidated shack.

Florence was at a loss for words and finding it extremely difficult to form a sentence that could do the barn justice. She knew that Jo had been a successful architect and she didn't doubt for a second that he could create beautiful things, but this was something beyond magnificent. She looked to her right. Jo still stood behind her, and she saw that George and Margot were next to them. George's eyes were sparkling and filled with tears, his cheeks glistening from those that had already fallen.

'My dear boy,' was all he could manage and which he repeated in a whisper a couple of times over.

Jo squeezed Florence's shoulder and ran over to kiss his grandad on the cheek before running forward towards the barn doors. The children stopped running in between the trees and the adults gathered a little closer as Jo and Sal swung open the gorgeous barn doors and revealed the inside.

If Florence had been shocked upon seeing the outside, it was nothing to how she felt the moment she lay her eyes on the interior. The rustic oak floor gleamed. Star-shaped glass lights hung from the strong wooden beams and at the back of the large rectangle structure, there was a grand pink curtain. Florence stepped forward with the crowd edging their way inside. Along the walls there were theatre posters and books prints. A room off to the side indicated that toilets had been put in as well as a small kitchen area that was closed off with bits of scaffolding still, but it was the curtains that Florence was drawn to, that were pulling her forward as the children broke into dances in the wide hall space.

Florence hadn't been aware of Jo following her, but when she stopped still in front of the curtains, she heard him say, 'Are you ready?' She looked over to him, a slight crinkle in her brow. This place was not for her, it was for George. Why was Jo asking her? She looked around nervously in search of her nanna and Jo's grandad and spotted them walking towards her. Jo nodded at his grandad like they were both in on some sort of big secret.

When Jo pulled on the long gold rope at the side of the curtains, they parted to expose a stage. An honest to goodness beautifully built and structured stage, with steps either side leading up to it and a glorious backdrop. Margot's hands shot to her mouth. George smiled so bright his ears blushed and Florence could once again feel the tears brimming on her lash line. It was as if Jo had pulled her castle in the sky down to earth.

'Jo, why?' Florence stammered. 'Why did you turn the barn into this?' she asked, tracing a hand over the edge of the stage.

'When I saw you that day looking up at it, there was so much passion, enthusiasm and delight in your eyes, and I knew you saw it for what it was meant to be. When I asked you how you envisioned it, you spoke in colours and other worlds. When we simply gave it a fresh coat of paint it didn't feel right; you saw so much more than that. You saw it as a flying saucer, a pirate ship, a portal to kids and adults' imaginations. You gave it many new lives, not just one,' Jo expressed.

'I love it fiercely,' Florence noted, her hands shaking with excitement at what she was looking at, though she had no idea what it meant.

Jo smiled shyly at Florence, that one bouncy lock falling over his eye. Then he took a stride over to his grandad, looked back at Florence and announced, 'Someone had the rather brilliant idea of Camp Calla Lily being used for book trails, fairs and writing retreats. All such fabulous ideas, but what do you suppose Grandad to summer camps, acting workshops for kids, and filling this place with energy, making it warm and welcoming again?' Jo asked, taking his grandad's hands in his.

'Well, I think that sounds like a marvellous plan. I could not be prouder,' George said, shaking his grandson's hand vigorously and giving Florence a mischievous smile. Jo beamed, his whole face lighting up with a smile. Cheers from the crowd as they listened to the news of what the barn and Camp Calla Lily would be offering broke into Florence's thoughts. She too had taken in what Jo had just asked his grandad, but the words were getting jumbled in her brain and she was unable to make sense of them. Summer camps and acting workshops for kids would mean a lot of work and more staff. Suddenly Jo was in front of her, bending slightly to look into her eyes, that one curl forever astray.

'The thing about the workshops is that I would need a teacher, someone who loves theatre, who has experience and might be interested in diving back into her passion and taking the lead with something like this,' Jo said, his charming side smile perfectly in place but his hazel eyes showing a hint of nerves awaiting Florence's response.

Florence looked at the stage then back at Jo. Her brain was quickly trying to compute what he had just suggested. Which, if she was not mistaken, was that she come and teach here at Camp Calla Lily and oversee this project.

The flutters in her belly made her feel as though she might take off at any moment. They were the happy excited wings that her nanna had been talking about earlier that morning.

'Yes,' she cried. 'Yes,' she cried again, flinging her arms around Jo. The words were out of her mouth before she had even had a single second to overthink or let her anxiety wash over her. Another round of applause made Florence aware of the others in the room. She released Jo and went to wrap her arms around Margot and George while Jo went to address the crowd.

'As you may have just heard, Camp Calla Lily are looking to host workshops and summer camps in the coming months, so we do hope you keep your eyes peeled for the latest news and that you will tell your family and friends and come along and see us in due time,' he told the room. 'I sincerely hope that you like the newly renovated barn and what it will soon be offering and once you've had a good look, if I can recommend making your way back to the main cottage, it will be time to get the evening's campfire underway. Thank you all again for being with us today,' Jo finished and was treated to a third round of applause and lots of congratulatory handshakes, as was Florence.

As the crowd mingled a while longer, Florence floated around the barn. She had bumped into Bronte and Ella who squashed her in a giant bear hug, in lieu of actual words, before heading away to see to the tepees, but she mostly kept to herself, for with every step around the barn Florence took, she felt dizzy with joy. Every corner of the place her eyes landed on made them sparkle brighter and bolder than ever before and she wanted to soak it all in.

When the crowd had dispersed a little time later, Florence could sense Jo was watching her. Ever since Bronte had encouraged her to listen to her heart, Florence recognised that it got very loud when thinking of Jo and louder still when she was near him. Right now, it was pounding in her chest and she knew it was her moment to speak up and let her heart do the talking.

'Jo,' she said, moving away from the window and making her way over to the stage. The stage – my gosh it was absolutely stunning – but she could not let herself get distracted. It wasn't too difficult to pull her focus back to the to the man she had very much fallen in love with. Jo was leaning against the woodwork in a white tee and navy waistcoat, which he had changed into quickly after the book trail and he looked dashingly handsome.

'Yes,' Jo replied meeting her gaze with a smile.

'This place is all my wildest imaginations come to life,' Florence told him, excitement in her tone as she stopped in front of him.

'Just because it's in our heads, doesn't mean that it can't be real,' Jo stated, making Florence's heart pound harder still, as she knew that was one of the reasons why she had fallen so quickly for this man. She smiled dreamily, taking in his gorgeous features, but before she could say any more Jo sprung forward, took her hand and galloped to the staircase at the front of the barn on the right-hand side.

'I have to show you something,' he said, delight clear in his voice. Florence giggled, as she tried to keep up with his large strides.

'How many more surprises can one girl take in a day, Jo Hadlee?' Florence asked with a laugh. Jo stopped on the foot of the staircase with a mischievous glint in his eyes.

'Just one more,' he said and went to turn around, before stopping and turning to face her again, 'for now.'

TWENTY-EIGHT

At the top of the staircase was where Florence decided that she should expect to be blown away by Jo each and every day of their relationship, be that a friendship or a romantic relationship. If she hadn't ruined her chances on the latter. She swallowed back the lump that rose in her throat with that thought and instead focused on what Jo was showing her and being present in the moment that she could tell he had been eager to share with her. It seemed that there was no end to Jo's creativity and his ability to bring visions to life, for she was now standing in the roof of the barn, which Jo had turned into somewhat of a replica of the annex in *Little Women*. There sat a table by the window, handcrafted and old-fashioned like the one she had envisioned all her life, every time her nanna had read her the story and each time she had read it herself. There was a large chest over by one wall and a comfy-looking armchair by the other. Candlesticks stood on a small coffee table and there were the new additions, not described in the book, but more for Jo's personal needs, of a bed and a bookshelf. In the far corner there remained a boarded-up room and a little scaffolding still.

'This might be the part that's a little selfish. I wanted a place where I could write,' Jo confessed while Florence stood there with her mouth open wide like a goldfish. 'And with not planning to go back to London, I wanted somewhere I could stay that didn't involve me getting in the way of business and staying in one of the huts,' Jo noted. He was rambling a little, which only endeared him more to Florence. It made her feel not so alone in her nerves. She wasn't meaning not to talk and let Jo's nerves stir in his stomach, but it was all a lot to take in: the barn, the annex, Jo staying at the camp, being closer to her.

Finally, she spoke up, taking her eyes off the quaint desk and resting them on Jo. 'I don't consider it selfish at all. I think it's absolutely magnificent and sophisticated. Oh Jo, you could write scripts for the plays. We can do productions for the children and invite the village. And you're moving here? What about London? What about being an architect?' Florence was aware that her words had started to pick up speed and she was asking an abundance of questions but there was so much she had wanted to tell Jo over the last five weeks, and it felt like now it was all coming tumbling out in this place where she felt truly inspired. 'I'll have to leave and go to college, but I promise I will work hard and do all I can with the workshops, fairs and camps and help you with whatever you need,' she added and when Florence paused for breath, she noticed Jo was smiling at her, that huge boyish grin that clearly said that he was pleased that she liked what he'd done with the place.

'Yes, to all of the above,' Jo said with a laugh. Then he rubbed the back of his neck. 'I can still be an architect, but I want to be here for my grandad. I wish to spend more time writing and creating and you made me see that this is the perfect place for that,' he explained. Then he clapped his hands together. 'You're going to college?' he asked, eyebrows raising behind his curls.

Florence walked over to the desk, moving her hand over the carefully carved woodwork. 'Yes,' she said with a confident nod. 'I start in September; I'm going to get my degree in teaching drama,' she told him and in one stride, Jo was right beside her, picking her up and twirling her around.

'That's amazing news, Florence. I'm so proud of you,' he said and Florence felt it. She felt that he more than most understood how huge this was for her and she embraced that feeling of being understood. As he twirled her around, she threw her head back and let laughter barrel out of her. When her feet were returned to the floor, she knew it was time.

Her parents were gone and the one man she had opened her heart to had broken it, but that was all in the past; right now she had to address it and admit her deepest fear.

'Jo, you can't promise happily ever after or forever,' she said and though she had wanted to be confident in this moment, it came out a whisper, her eyes drooping down to the floorboards.

Jo immediately flicked to the same page and after a moment's thought he said, 'Florence, no, I can't promise you forever, but I am promising you today. Today is all I can give you. I want to make all of our todays count. If one day we wake up and our todays have added up to forever, then I will consider myself to be an incredibly lucky man.'

Florence thought over Jo's words – there was a reason he was a writer; they were more beautiful than any book she had ever read and any dream she had ever had. She lifted her head to look at him. His piercing hazel eyes saw her, and she realised that in Jo seeing all of her, that in his eyes she saw herself too. The her that she wished to be and somewhere deep down knew she could be. With that thought she stepped forward closing the gap between them. Feeling braver than she had ever felt in her entire life, she reached up and caught a curl between her fingers. 'Is this the part where I am supposed to swoon?' she asked Jo playfully, the happy wings fluttering wildly now in her belly.

'If you could, maybe just a little so my ego doesn't bruise too much,' Jo said, with a sweet side smirk as he looked down at her, his hazel eyes not straying from her deep blue ones.

'I have fallen in love with countless fictional leading men. I have daydreamed about my Prince Charming, always feeling that he was safer kept in my head because when I did give it a shot it didn't work out quite so well. Then you came along and make-believe didn't feel so make-believe anymore and my daydreams don't feel so out of reach, but I'm scared, Jo,' Florence said softly, not taking her eyes away from his this time.

'Love is a scary thing, Florence,' he said before pulling out the battered book that he had been reading that first day she had met him when he had sat under the magnolia tree by her hut. Automatically Florence reached out and started to gently smooth out the creases and crinkled edges wondering where Jo had put the bookmark she had bought him.

'Each curved edge is a page that has spoken to my heart. Each wrinkle is from where it has been hugged tight to my body, always on my person. Each crease brings with it a memory from a moment spent diving into the pages. Love can cause a few bumps and bruises, but it's what life is all about. I realise this now. Passion and love for anything is what makes us feel alive,' Jo explained and Florence found herself wondering how she could ever have run from this man, for his eyes made her feel like she had found her home.

'You dream in what ifs, you see the world in what ifs, well, what if this: if you and me could be something more than just a friendship? What if it could be part of our fairy tale?' Jo added, placing the book on the small desk, and gently moving a finger over Florence's cheek. At his touch Florence's heart threatened to escape its cage, the wall around it well and truly shattered into tiny little pieces. She still felt fear but knew that sometimes you had to leap forward and take a chance on the things that you fear the most. A smile danced at her lips as she stood on her tiptoes.

'Jo,' she whispered, her lips an inch away from his.

'Yes,' Jo replied, the word coming out in a low grunt.

'What if I kiss you right now?' she asked, her voice coming out wistfully. She wobbled a touch on her tiptoes and so Jo leant down so she could return her heels to the floor and steady herself.

He moved one hand over her collarbone, the other cupping her cheek and said, 'I might just kiss you back.'

Both recipients were smiling broadly when their lips met for the first time. Florence had read every classic romance and had melted over the very first kiss between high school crushes, newlyweds, strangers, best friends, enemies, and long-lost lovers, but her kiss with Jo had to be her favourite – for what she had with Jo was very real; it was happening to her right at this very moment. If one thing could be said of the books she cared for so dearly was that Jo's soft lips and the passion in the way he kissed her sweetly yet taking his time, was as magical as the books say they were meant to be. This was her storybook kiss. She held on to Jo's waistcoat with one hand to keep him close, the other was tangled in his hair. She loved his hair and though it had been fun to ruffle it in jest during their friendly back and forth, it felt special to touch it with such desire cursing through her veins.

When Jo went to pull away from Florence for breath, Florence flicked open her eyes and when she saw him, his hair a touch wayward from where she had just ruffled it, his lips plump and eyes so vivid and filled with love and lust, she pulled him back into her tentatively, eyes wide and looking into his. When Jo leant down again, not taking his eyes off her, she kissed him again. Florence could feel Jo's heart beating erratically. 'You are the chapters I never want to stop writing, the book I never want to stop reading,' he whispered against her lips, barely breaking their kiss.

Seconds, minutes, hours, Florence could not be sure, had passed by the time they broke the second kiss and when Jo opened his eyes Florence gave him a thoughtful look.

He dropped a gentle barely there kiss on her lips, just because he could, and smiled before taking her hand and pulling her towards the staircase. 'Ma lady, we must go. I cannot have you miss the campfire,' he added picking up speed, jubilation etched on his handsome face. Florence skipped after him, holding his hand tight and feeling every bit a child about to embark on a great adventure.

Hand in hand they reached the campfire. Together they mingled with guests, dined on toasted marshmallows, and told ghost stories to the children, before Jo pardoned himself with his grandad and went to check in those guests who were able to stay over. It was the first time in an awfully long time that

Camp Calla Lily was fully booked, and the relief, pride and delight was evident on George's face.

'As a nanna I will always hope and wish that the look you have on your face right now never goes far. Being old and wise,' Margot said, pausing to give a playfully pointed stare at her own mention of old as she took a seat next to Florence before continuing, 'I know the world has its way of holding that smile captive sometimes and taking it from us in the cruellest of ways, but may you always have the strength to go and find it again. Promise me you will never stop dreaming or seeing the world as you wish to see it and know it can be.'

Florence rested her head on her nanna's shoulder as the last embers in the firepit fizzled and went out, only the moon and the lanterns keeping the area aglow with their light now. 'I promise,' she replied. Margot turned and kissed her precious granddaughter on the top of her head, and they stayed peacefully side by side until George's voice interrupted the low crackle of the burning wood.

'Margot, shall I walk you to your room?' When Florence looked up, she saw both grandad and grandson standing tall, hands behind their backs, watching both women with admiring glances. She stood up to help her nanna and hug her goodnight.

'Please, George. Lord knows it has been a minute since I was up this late,' Margot announced with a laugh, stepping back from Florence's hug. She gave her a warm smile. 'Goodnight, treasure,' she said before walking off arm in arm with George.

Florence and Jo watched their grandparents leave, their eyes then coming to rest on each other's. There was a magical charge in the air between them now. An electricity that seemed to represent their freedom to let themselves be together, but there was still an element of shyness, for they were both hopeless romantics and new to this romantic abandon.

'Can I assist you to your abode?' Jo enquired, in his regal tone. He held out his hand, his nose wrinkling with a cute smile. Florence stepped forward and placed her hand in his. Each time she had done this this evening, she noticed that jolt in her chest, that feeling of her heart expanding.

'I'd like that,' Florence said, interlacing her fingers in his as they began the short walk to her hut. They discussed the evening's events, the grand barn, the décor Ella had helped Jo find at a Charity Antique shop, and the book trail before arriving on Florence's deck. Florence looked up at the lantern over the door and her brows drew in, in thought. She turned to look at Jo.

'Jo, I can't stay here every time I come and visit. This hut can no longer be mine – you're going to need it for holiday goers, for customers,' she told him expressing her concern as she leant against the wood, the lantern above the door lighting up the deck with a sunset orange glow that highlighted the gorgeous hut, which she loved so much.

Jo's hands had gone into his pockets. He rocked back and forth on his toes and heels, curls falling in his face, his lips pursed in thought, before announcing, 'I have an idea. You can stay with me.' Once the words had left his lips, he then gave a more confident nod. 'Yes, you can stay with me at the barn. There is more work to do, I know. I'm putting in a tub and working out the electricity for upstairs, but it's all doable and liveable, but that is only if you want to. We can talk. We should talk about your visits, when you'd like to come and stay, how often you can come and stay. Maybe I can come and see you.' Jo's words raced out of his mouth.

Florence chuckled softly, stepping up to him and moving the curls out of his face. 'Hmm, sleepovers in the annex.' Florence tilted her head to one side, playfully scrunching up her nose.

'They would be the best kind,' Jo returned, as he let Florence move her fingers over his jawline.

'With bedtime stories?' she asked, her eyes narrowing at his.

'Every night,' Jo said, a small smile tugging at his lips.

'I'll think about it,' Florence noted, her own lips curving into a sweet grin.

'You do that,' Jo whispered as he leant down slowly, bringing a hand to gently cup the back of Florence's head. Hesitating for a flicker of a moment with their noses touching, they allowed their smiles to grow wider, savouring their closeness, before their lips met once more.

When they broke away from each other, Florence was the first to open her eyes. She played with the curl dangling in front of Jo's eyelids causing Jo's lips to curve into that delicious side smile of his, with the warmth of her touch.

'So, did you think about it?' he asked when he opened his eyes, making Florence laugh and playfully push him in his chest. Jo caught her hands and held them tight in his. Then taking a step back and not letting go, not wanting to leave her, he whispered slowly, 'Goodnight, Florence.'

She let one hand drop first, their eyes never leaving each other's, as Jo unhurriedly began releasing her other hand. With their fingertips touching as Jo backed off the decking, Florence returned, 'Night, Jo,' with a dreamy sigh.

Florence watched as Jo bowed stepping on to the grass. He gave a small nod, his lips were curved into a smile that crinkled his eyes, those eyes that shone with love and mischief.

Once he was a mere speck in the distance, Florence stepped inside her hut and tip toed across the room, being careful not to wake Bronte. When she reached the bed, she flopped down onto the quilt her knees having done that wobbly weak detail that she had read about in so many of her books.

EPILOGUE

The pale blue pastel cabin, which sat between the main cottage and the barn, emitted the most rich, aromatic smell of coffee around the grounds. Florence could smell it from the annex as it drifted in on the breeze that floated through the window. She licked her lips, being known to occasionally swap her beloved breakfast tea for coffee these days. She couldn't help herself, for Langston and Bronte brewed the most delicious blend. Florence then smiled, the smell signalling the start of the day and a very special one at that.

The fact that both Langston and Bronte were early risers like Florence meant that there was always fresh coffee and tea ready for her when she woke, that is on days when the Caffeine Heights hut was open and Langston and Bronte were on site. The moment the girls had returned to work after the spectacular barn opening, Bronte had shared the story of the event and regaled Langston with stories of her time spent at Camp Calla Lily and begged him to figure out cover for the café so that she could take him to visit. Langston had agreed and the four of them, Florence, Jo, Bronte, and Langston, had enjoyed a wonderful weekend together at the end of last summer. Langston, just as Bronte had done, quickly fell in love with the place and joined Florence and Jo's team of two in revamping Camp Calla Lily.

Jo and Florence already knew they wanted to host drama workshops and put on shows and events where children could unleash their imagination, read, craft and be whoever they wanted to be. Upon being mesmerised by the gorgeous pastel homes, Bronte had been a whirlwind of excitement and ideas and had asked Jo ever so nicely if he would make her a hut. At first, Bronte had put in a request for a hut in the shape of a unicorn, it then changed to a book and then she finally settled on the idea that Caffeine Heights have their own hut and for them be a part of the events. This idea had caused both Florence and Jo's heads to turn with them both thinking it a rather marvellous one.

After Jo had tied up loose ends in London, sold his flat and finished a project that helped him pay George's debts, things had been running more smoothly. George still grumbled about the money, but Jo had put his foot down, ensuring his grandad that once Camp Calla Lily started making a profit again that George could pay him back.

In the past year, Jo and a small team of friends had built an additional three new huts – pastel green, pastel lilac and pastel orange – for holiday makers. The green and lilac were bigger than the rest to accommodate larger families. The main cottage, with its eight guest rooms, had been booked up most weekends. In October they had hosted a special Halloween book trail and held a pumpkin carving event and Christmas saw the original huts occupied by couples enjoying the cosy and romantic festivities, dipping into the village to enjoy the Christmas markets and spending evenings at Camp Calla Lily curled up sipping on hot chocolate around the indoor log fires and occasional winter bonfire. The New Year had brought in individuals looking to cleanse and see in the New Year independently and surrounded by the peace and tranquillity the grounds offered.

Jo hoped that in the future they could build more family huts and look into a camp-style sleeping bunk for kids, but for now they offered day workshops that didn't require children to sleep over unless the whole family stayed at the cottage or in one of the huts for the weekend and made a holiday out of the weekend classes. Jo had put much of his own money in the renovations, while Florence had added decorations and stocked up the barn as she saw fit, insisting on doing it herself. Money had been tight, but the profit had slowly been growing. Likewise, Bronte and Langston had put savings aside, thrilled with their new venture in a mobile Caffeine Heights, though naturally Jo had lowered the price greatly for his friends, without them knowing. Since Langston's first visit to the camp, he and Jo had hit it off and Florence felt Jo would happily make such treats for people free of charge if he could. He had a kind soul like that and looked after the people he loved.

It was hard to get a word in edgeways when Jo and Langston were together, for they were always heads together deep in discussion over great poets and writers the likes of Ralph Ellison and Ralph Emerson, Langston Hughes, Maya Angelou and Oscar Wilde. But it was a joy to behold as both Jo and Langston inspired each other and had been filling out notebooks with their own works whenever they got a spare minute. Florence loved having Langston and Bronte around. Their hut opened for an hour in the morning and for two at lunchtime on weekends, to offer another food alternative than

Sal's Calla Lily Café. Sal had wholeheartedly welcomed a little friendly competition over the last few months, but he needn't worry for Caffeine Heights was to be the main food stop for the children's snack breaks and lunches so they didn't have to traipse up to the main building and disturb the other holiday makers in the café when the workshops were on, so there was business for everyone.

Jo was grateful and pleased to see the camp making money again and the difference in his grandad's demeanour was palpable. George still saw to the bookings, to allow Jo to focus on the grounds, but these days George had help with Margot often staying for weeks at a time. At first it was just the occasional weekend, but as Florence was busy during the week with school and working at Caffeine Heights, Margot had decided to venture to Camp Calla Lily to be with George so they could keep each other company.

Florence didn't mind; she didn't think her heart could grow any bigger but seeing her nanna so happy had made it so. Moreover, when time and work would allow, Jo would come to Manchester and stay during the week or come and pick her up after school on the Friday and they would drive down to Camp Calla Lily together. School had been going well for Florence. Though she was one of the older ones in the class, she got on with everyone as they all had such a flair for the arts that Florence loved to see. Jo was enjoying every aspect of working freely on the camp and being able to share and run ideas by his grandad. He was also making sure to take time for himself to write and had sent off his story, the one he had acted out to Florence the night of their campfire, to some publishers. He had made sure to give his leading man the happy ending that Florence had desired and Ella had told him bluntly that if no publisher should acquire it then he should self-publish it and she turn would proudly display it in the window of The Vintage Bookshop.

Jo had stuck to his promise of sleepovers and bedtime stories and each moment with him was a daydream come to life. As Florence stretched her arms above her head, looking around the annex from the comfort of their bed, she smiled as if she had just read a favourite chapter in one of her favourite novels, for this chapter of life she was currently participating in had to be her favourite yet. Her smile only grew wider when she twisted to her right and looked down to see Jo gazing up at her, his hair sticking out all over the place, his hazel eyes sparkling in the sunrise that beamed through the circle window behind her.

'Good morning, Florence,' Jo said in a bright and cheerful voice as he sat up, putting an arm around her, and kissing her cheek.

'Good morning, Jo,' Florence returned, leaning into his kiss.

'Are you ready for today?' he asked, playing with her sandy waves, his fingers grazing over her bare shoulder.

'I think so. There are nerves but at the same time I can't wait,' Florence expressed, dropping her chin on her shoulder where Jo's fingers were. She kissed one and he smiled.

'You're going to be fantastic and I will be the best assistant you've ever had,' Jo noted, leaning down to give her a gentle kiss on the lips.

'You will be the only assistant I have ever had,' Florence replied with a chuckle, feeling a warmth spread through her when Jo looked at her with hooded eyes and a cheeky grin. He kicked off the duvet and jumped out of the bed. Rounding to her side of the bed, he offered her his hand. Florence took it and Jo pulled her to her feet, spinning her around as though they had been transported to a ballroom and a grand orchestra were playing. Minutes passed as they floated around the annex, laughing, and moving in sync before they busied themselves in the small bathroom getting ready for the day.

Once dressed, Florence in a long and floaty pink sundress, Jo in black trousers and a white tee, they walked hand in hand out of the barn's clearing, through the dense forest of magnificent trees into the open hills towards Caffeine Heights. When they reached the pale blue hut, Bronte was just wriggling out of her and Langston's tent, which was nestled behind the hut, while Langston poured out four takeaway cups. Langston and Bronte always pitched a tent when they stayed over at the camp, not wanting to use up the accommodations reserved for guests and because they were both fond of sleeping under the stars. The cosiness of their sleeping quarters and with a little of the magic that Florence felt Camp Calla Lily possessed, thanks to her parents watching over the place, plenty of laughs and late-night conversations had meant that Bronte and Langston's relationship had flourished in these parts. Just thinking about it made Florence's heart swell.

Having been the best of friends for so long, Florence had felt that both Bronte and Langston were hesitant about ruining the relationship they had and so they hadn't rushed and neither she nor Jo had put any pressure on them by meddling. They had simply encouraged and supported their feelings, lent listening ears and positive notes and allowed destiny to do its thing.

'Good morning,' Florence said brightly as Bronte skipped over to the hut and took her cup from Langston, who always held hers in his hand until Bronte was ready to take it. Florence watched as their eyes connected. Bronte popped a sweet kiss on his cheek and Langston beamed and winked ever so casually before turning his attention back to Jo who was chatting enthusiastically about a recent poem Langston had written.

'Morning,' Bronte said to Florence after a long sip of the delicious roast, her cheeks rosy with a romantic flush. 'Are you excited for today?' she added as the girls took a seat at the picnic table.

'Yes. I think the excitement is outweighing the nerves right now actually. The barn is all set up. I have a vague plan and I have the best assistant in the world so...' Florence didn't finish her sentence, she simply shrugged playfully at Bronte who laughed in understanding. There was not a lot she could do now; the children were due to arrive at half past nine and only then could she really get a feel for how she would go about teaching. She had a mixed-age group from six years old to ten registered for today's class and so she knew a lot of the teaching would depend on getting to know the children and their personalities before any kind of curriculum was set in stone. She also wanted to find out what they liked, the kinds of books they read and plays they would be interested in performing; maybe they could merge a few together and create their very own brand-new version? Her mind wandered and she felt the happy wings in her stomach flutter.

'I still can't get over this place,' Bronte expressed with a dreamy sigh as she looked across the fields. The sun was rising above the lake causing beautiful rays to highlight the dewy grass, the pretty paint, and the detail of each hut. She still had one year left to complete her English degree and when not at school or writing her essays she was as busy as ever working at Caffeine Heights. But as the coffee shop had grown in popularity it had allowed her and Langston this escape to Camp Calla Lily, where, as much as Bronte loved their shop in

Manchester and it had been a dream come true, Bronte wished she could spend more time. However, Bronte very much believed in Jo and Florence's vision and hoped that once the workshops took off and they established their seasonal events and once she herself finished university, she could be the one to look after their coffee hut and get away from the city more. She and Langston had talked about the possibility of such a venture, but Bronte knew how much he worried about the shop and how difficult it had been to leave someone else in charge the weekends they were away, so she was aware it might be a little while yet before she could call Camp Calla Lily home. It was certainly a lovely goal to keep on the not too distant horizon.

'It is rather special,' Florence returned with a dazed smile as she paused to take pleasure in the sunrise and scope out the fields, where flowers opened up to the soft sunlight and the birds could be heard and seen flying from tree to tree during their morning chorus. 'Jo has worked so hard to revive it and I believe he's done a spectacular job; I never want to leave.' She chuckled to which Bronte raised her cup in agreement.

'This place is definitely magic. Did Olivia say she can make it next week?' Bronte asked.

Florence's smile grew. 'Yes, she and Drew will be here on Saturday,' she answered.

'I can't believe how excited she gets for the book trails. I think we've converted her to the book side,' Bronte replied, before letting out a soft chuckle. Florence wasn't sure if they had or if it truly was the magic of the camp that could make anyone's imagination come alive. The thought warmed her heart.

She couldn't wait for Olivia and Drew to visit and to have all her friends and family together. Mornings with her friends, breathing in the fresh air and enjoying her warm drink had become one of Florence's favourite things, it wasn't quite the same waking up to the brick walls and noisy cars back in Manchester, but she appreciated that all the same too. She had come a long way from being the girl who confined herself to her four walls and printed pages. Though the printed pages were not going anywhere anytime soon Florence was thoroughly enjoying her time at school and was not nearly as anxious about meeting new people anymore. Furthermore, having learnt so much already, she felt wildly more prepared for the day ahead.

* * *

Out in the field Florence heard the mighty roar of a dragon being slayed by an army of sword-wielding, howling knights. She and a small creature with emerald eyes raced around the barn collecting the precious gemstones, golden goblets, and sparkling treasure in a race against time. They couldn't let the knights see them; the dragon had been a distraction so they could make off with the treasure without being caught. They had to avoid the dungeons at all costs so they could deliver the goods to the evil witch so that she would release their fellow villagers.

Out of nowhere an eagle swooped in through the rafters, its loud cries alerting the knights who were celebrating over defeating the dragon. Florence saw one man look her way through the stone window. Their eyes connected and panic flooded her body. 'We have to move quick,' Florence whispered to the cute creature next to her. Picking up their pace, they threw the riches into their bag and Florence flung it over her shoulder. The noise of battle armour was getting louder as the knights trudged towards the barn.

Just as Florence and the tiny being reached the trapdoor, their only escape, the barn doors swung open and in poured the army of soldiers.

'What do we do now?' a trembling voice asked by Florence's feet.

Florence looked down at the little one by her side and smiled broadly. 'We must call out for our unicorns. Only they can save us now,' she said, feeling giddy at the thought of their unicorns coming to save them. The little face beamed, the emerald eyes sparkling with delight. 'After three, we face the soldiers and we shout out for help. They will hear us,' Florence assured her partner. 'One, two, three.'

Florence and her accomplice stepped out from where they were cowering over by the trapdoor. The knights halted and stood proud and tall; weapons raised. Nodding at each other, Florence shouted 'Silver' while her friend shouted 'Bob' as they looked up to the sky.

'Surrender now,' one of the knights yelled to an echo of agreement.

'Never,' shouted the little girl by Florence's feet.

'There's no way you can escape now. Give up the jewels,' came another cry from a different soldier.

'Wanna bet?' the little girl retorted. 'Our unicorns are on their way. I'd run if I were you,' she added, filling Florence with pride at her increasing confidence.

'Wait, what? No fair, they can't have unicorns.' Another solider spoke up causing Florence to stifle a giggle as the place erupted in huffs and another boy motioned, 'Unicorns can defeat everything with their magic. Why didn't we think of that?'

Just then the barn door opened, and Bronte skipped in. 'Snack time,' she sang to a chorus of cheers and clatter as the soldiers dropped their weapons. Leila tugged on Florence's dress and so Florence squatted down to her level. 'Miss Florence, can I keep my unicorn?' she asked, her eyes wide and twinkling.

'Of course. He's yours now; he'll always be with you,' Florence told her and was gifted with a small hug before Leila ran off to join the others who were lining up at the door at Bronte's request to make sure everyone was accounted for. When Florence stood up, she came face to face with a rather handsome knight.

'Unicorns huh? That's cheating,' Jo said, releasing his curls from his cardboard helmet. Florence reached up and picked bits of paper from his hair, smirking as she did so.

'You're just jealous because you didn't think of it first,' she said playfully.

'That much is true,' Jo said with a laugh. After a morning of introductions and crafts, the afternoon had been a blast. Following the children's lead, he and Florence had gone into battle, hunted for treasure and fought all sorts of mythical creatures. Florence looked radiant, the smile on her face never wavering. His heart tugged every time he caught sight of her with the kids, encouraging their imagination and joining in with their escapades. He too had been lost in their stories and was loving every minute. 'I think unicorns might be my favourite animal,' Jo said, placing his helmet with the others at the barn door.

'Why a unicorn?' Florence asked as she and Jo followed Bronte who had the children pretending to be animals as they hissed, growled, and roared over the hills towards Caffeine Heights.

Florence tilted her head to one side awaiting Jo's answer. He looked dashing and rugged after running around with the kids all afternoon and her heart beat a little harder.

'Because if you believe in something with your whole heart, it might just come true, and what a magical and wonderful thing to believe in,' he said causing Florence to stop in her tracks. She allowed the children to walk a little further ahead, knowing they were safe with Bronte, and turned to Jo.

'You think if you believe in unicorns enough, they will appear?' Florence queried with a sparkle in her eyes, knowing that she and Jo were once again on the same page.

'I know so,' Jo replied pulling her towards him. Florence let out a happy giggle before Jo leant in and brought his lips to hers in a moment that made Florence believe in unicorns, magic, and all the fairy-tale kisses that had ever happened and all those that were yet to come.

ACKNOWLEDGMENTS

My first thank you goes out to my former editor the wonderful Hannah Smith for being such a fantastic editor and someone who always makes me feel like I can do it. Thank you for championing Florence's story from the beginning and for your initial input in the editing process. I loved your advice and guidance in making Florence's story the best it could be. Thorne Ryan, my new and awesome editor, thank you for being so supportive and encouraging. Helena Newton, you are brilliant. I am forever grateful for your tweaks and changes and for catching all the things I might have overlooked. Lisa Brewster, thank you for such a beautiful cover that always brings a smile to my face. Thank you to the entire team at Aria Fiction; you are all amazing and I am incredibly grateful for all you do. Everyone at Aria who works to make my book what it is and helps to get it out into the world, thank you with all my heart.

Thank you to every reader who has picked up a copy of one of my books, you truly are incredible and fill my heart with so much love and I couldn't be more thankful to you for making my dreams come true and for allowing me to bring my stories to life. Each time a character or story connects with you, it means the world and I don't feel so alone. That connection is inspiring and is what motivates me and excites me to write more stories. A big shout out to Shelby, Kel, Nicole and Gem for never failing to make me smile with your reviews. Your support is everything.

Thank you Katie, Maxine, Rachel, Sam, Matt, Kayleigh and Amanda for being little balls of light and wonderful sources of positivity, inspiration and love.

And a massive, massive thank you to my incredible family who continually go above and beyond with their love and cheerleading. Jillian, Auntie Lynne, Auntie Georgina, Jo and June, thank you for reading my books and for always putting a smile on my face with your words of encouragement. It means the world that you enjoy the stories I write. Mum and Dad, thank you for always asking me how my writing is going, listening to my rambles and for being proud and impressed that I'm five books in. Chris, Kate and In, thank you for being huge inspirations to me each and every day. Kelly, Jen and Chris, it's truly hard to put into words how much your love and unrivalled championing means to me. You're with me during the good days and the bad days and never complain. I love you more than you know. To my grandparents, not a day goes by where I don't think about you. You continue to inspire me and I love you with every piece of me.

I'm sorry to anyone that I may have missed. If you are reading this, please know that I think you are absolutely phenomenal. I hope you have enjoyed Florence and Jo's story and that they inspire you to create the world you have in your mind and believe in fairy tales and the magic the world has to offer.

ABOUT THE AUTHOR

Lucy Knott lives in Manchester England, just around the corner from her childhood home and less than five minutes from her twin sister Kelly and brother in law Chris. She loves spending time with her family in addition to writing, reading and cooking Italian food. When not buried in a book, scribbling in a notebook or having dance parties for one to Harry Styles, she works as a teaching assistant.

Lucy loves to write uplifting stories that she hopes will put a smile on your face, fill your heart with joy, encourage you to embrace the awesomeness that you are and believe that any dream is possible.

Visit her website to find out more: www.theblossomtwins.com

HELLO FROM ARIA

We hope you enjoyed this book! If you did, let us know, we'd love to hear from you.

We are Aria, a dynamic fiction imprint from award-winning independent publisher Head of Zeus.

At heart, we're committed to publishing fantastic commercial fiction – from romance and sagas to book club reads and historical fiction. Visit us online and discover a community of like-minded fiction fans!